CRAVE me

Good Ol' Boys Book 4

M. ROBINSON

Crave Me

DEDICATION

To my VIP group

I love you.

I write all my books for you.

Thank you for being YOU.

Oh my God ladies…words cannot describe how much I love and appreciate every last one of you. The friendships and relationships that I have formed with you are one of the best things that have ever happened to me. I wish I could name each one of you but it would take forever, just please know that you hold a very special place in my heart. You VIPs make my day, every single day.

THANK YOU!!

ACKNOWLEDGMENTS

Boss man: Words cannot describe how much I love you. Thank you for ALWAYS being my best friend. I couldn't do this without you.

Dad: Thank you for always showing me what hard work is and what it can accomplish. For always telling me that I can do anything I put my mind to.

Mom: Thank you for ALWAYS being there for me no matter what. You are my best friend.

Julissa Rios: I love you and I am proud of you. Thank you for being a pain in my ass and for being my sister. I know you are always there for me when I need you.

Ysabelle & Gianna: Love you my babies.

Rebecca Marie: THANK YOU for an AMAZING cover. I wouldn't know what to do without you and your fabulous creativity.

Heather Moss: Thank you for everything that you do!! I wouldn't know what to do without you! You're. The. Best. PA. Ever!! You're NEVER leaving me!! XO

Silla Webb: Thank you so much for your edits and formatting! I love it and you!

Mitch Mckersie: Special thanks to my cover model! You did Austin justice and you're the perfect muse!

Jon Schueler: Thanks for the inspiration.

Brianna Partin: Thank you for making my dreams come true!

Michelle Tan: Best beta ever! **Argie Sokoli:** I couldn't do this without you. You're my chosen person. **Tammy McGowan:** Thank you for all your support, feedback, and boo boo's you find! I'm happy I made you cry. **Michele Henderson McMullen:** LOVE LOVE LOVE you!! **Roxie Madar:** Thank you for all your honest feedback! Love you! **Dee Montoya:** I value our friendship more than anything. Thanks for always being honest. **Clarissa Federico:** Thank you so much for coming in last minute and handling it like a boss. Your friendship means more to me than you'll ever know! **Rebeka Christine Perales:** You always make me smile. **Alison Evan-Maxwell:** Thank you for coming in last minute and getting it done like a boss. **Mary Jo Toth:** Your boo-boos are always great! **Ella Gram:** You're such a sweet and amazing person! Thank you for your kindness. **Kimmie Lewis:** Your friendship means everything to me. **Tricia Bartley:** Your comments and voice always make me smile! **Natasha Gentile:** Thanks for being gentle on my children and for all your amazing feeback. **Danielle Renee:** Thank you for wanting to join team M. **Kristi Lynn:** Thanks for all your honesty and for joining team M. **Pam Batchelor:** Thanks for all your suggestions and for also wanting to join team M. **Jenn Hazen:** Thank you for everything! **Laura Hansen:** I. Love. You. **Patti Correa:** You're amazing! Thank you for everything! **Jennifer Pon:** Thank you for all your feedback and suggestions! You're amazing! **Jen M:** Welcome back! I missed you! **Sandi George Laubhan:** I love all your feedback! Thank you! **Michelle Kubik Follis:** Welcome back! I missed you too! **Deborah E Shipuleski:** Thank you for all your quick honest feedback!

To all my author buddies:

T.M. Frazier: I fucking love you, you fucking Ginger.

Jettie Woodruff: You complete me.

Erin Noelle: I. Love. You!

The C.O.P.A Cabana Girls:

I love you!!

<u>To all the bloggers:</u>

A HUGE THANK YOU for all the love and support you have shown me. I have made some amazing friendships with you that I hold dear to my heart. I know that without you I would be nothing!! I cannot THANK YOU enough!! Special thanks to Like A Boss Book Promotions for hosting my tours!

Last but not least.

YOU.

My readers.

THANK YOU!!

Without you…

I would be nothing.

PROLOGUE

AUSTIN

I tied the belt tighter around my upper arm to stop the blood flow.

Squeezing my fist every few seconds to pump up my vein, it didn't take me long to find old faithful. It never did. I leaned back against the old, dirty, mold-infested couch, faintly hearing "Mad World" by Andrew Michaels somewhere in the dark, ominous background. The lyrics immediately brought back old memories— good times, happy vibes, when in reality there was anything but fucking happiness.

This wasn't who I'd always been.

Once upon a time, I tried to find my independence, and somewhere along the way, I found solace in the haze of dependency, which was what led me to that place in time.

I didn't bother to take in my surroundings.

It was always the same.

Familiar faces that blended together and never changed, always jonesing, always wanting, always needing, always craving.

More. More. More.

And never enough.

It wasn't about being high anymore. The euphoric, free feeling was long gone. All that was left was the pursuit. Day after day I was pulled down the proverbial rabbit hole with nowhere to turn, always trying to escape, chasing the non-existent dragon that only led to darkness.

It was too late.

Crave Me

It had me.

The addiction.

A tight grasp on my soul, pushing me further and further into the black abyss. What goes up, must come down. It's the law of physics, the code of life. I rode the high for as long as I could remember. I had been so far up that there was nowhere left for me to go but straight to the bottom. All I wanted was to drown out the feeling of my entire body caving in on me. Soothe the ache, throw fire on the chill, and ease the nausea.

The only thing I could do to feel as if I wasn't dying was…

To kill myself a little more.

I inserted the needle, welcoming the sting. My blood rushed in, and I slowly pushed down the plunger.

I wanted it to last.

I always do.

It was the best fucking part.

I pulled the plunger back out and watched with hooded, constricted pupils as my blood swirled in once again.

Heaven and Hell. God and Satan. Love and hate. It all blended together. Forming a clusterfuck of hope and despair.

Now…

Now, I squeezed my fist.

The rush.

Tingles from my fingers traveled up my arm and then, and then…

It hits.

Simultaneously my eyes closed and my head fell back against the couch.

I don't care that it's dirty.

I don't care that it smells.

I don't care about one fucking thing.

All the misery was gone in the blink of an eye. As if it wasn't even there to begin with. All that was left was the free, euphoric, and blissful feeling of pleasure that only this could ever bring me. My heart was full, filling in the hollow existence that was my life. The pain numbed.

Even if it was only temporary.

A few moments in time where the world faded into nothingness and I was swimming in an endless pool of possibilities. Not drowning in disappointment, judgment, and regret. Not feeling like I was dead inside, meanwhile I just killed myself a little more. I heard echoes everywhere. Colors blended together making it hard to focus on one thing. I blinked a few times and just like that...

I saw her face like I always did.

As if she was standing right in front of me.

Smiling.

Happy.

Laughing.

My whole world...

My girl.

My lips curled up slightly at the vision as I reached out for her. Wanting to touch her, needing to hold her, yearning to kiss her. Craving, God, craving to fucking love her.

"I'm sorry," I murmured aloud to no one but the illusion of my drug-infested mind. "I'm so fucking sorry," I repeated repentantly, longing for her to believe me.

Aching for her to love me again like she used to.

I don't know how long I sat there, staring at her beautiful face before my eyes, subconsciously rubbing the tattooed daisy that was placed over my heart. I couldn't take it anymore, and the desire won over the haze.

It was too powerful.

It was too vivid.

I grabbed my phone. "Baby," I said into the speaker. The ringing quickly followed, going straight to voicemail. I hung up and tried again. "Baby," I urged with desperation in my tone.

Still nothing.

I tried again and again and again.

I would try until the end of time if that's what it took for her to answer.

To talk to me.

To save me.

To crave me.

Time seemed to standstill, as my life slowly played out in front of me. Trying to balance somewhere in between the light and the darkness when all I could see was gray.

"What?!" she screamed into the phone, finally answering after I don't know how many failed attempts. "What the hell do you want now?"

"Baby." I breathed a sigh of relief.

"What do you want, Austin? Why are you calling me? We're over! I can't do this anymore!"

I shut my eyes and let my mind wander, allowing it to go to another place in time where she didn't hate me.

"I remember the first time I made you smile," I chuckled, as if it had just happened.

My nerves were on fire. The mere sound of her breathing through the phone was too intense for me. I hadn't spoken to her in such a long time. I licked my lips, my mouth suddenly dry.

"I remember when you used to smile just for me. Do you remember, baby? Do you remember what my love feels like?"

I heard her faintly breathing.

"Do you remember my hands on you? My lips? My tongue? The first time I made you come with my mouth? Do you remember all the times since? Tell me I'm not forgotten. Tell me you remember, baby."

Silence.

"I love you, Briggs. I love you so fucking much. You're killing me, don't you see that? I'm dying without you."

"No, Austin. You were dying *with* me," she rasped, knowing that it killed her to say that.

"The first time I saw your face, I thought to myself, damn, this beautiful girl is goin' to be the death of me. You were perfect in every way. I was a cocky son of a bitch who needed you then, as much as I need you now."

More silence.

"I had a dream about you, baby. I always fucking dream about you. In my dream, you had a ring on your finger. A ring I put there. You belonged to me. Only mine. Forever fucking mine. You were pregnant, Briggs. You looked so goddamn happy. I saw light at the end of the tunnel for the first time in years."

She sniffled into the phone.

"I made love to you. Slow, just the way you love. Taking my time to touch every last inch of your body. Memorizing every last bit of you. Making you come until you begged me to stop. I didn't."

"I can't—" she tried to interject, but I didn't let up.

"I kissed your stomach. Our baby. Letting my lips linger there, whispering sweet lullabies, letting her know Daddy will always be there. Baby, it was so real. For a second I gave you the one thing you so desperately wanted, the one thing I can't seem to give you."

"Why are—"

"After we were done, I just lay there with you and our unborn baby, both of you wrapped in my arms, the only place where you belonged. Unforgiving thoughts plagued my mind as I carefully moved you away from me, making sure not to wake you. I went into the bathroom and I got high. You found me. You always find me. Except this time... I died in your arms. You couldn't save me, but it didn't matter because the best part of me was already growing inside you. When I woke up, I was alone. I'm always alone, Briggs, even when you're near me. I can promise you the world. I can promise you a life. But even in my dreams, baby, I'm haunted."

"Jesus Christ, Austin," she wept. "Where are you?"

I opened my eyes, finally taking in my surroundings. As if I was being woken up from a dream within a dream. I couldn't tell what was real or lucid. Confused by my own reality. It was then that I looked down, the needle still firmly placed in my arm.

"Where are you?" she repeated with a shaky tone.

I shook my head, trying to find some clarity. "I'm so fuckin' sorry, baby. I love you, Briggs. I love you with everything that's left of me."

"Austin, where are you? Please, tell me where you are?" she whimpered, panic taking over.

I took a deep breath and murmured, "The place I hate."

Once again...

Pushing in the syringe.

Briggs

I drove with my heart in my throat like every other goddamn time before this.

I hated him.

I loved him.

I love him.

11

Crave Me

I slammed on my brakes, shoving my door open before my car was even fully shifted into park. The stench of the drug den immediately assaulted my senses, making me sick to my stomach that he was there.

I ran through the abandoned warehouse that he had told me about so many damn times on my voicemail. Ignoring the random junkies that were hollering at me, pleading for more drugs, begging for another hit. I tried my best to sideswipe the filth, piss, shit, and garbage all around me. I sprinted past the graffiti walls, covering my nose and mouth, trying like hell not to inhale the mold-contaminated air and decay that had taken over the shithole. Piles of trash surrounded the dirty mattresses and chairs, infested with rats and ghostlike junkies that appeared dead but could have been alive. I knew where I would find him. He always called from the same spot, leaving me voicemail after voicemail. Describing the back of the warehouse that looked over the harbor.

I turned the corner, and saw him. My once favorite maroon beanie placed securely on his head. I couldn't control my emotions.

I hated him in that second.

I despised the love I still had for him in my broken, fucked-up heart in that moment.

I slowed down as I got closer, my calculated steps slow and precise. I wanted to face him. I wanted to look into his eyes like I had done so many damn times before, even though I knew there wouldn't be anything but a hollow existence. A shell of the man I once knew gazing back at me.

The truth was eating me alive as if I was dying right along with him.

I couldn't do it.

Not anymore.

I stood behind the tattered couch, staring at the back of his head. He nodded off. The craving completely took over me, rotting its way into the empty space that now held his soul.

I shook my head in disgust and bewilderment with tears streaming down my face. This was all that was left of him.

No more I love you's.

No more I promises.

No more tomorrows.

No. More. Austin.

"Why?!" I shouted, my chest heaving and my heart breaking bit by bit. "Why do you do this to me? Why do you keep doing this to me?" I sobbed uncontrollably. "I can't fucking do this anymore! I can't watch you die! I can't watch you kill yourself more than I already have!" I bawled, my body shaking.

"I hate you! Do you hear me, Austin?! I fucking hate you!" I screamed loud enough to break glass.

Heaving, I leaned over and placed my hands on my knees for support, struggling to breathe in and out.

"Why do you do this to me? Please, Austin, please fucking enlighten me! I'm sorry! I'm so fucking sorry!" I whimpered hysterically.

He didn't try to comfort me like he always did. He didn't try to hold me, touch me, kiss me, or reassure me.

Lie to me.

Nothing.

I wiped my face, standing to look at him again. He hadn't moved from the place he sat. His body was lifeless.

"Austin," I murmured so low I could hardly hear myself. "Austin," I said a little louder.

My feet moved on their own accord. Inch by inch, I made my way around the couch, old needles, bags, and God knows what else crunching under my feet. I felt as though I was having an out of body experience. I was there, but I wasn't. Closing my eyes, I swallowed hard before I was standing fully in front of him.

"Please, God," I found myself saying as I slowly opened my eyes.

My body shuddered as I took in the needle that was still lodged into his vein, his eyes were closed, and his head leaned over to the side.

"No!" I lunged into action, tearing the syringe out of his arm and throwing it as hard as I could across the place I called Hell on Earth.

"No! No! No! No!" I repeated, grabbing his face, making him look at me. All the color had drained from his body, his lips turned blue.

"Austin!" I shook him. "Austin!" I shook him harder. "AUSTIN!" I slapped him across the face.

Nothing.

13

"Fuck! Fuck! Fuck!"

He wasn't breathing.

"Don't do this to me! Don't you do this to me again! Do you fucking hear me! Please! Don't leave me!"

I reached for my phone.

"9-1-1, what is your emergency?"

"He's not breathing. I don't know what to do! Please, please, help him!" I explained as much as I could to the operator, but my thoughts were scattered.

"Where is your exact location?"

"We're in the back of the warehouse overlooking the harbor by Wallace Street and Grant Avenue."

"Ma'am, help is on the way. I need you to calm down. Can you do that for me?"

"I don't know! He's not breathing. Please don't let him die!"

"Ma'am, I need you to calm down. You can't help him if you don't calm down."

I nodded even though she couldn't see me.

"Ma'am, are you still there?"

"Yes."

"I need you to lay him on his side with his knees bent for support. Make sure his face is turned to the side. Can you do that?"

"I think so."

I gently laid him down on the couch and did as I was told. My hands shaking the entire time.

"The paramedics are almost there."

The rest proceeded in slow motion.

Paramedics filled the vacant space, pushing me to the side. Narcan being injected up his nose. Paddles shocking him back to life.

"One, two, three, clear."

His body jolted.

"One, two, three, clear."

His body jerked again.

"He's breathing."

Laying him on a stretcher.

Rushing him into the ambulance.

Holding his hand the entire ride.

Emergency room...

Paperwork…
Insurance…
"Briggs," a familiar voice called out, pulling me out of my fog.
I cocked my head to the side.
"Briggs, do you remember me? I'm Aubrey's mom."
I nodded unable to form words.
"They're not going to let you go back there, honey. You're not immediate family. It's hospital policy. He's in good hands. I promise I will do everything I can to make sure he comes out of this alive. That being said, there's a chance he's not… he was dead for too…" She placed her hand on my shoulder in a comforting gesture with hesitation, unsure how to proceed. "Honey, you need to call his family as soon as possible, time may not be on our side today. They need to be here now."

I nodded again as she reassuringly squeezed my shoulder. I walked out the double doors of the emergency room, wanting some privacy. The cool breeze was a welcome feeling against my feverish face. The chaos all around me was too hard to ignore. I reached into my pocket for my phone and it was then that I noticed I was shaking. I couldn't form one coherent thought as I dialed his number. Shame and remorse submerged me, pulling me under, making it hard to breathe.

"Hello," he answered. I opened my mouth to say something, anything, but nothing came out.

"Darlin', are you there?"

"Dylan," I softly whispered his name into the phone. He was Austin's best friend, and the only one that knew the truth.

"Briggs? Are you alright?"

"I-it's Austin," I blurted out, my voice breaking, the words causing my stomach to turn.

"What?"

"It's Austin, Dylan. I found him. He called me after you did."

"Is he—"

"He OD'd. He's in the ICU. They don't know if he's going to make it," I informed him, my tone sounding distant and detached.

"Jesus Christ," he rasped. "What the fuck, Briggs? You promised me. You fucking promised me that you—"

"I'm sorry," I wept, tears streaming down my face. "I'm so fucking sorry."

"How did it get this bad? How has it come to this? How could you let this happen?" he roared question after question, looking for answers I didn't have.

I violently shook my head. "I tried. I swear to God I fucking tried! You have to believe me, Dylan!"

"No, Briggs. You didn't. You're the reason he's there. If he dies, it's on you, do you fucking hear me? You!"

I shut my eyes, my phone falling from my trembling hand, crashing to the ground. My body shuddering, knowing in my heart, he was right.

It wasn't always like this.

At least…

Not in the beginning.

CHAPTER 1

AUSTIN

"Austin, there you are!" my best friend Alex called out, running towards me with a huge smile on her pretty face.

Her name was Alexandra, but everyone called her Alex for short. She was only eight years old and thought she was one of us boys. Following us everywhere we went from the time she could crawl. Our Half-Pint shadow was our nickname for her.

"What are you doing over here on the dock all by yourself?"

I shrugged, not really knowing how to reply.

There were times that I wanted to be by myself. Alone with my thoughts where I could just let go and be me, without worrying about anyone else.

Where I wasn't just one of the good ol' boys.

Of all the people I knew, Alex would understand. Sometimes I felt like we had that in common, the need to escape.

It made things easier for me.

"Why do you have a fishing pole if you're not fishing?" She giggled, taking a seat next to me on the dock. "What are you writing in that notebook, Austin? You can't be doing homework, you hate school."

She leaned over to see and I casually closed it, picking up the fishing pole and casting it out in the water.

"Did you walk over here by yourself, Half-Pint?" I asked, changing the subject.

She rolled her eyes. "I'm not a baby, Austin. You're nine, that's only one year older than me and you walked over here by yourself," she sassed, making me grin.

"Is that right?"

"I know what you're thinking."

"Hey, I didn't say a word, but I'm a boy and you're not. So there *is* that."

She narrowed her eyes at me, giving me the signature Alex glare. There was no telling her she couldn't do something just because she was a girl. If you did, she would prove you wrong the second you laid out the challenge. Her willpower to prove her point had gotten her in trouble more times than I could count, but it didn't stop me from picking on her, mostly because I loved getting a rise out of her.

We all did.

Our eyes moved to the fishing pole when it jolted and arched.

"You got a bite! Reel it in, Austin!" she exclaimed as she bounced on the balls of her feet, clapping her hands with excitement.

I did, jerking my body back every few seconds, reeling until the fish was out of the water, flapping around everywhere. I stood, laying the fishing pole down on the dock. Squatting down to grab its scaly body with one hand, I used my other to pull out the hook from its mouth.

"I bet I can catch a bigger fish than you," Alex chimed in.

I grinned again, raising an eyebrow as I stood. "Oh yeah?"

She enthusiastically nodded.

"By all means, Half-Pint," I challenged, handing her my pole.

She smiled, big and wide as she removed her Chucks. The same black ones us boys started wearing instead of the pink ones her mom begged her to buy. She took a dramatic deep breath before sitting back down with her legs dangling over the edge of the dock, her feet swimming in the water. The exact same way I'd been sitting.

I shook my head and smiled at the image. I watched with a curious gaze as she sat with the pole out in front of her, placed between her legs, her hand ready to reel in a big fish. Determination was written all over her face. She would beat me, even if it meant she would have to stay there all day trying. Something about the way she looked in that moment inspired me. Before I knew it I was opening my notebook, turning it to a fresh page. She didn't pay me any mind, her attention focused solely on the task at hand.

I tried to capture how the lighting from the sun made the freckles on her nose more prominent and enticing. I watched as a few dark brown strands of her hair blew in the wind. The rest of it tied high on her head so she could fit in better with us. I watched the way she rubbed her lips against each other every few minutes, biting on her bottom one when she was done. How the boy clothes she was adamant about wearing fell off her thin, tiny frame, making her appear younger than she really was.

Nothing lasts forever.

There would come a time when she would shed the boy clothes, not wanting to look like one of us anymore. Blossoming before our very own eyes. Always wearing her long hair down with loose fitting dresses and flip-flops.

Still a tomboy at heart.

The scent of her sunscreen that I knew she put on every morning filled the air all around us. I smiled, enjoying this rare time alone with her. These memories were few and far between. I tried to capture every last detail of her, my hand running wild against the sheet of paper. Peering up at her every few seconds. She just had this natural beauty about her. I don't know how much time went by. I was in my own little world, and I loved it when that happened. My mind would shut off for a little while, and I could live in the moment.

That didn't happen very often.

Even at that young of an age.

I always felt older than I was. Even my thoughts were beyond my years, an old soul was what my mom called me. Maybe that's why being the youngest got to me so much. Having to try and do everything first, proving to the other boys and myself that I wasn't the last one. Regardless of how much bigger and older they were, I wasn't going to be the one left behind. It didn't stop them from trying to order me around, and as we got older, I'd tell them where they could shove it.

Putting an even bigger rift among our friendship, to the point that I no longer called them my brothers. My best friends.

Except with Alex.

Never with her.

She was what held all of us good ol' boys together, had been since she was born.

I continued to get lost in her, my hand not stopping for one single second. I could see her frustration growing with each passing minute. Not wanting to accept that defeat may be the inevitable, until finally she got a bite. Her face lit up and her body jerked forward from the force. She jumped to her feet for more leverage. I didn't stop drawing, I couldn't.

"Austin! I got one! I got a big one, too!" she celebrated, glowing from head to toe.

I laughed as she used all of her strength to reel it in. I could have offered to help her, but that would have only provoked her, and she would have pushed me away. She wanted to do this on her own. I would be lying if I said I didn't want to be the cause of her happiness.

The fish put up one hell of a fight; I'm surprised it didn't yank her into the water. It took her a while to reel it in, but once she did, the joy that radiated all around her was enough to make me put my pencil down and notebook aside.

I stood.

"Look! Look how big! I don't think you boys have ever caught one this big before!" she shouted, jumping up and down in front of me ecstatically.

"Well, I think you might be right about that one. Don't get used to that, Half-Pint," I teased.

She smiled, squatting down to take out the hook, exactly the way I taught her. I opened the cooler for her to stick it in next to my fish, but she hesitated and bit her lip, frowning.

"I don't think I want to keep it. I mean… it's so big. Maybe it could help one of the smaller fish fight off a big fish one day."

I chuckled, nodding.

She shrugged, trying not to look embarrassed as she threw it back in the ocean. She turned back around to look at me, but something else caught her attention. Her eyes widened and she gasped, looking down at the picture I just drew of her. I immediately reached down, closing and grabbing my notebook before she had a chance to snatch it.

She reached out, stepping toward me.

"Austin, please let me see," she begged with her big dark brown eyes gazing at me.

I couldn't say no to her.

None of us ever could.

I sighed and handed her my notebook. No one knew this about me, not even my parents. She carefully flipped open the cover, her eyes widening once again as she took in page after page of the pictures that I had drawn over the years.

"Wow," she breathed out. "Did you draw all these?" she questioned, peering up at me.

I nodded again.

She smiled, shaking her head as she looked back down, turning each and every page until she got to the drawing of her. Shock quickly replaced the smile on her face.

"Oh, wow." She softly touched the outline of her face and then her hair on the paper, paying close attention to every detail I carefully drew. "I didn't know you could even draw. How do I not know this? I know everything about you. Do the boys know?"

"No," I simply stated, nervously rubbing the back of my neck.

She didn't know how to feel about my response, I could see it all over her expression.

"Why are you hiding this amazing talent? I mean..." she gestured towards the notebook in her hands, "this is such a beautiful gift, Austin. You should share it with the world."

I shrugged, not used to getting compliments or praise, especially for something I didn't want anyone to know about me. She understood my silent response, nodding and closing the notebook. She handed it back to me.

"Do you not want anyone to know?" she asked what I was already thinking.

"Half-Pint—"

"It'll be our secret." She threw her arms around my waist. "I promise I won't tell anyone until you say I can."

I put my arms around her, kissing the top of her head. She hugged me tighter.

"Can you promise to show me more of your drawings? Can you share your talent with me, at least? Please?" she whispered, gazing up at me.

"I promise."

She nodded, hugging me one last time before she pulled away. It was then that we heard footsteps on the wooden dock, one big thud after another. We both peered in the direction of the noise.

"Bo!" Alex called out, her special nickname for him. "I've been lookin' all morning for you. I found Austin instead." She pointed in my direction.

He pulled her to his side, and she willingly went with love and adoration spilling right out of her. I looked back up toward Lucas and if looks could kill…

I would be dead.

Briggs

"Daddy, can I have this?" I asked, holding a dolly with sparkling purple hair, trying to look as cute and adorable as I could. My puppy-dog eyes always worked with Daddy.

"Your mom said no, princess," he responded.

"But, Daddy, I really need this, please, pleeeease, pretty please?" I begged, giving him the biggest pouty lip.

"Daisy, you already have hundreds of dolls that look exactly like that one," Mom chimed in.

"No, Mommy, I don't. She has sparkly purple hair," I said, raising her above my head so she could see and understand what I was talking about.

She grabbed her out of my grasp and I smiled big, thinking I won. It soon faded when she placed her back on the highest shelf that I couldn't reach.

"Mommy!" I stomped my foot on the ground.

"Daisy, don't you dare throw a temper tantrum right now. You have hundreds of dolls, you don't need another one," she reasoned.

"Daddy!"

"You heard your mother, baby," he soothed.

I rolled my eyes.

This was not the time for him to be calling me that. I grunted, "I'm not a baby!"

Did they not understand how much I needed that doll? She didn't know what she was talking about. I didn't have any like her. It was so unfair.

Ken didn't want to be with plain Barbie anymore, he wanted to be with Sparkle Barbie. She was ruining all my plans for the wedding of the year, a huge, purple, beautiful wedding. I crossed my arms and sulked the entire way through the store as she placed one stupid item after another in the cart.

Why did she get a book and I got nothing? Why couldn't she just not buy broccoli and get me my doll? I hated broccoli, even Daddy hated broccoli. Stupid Mom. Stupid broccoli.

She never let me buy what I wanted. Daddy never told me no. Sometimes I wished she wasn't around. That it was just my daddy and me. Life would be so much better if it was just the two of us, then Mommy couldn't tell me what I could and couldn't have. My daddy and I don't need a mommy. We would do fine without her.

I watched him pull out a wad of cash to pay for our groceries. There was a lot of money; we could have definitely bought my doll. She was just being mean.

"Daddy, please…" I pleaded, tugging on the ends of his shirt.

"Baby, we can talk about it later. I have to go. Daddy is running late for a meeting. You don't want me getting into trouble, do you?"

I could see it in his eyes, he wanted to say yes, but Mommy cocked her head to the side as if she was testing him. He looked down at me and shook his head no. He grabbed my hand as we walked out to the car, but I didn't want to leave, I wanted my doll.

"Daddy, please," I tried again.

"Daisy, ya no más!" Mom scolded in Spanish, "*Daisy, no more.*" I narrowed my eyes at her, giving her my angry face.

He buckled me into my booster in the backseat of his car. I hated that thing; I was a big girl. Daddy told me so all the time. I didn't need to sit in a baby seat. I was six years old, but my mom said that I was still under the weight and height, so by law, I still had to ride in one. I think she was lying, there was no law—she just wanted me to sit in one. Daddy gave me a kiss on the forehead and told me he loved me and closed the door.

He rounded the corner of the car and gave Mommy a kiss on the lips, telling her he loved her before he got into the passenger seat. I didn't want to sit behind Mommy, I wanted to sit behind Daddy. I kicked the back of her seat before she got in the car.

Daddy looked down at his watch after Mommy started driving.

"There's no way I'm going to make this meeting."

She sighed. "I'm sorry, Michael. I know how important this meeting was for you."

Her car had died on our way to the grocery store, so she called Daddy to come rescue us.

"It's my fault. I should've taken it in weeks ago. I've been so busy with this merger. I haven't had time for anything else. It's fine, I gave the tow truck driver our mechanic's address." He grabbed his phone and dialed a number. "Lesley, put me through to the board."

"Michael, where are you?" I heard someone say through the phone.

"I'm sorry, Dale. My wife's car broke down and I had to pick them up. I can—"

"Can you still make it?"

Mom looked over at him, nodding. Making a sharp turn that caused my body jolt to the right.

"Yes, I'm on my way now. In the meantime, let me bring you up to date on the building codes," he began.

"Mommy, I want to stay up and wait for Daddy to come home," I said, knowing he would have to go back to work.

"Daisy, why don't you ever make it easy on me? Huh? You know you can't wait up for Daddy. You have school in the morning. We will eat dinner and do bath time—"

"I don't want a bath. I want to take a shower," I interjected, gritting my teeth.

"Damn it, it's starting to pour." Mom ignored my comment.

Dad pressed a button and some lights came on.

"No, baby, bath time is easier on me," she added. "Por favor ya no me contestes así, *Please don't talk to me like that anymore.*"

"Yes, Dale. The figures need to match the proposal," Dad kept on talking, ignoring us both.

"But I don't want a bath." I kicked my leg against the booster seat, hitting the back of hers. She gave me a warning look through the rearview mirror.

Why couldn't she let me do what I wanted? I was a big girl. What was her problem? A bath and a shower were the same. They both got me clean. I stared out the window. I could barely make out the trees as we passed them. It really started to pour, and I could hear the drops coming down hard on the car.

"Oye, niña, quedate quieta," she ordered, "*Hey, little girl, quiet down.* You will get a bath," she sternly stated. "Is that a red light? Fuck, I can't see."

"Ooohhh! You said a bad word. Daddy, she's in trouble!"

"Daisy, enough!" Dad yelled at me, placing his hand over the phone.

Now they were both making me mad.

"No! I want a shower! I don't want a bath! I'm not a baby! I don't want one! I want a shower! I don't want a bath!" I screamed, kicking my leg against the booster seat over and over again, my feet slamming into the back of Mom's seat.

"Daisy Julissa Mitchell Martinez!" she roared in Spanish. "I swear if you say one more word..."

I didn't like it when she said my full name. It meant I was in big trouble.

"No! I don't care!"

"Daisy, you don't talk to your mother like that."

"I hate you both, I really hate you! I wish you would just go away and leave me alone!" I yelled, regretting it immediately.

She instantly turned around and looked at me wide- eyed with a tear running down her face. I had never said that to them before. It just came out. I didn't mean it, I loved them both. I felt really bad. I was about to apologize and tell her I loved them, but I was cut off.

"AMARI!" Dad yelled out, grabbing the steering wheel. "This fucking idiot—"

The loud crashing noise that followed made me want to put my hands over my ears as my body was thrown forward. The car spun, whipping Mommy and Daddy's bodies all around. I wanted to cover my eyes. I think I was screaming, or maybe that was my mom? My head hit something hard and my body felt like it was on a roller coaster ride, as we tumbled and tumbled and tumbled. I didn't know which way was up and which was down.

For a second, I caught a glimpse of Mommy's face in the mirror, and I swear she mouthed, "*I love you.*"

It all happened so fast, yet it played out in slow motion in front of my eyes. I heard glass shattering all over me, pieces flying through the air. The sound of crushing metal drowned out our screams.

When we finally stopped, an eerie silence filled the car. All I could hear were raindrops hitting what was left and rumbles of thunder in the distance. I was really dizzy and tired. It was hard for me to open my eyes, but when I did, what I saw…

Would forever haunt me.

***

A week went by before we stood in the pouring rain. A black umbrella placed high above our heads, a man I had only just met holding it securely in place behind us. I watched the raindrops fall, forming puddles all around us, shuddering with every single drop.

I looked up at the tall, big man who called himself my Uncle Alejandro standing beside me. Mommy told me all about him. She said he was her baby brother who loved me very much but he was a very busy man and couldn't come visit us. He always sent me gifts for my birthday and holidays so I always believed what my mommy had said. But now I wasn't so sure.

He never smiled.

He didn't laugh.

He barely even spoke to me.

I don't think he liked me very much, but I still wanted to reach for his hand to hold it. I still wanted him to wrap his arm around me so I could hide inside his big arms and feel protected from what was happening all around us.

I bowed my head in remorse and shame.

"Are you ready, Daisy?" Uncle Alejandro's rough voice filled the air from above me.

I nodded, lying. I wasn't ready. I would never be ready. It surprised me when he reached for my hand. My gaze quickly followed the length of his arm up to his cold, dark eyes that never held any expression or emotion.

"The real world is a fucked up place," he said in a neutral tone out of nowhere, making my eyes widen and my head jerk back by the way he spoke to me.

It didn't faze him. "It's better that you learn that now. You can't stay a little girl forever, Daisy."

"My name is Briggs," I declared.

No more Michael.

No more Amari.

No. More. Daisy.

A part of me knew he wasn't looking for an explanation. I didn't say anything as we stepped forward, taking one last look at where my parents were laid to rest. Knowing I got my wish.

I had put them there.

CHAPTER
2
AUSTIN

All the boys were like brothers to me. We grew up together in the small beach town of Oak Island, North Carolina. Our parents were all good friends since childhood, so it was only natural that we all became best friends with one another too.

Out of all the boys, I was always closest with Dylan McGraw. I don't know why, that's just how it was. As we got older, I guess I felt like out of all of them, I could relate to Dylan the most. You could maybe even go as far as saying I looked up to him in some ways, since he was a year and some change older than me. He was twelve, and I had just turned eleven. He never gave a damn about what anyone thought or said about him. He would tell it straight to your face, not caring if he hurt your feelings or not. He never judged me. I wasn't saying that the other boys did, but Dylan was different. He treated me like an equal.

Jacob Foster was the oldest of the boys, almost thirteen. That didn't stop Dylan from taking on the role of big brother to us all. Which was probably why I bumped heads with most of the boys and as we got older and our balls fully dropped, it only got worse. Jacob was the most levelheaded one and smart as all hell too. Which was interesting in regards to the girl he actually ended up with.

Then there was Lucas Ryder, who was only a year older than me. He was twelve going on thirty, and stubborn as shit. He had a smartass personality and sometimes he took it too far. We all loved to surf but Lucas was the most skilled, constantly riding into waves that had us all questioning his decisions. We butted heads more often than not. There were times that I thought our friendship wouldn't survive it. The animosity towards each other grew more and more as the years went on. Eventually, down the long, unexpected road of life, I wouldn't exist to him anymore.

We all looked out for each other in one way or another as kids. With all the time we spent together, our mannerisms and personalities crossed over from one boy to the next. It would have been rare if our traits hadn't blended together over time.

Except for Alex.

Alexandra Collins. Our Half-Pint. The prettiest girl I had ever seen, even at the age of ten. She was wise beyond her years. There was something about her that pulled all of us boys in, time and time again. Her childlike demeanor was something she never grew out of. No matter how old she got, she constantly looked at the glass as half full. Growing up, she became our confidant, biggest supporter, and best friend. We often forgot that she was a girl and wasn't just one of the good ol' boys like the rest of us.

When shit really went down, I could always count on Dylan. It didn't matter what it was or where I was, he was there at the drop of a dime. He had my back and I had his, but over the years I took our friendship for granted.

Years I couldn't get back.

Years I couldn't ever change.

As much as I wanted to...

As much as I tried.

After four months, we finally finished our tree house that we had been working on all summer. We messed around with Alex making her believe she wasn't going to be allowed up there with us, telling her it was for boys only. We even went as far as making a sign that said, "No Girls Allowed" written in Jacob's mom's red lipstick. Of course Lucas was the first to cave and let her in, which was no surprise to any of us.

We decided to crash in the tree house that night to celebrate it finally being done. Alex was getting her sleeping bag and pillow before we even got the last word out. It was late by the time she passed out next to Lucas. They had a special bond, something none of us could come close to, or even begin to understand. It was much more than a bond. It was more like two souls destined to be together, a deeper level of love for each other and not just in the friendship kind of way. Lucas and I had our issues, but I would be lying if I said I didn't envy him when it came to her.

I think we all did in our own ways.

"She asleep?" Dylan asked, nodding toward Alex.

"Yeah," Lucas replied, pulling up the blanket on her shoulder.

"I can't believe she found the magazines," Jacob groaned. "You think she'll rat us out?"

I laughed. "Nah, just don't piss her off anytime soon. What the hell did you think was going to happen? I told you not to bring them up here."

"That was not me." He pointed to himself. "It was that fucker over by you."

Dylan grinned. "Please, I was doing you dickwads a favor. I'm the only one that has actually seen a pair of tits in real life."

"Your mom's don't count," I joked.

"Go fuck yourself, Austin."

I laughed even harder, my head falling back. "Just sayin', brother."

"Yeah, and I'm just sayin' you can go fuck yourself," he chuckled back.

"You know better than to mess with Dylan's manhood. The boy's been kissing girls since our playground days in grade school," Jacob chimed in.

"Someone had to show you pussies how it was done."

We all laughed, looking over at Alex to make sure we hadn't woken her up. It was rare not to have her prying ears listening to everything we said. We tried our best not to say vulgar things around her, but we were just boys. Things slipped out of our mouths all the time. She was innocent and a true lady. Her mama did right by her, and it shocked the shit out of all of us that our filthy mouths never rubbed off on her, especially as we got older and cusswords became a thing of the norm.

Oh and getting laid, let's not forget about that one.

"Hey, I'll give credit where credit is due. My boy Austin here has already tongue-kissed a girl," Dylan said proudly, squeezing my shoulder.

A few weekends before we had all gone to a girl named Stacey's birthday party. Well, all of us but Alex, she never went to any parties. We ended up playing spin the bottle out on the beach when her parents went back inside. It was my turn to spin the bottle and it landed on Kimberly. She had braces and cut my lip. I lied to my mom telling her I bit it surfing.

"What have you done with a girl, Lucas? Jack shit," Dylan knowingly added.

"I'm sorry I have standards and won't make out with anything that just has tits and ass, Dylan."

He shrugged. "You forgot curves and blonde hair. I like that shit too."

"Does it have to be longer than yours?" Jacob goaded.

Dylan had blond hair down to his shoulders since he could walk. We all made fun of him for it. He looked like a damn girl, but they loved it.

"Just enough for me to grab onto something," he mocked, moving his hand up and down above his dick.

"Oh, bullshit! You haven't gotten head," I called him out.

"Yet," he arrogantly countered. "I know what I want out of life."

"A girl?" Lucas asked, surprised.

"Pussy," he simply stated.

We heard the rustling of a sleeping bag. Our heads simultaneously turned to where Alex was lying. She must have rolled over; she was still sound asleep. Once she was out, there was no waking her up.

"Which is more than I say can for you," Dylan challenged, whispering to Lucas.

"What's that supposed to mean?" Lucas answered, taken aback.

"What do you want out of life, *Bo*?" Dylan baited.

"Fuck off," he sneered.

All the boys laughed, except for me. Lucas didn't think anyone was watching as he longingly gazed down at Alex. Knowing that all he ever wanted was *her*. I bowed my head, silently praying they didn't ask me what I wanted out of life.

There was no way in hell I could give them an honest answer.

Briggs

Two years had gone by since I killed my parents.

Crave Me

They say that when you experience trauma, a drastic, life-alternating change, you're suddenly forced to grow up. Become wiser beyond your years. Mature in ways that didn't make sense except to the people who may have experienced similar events.

I knew that was the case with me.

I was eight-years-old and living with my Uncle Alejandro in New York. I had been taken away from everything I had ever known and was brought there, in a city full of buildings and no one to talk to.

Home.

He moved me across the country to start a new life, a life much different than the one back home in Washington.

No warmth.

No happiness.

No love.

I had a life back there. I had everything I could ever ask for. I lived in a home full of love and laughter. Pictures lined the walls of my home. The fridge was covered with my drawings. Daisies were always on our table.

My family.

I had none of those things there.

No friends.

No family.

No parents.

Uncle Alejandro hired a nanny to take care of me, but all she did was cook my meals, clean my clothes, and watch over me. She smelled funny and didn't say much. My driver, Esteban, was the only person who was actually nice to me and paid me any attention. He looked young and had been assigned to protect me. Uncle Alejandro used the word "bodyguard," but I didn't really understand what that meant or why I needed one of those, though I didn't dare question him about it.

My uncle had blue eyes like my mom, but that's where their similarities ended. She always told me he was her baby brother and he looked really young too. He was tall, so tall that it hurt my neck every time I had to look up at him. I was told I had to look him in the eyes, especially when he was talking directly to me. I was to do the same when answering him and only talk when spoken to. He didn't explain why, and I was once again too terrified of him to ask. He was built much bigger than my daddy, taking up almost the entire doorway when he walked through it. They were Colombian and he spoke with a slight Spanish accent, even though my mom didn't. His brown hair went past his ears and it was always slicked back, away from his face that also had hair on it. He wore nothing but suits with shiny black shoes that echoed down the halls in the penthouse.

I barely ever saw him and when I did, it wasn't for more than a few minutes. He always made it seem as if he had something better to do than pay any attention to me.

My mom lied.

Uncle Alejandro didn't love me.

Not even a little.

I was there because I had to be, not because he wanted me there. He didn't have to say it for me to know it was the truth. There were times that I overheard him speaking in Spanish, thinking I didn't know what he was saying. Little did he know, I was bilingual. Since I was a baby, my mom had spoken to me in Spanish and my dad in English. It was an ongoing joke in our family about how Mom would speak in Spanish only when she was talking about Dad, because he didn't understand what she was saying. She would pick on him and call him a "white boy" and he would always reply that she was his Latin Queen.

I smiled at the thought.

I only smiled when I thought about them.

Thinking about my mommy and daddy made my heart ache. It hurt so bad that sometimes I couldn't breathe. I was drowning in the misery I created, getting sent here as punishment for killing my parents.

Sentenced to a life of being alone.

I had no one else to blame but myself. It was all my fault. I woke up every night from nightmares and had no one to comfort me. No one to hold me and tell me that everything was going to be all right.

No one to tell me they loved me.

That's what hurt the most.

I had all of that before but...

I wished them away.

It only took a few minutes for my life to be ripped from me. I shook my head, trying to push away the images of my parents and the last time I saw them. It didn't matter. I didn't feel safe in the house that was now known as my *home*.

I cried a lot.

I cried more times than I could count.

"Daisy!" Esteban shouted, walking onto the back porch that overlooked the city of Manhattan.

It was the only place I felt like I wasn't dying, the lights of the oversized buildings resembled twinkling stars. I hadn't seen real stars since Washington. I quickly wiped away my tears, not wanting him to see me cry.

"There you are. I've been looking all over for you," he added, stopping when he caught me wiping my face. "Are you okay?"

I nodded, looking down at my hands that were now placed in my lap. I heard footsteps and assumed he left like I knew my uncle probably would have. I was surprised when I felt him softly grip my chin, making me look up at him. It was the first time I realized how kind his eyes were. They reminded me of my dad's, which only made my eyes fill up with more tears.

"Hey… it's okay," he soothed, crouching down and pulling me into his arms.

It was the first time anyone had hugged me in such a long time. The first time anyone showed me any kindness or love. Any sympathy. I leaned into his embrace, soaking it up as much as I could, knowing that it wouldn't last long, and silently praying that it wouldn't be the last time someone would hold me and try to make me feel better.

"Why are you crying?" he asked, rubbing my back every few seconds to reassure me that it was okay to tell him.

To talk to him.

To trust him.

I couldn't take it anymore, so I just let go. I cried, long and hard for I don't how long. He didn't let go or push me away. If anything, he held me tighter, letting me sob for as long as I needed. Whispering reassuring words to help ease my pain and the hurt I felt in my heart.

"I miss my parents," I finally let out, bawling even harder. "I miss my parents so much, Esteban. I can't breathe. I'm suffocating. I don't think I'll ever be able to breathe again. My heart hurts so much. It hurts so much every day," I sobbed unable to control my emotions and needing to tell someone.

To have them understand that I wasn't a bad child. I just made a mistake. A brutal mistake that cost me my parents' lives, the only love I'd ever known.

"I know, pequeña," he murmured, catching me off guard.

I sniffled, sucking in a few breaths before I pulled away, wanting to look at him. I didn't bother to wipe my tears. He had already witnessed me breaking down and held me in his arms. I could see my fresh tears wet all over his nice black suit jacket.

I immediately felt bad.

"You know?" I coaxed, sucking in a few more deep breaths.

He cocked his head to the side with a sincere, sad smile for me. "I know."

I bowed my head.

"It's okay. I understand. I lost my parents too."

That made me look back up at him.

"I was around your age when it happened. It took me years to recover, but I promise it does get easier as time goes on," he spoke honestly.

I could tell by his soft-blue eyes. I wanted to ask him what happened to his parents. I wanted to ask him if he ever felt whole again, if he ever felt love or happiness.

If he ever felt… safe.

Something told me that he did. His eyes spoke for themselves, and they answered all of my questions. Which only gave me hope that someday I might have that again, and for an eight-year-old girl, that meant everything.

"Yeah," was all I could bare to say, even though there was so much more that I was feeling.

Something told me that he knew. As if it was radiating off of me. He affectionately smiled and wiped away a few of my tears, before grabbing the handkerchief out of the front pocket of his suit jacket and handing it to me. I blushed as I took it. All of a sudden feeling shy.

He stood and I followed his lead, feeling even smaller than I already was.

"Hey," he coaxed, reassuringly squeezing my shoulder. "I cry sometimes, too. Shit happens, Daisy, whether we want it to or not."

I immediately peered up at him again. No one spoke to me like that besides my uncle, as if I was an adult and not a little girl. For some reason, in that moment, with him, by ourselves...

It made me feel better.

I smiled for the first time since my life drastically changed.

And it wasn't from the memories of my parents.

At least not that time.

CHAPTER
3

AUSTIN

The more things changed, the more they stayed the same. A year went by and it was already summer break again. The boys and I did our usual shit, except now girls started to hang out around us more often. The older I got, the more I started to shed my red hair and freckles from my Scottish heritage on my mom's side. I started to look more like my dad. My hair got darker, but you could still see an auburn haze running through it in the sun. Which only made my bright blue eyes stand out more. For some unknown reason, girls really liked that.

Not that I was complaining.

My skin evened out or maybe it was from all the time I spent in the ocean and sun, surfing and riding bikes. It was rare to find any of us indoors for very long.

We all knew it bothered Alex to share us with all those girls, even though she wouldn't admit it out loud. In a few short months, she would be attending middle school with the rest of us. It was the other boys' eighth year and my seventh. It was easy to spare her feelings when she went to a different school, but it was only a matter of time until she realized that we were all growing up. Seeing things she may not want to see. Experiencing things she may not be ready for. I hated the fact that she might feel like she was getting left behind and didn't fit in anymore, experiencing it firsthand.

We were all aware of Lucas and Alex's connection, it wasn't hard to miss. You would have to be a damn idiot to not notice it. I knew the boys were the real reason why Lucas finally asked Stacey out, a girl that had been pretty much on his balls for a while now. Lucas had his asshole ways like we all did, but he would never purposely hurt Half-Pint and this...

This would destroy her.

So when Jacob suggested that we walk on the beach to go to Alex's parents' restaurant, a place we all hung out at since birth, it didn't take long for me to put two-and-two together. Instead of calling him out on it to protect and look out for her like I should have, I went along with it. Mostly because it was easier that way, even though it didn't take away the piece-of-shit feeling that came along with it. Jacob and Dylan hated the mere thought of them having feelings for each other besides friendship, and that was where it all started...

The rift between us all.

Particularly for Lucas and Alex.

I saw them from a mile away and if I saw them, I knew the rest of them did too, especially Half-Pint. They didn't try to turn the other way and leave, we just kept on walking toward them. They were on a secluded part of the beach and the full moon only added to Lucas and Stacey dry-fucking the shit out of each other on the sand.

I watched Alex's face the entire time. The way her heart just broke into a million pieces, spreading out all over the sand for us to walk right over it. Jacob and Dylan didn't look at her once. They knew what they were doing. They wanted her to see it. In their eyes, they thought they were doing her a favor, blatantly showing her that Lucas wasn't good enough for her and didn't give a shit about her.

Bottom line.

It was fucked up.

"Damn, boy, get up in there all good-like and shit," Jacob interrupted as Lucas' hand was moving under Stacey's shirt.

His body instantly jolted off of hers, standing. "What the hell, Jacob?" Lucas roared, spinning around to give him shit.

I watched the entire thing play out in front of me like it was a goddamn soap opera. All the fight in Lucas immediately died the second he saw Alex with her head bowed and her shoulders slumped forward.

A kicked puppy.

And it took everything inside me not to beat the living shit out of all of them for putting her through this. For showing her that life was cruel. Bursting her bubble that we were her boys, especially Bo. I could tell that Lucas felt awful, but at the end of the day, he didn't know that he was in love with her.

He was a kid trying to be a man.

A guy...

We're fucking idiots.

Alex always knew. She just tried to deny it. Maybe knowing that he could never really be hers, and that...

I understood more than anything or anyone.

"Relax," Dylan interjected, bringing Lucas' pissed off glare back to him. "We're just passing through, heading up to Half-Pint's restaurant for dinner. By all means, keep goin'."

Dylan reached out for Alex's hand, and she quickly took it, her eyes locked on the sand, not looking at anyone, particularly not Lucas. Dylan nodded toward Stacey who was still sitting there, unfazed by getting caught.

"Bye, darlin'," he added as we walked off.

As I got older, it was harder to control my emotions, my anger most of all.

For the first time in our friendship, our brotherhood, I allowed it to completely take control. Not giving a damn about the outcome or the consequences.

"I'm going to use the bathroom," Alex whispered, barely loud enough for us to hear as we walked up to the restaurant.

Dylan nodded, letting go of her hand, and we stayed by the shoreline. I was the only one to actually watch her leave, making her way up the beach into the restroom where I knew she would probably be crying her eyes out. Proving to herself that she really was just a girl.

Before I could give it anymore thought, I turned around with my fist already in the air and punched whoever the hell was closest to me straight in the jaw.

It just happened to be Dylan.

He staggered backward, his grip firmly placed on the side of his face. Neither one of them batted an eye. It was as if they were both expecting it. Maybe even a little proud of the fact that I was defending our girl from the hurt they knew they caused.

Dylan spit blood onto the sand and peered up at me, Jacob following his gaze. Both of them standing tall in front of me with expressions I couldn't quite place.

"You're both fucking assholes," I gritted out through clenched teeth with my fists still at my sides.

"No shit, Austin," Dylan countered, shaking his head in disgust. "What the hell are we supposed to do? Watch him hurt her anyway? This was easier, alright? Like rippin' off a damn Band-Aid."

"That was fucked up and you know it!" I argued, stepping forward until I was an inch away from their faces. "That wasn't fair to either of them. You set them up."

Jacob sighed. "Austin, you're too young to understand."

"Fuck you!" I roared, only glaring at him. "You can pretend all you want that this scheme you orchestrated was the right thing to do, but you don't fool me. Lucas wasn't the one that hurt her." I stared back and forth between them. "It was you," I said, receding my steps, needing to get away from them.

"Both of you." I turned and left.

Alex was already walking out the front doors of the restaurant by the time I made it inside. I ran, grabbing her wrist, making her spin to face me.

She immediately gazed down at the ground. "I don't feel so good. I must have eaten something. My stomach hurts. My mom's going to take me home," she murmured just above a whisper.

"Half-Pint…" I coaxed.

Something in the tone of my voice made her peek up at me through her wet, spiky lashes. Neither one of us said anything. We just stood there in the parking lot of the restaurant in silence, knowing words didn't have to be spoken.

She knew.

I pulled her toward me, and she willingly came. She wrapped her arms around my torso, tucking her head underneath my chin. I held her tight against me, opening my mouth to say something, anything.

Nothing came out.

I kissed the top of her head instead.

"I love you, Half-Pint. I'm always here for you," I reminded her.

"I know. I love you, too."

She was the first to pull away, shyly smiling.

"You ready to go, baby?" her mom asked, walking up with Lucas' mom and baby sister Lily beside her.

She nodded.

"Hey, Austin. Jesus, boy, you get bigger every time I see you. To think you used to be the smallest one," her mom chuckled. "The boys are inside playing pool. I'm sure they're waiting for you."

I smiled.

Lily just stared at us with a gleam in her eye. Even at the age of six, she was smarter than all us boys put together.

"I'll see you later, Austin," Alex said.

I watched them leave, knowing that the next time I would see her...

She wouldn't be the same girl.

Briggs

"Can I play, too?" I asked the boy with the friendly smile.

My uncle had changed my school once again. In three years, I'd been to four different schools. I would start at one and be moved to the next with no warning. He never gave me an explanation, just that I would be attending a new school. Not that it mattered. It wasn't like I made any friends.

"No," he simply stated.

I frowned. "Why?"

I was a nice girl. My mom and dad told me all the time. My teachers back home all loved me, and I had lots of friends.

"Because you're that new girl Daisy and my parents said that I can't play with you or talk to you. I'm supposed to pretend you don't exist."

I jerked back, surprised by his response. I peered at all the kids that were standing around him, looking at me with the same expression. They were playing dodge ball, which happened to be my favorite game. I was really good, too. I could help them win since they weren't doing a great job at that.

"None of us are allowed to talk to you. You should just go back to where you came from because we don't want you here! You're a bad apple!" he shouted too close to my face.

Crave Me

I don't know what came over me, but fury rose from deep in my belly and my skin burned all over. Before I knew it I was raising my fist and punching him right in the nose. My eyes widened, shocked by my own outburst. I didn't have a violent bone in my body. I instantly felt awful when he leaned over and blood came gushing out of his nose. It was the first time I didn't use my words like my parents had taught me.

Shame replaced the angry feeling that had just taken over me in that moment. This wasn't who I wanted to be. My parents would be so disappointed in me, and that alone made me feel worse.

I heard some kids gasp and then others went running towards the teachers. I was going to be in so much trouble.

"I'm sorry," I blurted out, scared of the repercussions from my uncle. "Please, don't get me in trouble," I pleaded, trying to help him, but he shoved my hands away.

"I'm going to tell everyone! You shouldn't be here! You don't belong in this school! Your family, they aren't good people! That's what my parents told me! That's why we're supposed to stay away from you, and you just proved them right!"

I fervently shook my head. "That's not true! I'm a good girl. I'm sorry!" I yelled back, hoping he would understand.

"Get away from me!"

"Daisy!" Miss Anderson scolded, running up to us. "I saw you hit him, young lady. That is not acceptable behavior. You need to come with me to the principal's office."

I bowed my head, tucking my chin up against my neck. The tears were already forming in my eyes as I trailed behind her to face my punishment.

Except in that situation, the principal wasn't who I was concerned about.

They called my uncle a few times to no avail. The principal said I was suspended for a week. There was a zero fighting tolerance and my behavior would not be accepted at the school. I pleaded with him to give me another chance. I tried to tell him that this was the first time I had ever acted out like this, but he wouldn't let me explain. He didn't care that I wasn't the one who started it or that the boy was being mean to me.

Esteban picked me up shortly after. The school must have called him when my uncle didn't answer. They handed him an envelope with a letter that explained I wasn't allowed back on school property for an entire week after telling him what happened. Embarrassment couldn't even begin to describe how I felt about the whole situation.

I gazed out the window the entire car ride back to the house that wasn't my home. Never had been, never would be. I could sense Esteban's stare through the rearview mirror a few times, but I ignored every last glance.

"Well if it isn't my little fighter," Uncle Alejandro's rough voice filled the foyer when I walked into the penthouse.

I immediately froze in place, not knowing what to expect. I peered up at him, trying to keep eye contact like I was required to do. I stood there not saying a word, swallowing the lump that had suddenly formed in my throat.

Esteban closed the door behind him. The latching noise startled me.

"I'm... I'm sorry... Uncle," I stammered.

He folded his arms over his chest, cocking his head to the side and arched an eyebrow. Only emphasizing his tall, huge, intimidating stature.

"What exactly are you apologizing for, Briggs?"

He'd been calling me Briggs since the day I told him to at my parents' funeral, Daisy died in the car accident as far as I was concerned.

"For fighting or for getting caught?" he vaguely added.

I looked all around the room as if the answer was written on the walls.

"I told you to look me in the eyes when I'm talking to you, Briggs. I won't warn you again," he viciously spoke, snapping my attention back to him.

My mouth parted as I peered into his eyes like he ordered. My eyes widening in shock.

"I expect an answer. You're wearing very thin on my patience, little girl."

"I—"

"Señor." Esteban stepped forward, away from the door, interrupting me. "I'll vouch for her. The boy started it all."

Uncle Alejandro didn't make a sound. He didn't even move. His eyes shifted to Esteban who was now standing beside me. An eerie silence filled the room. It was then that I realized my uncle was like a venomous snake. You would never see or hear him coming but once he struck, it was too late.

You were dead.

His lip curled upward but not in a smile or comforting way. If anything it only added to the tightening sensation I felt deep within my bones that I swear radiated all around us. He nodded and then brought his right hand up to his jaw. Tilting his head to the side, he cracked his neck before placing his arms behind his back, holding them there. His eyes showed no emotion, no mercy, they were still dark and daunting as always. His expensive suit jacket perfectly in place, as he set one foot in front of the other with precise and calculated steps. His Armani dress shoes echoed off the tile floor, one stride after another, until he was up in Esteban's face, who didn't cower down either.

"If you cherish the legs you're standing on, I suggest you walk the fuck away."

I jerked back, stunned. My stare inadvertently moved to his hands that were still locked behind his back. Realizing he wasn't holding his hands behind him, they were firmly wrapped around the handle of a gun. More than ready to follow through with his threat.

"Señor," Esteban coaxed, "I believe you asked me to do a job, and I go where she goes." He nodded toward me.

My mouth dropped open and I shouted, "Uncle! I'm sorry that I got caught," I lied, praying that it would take the heat off Esteban.

Uncle Alejandro snidely grinned, ignoring my outburst. "La peladita te tiene cariño, Esteban," he mocked, *"The little girl is taken with you."* His glare never left Esteban's face.

"Con todo respeto, yo también," Esteban replied, *"With all due respect, I do too."*

My chest rose and descended with each word that fell from their lips, terrified of how this would end. Neither of them backed down. My uncle narrowed his eyes at him and swiftly moved his hands from behind his back, releasing his gun. I jumped when he started clapping, the sound deafening in the foyer. He stepped back from Esteban to finally peer over at me. My heart was beating a mile a minute.

It was now my turn to answer to him.

"Someone has a knight in shining armor, *Daisy.*"

He said my name to hurt me, to make me remember who I really was which was inferior to him.

"Briggs," I simply stated, hating that it had the desired effect he wanted.

I saw a gleam in his eyes that he didn't try to hide. Even though it was quick, I caught it. He put his hands out in front of him in a surrendering gesture, dramatically bowing his head.

"By all means, Briggs. Since we're all making fucking friends here, how about we cut the bullshit? Yo se que usted habla y entiende muy bien el espanol, peladita," he added, "*I know you speak and understand Spanish very well, little girl.*"

I didn't falter.

I couldn't.

He didn't want me to.

It was now or never. I could tell myself that two could play his game, but some place deep inside, a place I just figured out existed, so desperately wanted to please him. Maybe I was looking for approval, gratification, support, knowing deep in my heart that all I was looking for was…

Love.

"You never asked. You never ask me anything for that matter," I countered. "But I know all about you. My mom told me. You know? Your loving sister." Throwing that in there for affect.

His eyes glazed over for a split second, and then he blinked it away. Just like that, the cold obscurity in his dark blue eyes was back like it had never left, even if it was only for a moment.

"She loved you."

Another glaze. Another blink.

"She also said you loved me. 'Adored me' were her exact words, but since we're putting out all the *bullshit*," I cussed for the first time and it felt so foreign coming from my lips. I ignored the lingering sentiment and finally said, "You don't love me. You barely even like me. You tolerate me because you don't have a choice. I'm here because I have to be. Nothing more, nothing less. So let's not get it twisted. You're not the hero in this story. You're not the victim either. To me… you look more like the villain in an expensive suit."

He smiled.

Big and wide.

It lit up the entire room.

It was first time in three years that I saw the man smile, and I would be lying if I said it didn't make me happy that I was the reason behind it. He took a seat on the leather couch, with a look I couldn't begin to understand. He brought one leg up, resting his ankle on the opposite knee. His arms spread along the back of the sofa. The massive couch suddenly seemed small in comparison to my uncle.

"Bueno," Uncle Alejandro rasped. "I guess we can thank Esteban here for finally letting your balls drop. Trust me, Briggs, you're a Martínez, it's in your goddamn blood." He lowered his eyebrows, concentrating solely on me. "You scurrying around my home like a fucking mouse, a home I brought you into out of obligation to your late mom, might I add, ends tonight. Whether we like it or not, you're here to stay."

I took in his words for what they were.

My uncle was not a typical uncle. Maybe not even a typical man. He proved that then more than any other time. He was proud when I stood up to him and any other person for that matter. Taking pleasure in seeing my tough side that I never knew existed. He condemned all the traits my parents had implemented all my life.

That wasn't my life anymore, though, which only made all of this more confusing.

I completely forgot that Esteban was still standing beside me. He hadn't moved from where he was planted. He was listening to Uncle Alejandro as intently as I was.

"Let me tell you a little something about me," Uncle added.

He leaned forward, resting his elbows on his knees. Hands clasped in front of him in a prayer gesture, mockingly. He looked me up and down, slowly cocking his head to the side, an evil grin spread across his handsome face. Breaking the silence, he spoke with conviction,

"I'm your God, peladita. Driving the bus to Hell."

CHAPTER
4
AUSTIN

Two years went by, a few months short of my fifteenth birthday. The boys were surfing. The waves were supposed to be at an all-time high, they always were before big storms. On any other given day, I wouldn't miss the opportunity to surf either, but this day was different.

My dad was a prominent cardiologist and my mom was a pharmacist. They were the ultimate power couple. I told the boys I had to watch my nine-year-old brother, Hunter, while my parents worked late.

The truth was I just wanted to be alone.

I heard footsteps descending down the dock, and I didn't have to wonder who it was. Alex took off her flip-flops, pulling up her dress to sit beside me on the wooden plank, splashing her feet in the water like me. The day after we caught Lucas and Stacey on the beach, she showed up at church wearing a dress, make-up, and her hair down. It was her way of showing us that she was growing up too. I told you, she always had to keep up with the boys, reminding me that we were one in the same.

I glanced up from my drawing to find her with her very own matching notebook, beaming.

"Whatcha got there?" I asked, cocking my head to the side. An amused expression was evident across my face.

She shrugged not paying me any mind, turning the cover over to the first page, placing the notebook on her lap.

"I'm going to draw, too."

I perceptively nodded, letting her hold onto her pride, knowing that she was just trying to keep up with me.

We sat in comfortable silence for a while, just sketching and watching the blue waters.

Both of us lost in our own thoughts.

I peered up from my sketch when the sun started to set, catching a glimpse at Half-Pint's drawing from the corner of my eyes. She must have sensed me staring. She blushed, peeking up at me through her lashes.

Before I could think twice about it, I blurted out, "Is that your wedding?"

"Maybe," she softly whispered, suddenly appearing tinier than she actually was.

It didn't take long to recognize the man in the picture. I could see his dark hair and tall frame. The way she captured the look in his eyes when he stared at her and thought no one was watching.

Though I still asked, "Who you marryin'?"

She bit her bottom lip and replied, "Just a boy."

"Bo?" I stated as a question.

She closed her notebook, setting it to the side of her to look down at her feet that were now splashing in the water. Ignoring my question.

"Half-Pint, why do you do this to yourself?"

"What do you mean?" she retorted, still focusing solely on her feet.

"Hurting yourself. Wanting someone you know you can't have?"

"I don't know."

"Yes you do."

That made her glance at me.

"He kissed me," she revealed out of nowhere.

My eyes widened, surprised.

"Like... really kissed me," she emphasized, nodding to get her point across like it would change something.

When in reality, all it did was piss me the fuck off.

I didn't hesitate, viscously spewing, "Before or after he fucked around with Stacey?"

She gasped, shocked. Hurt was apparent all over her face by my response. Now, I was no better than the other boys. I did the one thing that I had avoided up to that moment.

I hurt her.

"They're making love?" she innocently questioned, her big brown eyes showing more emotion than I'd ever witnessed before. All glossy eyed.

"There's a lot more to fucking around than just sex, Half-Pint."

"Oh…" she paused for a few seconds. "So, they're doing the other stuff you're talking about then?"

I shook my head, annoyed with I don't know who. "Never mind." I closed my notebook and stood, wanting the conversation to be over. She immediately followed my lead.

"No! Don't do that. Answer me. Are they doing those things or not, Austin?"

"Ask him. Ask your *Bo*," I mocked.

Her eyes filled up with tears. I wish I could tell you that I felt bad, that I regretted telling her the truth she was so blind to see.

I didn't.

At least not that time.

"She's just a girl, Half-Pint. She's just a fucking girl."

She jerked back like I had slapped her across the face, and then she took a step toward me. Invading my personal space, the same one I wanted that day. She gazed deep into my eyes for what felt like a lifetime.

My truths that I hid…

From her.

From the boys.

From the world.

Especially…

From. Me.

Stared her blatantly in the face for the first time in our short complicated lives.

"Would you hurt me like that, Austin? Would you hurt me like Bo hurts me, just for a girl?"

I watched how her hair blew in the wind. How new freckles had formed on the bridge of her nose from the sun. How her lips were parted and her body slightly trembled, waiting on pins and needles for my response. The smell of her sunscreen and cherry lip-gloss assaulted my senses, leaving a sense of longing for the little girl in pigtails. The same little girl that would follow her good ol' boys around everywhere we went.

I took in every last detail we loved about her.

"Yes," I lied.

That was my first and biggest mistake.

Briggs

I was almost twelve years old and settling into my new life. Another three years had flown by. The life and memories I once knew went right along with it. Everyday I remembered my parents less and less. Everyday another piece of my heart went missing, disappearing and leaving me with nothing but the hollow, empty space that formed in its place.

I read and I wrote a lot.

I had a huge collection of books. My otherwise neat room was filled with stacks of novels. Stories that were poured out of someone's heart and soul onto a piece of paper for another person's enjoyment. These books were my freedom.

Sometimes the books were about epic love and other times they were deeper than that, life lessons on yellowed paper. My collection was quite impressive thanks to my uncle who spared no expense to indulge me. I loved getting lost in the fictional worlds of the author's creations. It took away the pain from my own.

My way of escaping.

My book friends.

Where I was loved, cared for, and cherished. Where there's always a happily ever after and the hero always ends up with the heroine. Those were my favorite kinds of stories.

Except, my story wouldn't be one of those, and I knew that even then.

I'd been writing in a journal for the last few years. At first it was memories of my parents so I wouldn't forget them, but then somewhere along the way I began writing about my feelings and emotions.

My journal became more therapeutic than a remembrance of the people I tried to keep so deeply in my heart.

Esteban caught me writing a few times, and to my surprise, he never asked to read what I wrote. He never even asked what I was writing.

He just called it, "The window to your soul." Which was all he ever said about it.

Esteban was a man of very few words, but when he did talk, it meant something. I really liked that about him. He never felt the need to fill the silence with meaningless banter. So when he said something I really listened, appreciating the wisdom he may have to offer.

I'd changed schools four more times in the last three years and at the rate I was going, there wouldn't be any more schools to transfer to. A few things changed with my uncle for the better I guess. He was around a lot more, and we ate dinner together a few nights a week. He asked me how my day was and if there was anything I needed or wanted. That was pretty much the extent of our conversations, but at least he tried.

"How was class?" Esteban asked, pulling me away from my thoughts.

I started taking a creative writing course outside of school. The instructor was nice and most of the students kept to themselves, lost in their own thoughts about what they would be writing on the blank pages of the notebooks placed in front of them.

"It was good," I answered, looking at his face in the rearview mirror as he drove.

"I bet you write better than all your friends."

I scoffed. "You're my only friend, Esteban."

Our eyes locked through the rearview mirror.

"You listen to me, and you're there when I need you. I guess you're my chosen person," I shyly smiled.

He didn't falter. "I'm not your friend, Daisy," he informed, catching me off guard.

My happy moment was quickly replaced with disappointment.

"I'm your bodyguard and driver. I work for your uncle. Don't ever forget that," he rudely added, focusing back on the road in front of him as if I didn't exist.

He'd never treated me like that before, and I tried to hide my tears because in my mind I thought he was my friend.

Crave Me

The only one I had.

CHAPTER
5

AUSTIN

"That feel good, baby?" I groaned into her ear, rubbing her clit in slow progressive circles.

For the life of me I couldn't remember her name.

Jennifer, Jenny, Jen something?

It's not like I was looking to date her, take her to the goddamn prom, or God forbid, back home to meet my mama.

Her body shuddered beneath mine the harder I moved my fingers on her pussy. She was so fucking wet, and I resisted the urge to bring my fingers up to my mouth to taste her. I claimed her mouth instead, mostly to drown out how fucking loud she was. Not that it mattered how loud we got, the music from the party downstairs was blaring through the speakers below us.

"Right there," she panted against my lips.

"Here?" I taunted, thrusting two fingers inside her.

One thing changed after that day on the dock with Alex almost a year ago. One very important thing.

I didn't give a fuck anymore.

Zero. Fucks. Given.

"Fuck 'em and chuck 'em," was Dylan's motto. I decided to adopt his attitude, and I swear to God it made my life so much easier. No stress, no drama, no worries. No more of the emotional bullshit and baggage that ran my life with *Half-Pint and her good ol' boys*.

I did what I wanted. When I wanted. How I wanted.

If you didn't like it…

You could go fuck yourself.

Being a pansy-ass follower got me nowhere, and at least now I didn't have to pretend to be something I wasn't. I didn't have to march in line with my dick tucked between my legs waiting for the boys to realize I was just like them. Proving to them…

I was.

I let myself go and enjoyed what life had to offer. I spent way too many years caring about what other people wanted, what other people thought, what other people expected. Years of pent-up frustration came coursing out of me.

I'd been caught inside of a wave for far too long. It was only a matter of time until I wiped out.

"Harder, faster," she moaned, rotating her hips against my hand.

Her pussy got so damn tight as I fucked her with my fingers. Her mouth parted letting a moan escape. Her soft, wet tongue peeked out, licking her lips, biting the bottom between her teeth. I took in her soft glow, her rosy cheeks, the subtle sweat pooling at her temples. Watching her tits bounce with each thrust of my hand, the way her back would curve each time I hit her sweet spot. Her hands fisted into the blankets beneath us and her body arched just slightly at the last second as she came all around my fingers.

My dick throbbed and my balls ached.

She smiled, opening her eyes. "Your turn."

"Is that right?"

She nodded, pressing her hands against my chest to flip me over and straddle me. I assumed she was just going to suck my cock, so when she grabbed a condom from her purse, I pretended that I wasn't taken aback. She unbuckled my belt and pulled down my jeans, followed by my boxers. My shirt was already off. My hard cock sprung free, smacking against my stomach.

"Wow," she breathed out.

My dick twitched from the praise.

She seductively smirked as she slid her way down my body. Slowly kissing along my abs, only stopping when her face was just above my cock. She looked up at me through her lashes, grinning with glazed eyes and an allure I had only just witnessed. She slipped the head of my dick into her awaiting mouth, using her hand to work my shaft. I lay back with my fingers laced behind my head, watching with hooded eyes as she sucked my cock like she had something to prove, enjoying the sensation she stirred in my balls.

It was almost too much.

I gripped the back of her neck and pushed her head lower down my shaft until she gagged, making me groan from the vibration. She released my dick with a pop and tried to hand me the condom. I shook my head no. She understood my silent order and ripped it open with her teeth, sliding it down my length in one swift movement.

Crawling up my body in a slow, steady stride, she hovered above me, waiting in anticipation for my next move. I didn't falter. Grabbing my cock, I angled it toward her opening and she effortlessly slid down. Her pussy was so fucking tight. My eyes shut and my head fell back against the pillow, taking in the feeling of her warm heat wrapped around me. I clutched her hips, gliding her down my shaft.

"Fuck," I growled, loud and hard.

"Jesus, you're as big as some of the seniors. Are you sure you're only a freshman?"

I ignored her stupid question. Leaning forward, I pulled her toward me by the nook of her neck, our lips collided, rough and eager. I sucked her tongue in my mouth when she started to ride the shit out of my cock. Back and forth, up and down, keeping a steady rhythm like a goddamn pro.

"Fuck... you feel good," I groaned in between kissing her.

It fueled her desire to work me over harder and more aggressively, each sway of her calculated hips hitting every spot that drove me closer and closer to the edge of release. I couldn't hold back any longer, it felt too fucking good. I flipped us over, needing to control the movements before I blew my load in less than a few minutes.

She placed her legs on my shoulders. "Like that. It feels so much better like this," she panted, mimicking my breathing.

I pounded the fuck out of her tight, wet pussy, in and out.

Forcefully.

Urgently.

Demandingly.

I took what I needed, and she gave what she wanted.

"I'm going to come," I huskily groaned.

"Me too, I'm almost there," she moaned loudly.

The second I felt her tighten around me, I came so fucking hard that I saw stars. I fell on top of her, sweat dripping from both our bodies, her legs sliding off my shoulders. We both lay there breathless, our hearts beating rapidly, lost in our own thoughts I was sure. I pulled out my cock and got off the bed, walking into the bathroom to get rid of the condom.

When I came back in the room, the smell of smoke assaulted my senses. She was sitting up against the headboard, a thin white sheet covering her body. She looked like an angel, even though I knew she was anything but. Her thumb and index finger held what appeared to be a rolled up cigarette firmly placed between her lips. She sucked in, long and hard, holding in the smoke for a few seconds before exhaling slow and steady.

There was something seductive about the way she did it. I stood there and watched her take another drag, observing the picture that was being painted in front of me with a hypnotic allure that drew me toward her, instead of leaving the room like I probably should have.

"Want a hit?" she purred, extending her hand out in my direction.

I'd never done drugs before, but that didn't stop me from contemplating doing it. I sat next to her on the bed, not bothering to get dressed.

"Sex and weed are always a great combination," she added, taking one more hit before handing me the joint.

I took one last look at the random chick in front of me and then closed my eyes.

All I saw was *her* face.

Bringing the joint up to my lips, wanting to forget that I just had sex for the first time with a girl…

I didn't crave.

Briggs

I stared down at the blood on my panties for I don't know how long. Thinking maybe if I looked at it long enough it would magically disappear or something.

It didn't.

I was twelve and I had just gotten my period for the first time. I didn't have a clue what to do about it. It wasn't like I had a mother or any other female around to guide me.

I lived with men.

Normally, I probably would have asked Esteban to help me, but ever since that day in the car, he barely spoke to me anymore.

I was a job to him, and he started treating me like one.

I jumped suddenly from a loud, hard knock on the door.

"Briggs? What the hell are you doing in there? You've been in there for almost an hour," Uncle Alejandro barked through the door, surprising me that he even noticed.

I didn't answer him. What was I supposed to say? I glanced around the bathroom hoping the floor would swallow me whole. I wasn't that lucky. I immediately pulled up my panties and slid down my skirt. Taking a deep breath, I opened the door, but my eyes remained down on the ceramic tiled floor.

"What the fuck?"

"I'm bleeding," I murmured.

"Peladita, what part of look me in the eyes when I'm talking to you is so hard for you to fucking understand?"

I instantly looked up at him with annoyance written all over my face. Head cocked, nostrils flaring, lips pursed, with my hands in fists at my side.

"Is that all you care about? Fine! I'm looking you in the eyes and telling you I'm bleeding! Better?"

Maybe my period made me stupid?

"You watch your fucking tone with me, little girl," he sneered, looking me up and down. "What did you do? Cut yourself?"

I scoffed. "No I didn't cut myself! I'm twelve years old and a female! You're a smart guy, put two-and-two together!"

He opened his mouth probably to yell at me, but quickly shut it when he realized what I was implying. He did it a few more times, looking at me speechless, which only added to my frustration.

"Are you just going to stand there and be all... *you*?" I asked, pointing at him. "Because the longer we stand here, the more the blood keeps coming—"

He put his hand out in front of him, shushing me. "Enough."

"Well… then help me. I don't know what to do," I pleaded with desperation in my tone.

"Why are you telling me this? Why don't you tell your nanny? She's a woman."

I sighed. "She doesn't like me."

"And you think I do?"

His words didn't faze me. The feeling was mutual.

"In this case, you're the lesser evil."

Without another word he pulled out his phone, turned around and started to walk away, completely ignoring my rant. I followed close behind, assuming I was supposed to. He made his way into his office, still not acknowledging me. I sat down in one of the chairs in front of his desk.

"Don't get too comfortable," he snapped.

"Si, señor," Esteban announced, walking into the office before I could give any thought to what he'd said to me.

Oh, God. Please, please, please, don't let him do what I think he's about to…

"La pelada se desarrolló," Uncle crudely revealed, *"The girl just got her period for the first time."* His phone rang. "She's your job. You deal with it." He nodded at Esteban, answered his phone, and left.

I sat there in shock, completely silent. Embarrassment couldn't even begin to describe how I felt. I wanted the floor to cave in and swallow me whole. I stared at the doorway for I don't know how long after he left. My face burned from humiliation and anger that he would do this to me. I finally glanced over at Esteban who was frozen in place, awkwardly rubbing the back of his neck for comfort.

He did the same thing my uncle did. He opened his mouth a few times to say something, but nothing ever came out.

"So… are you…" He narrowed his eyes at me, confused. "I mean… does it… what… *fuck*," he stressed the last word and it was the first time I heard him cuss.

"I don't know."

He cocked his head to the side.

"I mean…" I shrugged. "I don't know what to do."

"Me and you both, kid." He laughed nervously.

"Do you happen to have a wife or girlfriend, or someone I could maybe talk to?"

He shook his head no.

"No friend that's a girl?" I added, stunned.

He shook his head no again.

The realization that Esteban and I might've had more in common than I thought was a bigger rude awakening than getting my period.

"Can you walk?" he asked, pulling me away from my thoughts.

"Yeah, I got my period, I'm not incapacitated."

We both grinned.

"Come on, smart ass. I guess we could go to the pharmacy. We can't be the only dummies that have ever walked in there with this problem."

I went to the bathroom before we left to add more toilet paper to my panties. I felt like I was wearing a diaper the entire time, but to my surprise the pharmacist behind the counter was very understanding. She said her daughter was around my age and she went through the same thing with her a few days prior.

I breathed a sigh of relief.

She didn't ask me any questions as we walked down the feminine aisle. She just stopped every few steps to show me all the different kinds of tampons and pads I could use. Explaining which ones she thought would be best for me. She even went as far as pulling out a pamphlet that demonstrated how to insert it. She told me that I needed to start seeing a gynecologist because I was becoming a woman and the doctor could further explain what would start happening to my body.

"Everything okay?" Esteban asked as he saw us making our way back to the counter.

She put her arm around me in a comforting gesture. "Everything is perfectly fine. It's nice of you to help your sister out, we don't see that often, it's usually the moms that deal with these kind of situations," she said.

"He's not my—"

"No problem," he cut me off.

I didn't give any thought on why he interrupted me. I'd had enough drama in the previous few hours. I took a long, hot shower when I got home, threw away my ruined underwear and used the dreaded tampon. Wanting to forget about the day from Hell.

Wishing my mom was there with me.

I gasped, placing my hand over my heart when I walked back into my bedroom. My uncle was sitting on the armchair in the corners of my room.

"Don't you knock?"

"It's my home," he simply stated.

"Yeah, well it's my bedroom," I responded while holding onto my towel for dear life.

He was over to me in three strides, almost knocking me over.

"I'm going to overlook that you're acting like a disrespectful *puta* because of the changes you're going through." He leaned in close to my face. "But if you speak to me like that again, I have no problem letting you meet the man behind the expensive suit."

I jerked back, swallowing hard. Immediately understanding his subtle threat.

"Now," he stepped back and I let out the breath I didn't realize I held, "Esteban says everything was taken care of."

I bit my tongue and just nodded.

"I've made an appointment with the female doctor for you."

My eyebrows lowered. "How did you—"

"It's next week. After you're done with that bitch-causing thing."

With that he turned and left.

I changed into some sweatpants and a t-shirt, getting ready to climb into bed when I saw a glass of water and two Ibuprofens sitting on my nightstand next to my book.

I chuckled, shaking my head in amazement.

CHAPTER

6

AUSTIN

The boys, Alex, and I sat around the fire pit on the beach, bullshitting and shooting the breeze. It was the annual Fourth of July festival in Southport. The entire street closed down for the parade and firework display.

After the festivities there was always a party happening down at the beach. We were spending our last night together before the boys left for Ohio State in the morning, leaving Alex and I behind.

"I can't believe you boys are leaving me," Alex whispered in a sad voice.

She was sitting between Lucas and Aubrey, Dylan's girlfriend. Normally Lucas would have pulled her to his side, comforting her and she would have leaned into his embrace. Appreciating his comfort and loving his warmth, except too much had happened between them now.

A lot changed in the last two years, including Alex having a new guy friend.

His name was Cole Hayes. He was from California, vacationing with his parents in Oak Island for the past two summers. Alex started working at her parents' restaurant the summer before she entered high school, and as luck would have it, he happened to sit in Half-Pint's section one afternoon, while we were surfing. He'd been a pain in the ass ever since.

She chose to work, for reasons that I already knew, but she never voiced.

When I saw Alex walking down the beach with Cole beside her an hour prior, I was shocked to say the least. She never went to these things. Parties weren't her thing.

"You still have me, Half-Pint," I reminded her, sitting on the other side of the pit.

"Thank God for that," she breathed out, "or else I would be completely losing it."

She crawled her way over to me, wrapping her arms around my waist. Her face tucked securely against my chest. I kissed the top of her head as she lay in my arms. I could sense Lucas' glare, but still felt the need to look up at him. To my surprise it wasn't a look of jealousy or anger like I expected.

There was longing.

As if I held his entire world in my arms.

For the first time we were on opposite sides of the fence, and I would be lying if I said it didn't make me feel good to finally be the one that wasn't standing on the wrong side.

I never imagined anyone could break Lucas and Alex's bond. I would have bet my life on it. There were plenty of boys that were interested in Half-Pint throughout the years, but they all knew she came with baggage.

Four of them.

Cole showed up out of the blue one day, making it known that he was interested in our girl and not giving a shit what we thought about it. I didn't know whether to beat the shit out of him like the boys wanted to or shake his goddamn hand.

He was in love with Alex. It didn't surprise me. Alex was hard *not* to love. He put up with all of us boys because she didn't give him a choice.

At the end of the day we would always be her good ol' boys and for some reason...

That had always been good enough for me.

Dylan hugged Aubrey closer into his chest. Her back pressed up against him with her head tilted to the side, resting on his shoulder. Both of them watched the flames of the fire, lost in their own thoughts.

Dylan had started showing interest in the new girl, Aubrey two years ago, and to be honest, I was still dumbfounded by it. He was a bigger whore than I was. He pretty much chased her down until she finally gave in, challenging him to keep his dick in his pants for a month before she agreed to go on a date with him.

They'd been together ever since.

What once was a happy-go-lucky relationship turned into something volatile a few years later. Only proving to me that love was a bunch of fucking bullshit.

And Jacob, well… he was another story. One that I would learn soon enough, showing me how much of a hypocritical son of a bitch he really was.

Alex took a sip of her drink.

"Take it easy on that," Lucas warned, his eyes still intently placed on us.

Alex wanted to forget, she wanted to rebel, she wanted to prove something to us, and that's why she was drinking in the first place. As much as I hated to admit it, Lucas was right. But I was the last person that had any right to tell her what to do, so I just grabbed the drink out of her hands and finished it off for her instead.

Yeah, I'm a fucking hypocrite too.

"Ugh," Alex protested. "I'll just go get another one."

She stood, losing her balance. Aubrey grabbed ahold of her.

"I'll go with you." She knowingly winked down at Dylan.

Aubrey loved our Half-Pint, too. Her and Cole were both seventeen like me, and going into their senior year of high school as well. To be honest, I really liked Aubrey. She was good for Dylan, kept him on his toes and put up with all his bullshit. He was lucky to finally find someone who would. Aubrey was the best thing to walk into his life. They were meant to be together.

We watched them leave.

"You alright over there, McGraw?" I asked Dylan who was gazing at Aubrey with the same yearning that Lucas displayed over Alex.

"Just fuckin' peachy, brother," he replied, shaking his head. "How about you? How you holdin' up? You ready to run this fuckin' town without us?"

"Been doin' that since the day I was born."

We all smiled.

"I know. I taught you well," Jacob chimed in, cracking his neck.

I chuckled. Lucas still hadn't taken his stare off Alex. He wasn't paying us any mind.

"You're the last one left, Austin," Dylan said out of nowhere, catching me off guard.

I turned from the fire to look at him, not sure where he was going with this.

"I know we all give you shit for being the youngest and you used to be the smallest. Come to think of it, there was a time I thought Half-Pint might be bigger than you." He grinned.

"Asshole," I muttered, holding back my own grin.

"But you grew up," he added with a sudden serious expression. "And you're up, brother. We're not goin' to be around, and Half-Pint is gonna need you now more than ever. Especially since this is her last year before she's really alone."

I nodded, understanding.

"She's your responsibility. You watch out and take care of our girl," Jacob added.

"Of course," I vowed.

Jacob nudged my shoulder. "Won't be the same without you, bro."

"Ain't that the truth." Dylan stood. "But enough of this sappy shit, I feel like kicking someone's ass in a game of beer pong."

"You're on, fucker," Jacob challenged.

Dylan stopped in front of me to do our usual handshake, patting me on the shoulder. Jacob followed his lead and they left.

Lucas and I found ourselves sitting in uncomfortable silence for what seemed like a lifetime, staring at the flames and the sparks soaring up into the dark sky. There were no stars out; there was barely a moon. The wind blew all around us, mimicking the waves of the ocean. I immediately wondered if the boys would miss this.

It was all we'd ever known.

All I knew was that I wanted out of this town.

"You know they're right," Lucas declared, breaking the silence and bringing my attention back to him.

His intense stare hadn't wavered from Alex, who was giggling like a little girl, hanging all over Cole.

"She's drunk," he stated, taking the words right out of my mouth.

I shook my head, taking a deep, long breath, not knowing how to reply.

"Fuck," he whispered to himself, bowing his head and running his hands roughly through his hair.

"Lucas—"

"I didn't think it was going to be this fucking hard… leaving her. With you."

"We all love her. Just as much as you do."

He peered up at me with a look I recognized and understood all too well.

I didn't falter. "It was your choice to go away to college. No one put a fuckin' gun to your head, ordering you to move to Ohio. You're leaving her… with me, because *you* chose to. So if that's eating away at your conscience, it's no one's fuckin' fault but your own."

He scoffed. "That girl over there," he gestured toward Alex, who was still draped over Cole, "is my fucking world, and don't you ever forget that," he roared through gritted teeth.

I chuckled, shrugging. "I'm not the one leaving her, *Bo*," I declared, adding fuel to the fire.

He jerked back like I had hit him. "Tread carefully, Austin," he sneered, standing, taking a step closer to me.

I stood too. We were a foot apart. It didn't matter that there were people everywhere around us, neither one of us backed down. For a few seconds in time we forgot that we were brothers, best friends, playing on the same damn team.

"Get the fuck out of my face, Lucas," I cautioned through gritted teeth and a clenched jaw, ready to knock him on his ass if needed. "She's better off without you here, but don't you worry, Bo. I'll take care of our girl."

"You, son of—"

"Hey…" Alex wobbled, stepping in between us. "What's going on?" she slightly slurred with a lazy smile.

I pulled her toward me before she fell, bringing her into my arms. She rested her head on my chest and wrapped her arms around me, sighing contently.

Lucas glared at me one last time before stepping back, surrendering his hands, placing some much-needed distance between us.

"Where you going, Bo? You's not supposed to leave until tomorrows. I don't want you to leaves," she jumbled; completely oblivious to what was going on with us.

"I'll always come back, Half-Pint." Lucas backed away, pointed his finger in my direction and warned, "Don't fuck it up."

Alex peered up at me, distracting me from Lucas. She had glossy eyes, rosy cheeks, and a sluggish smile. Obviously, having a hard time focusing on my face.

"You changed, Austin," she said out of nowhere, catching me off guard.

"Half-Pint—"

"You used to be such a nice boy. A very, very, very nice boy. You's not that boy anymore and that makes me sad."

"Alex, you're drunk."

She slowly nodded. "I don't like new Austin's. He uses girls and causes troubles. That's not you. Not my boy. Brings him back." She hugged me closer, her face pressed into my chest. "Mmm kay?"

I kissed the top of her head. Looking over at Lucas who hadn't moved from the place he stood. Only confirming her boy was gone.

And he wasn't coming back.

Briggs

"Oh, come on, Esteban! Just watch the movie with me," I coaxed, patting the couch next to me. "It's Friday night, and we both know you don't have any friends," I teased. "What are you going to do? Go hide out in your room? Come on, I know you want to. What guy wouldn't want to watch *The Shining*?"

He raised his eyebrows.

"It's almost Halloween. I'm trying to get into the spirit. Hang your gun up and take a load off. See what I did there? Gun, load?" I wiggled my eyebrows.

He chuckled, shaking his head.

"My uncle's gone and who the hell knows when he'll be back this time. So, you don't have to play guard dog for me tonight. I ordered a pizza. I have popcorn, gummy bears, and snow caps," I said, pointing to the assortment of snacks on the coffee table. "All food groups. Plus, we don't have to go anywhere. Now sit down and watch the damn movie with me."

He looked at me skeptically and then sat down on the other couch.

"When did you become so bossy?"

"Peer pressure. I'm around my uncle all the time. I'm far too sensitive," I stated, pulling my blanket over me and popping a gummy bear in my mouth.

He laughed, big and throaty. I smiled, biting my lip.

"Why do you pretend you don't like to hang out with me? I'm kind of a big deal."

"I'm not your fri—"

"Yes, I know. We're not friends. You work for my uncle... yada, yada, yada, I got it. But," I paused for effect, "you're my bodyguard-slash-driver, so that means you work for me, too." I grinned all proud of myself.

"When did you get so smart?"

"It comes with age."

"You're fourteen."

I shrugged. "Yeah, but I've been through a lot. It's kind of like dog years, so I'm really like a hundred and something," I explained, counting on my fingers.

"Ninety-eight," he answered.

"That's what I said."

The last few years had been uneventful, we'd all fallen into a comfortable routine, and I was thankful for that. God knows I had enough drama to last me a lifetime when I first moved in. I guess Esteban was right. Things did get easier as more time went by, I just hadn't figured out if that was a good or bad thing.

It had been two years since I'd last changed schools. I wish I could tell you that I was happy staying in one place, but it didn't change the fact that I was alone. I hated school. I hated my teachers. I hated the students. Nothing about my life was normal. I had no parents, no friends, no one to talk to. I was around men and adults all the time, and I began to think that was maybe the reason I stopped trying to make any friends.

It was pointless.

I still read and wrote a lot. I spent most of my time with the fictional characters I'd grown to love from the pages of my books.

But with age came wisdom or however the hell you say that… I knew my uncle was involved in some sort of shady-ass shit. I had a bodyguard who hardly let me out of his sight for more than a few minutes, and that was only when I had to use the bathroom or we were in the penthouse. There was also the fact that every man my uncle brought around, which seemed to be few and far between, were all packing heat.

Every. Last. One.

The pizza arrived shortly after I ordered it and Esteban insisted he'd go get it from the door. He set the pizza on the coffee table while I went and grabbed us some sodas. I smirked, nudging him with my shoulder when he moved to sit beside me, so that he was closer to the food.

No one warned me that *The Shining* wasn't your typical horror movie with a killer who was an actor dressed in costume and made up like Freddy Kruger or Jason. I was prepared for that. The storyline in this movie could actually happen in real life and that scared the absolute living shit out of me.

At one point, I jumped and screamed so loud that I pretty much ended up in Esteban's lap. To tell you the truth, I wasn't even embarrassed about it. I even considered staying in his strong arms. I'd known Esteban for eight years. As much as he reminded me that he wasn't my friend, a part of me knew that he was. It was just part of his job to tell me that he wasn't.

At least that's what I hoped for.

I was a young girl, a teenager well on my way to becoming a woman. It was easy to get lost in the romance fantasy that I read in my books and imagine real life being that way. Over the last few months, I'd found myself thinking about Esteban in ways that I never had before, in ways that I probably shouldn't have.

But that still didn't stop me.

You couldn't blame me. It's not like I was around guys my own age. They steered clear of me as much as my uncle did. Esteban was handsome with blue eyes, tan skin, and dark brown hair. He was as tall, built, and muscular like my uncle and only wore suits like him too.

"What are you thinking about over there?" he asked, startling me away from my thoughts.

"Mmm?" I replied, tearing my eyes away from the movie to look over at him, heat spreading across my cheeks.

"You went from being scared to lost in thought."

I narrowed my eyes at him and blurted, "Shouldn't you be watching the movie instead of me?"

He cleared his throat and peered back at the TV.

"I don't know why I said that," I whispered, loud enough for him to hear.

Esteban suddenly stood to leave. I knew what he was doing. He wanted to put some distance between us.

I shocked us both when I shouted, "No!" Gripping his wrist, I held him in place.

He looked down at my grasp.

"Please don't leave."

Our eyes locked and I immediately let go.

"I'm tired of being alone, Esteban," I admitted out loud for the first time. "I don't have any friends. I barely see my uncle. I have no one." I shifted on the couch to face him. "I know you said you're not my friend, but... that doesn't mean that I don't see you as one. You're the only person I have."

He frowned. Esteban wore his emotions on his sleeve. I could physically see his heart breaking for me. I hardly knew anything about him, but for some reason I felt like I knew everything.

"Daisy—"

"Briggs. Why do you insist on calling me Daisy?" I questioned, surprised with the turn in events.

"It's your name," he simply stated.

"Daisy died the day she killed my parents. She doesn't exist anymore."

He jerked back, stunned. "It was a car accident. You had nothing to do with that."

"I caused it."

"The driver in the other car caused it."

I shook my head no. "That's not how I remember it."

"You had nothing to do with your parents' death. Do you understand me? Nothing," he argued in a stern tone I'd never heard before.

Crave Me

I stood, looking deep into his eyes, and spoke with conviction, "Have you ever killed anyone?"

CHAPTER 7

AUSTIN

I had been staring at the letter on my desk all morning. It didn't look as pristine as it did three months ago. I don't know how many times I had folded and unfolded it. Reading the same lines over and over again, still not finding the courage to bring it up to my parents.

"It is our pleasure to inform you that your application for admission to the School of Art and Design at Pratt Institute for the Fall Semester has been approved. We congratulate you on your acceptance and look forward to having you begin your professional studies at Pratt."

I never in my wildest dreams thought I would get in. Not a chance in hell they would accept my application. I had known about Pratt, School of Art and Design, since I was a kid. Anyone with the kind of passion I had for drawing knew that this was *the* school to attend if you wanted a career in arts. They were the number one art school in the US, receiving thousands of applications. Getting in was a miracle itself.

My parents had been on my ass about college and applying to schools for months. I finally applied to a few, including Ohio State, just to get them off my ass. The truth was I didn't even want to go to fucking college, but Pratt…

That was different.

Being the number one art school, I thought maybe that bit of information would sway my parents' opinion on the subject. So I applied. My GPA was decent, even though school wasn't really my thing. I had already started a portfolio of my drawings, years of

71

adding sketches upon sketches into it. All I was required to do was send in my application with a few sketches, some letters of recommendation which my art teachers were more than happy to provide, and an application fee. I shoved my packet into the mailbox one morning before school and didn't give it a second thought.

I started to check the mailbox on a daily basis so I could intercept the mail from the schools I had no interest in attending. I would throw away the response letters without even opening them. I didn't care if I got in, I wasn't going to Stanford or Florida State or whatever other fucking school they made me apply to. I tried to voice my opinion, but I could never get a word in, and if I did, it went in one ear and out the other.

My parents weren't bad people, but they were overachievers. Always needing the best of the best and wouldn't settle for anything less. Out of all of our families, mine was the best off financially. My parents' had to have nice things. We lived in a big house in a high-end, gated community. They were VIP members at the country club. They had new cars every year. We went on expensive vacations.

The whole nine yards.

To me, they were just keeping up with the Jones'.

I couldn't tell you how many times the boys and Half-Pint's parents fucked with my parents. Saying that they worked too much, that we didn't own our things, they owned us.

I knew that at the end of the day they wanted what was best for me. Not thinking that maybe I already knew what that was. They were suffocating me and they didn't even realize it. In their eyes, everything was the way it was supposed to be.

Which was why I had been holding onto the acceptance letter for the last three months, debating on telling them. Praying every day that they would be supportive of my decision, even though I knew in my heart that they would shut it down. All my life I felt like my parents, the boys, and maybe even Alex, were all trying to mold me into something I wasn't.

Something they wanted me to be.

I never felt accepted, I never felt good enough, and that's what killed me the most. That's what ate away at me, piece by piece.

At the end of the day... I needed to make myself happy. Life was too short, you only lived once, and all that other bullshit.

I wanted to make the best of it.

I grabbed the letter off my desk along with my art portfolio. No one knew about my talent, except Alex. I wanted to keep it to myself, and maybe that was my first mistake. For the first time in my life, I had to show everyone who I was, and I was scared shitless. I would start with my parents, they loved me and I knew that. I just hoped they loved me enough to let me come into my own.

If I wanted them to accept me for who I was or who I wanted to be, I guess I should start by giving them a chance.

"Austin, there you are, honey, I was about to call you down. Dinner's almost ready. Will you help me set the table?"

I nodded, placing the letter and portfolio on my chair. We sat down shortly after for dinner, and I waited until my dad asked me his usual dinnertime questions.

"How was school?"

"Fine."

"Have you heard back on any more colleges?"

"Honey, I thought we decided he was going to go to Ohio State with the boys?" My mama interjected. "It's a great school, and he wants to be with his friends. I think it'd be good if they all stayed together. You know Austin has always needed a leader."

My eyes widened, but I quickly recovered, glancing over at my thirteen-year-old brother, Hunter. He shook his head, just as shocked as I was.

"Darla, it would be good for the boy to broaden his horizons. He can't always be following around the boys. He's never going to come out of their shadows."

"I know, honey, but he needs them. He's always needed them. They will look out for him. They always have."

I scoffed, "You guys do realize I'm sitting right here, right?" They always did this, talking about me like I wasn't in the damn room. "Can't you wait until I at least leave the room to point out more things I can't do?"

"Austin," Mom coaxed. "We don't mean it like that. You're the baby of the group. The boys have always been… well you know, honey. More mature and stuff. It's normal for us to worry."

I scoffed, "*Mature*? Are you for real?"

"Austin, watch your tone," Dad ordered.

Crave Me

I would never rat out my boys, but fuck… if my parents only knew.

"I'm sorry."

Mom smiled and Dad shook his head. Now was as good a time as any.

"About college," I said, wiping my mouth with my napkin, bringing their attention back to me. "I got accepted into another school. One that I really want to attend."

They beamed. I'd never said I wanted to go to any college before.

"It's in New York—"

"We didn't know you applied to NYU. That's an amazing university. I'm so proud of you, Austin!" she rambled on.

"Brooklyn, New York," I clarified. "It's Pratt Institute, School of Art and Design."

They both jerked back, confused.

"It's actually the number one art school in all of the country, and I honestly don't know how I got accepted but," I set the letter in front of them and finished, "I did."

My dad picked up the letter off the table and read it over, with Mom hovering over his shoulder to read too. Both of their faces void of any emotion.

I waited.

"Art school, Austin? Where is this coming from? You've never showed any interest in arts," she stated, smiling, holding back a laugh.

"Actually, I have." I sat up in my seat, grabbing my portfolio that was sitting beside me.

My heart was pounding and my palms were getting sweaty. I swallowed the lump in my throat and pulled back the cover, showing them the first few sketches. Their faces were the blank canvas I was used to drawing on. They took in the sketches that had bled out through my hands.

But I still couldn't read them at all. My mom grabbed the notebook from my trembling hands and continued turning pages, one after the other. Running her fingers over the illustrations. Realizing what I had kept from them.

"I've been drawing since I could hold a pencil, Mom," I added, trying to gain a response. "My art teachers wrote my letters of recommendation. I actually think they were the reason I got in. They've been telling me I have a God given talent since elementary school—"

"They never told us," Mom interrupted, taken aback.

I shrugged. I wanted to say it was because they never bothered to go into their rooms during parent night. That they always said electives didn't matter, but I bit my tongue. It wouldn't help my case. Mom flipped page, after page, after page until she was almost to the end.

Nothing.

"I have some more sketches up in my room. I'll go—"

"No," Dad snapped, locking eyes with me.

"I'll just be a minute—"

"I don't need to see anymore of this garbage, Austin. Is this why you're an average student?"

He pulled my portfolio out of my mom's hands, throwing it in the middle of the table. It rattled the dishes.

"Dad, it's not—"

He put his finger up in the air, silencing me. I swallowed hard.

"Money on tutors, money on after-school help, afterschool SAT practice courses, do you want me to go on? We have spent thousands of dollars to get you the best education, and *this* is why you're always struggling? Because you spend more time on a hobby? You wasted all this time with your head up in the goddamn clouds, when it should have been focused on your homework?"

"Joseph…"

He put his hand out in front of my mother, silencing her as well.

"This is an out-of-state private school, Austin. You think we're going to pay for that?"

"I don't know, Dad. You were going to pay for the other ten out-of-state private schools you made me apply to."

He leaned back into his chair, shaking his head. "Yes. For an education. For a profession. For your future."

"This is my future. This is what I want to do with my life," I argued through gritted teeth, anger began to take over me.

"To become what, Austin? A starving artist? Who will always depend on us to pay his bills? What will you do in your long-term future, Austin? Do you think an arts degree will help you raise a family one day?"

"Dad, that's—"

"Hunter, go to your room," he ordered, not letting my brother finish. "The last thing I want is your brother rubbing off on you."

"Dad—"

"Hunter, just go!" I broke in, giving him a sympathetic stare.

He left.

"Austin."

I glanced back at my dad.

"We're not paying for this. Do you understand me? You're not going to Pratt, end of story. I realize now that you don't even want to bother with college, so I won't force you to go to an Ivy League school. It would be a waste of your time and my money, but so help me God, you will go to Ohio State and get some kind of a degree that will earn you a living. If you choose Pratt, you will have to carry your own weight."

They were killing my soul, crushing my dreams without even batting an eye about it. I immediately resented them for trying to mold me into their liking, not mine.

"How am I supposed to pay my way? I can't even apply for financial aid. You don't think I've looked into it? You guys make too much money. You're literally my last resort. Why can't you use my college fund for Pratt? I will even get a job and rent an apartment on my own. I'll take care of all my own expenses. All I ask is for you to pay for my school. Please… I've never asked for anything. This is important to me. This is what I want for *my* future."

"This conversation ends now, Austin. I've said my piece. End of story."

They weren't taking this away from me. Not now. Not ever. I had never disrespected my parents; I was raised better than that… but in that moment, in that second…

They weren't acting like my parents.

They were complete fucking strangers.

"And here I thought you would actually be happy and excited for me," I mocked.

He shook his head, disappointed. "*Happy and excited for you? To see you want to throw away your life? On a hopeful dream that won't get you anywhere but asking for spare change on the side of* the road? Unbelievable. How about you show your mother and I some respect? For everything we've done for you."

"I didn't know that respect was earned off my major, old man. That's a lot to ask of a college. Don't you think?"

"Austin..." Mom warned.

I laughed, "I'm sorry. I forgot. I still live under your roof. I follow your rules or else. You remind me daily. I should have it memorized by now."

He instantly stood and was over to me in two strides. Right in my face, grabbing my t-shirt in his fist.

"Listen to me. If it weren't for your mother, I would cut you off the second you graduate from high school. But I'm giving you a chance to straighten out, even though all you do is cause trouble. Whether at school, with your teachers or classmates, or all the girls you hang around with. We give you everything. Everything and you shit all over it. I'm surprised you haven't knocked someone up yet."

I snidely smiled. "Well, you did one thing right by me. You taught me that I should always wrap it up. Congratulations, I know how to put on a condom."

He didn't falter. "You make it hard to want you as my son," he viciously spewed, instantly regretting his words.

My mama's jaw dropped, surprised by his outburst. I would be lying if I said it didn't shock me too. He just confirmed what I always knew. I was a fuck up in their eyes. Not worthy enough to be their son. All I ever wanted was for them to accept me for who I was and welcome me with open arms.

And this was exactly why I spent my life hiding behind my secrets. I knew... I knew they wouldn't accept me. Except, I never thought it would hurt this goddamn much for them to confirm what I already knew in my heart.

"Wow..." I stepped back out of his grasp. Hands surrendered, head shaking.

I could see it in his eyes. He wanted to apologize, take back his hateful words. But that wasn't my father. He remained the solid man he always was. Breathing heavy with flared nostrils and a look of pity on his face.

I backed away from the situation before I really said something I regretted.

"Run along, Son. Which one of your girls or parties am I paying for tonight? Huh?" he yelled as I stormed out, slamming the door behind me.

I walked around aimlessly for a while until I remembered the boys were in town for the weekend, and I knew just where to find them.

"What the fuck is wrong with you?" Dylan asked, as I walked up to him and the rest of the boys on the beach. "You look like someone just took a shit in your cereal."

I handed him the letter, too pissed off to explain. If anyone could understand, it would be the boys. Dylan lowered his eyebrows, taking it out of my hand. Jacob and Lucas hovered around him to read it too. I stood there drawing circles in the sand with my foot, glancing up at their expressions.

Wondering which way this would go.

"Art school?" Jacob questioned, looking back up at me. "When the fuck did you learn how to draw?"

"Doesn't fucking matter. My parents won't pay for it. Looks like I'm going to Ohio State with you guys."

"Austin, come on, man… do you honestly want to go to art school? Or is this you just trying to rebel over something else?" Lucas chimed in.

"Art school sounds like a whole bunch of pussies, drawing out their feelings and shit. That's not you. Besides, what the fuck are you going to do with an art degree?" Dylan added.

"What the hell do you know about art school? Have you been there?" I snapped.

They laughed.

They fucking laughed.

"This is a joke right? You're fucking with us?" Jacob chuckled. "We all know you want to come to Ohio State, Austin. We're there. You've been following us around since you could walk."

I jerked back like he had hit me. "Wow…"

They faltered, their expressions quickly changing to something I couldn't quite place.

"Is that right? I've been following you around. Good to know."

"He's just fuckin' around. Why you being such a pussy? You bleedin' out now?" Dylan laughed some more. "Don't go turning into a bitch on us, now that we're not around to man you up."

I couldn't believe this. I go to my boys. My brothers. My best friends for some goddamn support and they proceed to add to my parents' theory, pointing out everything I have ever felt.

Every last one of them.

Tearing into my insecurities. I wasn't expecting that.

Not. Ever. That.

"Fuck you! Fuck all of you!" I roared, turning around to leave. "All of you can go fuck yourselves. Thanks for the support, bros."

"Austin! Stop being such a bitch! We were fuckin' with you!" Dylan called out behind me.

I didn't bother to look back.

It was pointless.

The damage was done.

Before I knew it, I was sitting on the dock, feet dangling in the warm water. Looking off in the distance, reflecting on the day's turn of events. Wishing that I had my notebook to take out my frustration on a blank sheet of paper. Getting lost in the world of my illusions, creations, and art. But all I could do was sit there and dwell on what had just happened.

With my parents.

With my friends.

I was alone.

I hated myself for letting down my guard, allowing them to see my truths I hid so well for so many years. That it became second nature.

I wanted to hit something.

I wanted to scream.

I wanted to run away.

I wanted to make this fucking feeling go away. I'd give anything to bring back my not giving a fuck attitude that I had gotten so used to. Seeking comfort in myself.

All I ever had was that.

I owned it.

Now that was torn away from me.

I stood, pacing the dock, running my fingers roughly through my hair. My anger and nerves set on fire. My body scorching hot, my adrenaline pumping so hard that all I could see was red, and all I could feel was blue. I wanted to claw out of my skin for being so fucking stupid.

I paced around the dock, desperately trying to work off this emotional bullshit. When I heard footsteps coming toward me, I didn't have to look up to know who it was.

Alex.

Half-Pint.

Her…

She was always there for me. Always knew when I needed her. The one person that I could count on, the one person that loved me wholeheartedly.

No matter what.

I peered up and there she was. Wearing a white dress, looking like an angel, so genuine and pure. The Heaven to my Hell, or so I thought. Her hair cascaded down her face, her back, her breasts.

I wanted to get lost in her…

"Hey, you okay?" she asked, taking in the desperation playing out in front of her.

My yearning for someone I shouldn't be thinking about. Someone that wasn't mine and never would be.

"How the fuck do you always know when I need you, Alex?"

She smiled and her entire face lit up. "It's because I love you."

I threw caution to the wind and cupped the sides of her face. Her eyes widened before I pulled her toward me, not giving it a second thought.

I kissed her.

For a second, my lips touched hers. For a moment, I felt the pain go away. Reality disappeared that instant. It didn't last long and a part of me knew it wasn't going to.

Her hands pressed against my chest, shoving me away, making me stumble backwards on the dock. Feeling the loss of her warmth immediately.

"Austin!" she shrieked out, backing away from me with a look of disappointment on her face. "What are you doing?"

"Fuck!" I called out. "I'm sorry. I'm so sorry, Alex. I shouldn't have done that."

She shook her head side-to-side, lost in her own thoughts. Not knowing how to reply. Not knowing what to do or how to move forward.

"Austin," she barely whispered.

"I know, Alex… you don't have to say it," I managed to respond.

We stood there for I don't know how long, staring aimlessly at each other. And then… she just turned around and left. Walked away from me without another word.

I bowed my head.

Feeling lost. I knew she wouldn't tell anyone. She would take this to her grave, as would I. She wouldn't break the bond between the boys and I.

But that didn't mean.

I didn't just break the bond between her and me.

Briggs

"Daisy."

I heard someone whisper in my sleep. I rolled over toward the voice.

"Hmm…" I groggily opened my eyes, wiping sleep from my face. "Esteban?" I muttered, blinking away the darkness and looking around confused.

"Everything okay?" I immediately asked, taken aback. He'd never been in my room before.

"You need to get up and come with me," was all he said before he started making his way out of my room.

I scratched my head, not understanding what was going on. I pushed off my covers, swung my legs over the edge of the bed, and stood stretching. Making my way into the bathroom to brush my teeth and wash my face. I tied my hair back in a ponytail as I walked out of the bathroom to find Esteban leaning against my door. He didn't say a word. He just stared out in front of him like he was lost in his own thoughts. His composure read of a man on his way to his execution. A man I'd never met before.

And that scared me more than anything.

"Is everything—"

"Come on," he interrupted, pushing off the door and walking away.

I followed behind him, trying to keep up with his pace. The sound coming off his black dress shoes echoed through the dark, narrow hallways, mimicking the pounding of my heart and the ringing in my ears. The silence was deafening all around us. I never realized how quiet the penthouse was at night. Our shadows simply heightened the darkness lurking in the corners. It didn't even seem like it was that late.

One stride for Esteban was three steps for me. I know because I counted. It was the only way to keep my breathing somewhat steady.

One stride.

Three steps...

One stride.

Three steps...

One stride.

Three steps...

I followed him through the swinging door that led to the kitchen. The strong, pungent smell of bleach assaulted my senses. My hand immediately rose to cover my nose and mouth. Esteban didn't bat an eye, too focused on his task that led us to the service elevator. He pressed the button and within seconds it dinged. The doors slid open as if it had been waiting there for us the entire time.

He stepped in while I stayed frozen in place. My heart pounding so profusely that I found it hard to breathe. My lips parted and my chest heaved with each passing moment that escalated between us. Panic began to set in and my mind started running wild. I anxiously tried to gather my thoughts, but they were as stuck as my feet were glued to the floor beneath me.

"Get in," he ordered.

The unfamiliar harsh and demanding tone only added to my fear. For a quick second I wondered if he could smell it.

I didn't budge.

I couldn't.

"Why?" I blurted, finally finding my own voice.

"Get. In," he repeated and my body began to shake.

I stared into his dark, soulless eyes. I took in his daunting, eerie composure, the way his hands hadn't left his sides, not hiding the fact that he was strapped. Which he never was inside the penthouse.

I took in every last detail.

From the new cut he had just above his eyebrow, to the slight wrinkle of his black suit jacket. How the first two buttons of his black dress shirt were missing, and how his stare hadn't wavered from mine.

Not. Once.

Reminding me of my uncle.

"Are you going to hurt me?" I found myself asking, needing confirmation, but knowing it didn't matter. He wouldn't tell me the truth.

Esteban would...

But he wasn't Esteban.

"Get. The. Fuck. In," he gritted out.

I swallowed hard before placing one foot in front of the other, standing on the opposite side of the elevator. The furthest spot away from him. He didn't falter, punching one-zero-one-seven into the keypad, like he wanted me to see it and then button B.

My mom's birthday?

His eyes stayed focused in front of him, and my eyes stayed locked on the side of his face. I jumped when the elevator dinged again, immediately shutting my eyes as hard as I could. Desperately wanting to pretend that this was just a bad dream. A nightmare that I would soon wake up from, finding no one was there to comfort me, but myself. I used to loathe that feeling, and now for the first time I craved it.

I heard the doors open and I involuntarily took three, reassuring breaths.

One...

In and out.

Two...

In and out.

Three...

In and out.

I was struck with a coppery scent and I knew that as soon as I opened my eyes, my life would never be the same again. The smell of fear and bodily fluids were all around me, there was no mistaking it.

For some reason I thought about the last time I was happy. Slowly, cautiously opening my eyes, holding onto that feeling for as long as I could.

"Por fin," Uncle Alejandro broke the silence, "*Finally.*"

I swear on everything that was holy, my heart stopped beating. All the feelings, all the emotions were gone in a flash as if they had never been there to begin with.

I was there, but I wasn't.

"Venga," Uncle ordered, "*Come.*"

My eyes widened as I came face-to-face with something straight out of a horror film. My blank stare went to the man. A man I'd never seen before. His head was draped over, his arms tied behind his back, and his legs strapped to the steel chair he was sitting on. A plastic visqueen-lined area beneath him. Silver duct tape sealed his mouth and eyes. Blood dripped down his bruised and bloody face. I looked around at my uncle's men. They wore their sadistic expressions and bloody knuckles proudly, no hint of remorse, no sign of guilt. They were showcasing their handy work.

The man was beaten within an inch of his life.

I looked from the man who was alive but appeared dead to Esteban who was standing at the far corner of the basement. Once again the man I knew. Except this time, he looked as broken as I felt.

The shame and remorse eating him alive.

Me.

"I bring you a gift, and this is how you react?" Uncle voiced, bringing my gaze back to him.

He was leaned up against the wall behind the man in the chair. His arms folded over his chest, one leg draped over the other. The sleeves of his shirt were rolled but there wasn't a hair out of place.

"A gift?" I whispered, loud enough for him to hear.

"Briggs, I won't tell you again. Come here."

I stepped off the elevator and the doors closed behind me.

I shuddered, suddenly cold.

My uncle smiled. "Are you scared?"

I didn't know what to say, so I didn't say anything. I had to dig my nails into the palms of my hands to keep from passing out.

"You're my niece, the daughter of my only sister, who I loved very fucking much. I would never physically hurt you. Don't you ever fucking offend me again by letting that thought cross your mind."

I blinked, taking in his words. The concrete floors were callous beneath my bare feet, the sounds of a furnace echoed through the huge, damp, concrete basement.

"Do you understand me?" he added.

I peered down at the man in the chair, ignoring his question. My uncle followed the direction of my stare.

"It was a hit and run."

Our eyes locked.

"And this," he nodded at the man in the chair, "is the man who ran," he stated, answering the question in my mind.

My eyes scanned his body, confused and overwhelmed by the turn of events. I couldn't look away from the man's gruesome appearance. His chest was in worse shape than his face. Blood was covering his whole torso. I looked closer and sucked in a breath.

Amari.

My mom's name was carved on his skin, peeking out through his ripped, button down shirt on his chest.

My uncle jerked his neck toward Esteban, who understood his silent command. He made his way to the man in the chair. For a second, Esteban's eyes pleaded with me to forgive him for what was about to happen. He roughly ripped off the tape from his eyes and then his mouth. Throwing a bucket of water on his face and the man stirred into consciousness. Gasping for air that wasn't available for the taking.

Esteban quickly retreated back to the corner of the basement. I could have sworn I saw him make the sign of the cross before the sounds of the man waking up brought my attention back to the situation.

He immediately started screaming and thrashing around. My uncle didn't pay him any mind. For the first time in my life, I fought an internal struggle between right and wrong.

"You didn't kill your parents, Briggs. He did," Uncle reminded, fueling my battle of good versus evil.

My heart.

My mind.

My soul.

"LIAR!" the man yelled out.

I jumped, craving to place my hands over my ears, my eyes.

To hide.

To crawl into that empty space I'd been living in for years. To seek refuge within myself was the only way I knew how to survive.

"YOU'RE A FUCKING LIAR!" he screamed bloody murder, whipping around even harder, faster, almost making the chair fall over.

No one paid him any mind as I visibly struggled with my conflicting emotions.

Unforgiving.

Merciless.

Remorseless.

Please, God...

One right after the other.

"It's midnight," my uncle said, settling his stare on the man.

The rest played out in slow motion.

My uncle raised his gun, pointing it directly to the back of the man's head. The man stopped moving as if he knew. All of the fight in him was gone.

Locking eyes with me instead.

I screamed, shaking. "No! No! No! You don't have to do this!"

"Happy fifteenth birthday, *Daisy*."

And with that...

He blew his fucking head off.

CHAPTER
8

AUSTIN

"Hey," I greeted, walking up to Alex from behind.

She turned to face me and smiled shyly. "Hey."

I hadn't seen her much since that day on the dock. There was no point to it. I fucked up and she knew that.

I sat down next to her on the bench, surprised to find her at the pier. It wasn't a place she came to often. I had been hanging out at Charlie's house all day, throwing back a few drinks and shooting the shit.

"Whatcha doin' over here by yourself?"

"I don't know. Sometimes I come here to think."

I understood that all too well.

"About Lucas?" I blurted without thinking.

She immediately looked over at me, shocked and dismayed. I reassuringly smiled with an arched eyebrow and a mischievous look on my face. The last time we talked about her and Lucas was half a decade ago. Never once bringing it up after that day on the dock. Maybe she thought I forgot, or maybe she pretended like it never happened. Whatever the cause may have been, a lot had happened since then.

I wasn't the same boy anymore.

And she wasn't the same girl.

"It's okay, Half-Pint, I'm not Jacob or Dylan. All I want is for you to be happy with Lucas, with Cole, shit even with a chick if that floats your fancy."

She chuckled, shaking her head. "No girls."

I laughed, "A guy can dream, right?"

She grinned, nudging me with her shoulder. "How long have you known?"

All our lives. "Long enough."

She nodded with understanding as she turned to look back out over the water.

"The boys—"

"I know," I interrupted, already knowing what she was going to say. "In all fairness though, they're just looking out for you, Alex. It's what we've always done. It's not coming from a bad place. You know we love you more than anything."

"I know."

The boys had definitely done some damage when it came to their relationship, and maybe I had my part in it too. Over the last year I thought a lot about my childhood, about the things I couldn't change and for the first time…

I didn't want to.

Every memory, every moment, every life event brought me to this place in time where I was content and comfortable in my own skin. Finally, finding some solid ground to the rocky foundation that had always been placed beneath me.

"I don't think you do. I know you, Alex. I've known you as long as I've known them. You and Lucas have always had a special unbreakable bond. When I was a kid, I used to be jealous of your relationship. It wasn't because I wanted you in that way or anything, it was more because I never had that connection to anyone. You're like my little sister and that applies to all of us," I revealed, knowing it was the effects of the booze I'd been drinking all day.

Part of what I said was true and part of it wasn't.

Half-truths, so many lies. Too many lies.

But I still found myself saying them because it was what she needed to hear. And at the end of the day, she was all that ever mattered.

To all of us.

"Except you and Lucas complete each other. You balance each other out in a way that we all do for one another, but you had your own dynamic going on."

She nodded in understanding.

"As the youngest, I've always felt like the odd man out with the rest of the boys. I guess that's why I try to do everything to the extreme. I need to make up for it or something," I admitted out loud.

I had nothing to lose anymore.

I'd lost it all already.

When I realized that, was when I started living.

"Austin," she murmured, completely surprised by my outburst. "I never knew you felt that way."

I shrugged. "I'm good at hiding things, we have that in common. The boys have never made me feel like that by any means, at least not on purpose. It's still there, though. You know Lucas always tells me that we're a lot alike, and I never understood what he meant until they left," I paused, reflecting on what I was about to confess to her. The alcohol making it easier to do so. "Both of us wanting to be one of the boys."

She gazed at the side of my face. "I've never thought that about you. Not ever."

I nodded. "And I've never thought that about you, but it doesn't change the fact that you felt that way, does it?"

"No," she half-whispered.

I smiled sadly and bowed my head for a few seconds, only looking back up when I was ready.

"I graduate in a few months."

"Three months," she stated, like she was counting down the days until she would really be alone.

I glanced at her, smiling, and it eased the worry she felt in her heart.

"You going to miss me, Half-Pint?"

"Always," she bellowed, her eyes blurring.

I wrapped my arm around her shoulder and pulled her into my chest, kissing the top of her head and letting my lips linger. I had eaten some food and put some gum in my mouth before I left, to cover up the stench of alcohol. Alex was too innocent and naïve to realize I had been drinking. Which only made me pull her closer to my chest.

"I will always be here for you, it doesn't matter where I am. I will always take care of you, and I will always love you. You're my Half-Pint," I vowed, my voice breaking.

As hard as it was for her to know that I was leaving her, it was just as hard for me to be leaving her. Even though I wanted nothing more than to get the fuck out of this town.

She sniffed. "Ditto."

"One day we won't care what the boys think about us or what we do. On that day, we will both be extremely happy," I said, silently praying it would be true.

That was the hardest pill to swallow.

"So…" I brushed off the sentiments. "It's Saturday night and Charlie's throwing one of his raging parties. Let's go," I urged, standing up and reaching out my hand for her. "No," I coaxed, shaking my head before she could answer. "I don't want to hear your bullshit excuses about this or that. You will have fun with me. You will drink. You will dance. You will party. And that's a fucking order."

She giggled and rolled her eyes. "Okay."

I wanted to spend one night with her where I didn't think about tomorrow or the next day or the day after that. How things might change between us after I left. How we may not be as close to one another as we had been this last year without the boys around.

I wanted one night where we could both let go.

Be free.

Show her how much fun it was to just not give a fuck anymore. What anyone thought, wanted, or needed. To see that life didn't start and end with her Bo. That there were other possibilities in this world where she might be happy, and I wanted to take pride in being the one person that opened her eyes to that.

I drank.

She drank.

I danced.

She danced.

We laughed.

We smiled.

We lived in the moment. Where it was just me and her. And it was one of the happiest days of my life.

"Stop walking so fast," she rambled, holding onto my hand tighter.

"Stop walking so slow," I replied, slightly slurring.

"Hurry your asses up!" Jason yelled from in front of us.

"Where are we going?" she asked, already forgetting what I told her.

"The cops are coming. The party is being relocated."

"Oh yeah," she giggled, and it was the sweetest sound I'd ever heard.

I opened the passenger door for her and closed it when she was safely seated inside. I ran over to the driver's side, jumped in, and threw my car into reverse. Her body jerked forward from the momentum, and she started to giggle.

"Turn the music on," I said.

She had a hard time finding the knobs, fidgeting from one to the other.

"Half-Pint, you're drunk," I chuckled right along with her.

"I love this song!" she shouted when she found the station she wanted.

I watched her dance around in her seat, singing at the top of her lungs. I'd never seen her so fucking happy before, and I would be lying if I said it didn't make me love her just a little bit more.

I banged on the steering wheel, dancing right along with her. The music switched over to a slower song as we pulled up to a red light.

I caught her leaning back in her seat, lazily looking over at me from the corner of my eye.

"I love you, Austin. I love you so, so, so much."

I looked over at her and spoke with conviction, "I love you more. I will always take care of you and don't you ever fucking forget that. Now put your fucking seatbelt on."

"Oh yeah." She sloppily grabbed the strap behind her head as I started driving again.

"It won't go in the buckle," she giggled again.

"Here." I took it out of her hands. "Grab the wheel."

"Mmmkay."

The car started swerving a little.

"Austin, I don't think I should be doing this."

"I'm almost done."

I would never let anything happen to her. I didn't care how long it took me to put her goddamn seatbelt on. I wouldn't stop until she was safe.

I felt her looking down. "You need to put your seatbelt on, too," she hiccupped.

"Done," I stated, ignoring what she said.

She smiled at me before facing forward as I grabbed the steering wheel again. We went back to dancing around.

"Austin, you pussy, can't you drive faster than that?" Jason shouted out his car window next to us. "If I beat you to the woods, you pay for all the beer."

"You're on!" I yelled back.

"I don't think—"

"Hey," I interrupted. "What were the rules?" I reminded with a huge smile on my face.

"To have fun," she beamed.

I turned the radio up louder and pushed down the accelerator with my foot. She danced around some more and I focused on driving faster than him. I hated when my friends thought they could do something better than me. That only added to my will to kick his fucking ass.

The paved road ended and we had to drive through the woods till we reached the party. My car started to recoil from the dirt and grass, making her body jolt all around. I went faster, wanting this to be over and for her to be comfortable again. She pressed her hands against the dashboard, trying to hold her body steady from the impact around us.

I expected it when she yelled out, "Slow down!"

"We're almost there!"

I could sense she was scared. Which only pissed me off further and fueled my need to beat him for making me cause her any distress.

She turned down the radio.

"You're going too fast."

"Relax, we're fine," I soothed.

I knew these woods. We were fine. I'd been partying in them for years. She gasped every time I took a sharp turn. The cars headlights only illuminated a few feet out in front of us, so I could understand why she was hanging on the edge of her seat. I decided to take a short cut and swerved left and then right. We would get there faster that way and then we could go back to having a great night. Like none of this bullshit had happened.

When I saw the clear path in front of us, I heard her breathe a sigh a relief, and I knew I had made the right decision.

Except it was too soon…

My heart dropped and pure panic took over, locking up my senses. A tree laid out in front of us a few feet ahead, probably a result from one of the last few hurricanes.

"AUSTIN!" she screamed bloody murder.

It vibrated throughout the car, and I immediately looked over at her with regret and sorrow written clear across my face. I slammed on the brakes, but it was too late. The tires spun in the mud, causing us to slide closer and closer to our destiny that waited with open arms. Alex's screams and the sounds of branches whipping by filled the small, vacant spaces. She instinctively placed her arms over her face, and my whole life flashed before my eyes within seconds.

My parents…

My brother…

The boys…

Alex.

Half-Pint.

Her.

That's when I remembered I didn't have my seatbelt on. It was her life or mine.

Hers or mine.

Hers or mine.

Hers or mine.

I. Chose. Hers.

Everything from there on out happened in slow motion. I threw my body towards the passenger seat, placing my arms over her tiny frame, desperately trying to hold her back. Glass shattered all around us as metal screeched at our sides. I felt my body being thrown backward as if I was flying through the air.

I shut my eyes and awaited my fate, praying to God for the first time in my life, to please, please…

Save her.

And then…

Everything. Went. Black.

Crave Me

Briggs

There's no way to describe someone's brains being blown out of their head, splattered on the floor and walls. Time just seemed to stand still, nothing moving, including me. Sour bile burned in the back of my throat, threatening to surface. There was an unfamiliar smell lingering in the air. Whether it was the scent of blood or death, I wasn't sure, but I would never forget it for as long as I lived.

It was now a part of me, burned into my senses whether I wanted it to be or not.

My eyes floated to a coolness I felt on my arm and I flinched sending the white matter to the floor after realizing what it was. That's when I noticed my shirt. Red speckles splattered all over my white Superman tee. A sight I would never be able to un-see. A feeling I would never be able to un-feel. Despair washed over me, like when my parents died.

Adding to the pile that would forever haunt me.

The guy was dead, his blood not only on my clothes but also my hands. Another life lost because of me. I didn't know how many more deaths my soul could handle.

I was doomed.

I would burn in Hell one day.

I might not have been the one who pulled the trigger, but it didn't change the facts.

Uncle Alejandro did it for me.

That didn't make it any better.

If anything, it only made it worse.

My eyes jerked in rapid movements, imprinting the gory details of the evening into my mind, my memory, and my soul.

Their nonchalant faces taunting me, like they didn't have a care in the world.

The kickback from the gun as it jerked back my uncle's arm.

The flash behind it.

The sound of a bullet as it blasted through his skull, lodging into the steel door of the elevator, only a few inches away from my face.

The ringing sound in my ears caused from the blast, left me thinking I was deaf.

Blood...

Brains…

The God awful stench, *imprinted.*

All of it.

I took off like a bat out of Hell. I didn't think twice about it. I ran on pure emotion and adrenaline, trying to seek shelter anyway I could. I punched the code into the service elevator as if my life depended on it. The scene wouldn't stop playing out in front of my eyes, over and over in my mind.

On instant replay, I was powerless to stop it.

My heart pounded out of my chest and the walls felt like they were caving in with each passing second. The elevator dinged, the doors slid open and I was back in the kitchen. I pushed off the wall and ran as hard and as fast as I could for the front door. My legs burned and my body ached. I immediately tried to open the door, forgetting that it was still locked. I turned the knob, but it wouldn't budge.

"What the fuck?!" I screamed out, barely being able to hear myself. "Fuck!" I yelled in frustration, banging on the door.

Panic set in, I couldn't leave.

I never opened the door or left the house by myself. It took me a second to find the alarm that was on the far wall behind me. Stumbling on my own two feet, I almost fell to the floor running to it. My hands shook the entire time I punched the code in from the service elevator.

Nothing.

"Fuck!" I screeched out, punching it in once again.

Nothing.

I shuddered, resisting the urge to throw up. "What the fuck?!" Swallowing hard, my mouth suddenly dry.

I backed away from the alarm and turned my efforts back toward the door.

"SOMEBODY HELP ME! SOMEBODY PLEASE HELP ME!" I screamed at the top of my lungs, over and over again, fists pounding as hard as I could. "PLEASE! PLEASE!"

I begged until my voice was raw, my throat burned, and my resolve broke.

Nothing.

No one.

I looked around the room and realized I was alone. No one had chased after me, no one was behind me, no one followed me.

I ran into my room, slamming the door behind me. I frantically looked around, trying to gather my thoughts. I needed to lock myself away, I quickly shoved my dresser in front of the door, making sure it was secure.

It was a useless precaution.

If my uncle wanted in, he would get in.

I was hyperventilating, held captive in a house that was supposed to be my *home*. I had nowhere to go, nowhere to turn, nowhere to run.

I had no one.

I fell to my knees, welcoming the sting from the impact. I sat there and let everything I was holding in go.

I bawled for my parents.

I cried for that man, even though I shouldn't have.

I sobbed for what I was forced to witness.

Most of all, I wept for the fact that he killed that man for me.

"Happy fifteenth birthday, Daisy." Echoed in my mind, followed by the blast over and over again.

I don't know how much time went by before I crawled my way into the bathroom and forced myself to look in the mirror. The girl looking back at me was still covered with the man's blood and remains. I stepped back, pulling off every last piece of clothing. Throwing it right in the garbage where it belonged.

I stepped into the scorching hot shower, wanting and needing it to wash away all of my sins. Pressing my forehead against the tile, I just stood there, watching the stranger's blood paint the shower floor red and then go down the drain. Taking the last bit of innocence I had with it. I stayed in there until the water was frigid cold, which was a nice change to the burning of my skin.

I put on a tank top and some cotton shorts, grabbed the comforter off my bed and curled up on the floor in the furthest corner of the room. Far away from the door.

Waiting for the knock that I sensed was coming.

Never expecting who was on the other side.

CHAPTER
9

AUSTIN

"When is he going to wake up?"

Why can't I open my eyes? Why can't I feel my body? Why am I so tired...

"Austin, can you hear me? The doctor says we need to talk to you. That you can hear us, and it will help you come out of your coma."

Coma? I'm in a coma? Where is Alex? Someone tell me where Alex is? Why am I so tired...

"You look good today, baby. My boy's got some color again. You're looking like your old self. Come back to us please. We're all waiting here for you. Open those bright blue eyes."

Where is Alex? Please, someone tell me where Alex is? I need to know if I killed her. I can't live if she didn't. Why am I so tired...

"We've seen a significant decrease in the swelling on his brain. The medically-induced coma is doing its job, and like I said before, it's just a waiting game now."

My brain? What the fuck is wrong with my brain? Why can't I wake up? Open your eyes, Austin! Open your goddamn eyes! Why am I so tired...

"Austin... you need to wake up now, okay? You can't leave me. I love you. Please... come back to us."

Half-Pint.

Alex.

She's alive.

And now...

Now I can finally sleep.

"His eyes! Did you all see that? Oh my God, his eyes are opening. I think he's waking up! Honey, honey, can you hear me?" Mom asked.

My eyes fluttered open, trying to shake off the haziness of my mind. Blinking away the darkness and welcoming the light that showed me I was alive.

"Water," I softly murmured. My lips were so chapped it hurt to move them. My throat so dry I could barely swallow.

"Oh, my God! He's talking! He's up! Dylan, go get the doctor! What, baby? Say that again."

I felt her lean down by my face.

"Water," I whispered into her ear.

I heard the shuffling of feet, but had to shut my eyes again, the lighting in the room was too bright. All I wanted to do was keep them open, but they burned.

"Open your mouth, baby."

I did and the second I felt the straw on my lips I sucked, drinking it all down in one, long gulp. I couldn't fight the drowsiness even though the last thing I wanted to do was sleep. I felt like I had been sleeping for years. I heard voices, questions being asked, and felt hands stroke my face, arms, and chest. Before I could give it anymore thought or fight it off any longer…

I passed the fuck out.

I had no idea how much time had gone by when I woke up next. I felt better but groggy and disoriented as all hell. The doctor, which happened to be Aubrey's mom, asked me so many damn questions that it made me want to go back to sleep to keep from answering them.

"You've suffered severe trauma to your brain, Austin," her mom reminded.

"No shit?" I sarcastically replied, wanting the hell out of this bed and hospital.

"Austin," Mom reprimanded.

"You have several broken ribs, burns, and deep cuts on your face and all over your body. Some will heal, but most will scar. You flew out the windshield. They found your body almost seven feet away from the car. God, Austin, you're lucky to even be alive. If it hadn't been for the grass and damp dirt from all the storms we've been getting lately…there's no doubt in my mind you would have died."

My mom bowed her head while my dad took a deep breath.

"We had to operate on your brain to stop the bleeding and put you in a medically-induced coma to reduce the swelling."

My hand subconsciously went up to the side of my head where I felt the bandage. My hair shaved around it.

"I guess that explains the killer headache," I said.

"You've been in a coma for a week. That's normal. But, Austin, it's going to take some time for you to heal. We haven't tested your physical skills yet. There's a chance that you may need physical therapy. You have several fractures in your back and on your legs. Your motor and mental skills seem to be okay, but that could also change as the days go by. We will be watching you closely for the next few weeks."

"Weeks?"

"Yes. You won't be medically discharged for a while, so you might as well get comfortable. You're not going anywhere."

I took a deep breath, hating that she said that, and immediately touched my ribs.

Fuck that hurt.

She walked over to my bed and handed me what looked like a controller.

"You're on a morphine drip. At least for the next few days until we've figured out where your pain is centered and how high your tolerance is. Then we can switch you over to doses throughout the day. When the pain is too much, you press this button. Okay?"

I nodded, tucking the controller at my side.

"I'm serious, Austin. No playing Mr. Tough Guy. You just had a dosage not too long ago so that's why you're feeling somewhat stable. But I promise you once the pain kicks in, it will be unbearable, you—"

"I got it."

She nodded again, giving me a worried look.

"Do you remember anything? The accident? Do you remember what happened?"

All eyes fell on me. I couldn't tell if their expressions were hopeful that I would or optimistic that I wouldn't remember.

Drinking with Charles all day.
Finding Alex on the pier.
Dragging her to his party.
Dancing.
Laughing.
Drinking some more...
Driving drunk.
Racing Jason.
Woods...
Driving faster and faster and faster.
A shortcut.
A tree.

"Half-Pint?" I stated as a question.

She lowered her eyebrows. "Austin, do you remember?"

I peered around the room and then it hit me like a ton of fucking bricks.

Almost. Killing. Alex.

I swallowed hard, trying to control my breathing. My emotions. The machine that I was hooked up to suddenly started making a lot of noise.

"Austin, it's alright. She's okay, she's—"

"Right here," Alex broke in.

I blinked a few times. I wondered if it was just my dazed and confused mind playing tricks on me. She was in a wheelchair, Lucas standing behind her. Her hands firmly placed on her lap. She looked so tiny in that chair, her beautiful face covered in nothing but bruises and cuts. The hospital gown did nothing to hide more of the same on her body.

I sucked in air that wasn't available for the taking. My eyes now wide, my body now shuddering.

It took everything inside me not to breakdown.

"I'm fine," Alex coaxed as if she knew what I was thinking, what I was feeling.

What I needed to hear.

"Answer the question, Austin," Lucas demanded, bringing my attention to him. "Do you remember what you did?"

"Bo, that's—"

"I'm sorry," I found myself saying. "I don't. I don't remember anything," I lied.

Not because I was scared of the consequences.

Not because I was afraid of facing the boys, my parents or even the cops.

Not from any of that.

I was fucking terrified that if I told her the truth, that if Alex knew I remembered almost killing her, she would never look at me the way she was looking at me right then and there. And I would lose the only girl that ever mattered to me.

The girl I was supposed to protect.

The girl that I vowed to never hurt.

My best friend.

"Alex, you shouldn't be up. You need—"

"I'm fine," she reprimanded with a stern tone. "I'm not leaving until I talk to Austin. Alone. Now, if all of you could please give us a few minutes."

Aubrey's mom looked back and forth between us. "You have ten minutes."

Everyone left, much to Lucas' disapproval. He lingered at the door before disappearing into the hallway. Alex got up off the wheelchair to shut the door. I opened my mouth to stop her.

"I'm fine," she interrupted, walking over to me. Sitting on my bed, right next to my waist.

The guilt was eating me alive with each passing minute.

I couldn't take it anymore and instantly pulled her into my arms, hugging her as tight as I could. I didn't give a fuck how much it hurt my ribs. I was so grateful that she was alive.

That I didn't kill her.

She willingly came. Wrapping her arms around my neck. For the first time I was the one to tuck my face into the side of her neck. Needing comfort, reassurance, and love.

Needing her.

Even though I didn't deserve any of it. Not after what I did.

"I'm so sorry, Half-Pint. I'm so fucking sorry," I openly bawled not being able to hold back.

"Shhh…" She rubbed my back. "Shhh… Austin. I'm fine. It wasn't your fault and it doesn't matter. We're alive, and I love you no matter what. Shhh…" she soothed, whispering reassuring words, over and over again.

All lies.

Every last one of them.

But I didn't stop her.

I broke down until I couldn't anymore.

She told me that she didn't remember anything either. She told me that everything was going to be okay. She told me that she loved me over and over again. She told me everything I wanted to hear, everything I *needed* to hear. It should have made me feel better.

It didn't.

After she left, I sat there by myself. I couldn't get my mind to shut off, I couldn't get my feelings to stop attacking me, turning on me and making me feel like a bigger piece of shit than I already knew I was.

Regret...

Remorse...

Shame...

Almost. Killing. Alex.

I reached for the morphine drip.

And pressed the button.

Briggs

I jumped as soon as I heard the knock on the door. The loud noise startled me even though I knew it was coming at any moment. It still didn't prepare me. Nothing did. I held in my breath the entire time not wanting to make a sound, trying to remain calm in the chaos. Not allowing it to take me further and further into the black abyss. Praying that my uncle would accept my silence and just go away. I jumped again with the second knock, my nerves were on fire and all that did was pour gasoline on the fear that had taken up residence in my body, igniting it more.

"Daisy..."

My heart dropped.

The pounding rhythm immediately subsided and it was replaced with an unfamiliar feeling. A feeling I couldn't quite place, it didn't scare me, but it didn't comfort me either.

"Daisy, open the door. It's me."

It's me.

M. Robinson

He said it like it made a difference, like it took away the last few hours of my life, like he didn't play a part in the turn of events tonight and like he wasn't one of the reasons I was there in the first place. As if saying "It's me" made it all go away and magically better. Trying to put a Band Aid on my soul, when it was already broken beyond repair.

"Daisy, please... just open the fucking door," he wallowed, his voice wrecked and torn.

My feet moved on their own accord, my body being pulled by a string. Drawing me closer and closer to the door. Before I knew it I pushed my dresser out of the way and turned the knob. I instantly jerked back, assaulted with the strong scent of alcohol. Esteban was leaning on the wall beside my door, one arm propped up with his forehead pressed against the drywall, his other hand still in the air ready to knock again.

It took him a second to realize I had opened the door. Angling his head slightly to look at me, we locked eyes, our expressions mirroring each other. His eyes were bloodshot and swollen. I couldn't tell if it was from crying or from the bottle of whiskey that was still firmly clutched in his grasp. We stood there for a while not saying anything. Words weren't necessary. Our eyes spoke for themselves.

And his spoke volumes.

"I'm so fucking sorry," he breathed out. Desperation and sadness written all over his face, I had never seen him like that before.

It physically pained me to see him that way. The once strong, solid man was gone. All that was left in his place was a man nearly on his knees begging for forgiveness.

"Where is *he*?" I asked, needing to know.

"Gone. For now, anyway."

"How could you do this to me?" I whispered, my eyes filling with fresh tears.

He shook his head, averting his eyes to the floor. Not able to look at me anymore.

"Did you think I had a choice, Daisy? We're more alike than you realize," he paused to let his words sink in. "This life. It's yours whether you want it to be or not. It's the shitty cards you were dealt. All you can do is embrace it, because if you don't, it will bury you alive. I could have warned you. I could have told you to leave. I could have done a lot of things… but in the end, it doesn't matter. You're already nailed to the cross."

I vigorously shook my head.

Back and forth.

Back and forth.

Back and forth.

"Fuck you," I scoffed, snapping his attention back to me again. "Do you hear me? Fuck. You!" I screamed not caring who heard me. Tears streamed down my cheeks and fell to the floor between us, along with my jaded heart and fucked up soul.

I turned around and went back into my room, needing to sit down. I sat on the edge of my bed defeated, hating that he was right, hating that I had no choice, hating that this was my life now.

I hated my uncle, but I hated myself even more.

I bawled. I sobbed so hard that my body convulsed and I couldn't breathe. The walls were crashing down all around me. Hyperventilating and sucking in air that wasn't available for the taking, drowning in my own despair. Asking God why, why I deserved this? Beginning to think he didn't even exist.

I felt fingers caress the side of my face, wiping away my tears that kept falling, one right after the other. I peeked up through wet lashes and blurry eyes, Esteban was on his knees in front of me.

"I'm so fucking sorry," he rasped, his own voice breaking.

That's when I really lost it.

That's when it really hit me.

It was all a lie.

No God.

No family.

No love.

I was all alone. Abandoned. By myself.

I trembled, my body giving out on me. Any ounce of strength I had left, vanished. He pulled me into his strong, solid arms. A place I was so familiar with. The only comfort I've ever known since the day I died. I sobbed uncontrollably, my vision blurred and my throat locked up, becoming so raw, so dry, so torn into pieces that I would never be able to be put back together. He held me tighter, trying like hell to save me from myself.

"Please… please…" I begged, shuddering against his chest.

I wanted something, anything, to keep me from feeling the emotions that were dragging me down, deeper and deeper into the pits of Hell.

Standing right by my uncle.

Where a part of me knew I belonged.

"What can I do?" he commiserated, pulling back, placing his warm hands on either side of my face, to look deep into my eyes. "Tell me, what I can fucking do and I will do it, Briggs. For you."

It was the first time he ever called me that and I would be lying if I said I didn't yearn to hear him say Daisy.

I blinked away my tears, swallowing back the sobs to gaze at the only man who has ever given a damn about me. The only man who had ever been my friend, my protector, my confidant, my everything.

He was all I'd ever known.

"I want to be the hero of my own story, Esteban. I crave to feel what they feel even for just a night, and you're the closest person who resembles affection in my life," I half-whispered.

I leaned in on pure impulse and looked into his vacant eyes, searching for something. I felt him lightly gasp before I brushed my lips against his, kissing him. My inexperienced lips moved against his for a few seconds before he finally started to kiss me back. It was the first time I had ever kissed anyone. It felt different than I had imagined it would, a sensation like nothing I could ever describe and for a few fleeting moments it took away the pain in my heart.

He shook his head, pulling away from me, pushing me back and I whimpered at the loss of his lips.

"We can't do this."

"You want to make this better? Me better? I need you to take away the bad, silence the chaos in my head. Please…"

His conflicted stare never left mine as I reached for his shirt. He didn't say a word or move a muscle when I started unbuttoning it one by one until it was fully open. I took in his hard naked chest for the first time, the contours of his abs, his tan skin that was so much darker than my white complexion.

I reached for the bottom of my tank top and his hand instantly stopped me.

"Daisy," he warned in a voice I didn't recognize.

105

"I know… this doesn't change anything. I'm not looking for you to whisper sweet nothings in my ear, Esteban. I don't need you to make love to me. I know where we stand. I just need this from you right now."

It's never this hard for the heroines in my books. They make it seem so easy.

Am I wrong? Is this a mistake? Am I going to regret this?

I closed my eyes and pulled my tank top over my head, before either of us gave what I'd just said anymore thought. Tossing it aside, I felt a chill on my bare breasts. I reached for my cotton shorts and slid them down with my panties, flinging them both aside as well.

When I was fully undressed, I took a deep breath and opened my eyes. I would never forget the look on his face for as long as I lived. It was the first time anyone had ever looked at me like that.

"You're beautiful," he coaxed with hooded eyes and a sad smile.

I blushed, not used to the praise. I could sense his resolve as his eyes took me in. I could feel his thoughts raging a war in his mind, so I leaned in again before he could give it anymore thought. Taking away the need to feel anything other than what was wreaking havoc on my soul.

I leaned back against the bed, bringing him with me. My hands pressed against his chest when I felt his weight on top of me. I ignored the smell and taste of alcohol that radiated off his breath, knowing that it was impairing his decision between right and wrong.

I wanted this.

I needed this.

It was wrong, but it didn't matter because in that moment it felt right, and that's all that mattered to me.

We kissed and touched each other, getting lost in the moment, getting caught up in the way we were making each other feel. His hands were everywhere and all at once, like he couldn't decide where he wanted to touch me the most. I sought comfort in the false illusion he was letting me have, and reality hit the second I felt his dick at my entrance. It all became clear that this was really happening.

And I welcomed it with open arms.

He leaned his forehead against mine and groaned, "Are you sure? This is what you want?"

I smiled against his lips, nodding. Kissing him hard once again. He thrust in slowly, and carefully, knowing that this was my first time. I held back the urge to whimper, not wanting him to stop but to keep going and make me feel the promises of what his hands already brought me.

When he was fully inside of me, he let out a deep, long breath. "Are you okay?" he murmured in between kissing me.

I nodded again, not being able to form the words for what I was thinking, let alone feeling. The sounds of our bodies coming together echoed in the room, filling the silent void. Once the stinging diminished, a new bubbling feeling crept into my lower abdomen.

I moaned and my head fell back, allowing him to kiss, lick, and suck.

His hand reached down between us to touch me and I swear I thought I was going to die.

Right then and there.

"Oh my God," I panted.

I couldn't take it anymore.

The way his thrusts devoured me, the way his fingers played with me, the way his kisses consumed me, was far too much for me to control. The room started to spin and my breathing faltered. I felt like I was coming apart and being ripped open all at the same time, barely being able to control my movements, let alone my breathing.

I made all sorts of noises that seemed foreign coming out of my mouth. The room caved in on me, as spasms consumed my body, taking me to the edge and all I wanted to do was fall.

I was almost there…

So close…

Just one more…

"Ah—"

"YOU, MOTHERFUCKER!" Uncle roared, taking something else away from me.

I screamed, jolting out of my skin. Esteban was roughly ripped away from me and I saw his body being thrown across the room. His back hit the wall so hard it tore through the drywall. My uncle didn't falter, he picked him up and slammed him up against the doorframe, and I heard a loud crack.

I was frozen in place with the sheet covering my naked body. I sat there watching my only friend, get ripped away from my life.

I couldn't move.

I couldn't speak.

I couldn't tear my eyes off the brutal scene in front of me. As if I was watching a train wreck unfold and not being able to look away.

"YOU PIECE OF FUCKING SHIT! AFTER EVERYTHING I'VE DONE FOR YOU!" my uncle roared, picking him up off the ground again and punching him in the face repeatedly.

Esteban's body lay lax against my uncle's strong grip. He punched him in the stomach causing the beaten man to fall forward, crumbling to the ground. He bent down flipping him onto his back and straddled his waist, beating him to an inch of his life.

Because of me.

More blood on my hands.

"NO!" I screamed, loud enough to break glass. "PLEASE! STOP! PLEASE I'M BEGGING YOU! I'LL DO ANYTHING! ANYTHING!"

My uncle ignored me and continued his assault on Esteban's face and body. When he finally stopped to stand, I breathed a sigh of relief, thinking I'd won. That I got through to him.

I didn't.

He reached into the back of his slacks and pulled out his gun, aiming it right at Esteban's head.

"NO!" I cried out.

I lunged into action, jumping off the bed and throwing myself in front of the gun. That was now placed directly on my forehead. My body shielding what was left of Esteban's life.

"Get the fuck out of my face," he gritted through a clenched jaw.

"No! Please! Please! Please! I'm begging you. It wasn't his fault." I got down on my knees, tucking the sheet under my arms, setting my hands in prayer gesture out in front of me. "I'm begging you, pleading with you on my hands and knees to please not do this! Please, Uncle! You don't have to do this!" I bellowed through tears.

He scoffed. "You think your pitiful performance is going to work on me? You don't know me, peladita. Get the fuck off the floor before I make you, and trust me, you don't want it to come to that."

I shook my head. "No."

He cocked his head to the side as if no one had ever said that to him.

"You look like a fucking whore on your knees. NOW, GET THE FUCK UP!"

I shook my head again. "No."

"What? You love him? You love that piece of shit?" He pointed to Esteban's lifeless body.

I swallowed, hard. "No, Uncle. I don't," I answered the truth.

His head jerked back, stunned. He believed me.

"So, you are a whore," he stated. "Your mother would be so proud."

I frowned not wavering. "Please. Please, don't do this. Not for me, okay? You don't have to do shit for me. Do it for my mom. The only sister you had. The one you loved so fucking much," I reminded, throwing the words he spoke hours ago back at him.

His eyes glazed over as he narrowed them at me. For the first time he didn't hide the fact that the mere mention of my mother could bring him to his knees.

He slowly lowered his gun, but didn't holster it.

I exhaled for what felt like an eternity. He grabbed his phone from his pocket and walked towards my window. I immediately turned to check on Esteban.

I placed his head on my lap and caressed the sides of his bloody, bruised face. Barely recognizing the man who was in my arms.

"Hey…"

He stirred.

"You're going to be okay…" I coaxed.

"Venga a recoger a este hijo de puta antes de que yo lo mate," Uncle roared, "Come get this son of a bitch before I kill him."

He hung up, placing his phone back in his suit jacket, still facing the big, bay window in my room with his back to me.

After all these years, after all this time, I wanted to know what he was thinking. What he was feeling. I wanted to know his story. What made him the way he was? If he was ever a kind person… a loving man… a scared child…

I shook away the thoughts when I heard footsteps ascending down the hall. The same two men I'd met in the basement walked into the room. My uncle took one look at them and then nodded toward Esteban, turning to face the window once again.

They quickly picked him up, dragging him away from me. Taking the blanket off the bed and wrapping it around him. He was half-conscious when the men stood him up, but he was still hunched over, reeling in pain. They placed his arms around their necks for support.

Esteban opened his eyes as much as he could. Wanting to look for me I was sure. The men didn't allow him any time and I wasn't stupid enough to say anything to him. They carried him towards the door, leaving me to wonder if I would ever see him again.

It didn't matter. He was alive.

"You know what?" Uncle said, bringing all of our attention back to him.

The men holding Esteban spun to face him.

My uncle turned around and narrowed his dark, daunting, soulless eyes directly at Esteban.

"I changed my mind," he simply stated.

And before it registered what he just said. He lifted his gun and shot him.

"NO!" I yelled out, placing my hand over my mouth.

Hearing him groan out in pain, it was then I noticed his leg was gushing blood and my hand fell to my heart.

Relieved.

"The next time you *fuck* with what's mine, Esteban, the bullet will go in your fucking head."

With that the men turned and left, leaving a trail of his blood on the floor.

"Briggs," Uncle announced and I glanced over at him with nothing but hatred in my glare.

He was lost in thought, staring at my shed innocence that stained the sheets on the bed. He walked over to me, every step precise and calculated with the same vicious expression on his face. He roughly gripped my chin, making me look him dead in the eyes. He looked at me like I had been reborn, like I was no longer a little girl and said,

"You're a Martinez now."

CHAPTER 10

AUSTIN

One thing I knew for sure…

I fucking hated school.

I sat in my freshman Psych class not paying any attention to the lecture, too distracted checking out the chick sitting one row below me in the auditorium. Her tits were on full display, making me want to bury my face in them and motorboat the shit out of her.

I grinned, biting the edge of my lip.

The best thing about college was the pussy and parties. The rest was just kind of a blur. I barely ever went to class, too hungover from the night before to give a shit about anything before noon.

That's when my day started, most of the time I woke up alone, but I never went to sleep that way.

Not that we slept…

After the accident, I had a lot of time to make up for staying in the goddamn hospital for a month. Not to mention the countless fucking hours of physical therapy that followed shortly after my stay. I wasn't miraculously cured, my back still hurt like a son of a bitch whenever I worked out.

Thank God for pain pills.

My hair had grown back, covering the massive scar I had from surgery. I grew out my facial hair to cover the ones on my face. The only visible scar was a small one down my eyebrow, glass sliced right through the hair and left me with a missing patch. I had some wicked marks on my arms, back, chest, and legs, which I was self-conscious about at first. They were my motivation to start a daily regimen of working out at the gym like my life depended on it.

I accepted the fact that they were a part of me now, forever etched into my skin.

A daily reminder that I'd fucked up.

To my surprise the scars got chicks all hot-and-bothered, something about making me look like a bad boy. They were on me like bees on honey.

College was like sex Heaven on steroids. Chicks liked to experiment, they wanted to embrace their sexuality or some bullshit and I had no problem being their fucking subject.

I had missed so many days of my senior year after the accident that I had to take summer classes to graduate. They let me walk with my class though. I didn't give a shit about any of it, I did it because it made my family and Half-Pint happy to see me walk across the stage and receive my diploma. My mom hung it proudly in her office, saying that my college diploma would go right next to it someday.

It was just another piece of paper that I could wipe my ass with as far as I was concerned. That's how much school meant to me.

The boys and I saw each other here and there, but not nearly as much as we used to.

So much had changed.

So much had happened.

I spent my freshman year in the dorms instead of living with them. The plan had been to move in with them after graduation since they planned on getting a bigger apartment for all of us.

That was shot to shit real quick.

"Jacob and Dylan may have forgotten what the fuck you did, Austin, but I haven't. And I won't," Lucas argued during my graduation party.

I didn't say anything because what could I say to that. He was right.

"Lucas, calm the fuck down. He fucked up. He knows it. With the hours of community service, the legal fees, and his license being suspended for a year, not to mention the physical scars, I think it's enough of a daily reminder for him," Dylan intervened, holding him back with his forearm.

"He almost fucking killed her! She was in a goddamn coma!" He shoved Dylan's arm away, pointing at me. "You stay the fuck away from, Alex. Do you understand me? Stay the fuck away from her!"

"I can't do that," I countered, not backing down.

He stepped closer to me. Our faces were an inch apart. Dylan and Jacob standing right beside us, waiting to step in.

"You may not remember what you did. But that doesn't change the fact that you're a fuck up," he gritted out. "We give you one thing to do! One fucking thing! Take care of her. Just take care of her. It was fucking simple! You couldn't even do that! I'm tired of making excuses for you. You're lucky I don't bury you alive."

I held my chin higher. "So much for being brothers, Lucas."

He scoffed, shaking his head. "You're not my brother."

I looked him up and down.

He stepped away from me, adding, "Not anymore."

I swallowed hard, blinking away the hurt I felt in my heart.

"Give him time, Austin. He'll come around," Dylan coaxed.

I nodded.

"Dylan's right. You know Lucas... he's hotheaded and stubborn as all hell. When he's ready, he'll forgive you. He'll get past this. "

"Have you?" I blurted, already knowing the answer.

They both looked at each other and then back at me, the truth written clear across their faces.

"Exactly."

"Hi," the girl with the tits from class greeted, pulling me away from my thoughts as I walked out into the parking lot.

I glanced over at her and she smirked, playing with the ends of her hair. I immediately envisioned pulling it while I was balls deep inside her. Gripping it back by the nook of her neck as I fucked her doggy style.

My cock twitched.

"Hey there." I smiled.

"You want to hang out?" she asked, doing that thing chicks do with their lips. A pout that she seemed to have perfected, making me wonder what they would feel like wrapped around my cock.

"I have some weed back at the sorority house. We could smoke, talk, you know... whatever."

I was about to say something when my phone rang. I grabbed it out of my pocket to see who was calling me. Alex's smiling face illuminated the screen.

"He almost fucking killed her! She was in a goddamn coma!"

I hit ignore.

"Lead the fuckin' way, sweetheart."

Briggs

Alejandro Martinez.

I never understood the importance of a name. It wasn't until after that night three months ago that I learned that names carry a heavy load.

The connotation behind a name, and not just any name…

My name.

Martinez.

"Damn! I love your hair," the girl behind the counter all but screamed as I walked into the tattoo shop. "How did you get such a vibrant purple? Oh my God! I would kill for that!"

I ignored her compliment and looked around the room, stopping when I spotted the guy in the back corner covered in tattoos. When he felt my gaze on him, he peered up and we locked eyes. I internally smiled.

I recognized those eyes.

I walked toward him, never breaking our connection. The tattoo business card that I found on my uncle's desk safely hidden in my pocket.

If you wanted to know the truth about someone…

The secrets that lurk in their dark corners.

What they're feeling… what they want… what they need…

The depths of their soul.

Just look them in the eyes.

They never fucking lie.

I handed him the piece of paper that I had clutched in my tight grasp. He took it from me and looked it over, jerking his neck back with a fascinated regard.

"You want this tattooed?" he asked. His gaze still intently placed on the drawing in his hand.

"Yes."

"Where?"

"From the nook of my neck, down the center of my back, stopping in the middle." I pointed to the sketch. "These I want on each of my shoulder blades, cascading down the sides of my entire back."

He shook his head, mockingly. "Sweetie, this is an intricate tattoo. The detailed outline will take several hours, not to mention several sessions to do the color and shading. The pain alone can be unbearable." He handed me back my drawing. "How about just a butterfly or something?"

I cocked my head to the side and narrowed my eyes at him. "I got nothing but time, *sweetie*."

He arched an eyebrow. "How old are you?"

"Old enough."

"Oh yeah?" He nodded at me. "Let me see your ID."

"Alejandro Martinez is my ID."

His eyes widened, it was quick but I saw it. I knew he would recognize the name, having an appearance of a man who was just released from prison.

"And trust me, he won't give a fuck," I added.

He stood up and gestured toward the chair in front of him. I sat down, waiting for him to get suited up. It didn't take long for him to have everything ready. Pulling over the curtain to give us some privacy, he laid down the table and patted it.

"You can change in the bathroom. I have a smock in there you can use, just leave the opening in the back."

I smiled, grabbing the hem of my shirt.

"I'm not shy, I don't need the bathroom. Be a gentleman and turn around."

He smiled back at me, spinning the chair that he was sitting in. I threw my shirt and bra on the counter and laid face down on the table. I heard his movements and the sliding of his chair on the tile floor. I felt his warm hands, rubbing alcohol all over my back.

"This your first tattoo, little girl?"

"I don't know, is it yours, big boy?"

He softly laughed behind me. The vibration causing my back to stir.

Crave Me

"You sure about this? Once the needle hits your skin. There's no going back."

I looked at his reflection through the mirror to my right and then back at my own reflection and said,

"There's no going back for me. Only forward."

CHAPTER
11

AUSTIN

I got kicked out of the dorms a few months into my sophomore year of college for smoking pot. I was surprised that it took that damn long for the resident advisor to smell it coming out of my room. It was just some damn weed. It comes from the earth for God's sake. It was already legal in several states.

I didn't understand why I was getting so much flack for it. The parents on the other hand, lost their shit because of this.

I moved into Dylan and Jacob's apartment, as Lucas happened to be moving back to Oak Island. His mom was diagnosed with stage three-breast cancer, and he'd ended up knocking up some chick.

It took everything inside of me to bite my goddamn tongue, knowing the news nearly killed Alex.

Karma's a bitch.

We all took the news of his mom getting cancer pretty bad. I was the last one to find out. They waited until I was visiting to sit me down and tell me. It was Lily's, Lucas' baby sister, sixteenth birthday. For some fucked up reason they thought that was the best time to tell me. I barely let the news settle before I called up some random friends that night and got shitfaced at The Cove downtown.

The night was full of fucking surprises.

Just one right after the other.

Dylan and Jacob promised Alex we would come visit her in California for spring break. Between the news of Lucas' mom and his bundle of joy being born soon, she needed her boys. At least that's what she told them. It was her freshman year of college. She was living with Aubrey in an apartment, both of them attending UCLA. The same college Cole was attending.

Which was more than just a coincidence, even though she said he had nothing to do with it, and the sad part was…

I believed her.

We left Half-Pint's apartment before sunrise our last day in California to go surfing. We rented some boards for the day, since we didn't have ours. I hadn't been on a surfboard since before the accident. It was the best feeling in the world. I loved being back on a board, watching the sun come up. There was nothing else in the world that compared to being out in the water when no one else was around. Watching life just come awake right before your eyes. It was the most peaceful feeling. Once the sun came up, a light breeze kicked up, causing the wind to blow against my face. Tasting the salt water and sand. Being one with Mother Nature and all her glory.

By noon my back was killing me, the throbbing sensation radiated everywhere and all at once, almost crippling me. I barely made it back to the shore, the white water had to drag me back in. I actually had to lay there against the current. The pain was unbearable. My back spasms were so fucking bad. I didn't think I would be able to move again.

"What the fuck you doin'?" Dylan asked, hovering above me with his board under his arm.

"Relaxing," I simply stated, glaring up at him through silts in his eyes.

He reached out his hand to help me up and I grunted in pain, leaning over once I stood.

"You alright?"

"Just fuckin' peachy," I rasped out.

I stood, breathing through the pain. In and out, slowly moving my body to an upright position.

"Austin, you're not going to your physical therapy anymore, and you're popping those painkillers like fuckin' candy. It's masking your pain, it's not fixin' it."

"Jesus Christ, man. It's not even noon yet and you're on my balls. You guys don't fucking get it, you don't know what it feels like after that physical therapy bullshit. I can barely walk and I'm in bed for days after one session. I can barely take a goddamn piss without holding myself up against the wall."

"No shit. But the more you do it, the easier it will get."

"You want to hold my cock too, McGraw? Would that make you feel better? Last time I checked you didn't have a medical degree and you hadn't flown out the window of a fucking car," I argued.

"Whose fault is that, Austin?" he spewed, regretting his words immediately.

"This was a good talk. I'll see you back at Alex's apartment."

I took a cab back to Half-Pint's place, leaving the boys to surf some more. I hadn't gotten my license back yet, not that it mattered. I wouldn't be able to drive in my current state of pain. By the time I flagged down a cab, I was seeing stars from the severity of the throbbing. Of course I didn't bring enough painkillers with me either. I honestly didn't think surfing would take me down like that.

I paid the driver and slowly made my way into her apartment. As soon as I opened the door, the sound of someone moaning tore through the foyer. At first I thought it was Aubrey, but she barely left her room, avoiding Dylan like the plague. They'd broken up suddenly almost two years ago, and things were still awkward between the two of them.

"Cole, you have to stop, we can't do this right now."

I stopped dead in my tracks as soon as I heard her voice. All the blood drained from my face.

"The boys could come back any second. I don't want them to find out this way," Alex pretty much panted every word.

"They're surfing, darlin, just lay back and enjoy what I do to you."

My feet moved on their own accord. There was no stopping it. Her door was cracked open and what I saw was almost as crippling as the pain in my back. Cole was on his knees on the side of her bed, his face buried between Alex's legs.

I scoffed, backing away from the door before they heard me. I'd never be able to look at Alex the same way again. My heart broke a little more that day. Any illusions I had all these years were shattered in that moment, and it wasn't because of Bo or Alex. Realization hit me like a ton of bricks.

I was never a choice.

I wasn't even in the running.

I was never good enough.

I took a quick shower, downed some painkillers, and got the fuck out of there. The last two nights I had hooked up with some random chick. As luck would turn out, she loved my cock and welcomed me with open arms when I knocked on her door.

All I wanted to do was forget, so I spent the entire day wrapped up in her pussy.

Doing just that.

"You going to the fraternity party tonight?" she asked, laying her head on my chest.

I shrugged. The last thing I wanted was to be around Cole, Alex, and the good ol' boys. I wouldn't mind staying right where I was, going another few rounds with her.

She peeked up at me through her lashes. "You want to have some fun tonight?"

I grinned, thinking she read my mind and was talking about fucking again.

She rolled over and grabbed something out of her nightstand drawer. She placed two blue pills with an engraved star stamp on my chest.

We locked eyes.

"You want to fuck like a God?"

She swallowed the two pills that were in her hand and before I could answer, she ordered, "Open your mouth and follow me down the rabbit hole. I promise to be gentle," she purred.

My mouth parted, answering the question for me. I swallowed back the pills and waited...

***

"What are you on, Austin?" Alex asked, sitting on the hood of her car. I stood in front of her keeping my distance.

My eyes were so fucking dilated. I had a hard time focusing on her face and not on the streetlights behind her. Everything was breathing, thriving, and vivid. I couldn't focus on more than one thing without my eyes twitching and my body feeling alive. Like I had woken up for the first time, like I was living for the first time, like I was seeing clearly for the first time. The thought alone made me take a breath from the sensations that coursed through my blood.

After the chick and I fucked each other's brains out, she wanted to check out the party. I just wanted to move, I couldn't stand still. I walked into the party for a few minutes and walked right back out as soon as Alex and the boys walked in. There was no escaping them.

My back didn't hurt.

My heart didn't hurt.

Nothing fucking hurt anymore.

It didn't take long for Alex to follow me outside.

"Just weed, Half-Pint, relax. You sound as bad as the boys," I stated.

"I'm worried about you," she coaxed.

I laughed. *Yeah, you looked so fucking worried about me while Cole was eating you out.*

"Don't be, I'm fine." I leaned in close to her face and spewed, "Now, you and Cole? You fucking him, Alex?" Having no filter.

The drugs had taken over, and I welcomed the feeling with open arms. Spending way too many years keeping my mouth shut for everyone else.

She gasped, jerking back. "Jesus, Austin."

I rolled my eyes, walking away from her, needing to move again. My body tingled everywhere.

"Oh, come on, Alex, we're not kids anymore. I know you get... wet," I crudely baited. Not giving a fuck anymore.

She immediately jumped off her car, walking away from me. I grabbed her arm a little too hard, just wanting to stop her.

"Oh my God, stop! I'm joking. Calm down."

"Let go of my arm," she harshly demanded.

I did.

"You're lying. What are you on?" she repeated, sounding like a damn broken record.

I sighed, wanting her to stop asking and blurted, "Ecstasy."

"Why? Why are you doing this?"

I smiled big, backing away. "Why not, Alex? You only live once. Might as well fucking make it count, right?"

"Austin," she murmured, trying to reach for me.

I pulled back my arm, already knowing what was coming. There was no way in Hell I was letting her ruin my high. After everything I'd been through the last few years, I fucking deserved it.

"No! Don't look at me like that. I'm having fun."

She eyed me, disappointed in my behavior.

I put my hand out in the air, surrendering. "Fuck it. I'm out of here."

"Austin!" she shouted after me, but I ignored her and kept going.

I walked around aimlessly for I don't know how long. There was a park up the road I found myself wandering toward. I wanted to look at the stars. Be in the moment. Fucking forget about her. Fucking forget about all of them. I laid down on the slide, tucking my arms behind my head, and peered up at the sky.

Lost in the beauty of the world.

The silence all around me.

The quiet before the storm...

"What the fuck, man?" Dylan roared, walking up to me with Jacob beside him.

That didn't take long. "Nice of you to join me, boys, but if you came here to lecture me, I suggest you turn the fuck around. I'm not going to take any shit from either one of you," I calmly stated, causing them to jerk back from the impact of my response.

I was in no fucking mood for more bullshit. I just wanted to look at the goddamn stars.

"Jesus Christ, Austin," Jacob rebutted. "What are you doing? This isn't you."

I scoffed, standing up right in front of them. "Who am I? Huh? You tell me, boys, because I have no fucking idea anymore. I have spent the last twenty-one years of my life marching in line with all of you. I'm done. Do you hear me? Fucking done."

Today was the last straw...

No more going back for me.

Just clear skies ahead.

"What the hell are you talking about? You're not making any goddamn sense," Dylan countered, folding his arms over his chest. "Fuck, man, we know you went through some shit with the car accident but—"

"You don't know a goddamn thing. Your head's been so far up Aubrey's and every other girl's pussy, you can barely see straight."

Dylan immediately stepped toward me ready to throw down, but Jacob placed his arm across his chest.

"Relax," he ordered in a rough tone, looking back at me. "This the way you want to play it? We're your friends not your enemies, asshole. You need to remember that while you're on this path of self-destruction that you so intently feel like continuing. What's next? Cocaine? Huh? What's it going to take for you to get your fucking shit together, Austin? Rehab? Fucking overdosing? Do you have a fucking death wish, bro? Please tell us so we know what to expect from your path of God-knows-what."

I snidely smiled. I was done fucking protecting them. They wanted to act like I was the fuck up. They wanted to pretend like they were so fucking perfect, well then they had another thing coming.

Lucas with his God-given attitude of never hurting Alex, when all he did was that. Knocking someone up killed her in ways I couldn't have done in the car accident.

Dylan fucking anything with tits and an ass, flaunting it in Aubrey's face, not giving a shit about the hurt it caused her.

And then Jacob… fucking Jacob.

"That's… fucking… rich… coming from you, Oh, Mighty Jacob." I shook my head with a devious stare directed only at him.

I could see Dylan from the corner of my eye. He seemed just as baffled as Jacob was. They really were fucking clueless, such goddamn hypocrites. Acting like they were better than me, when they were anything but.

"You want to judge me and point fingers? People who live in glass houses shouldn't throw stones…" I mocked in a tone he didn't appreciate.

"Stop speaking in code and just fucking spit it out already," Jacob demanded.

"You want to talk about how I'm living my life? Tell me that I'm fucking up? Well, shit, Jacob, why don't you look in the goddamn mirror?"

He jerked back like I had punched him in the face, and now I was going to take him down.

"I saw you. I saw it all. I was there that night."

"What night?"

"The Cove," I simply stated.

His eyes widened, all the color draining from his face.

"What's the matter, Jacob? Cat got your tongue?" I taunted.

Dylan looked back and forth between us. "What the fuck is he talking about?"

"Should I tell him?" I baited, nodding toward Dylan.

I knew the night was replaying over in Jacob's mind as I stood in front of him.

"Oh, come on, Jacob, we're all friends here, right? Isn't that what you just said to me. What are secrets between friends?"

"You don't know what you're talking about," he finally gritted out, his jaw clenching.

"I don't? Well, then why don't I refresh your memory and let Dylan decide if I'm right or wrong. You see... Dylan," I ridiculed, still only looking at him.

"Jacob here isn't who he thinks he is. Holding himself up on a goddamn pedestal when he should be buried in the ground for what he wants to do. See, I was in town a few weeks ago, hanging out at The Cove downtown. I saw someone that looked like Lucas' baby sister and to my surprise it was actually her."

Dylan shut his eyes like he knew what the next words out of my mouth were going to be. It was then I realized we all kept secrets from each other.

"So, of course, I made my way toward her. She was dry humping some cocksucker on the dance floor. I would have never thought the girl I saw as a little sister my whole life could move like that. It made me sick to watch it. What did it do to you, Jacob?"

His fists clenched at his sides.

"Then out of nowhere I see this guy haul ass through the crowd. I'm getting ready to throw down if some other motherfucker even lays a finger on her. Except, I'm nearly knocked on my ass when I see Jacob appear like her knight in shining armor. Isn't that right? After you proceeded to kick the guy's ass, I'm about to walk over and pat you on the fucking back for a job well done, but Lily shoves you and takes off like a bat out of Hell. Jacob here not far behind her."

He tried to remain calm, but each word that came out of my mouth made him more aware of how fucked up the situation was.

"So I followed you. Both of you. Would you like to tell Dylan what I saw? Or should I do the honors?"

He shut his eyes, the shame immediately filling his body.

"I watched you pretty much attack her in a parking lot on the side of a goddamn SUV. Tell me, bro, do little girls get you hard?"

"Enough," Dylan interjected, taking the words right out of Jacob's mouth. I didn't know if it was for his benefit or Jacob's, but I assumed it was both.

"Yeah... try watching it. Maybe Jacob can give you a private show like he gave me?"

"Austin," Jacob warned on his last thread.

I cocked my head to the side. "Or do you only get hard when you think no one is watching?"

He narrowed his eyes at me. I didn't falter.

"It's all good, Jacob, as long as there's grass on the field, I say play ball."

He cold-cocked me straight in the jaw. My face swayed back from the impact of his fist, but my body didn't move. I was expecting it. Bracing myself for it.

"You can say whatever the fuck you want about me, but you talk about Lily like that again, and I will lay you the fuck out, Austin. I don't give a fuck who you are." He shook out his hand, the pain traveling up his arm.

I leaned over, spitting out blood on the grass. Glaring up at him. "Truth hurts don't it, motherfucker?"

He stepped toward me and Dylan held him back, stepping in between us.

"Get out of here, Austin," Dylan ordered.

I looked at him, surprised and dismayed. I couldn't believe after what I told him he was taking Jacob's fucking side. I know I only saw Jacob kiss Lily against the SUV that night but fuck, if that would have been me instead, they would have crucified me.

"The Good Ol' Boys, huh? Yeah... you don't have to tell me twice," I viciously spewed, backing away still facing them.

I wanted to remember them just like that. So if I ever missed home, I would always remember that there was no home.

To go back to.

Briggs

I swallowed two blue pills stamped with stars and I wanted to dance. I couldn't remember the last time I closed my eyes for more than a few seconds other than to feel the euphoria coursing through me. I rode the high for as long as I could.

Hours...

Days...

It all blended together.

The crowd of the club got louder, heavier, deeper.

Except when you're a Martinez, you don't worry about any of that. You're up in VIP, in a private section, closed off, partying with whoever the fuck you want.

I brought the party.

I stood on the balcony swaying my hips, watching the people dancing below through dazed and tainted eyes. Loving life, living in the moment, letting the beat take over them.

Not a care in this fucked up world.

The darkness in my soul consumed me, overshadowing the high that I so desperately wanted to hold onto.

All that was left was emptiness.

Next thing I knew I was opening my car door, my sound system blasting '*Silence*' by Delirium through the speakers. Thumping loud and hard into my veins, mimicking the pounding in my heart and the ringing in my ears. As if she was talking just to me.

Just. For. Me.

Feeling *me*.

Possessing *me*.

Silencing me.

I pulled my car over on the side of the road. I grabbed my ear buds and plugged them into my phone, slipping it into my back pocket. Not wanting the music to stop as I walked toward the Brooklyn Bridge. It was one of the oldest bridges in New York, and it captured my attention as a child. There was something about the bright lights of the city reflecting off the East River, the sounds of traffic flying past as you walked along the pedestrian path. No matter the time or day.

It was alive.

Breathing for me.

One of my only fond memories was driving on the bridge as a child, shouting at Esteban to look up every time we were about to go under the double arches. I would hold my breath until we passed through what looked like angel wings, making wishes that never came true.

I got lost in the beat of the music blasting through my ears, mesmerized by the meaning of her words, pulling me closer and closer to the angel arches. My feet moved on their own accord, my body and mind following close behind my deliberate steps.

I dropped out of school the day of my fifteenth birthday. I knew my parents would be rolling over in their graves. Their only daughter… a high school dropout. They weren't around though, so now I followed Alejandro's footsteps. Whether I wanted to or not. Two years since I embraced being a Martinez, sitting next to my uncle on the bus to Hell.

And already it felt like an eternity nailed to the cross.

I took in the beauty of the Heaven in front of me, standing right under the angel, looking over the edge and gazing down below. Cars flew by faster and faster, headlights blurring into the night. They appeared so small, so powerless, almost like they weren't real.

The soft strumming of the chorus immediately assaulted my senses, making the hairs on my arms stand at attention. The thumping from the ear buds vibrating against my core. It was a warm night but I suddenly felt cold all over, chills running through me. I closed my eyes reeling in the emotions, the feelings, and racing thoughts that attacked my mind at rapid speed.

One right after the other.

They were devastating and merciless.

I grabbed onto the cold railing, taking a deep breath as the wind blew against my face, producing a new high I had yet to experience. I rested my head back relishing in the vibrations against my soul. I had no control over my body, placing one foot on the railing, the other slowly after.

The music was smooth like silk, but raw like nails, clawing at my skin, burrowing inside me, making itself at home.

My mind.

My body.

My soul.

I climbed through the wires to stand on the rusted ledge, steadying myself once my feet met my hands. Gradually balancing before slowly standing tall. My thoughts bleeding off of me right onto the oncoming traffic. I felt the vibes all around me even though I still hadn't opened my eyes to take it all in.

I was caught up in the silence, I could finally believe. Lifting my arms out beside me like an angel ready to fly away. Riding the white wave to my sense of wonder.

Freedom.

I sucked in deep breaths, my heart beating so fucking hard. I thought the pounding would knock me over from the force of my own rage. The song hitting it's all-time high and just when the thought of letting go came over me.

Giving into the release.

The beat slowed, the song coming to an end. The chaos quieted down all around me.

I opened my eyes.

Gasping.

The force so powerful, so crippling, so fucking real that it jerked my body back against the wire cables, my hands immediately gripping the iron ropes to the point of pain.

For a moment I had silence.

For a second I found my peace.

Even if it almost just cost me…

My life.

CHAPTER
12

AUSTIN

It had been a month since I dropped out of college.

It had been a month since I left and hadn't looked back once.

It had been a month since I started living.

I got the fuck out of California, leaving all the bullshit behind. I took the first flight available to Ohio, not bothering to tell anyone. As far as I was concerned no one existed to me anymore. The only stop I made was by our apartment to grab enough shit to fit in my duffle bag. I went straight to the airport and picked the next flight departing, getting the hell out of Ohio.

Which happened to be Miami, Florida.

I met some random chick on the plane and followed her back to her apartment, where we fucked for the next three days. I didn't mind, she had nice tits and let me fuck them, too. Plus, it was a place I could crash for a few days till I got my shit together.

My phone was blowing up with phone calls and text messages from everyone and their mother. After a week of not answering or replying you'd think they'd take the goddamn hint, but it only made them bother me more.

I replied to one text.

"I'm fine, Half-Pint. I'll keep in touch when I can. Goodbye."

And I threw away my phone.

I was living off odd end jobs, here and there, enough to get me through without settling any roots. I was technically homeless, crashing with friend's that I met partying or a new pussy's bed, more often than not.

Crave Me

I was having the time of my life.

I lit my cigarette as we walked into the party, blowing smoke into the air. The pretty blonde I picked up at the bar said she was going to some house party on South Beach.

Never being one to pass up a good time, I decided to go with her.

We arrived around one in the morning, having a few drinks while she eye-fucked the shit out of me before leaving the bar. The house was packed by the time we walked in, barely enough room to pass through the crowds of people as I followed her to the makeshift bar.

"What's your poison?" she asked.

"Whiskey neat."

She cocked her head to the side. "A Jack Daniel's boy, huh?'

"Yes, ma'am," I drawled out with a grin.

I had already forgotten her name. Nothing new for me, chick's faces and names always blended together. I never stayed around long enough or cared enough to remember who they were.

"Ma'am, huh?" She flirted.

"I'm just a Southern boy," I simply stated.

She slowly nodded. "Is it true what they say about boys from down South?"

"Depends who you're asking." I smiled.

She introduced me to some of her friends she found inside. We hung out, drinking, dancing and shooting the shit about nothing in particular. I needed a break from the stifling atmosphere. Excusing myself, I made my way out onto the empty balcony, wanting a change of scenery. It was hotter than Hell in there, and I wasn't a fan of big crowds to begin with.

I lit the blunt that was in my pocket, sucking in a deep, long breath, holding it in. I leaned against the railing, resting on my forearms, overlooking Miami Beach. Taking in the soft lure of the waves from the ocean, the moon smiled down on me like a Cheshire cat. There was mixture of smoke and salt in the air surrounding me. The beach brought back such a familiar feeling, and for the first time a sense of longing came over me.

I blew out the smoke in my lungs.

The music from inside changed over to this seductive, alluring beat. A soft voice followed with lyrics about her head being a jungle, and I could relate to that feeling. Something about the song made me turn around and look back inside.

The dance floor wasn't as packed as it was before. People were still everywhere, dancing, hooking up, and having a great time without a care in the world.

Someone caught my attention. I narrowed my eyes, trying to get a better look at the girl in the center of the dance floor with her back to me. Long, vibrant, purple hair cascading all around her as she seductively swayed her hips to the beat. Making love to the music in a way I had never seen before.

She possessed the music; the music didn't possess her.

She was wearing a gray cotton, backless, belly shirt that was held in place by a simple, thin string, tied in a bow across the center of her back. Her ripped up jeans hung low on her hips, the hem dragging on the floor beneath her. She was covered in tattoos. One sleeve completely finished on her left arm. Her right arm halfway there with a few places of creamy, white skin peeking through.

But the tattoo on her back was what had my attention. It was a masterpiece. I had never seen anything like it before.

Intricate, mesmerizing, dark, yet the most beautiful thing I had ever seen. It had a pin up style angel drawn in the center, starting at the top of her spine and ending down the middle of her back. The angel's head was bowed not revealing her face, hands placed out in front of her, clasped in a prayer like gesture. Purple hair, flowing wild and free.

The wings attached to the angel, spread out on each of her shoulder blades, descending all the way down both sides of her back. Narrowing in on her tiny waist. The wings were so fucking detailed. I imagined she must have spent hours upon hours and several sessions lying on a table.

The wing on the right side of her back was so pure and white, illuminating to the eye. I had no idea there could be that many shades of white all intermixing, creating the feathers texture. Hints of silver were interlaced with the white making it really standout. Each feather was perfectly placed, every stroke immaculate.

While the wing on the left side was clipped, made up of dark shades of black with red bleeding through the empty spaces. The feathers were tarnished, broken, all out of place, and moving in all sorts of directions. Some were missing, some hanging by a thread. The same flawless, distinct texture, and shading as the right wing.

They were contrasting and contradicting to say the least.

Baffling even.

I stood there amazed and in awe of the story and mystery before me. Desperately wanting to unfold it. I wanted to find out if every piece on her had a meaning, a significance behind it. The girl was a dancing paradox and I couldn't tear my eyes away from her, even if I wanted to.

And I didn't want to.

Her hands slowly worked their way up her body to her head, running her fingers seductively through her hair, holding it up in place. I wanted to sink my teeth into her luscious ass. The way she moved, the way she swayed, the way she danced was so unbelievably fucking sexy, but it wasn't like every other girl I was used to seeing.

She wasn't dancing for anyone but herself.

She rocked her hips, spinning to the beat of the music, finally turning to face me.

I. Stopped. Breathing.

She was fucking beautiful. Describing her wouldn't even do her justice.

Her eyes were shut, oblivious to all the eyes that were fixated just on her. She didn't give a fuck who was around, who was talking, who was dancing.

All her facial features were pronounced and prominent but perfect for her. Her mouth was pouty and plump, seductively biting on her lower lip as the song came to an end. I swallowed hard, my mouth suddenly becoming dry. My gaze traveled down her body, her breasts were full, big, and perky as fuck. She wasn't wearing a bra, and I could see her nipples peeking through her top. She had the tiniest waist with her hips slightly curving out.

An hourglass figure, exactly how I liked it.

There were tattoos down the sides of her stomach, one on her lower abdomen, and a few cursive writing pieces scattered around. The one on her collarbone caught my attention the most and I wanted to know what it said. My eyes wandered back up to her face at the exact same moment the song ended.

The vision in front of me opened her eyes, and I sucked in a visible breath. I'd never seen eyes so bright and blue before. She looked so angelic, even though I knew she was anything but pure.

She cocked her head to the side, narrowing her eyes at me. Taking me in as much as I took her in seconds ago. The music changed over to a faster beat, and the dance floor was once again filling quickly. The crowd of bodies started to surround her, but she didn't let that deter her regard over me. Slowly, she walked toward me, parting through the men and women dry fucking each other on the dance floor.

Never breaking our connection.

I was leaning against the railing, one leg placed over the other. The blunt still between my thumb, index, and middle fingers. My other hand placed inside my pocket, rubbing my fingers together, imagining the way her skin would feel beneath them. Patiently and calmly waiting for her to say the magic words that would allow me to touch her.

To feel her against my skin.

Along my mouth.

Around my cock.

She was intoxicating as much as she was suffocating.

I took in the way her hips swayed, the way her tits bounced, and the way she licked her lips, making my dick twitch at the sight.

She stepped out onto the balcony, closing the sliding door behind her to lean up against it. Angling her body in a way that only made me want to devour every last fucking inch of her silky, white skin. The smell of weed, salt water, and something else, something tempting, something sinful, something *her* surrounded us.

Was now my new favorite scent.

Without saying a word, she gradually eyed me up and down with a fascinated glare. She took me in inch by inch until she stopped, reaching her desired destination. I followed her stare down to my hand still not moving from the place I stood. Grinning like a goddamn fool when I realized what she wanted.

"Can I have a hit?"

I peered back up at her.

"Pretty please," she added in a seductive tone, biting her bottom lip.

I didn't give it a second thought. I pushed off the railing, taking the blunt to my mouth and sucking in long and hard. Striding over to her in four, determined steps. Her gaze didn't waver from mine as I leaned in close to her pink, pouty mouth, catching her completely off guard. Caging her in with my arms. Her eyes widened but she didn't push me away. I parted my lips, slightly letting some smoke escape and that's when she realized what I was doing. She mirrored my direction, and I slowly, softly blew out the smoke from my lungs into her awaiting mouth.

I saw something familiar in her eyes, something I had always seen in mine, reflecting back at me.

Pain.

A raw and dark painful ache, exactly like the pain I had been carrying around my whole life. I felt it in my skin, in my heart, and in my soul that this girl was different. She was like a diamond, smooth but with sharp edges. Our lips touched ever so lightly the entire time.

I knew right then and there…

This girl.

This. Fucking. Girl.

Was going to be the end of me.

Briggs

Have you ever met someone that you felt like you already knew with every fiber of your being? Knowing it was physically impossible, knowing it was the first time you had ever laid eyes on him, knowing that he was a complete and utter stranger.

But, feeling it in your heart, in your mind, and in your soul that this person was a part of you. Someone you possibly met in a previous life, someone who may have meant something to you.

I locked eyes with the guy across the room and a sense of deja vu hit me, I felt like I had seen him before, his presence was comforting and intriguing, although in my head I knew he was a complete stranger. I felt a pull towards him, like he was a piece of a puzzle that was missing from my life.

I knew something was brewing.

Something big.

Important.

Life-changing.

The way he looked at me consumed me in ways I never thought possible. There was a predatory yet captivating glare in his eyes. As

M. Robinson

if I was the answer to every question he ever had. His eyes were blue, maybe green, but mostly blue. I couldn't tear my eyes away from his, they were so bright, so blinding, so fucking true.

The scar on his eyebrow caught my attention first. There was a patch of hair gone, sliced right down the middle, and left in its place was the memory of what made him almost lose his eye. If it had been a few centimeters lower, it would have been gone like the hair.

His skin was slightly tan from the sun, but I could see a few freckles peeking through on the bridge of his nose and on the sides of his cheeks. He had facial hair all around the lower side of his face, I guess you could call it a beard.

He had dark brown, spiky hair, and with the lighting above us I could see hints of red scattered around. My eyes moved on their own accord from his face down to his body. It was then that I realized how big he was. His white V-neck shirt pressed tightly against his chest, while the sleeves barely held in his strong, defined, muscular arms. I had the sudden urge to feel them wrapped around me. He was tall, way taller than my five-foot-four frame. He had to be over six feet of solid muscle.

He was devastatingly handsome.

In a bad boy I want to fuck every part of you kind of way.

But that wasn't what captured my attention. It was his scars. There were several down his arms, some on his neck. I only imagined he had to have more. They had to tell a story and I instantly wanted to see and touch every single one of them, as if they would tell me what happened to him.

He hadn't moved from his place in front of me, still caging me in with his arms. I began to think his feet were glued to the floor beneath him. Smoke billowed up all around us, only adding to his tempting allure.

His lips were smooth when they brushed mine. I felt the sudden urge to feel them against me again, but deeper that time.

I bit my lip at the thought, and his eyes glazed over.

"What's your name?" he asked, seeming caught off guard by his own question. Like he had never asked for a girl's name before.

For the first time since my parents died, I wanted to say...

Daisy.

I opened my mouth to reply but quickly asked, "What's yours?" instead.

He smiled, big and wide. Displaying perfect white teeth.

"Austin."

I noticed there was a slight southern drawl to his voice and had to resist the urge to ask him where he was from.

He raised his scarred eyebrow at me, waiting for my response.

"Briggs."

He cocked his head to the side not sure if I was telling him the truth. I wasn't used to telling people my name, it felt so foreign leaving my lips. I never had a reason to voice my name, people around me already knew. My little black cards were the reason why I was there. I went where my uncle ordered me to go.

"Is that your last name?"

I shook my head no.

"Your parents named you Briggs?" he questioned with a hint of teasing in his tone.

"Your parents named you Austin?" I fired back with the same tone.

He chuckled. "Feisty."

Standing upright, moving away from me and taking his warmth with him. I immediately missed it.

He hit the blunt again and then handed it over to me. I tried to hide my disappointment, I wanted to feel his lips on mine again. I shook away all the new and unfamiliar feelings, stepping away from him to walk over to the railing.

I hit the blunt a few times, waiting for him to join me. It took longer than it should have, and I was suddenly subconscious about what he was thinking that made him waver and stay by the sliding door where I left him. When I felt his presence next to me, I thought he would lean over the railing to look out at the water like I was.

He didn't.

He stood close beside me, leaning up against the railing, his left forearm holding up all his weight. His eyes placed intently on the side of my face, looking through me. Not at me.

I cleared my throat and swallowed hard. My heart beating rapidly with the effect he was having on me.

"So, *Briggs*, you from Miami?"

My nerves were set on fire. A hot blaze ran steady through my body. It was like nothing I had ever felt before. He had me questioning who he was and how he had this hold on me. I hated and loved the newfound feeling he was producing deep within my core.

It was mind-boggling.

I had been around some of the most powerful, corrupt men in the entire world and didn't bat an eye. They didn't even fucking faze me anymore. Yet, there I was anxious and nervous about a guy I had only just met. Acting like the teenage girl I was supposed to be and not the fucked up prodigy I'd become.

The connection and pull he had on me was making me want to reveal my truths, and that scared the shit out of me.

"How old are you?"

I shrugged, unable to find my voice.

I knew I was making a complete ass out of myself, but I wasn't used to talking to ordinary people. All the acquaintances in my life were business transactions.

I handed him back the blunt, not answering his questions.

He eyed me cautiously.

It was too much to take in, and I was making a fool of myself anyway. I pushed off the railing.

"Thanks for the smoke," I said with a nod.

I didn't give him time to answer. I quickly turned to leave, but he caught my arm, stopping me.

Our eyes connected.

"Where you goin'?" he asked, as if his whole world was about to walk away from him.

I smiled. I couldn't help it.

"I got a smile," he added, reaching out with his other hand like he was catching my expression in the air and placed it near his heart.

"I'll keep that one. Who knows when I'll get to see it again."

I laughed, giving him a huge smile that time. He groaned, setting his hand over his heart again, bowing his head in a dramatic gesture.

"Now, you're just tryin' to kill me, baby."

Baby...

I blushed, grinning like a damn schoolgirl. When he unexpectedly pulled me toward him, for a brief moment I thought he was going to wrap me in his arms, but at the last second he set me right next to him by the railing.

"What's a guy got to do around here to get you to talk to him, huh?"

I shrugged, that time I was just fucking with him.

"Damn, I take two steps forward and three steps back. I won't complain... I got a smile, didn't I?"

I grinned.

We passed the blunt back and forth a few more times in comfortable silence and then he threw the roach over the railing.

"Where you from, Austin?" I blurted what I had been thinking since the second I laid eyes on him.

His mouth dropped open in another dramatic gesture. "Wow. She speaks, I had no idea. I was beginning to think it was me." He smiled. "I do believe I asked you first though. Nice try."

He reached over, softly gripping the back of my neck, smirking at me. I realized pretty quickly that he liked to have his hands on me in one way or another, and I recognized even faster that I liked it.

"North Carolina," he answered, anyway.

"Ah." I nodded. "A down South boy. I guess it's true what they say about Southern charm."

"Baby, you have no idea. I'm just getting started."

I didn't falter, I loved the way he was looking at me too much. "Washington," I revealed, shocking myself.

My eyes immediately widened by the truth of my response. It just came out of nowhere, a slip of the tongue. The last time I said I was from Washington my parents were alive and I was six years old.

"Hey..." he coaxed, taking in my stunned expression.

He took his finger and lifted my chin to look deep into his eyes. I shook my head, stepping back and away from him. He cocked his head to the side confused by the turn in events.

This was too much. He was stirring up too many emotions in me.

I couldn't do this. It wasn't fair.

Not to *him*.

I wasn't meant to be this person. Maybe I was in another life, maybe in another time, maybe in another world. In this one, I was a Martinez.

So I just turned around...

And left.

CHAPTER
13

AUSTIN

I looked for her.

Briggs.

I couldn't find her anywhere. It was like she fell off the face of the earth or was a figment of my imagination. I spent two weeks, two fucking weeks trying to find her in Miami clubs, bars, and random house parties to no avail. I gave up my search, losing all hope in finding the blue-eyed angel.

The first place I traveled outside of Miami was Washington. I didn't even realize it until I was getting off at the bus stop, I was in Brigg's home state. My subconscious must have taken over, thinking it would be easy to find the girl with purple hair and tattoos among millions of faces.

The girl I knew nothing about but her name. I couldn't get her out of my head. I gave up searching for her after a few weeks, even though I didn't want to.

I'd met a few young transients like me, traveling with just the clothes on their backs and the bag over their shoulders. Wanting to see the world and everything life on the road had to offer.

I learned pretty quickly that money runs out fast, and there were times I slept under a bridge, on the beach, or in an alley. I had been fucked with a few times, so I realized safety was in numbers. I had been to Colorado, Nevada, and Louisiana, to name a few, in the last six months. I left Ohio eight months ago and never looked back. I had sent a few postcards to my parents and Alex from random places over the last eight months, but I hadn't spoken to anyone since I left.

Now I was in Michigan freezing my fucking balls off in the dead of winter. One of the guys I was traveling with wanted to see The Great Lakes and snowboard Boyne Mountain. The second we stepped off the train I regretted my decision immediately. Why the fuck anyone would want to live in this miserable cold was beyond me. I usually worked construction or bartending to make some money wherever we traveled, depending on what was in demand.

In Michigan… there was no work.

We found ourselves in Detroit under an overpass on I-75 with a can and match. We lit a fire and it still wasn't doing anything to appease the subzero air all around us.

"We're going to fucking freeze out here," Heather said as her boyfriend Ross hugged her tighter into his body trying to generate more warmth.

They'd started traveling with us about three months before. We met them in Las Vegas one night when we were fucked up on the strip. There were six of us now, and she was the only girl. I would be lying if I said I wasn't jealous of their relationship. They always had each other's backs, no matter what. It was easy to get lonely traveling around from place to place.

I never thought I would want to share this experience with someone.

That was an unexpected surprise.

"She's right, we're going to fucking freeze," I stated, trying to blow warm air into my hands.

It was no use. Nothing would work, it was just too damn cold. The pain pills I bought off the street weren't even numbing me up anymore. My back ached from the frigid weather. I never believed it when people said the cold could fuck with your bones.

"Fuck this." I stood, walking away. "I'll be back."

"Where you going?" Mike called out behind me.

"I'll be back," I repeated, debating if I was really going to do this.

I saw an ATM up the road earlier in the day, and I would be lying if I said it didn't cross my mind to stop at it as soon as we walked past it. If it wasn't so goddamn cold I would never even think about doing this, but we were going to die out here tonight if we didn't find a warm place to sleep. I pulled out my wallet from my back pocket, opening it up to grab my ATM card. The same one my parents gave me when I left for college. I hadn't used it once since I left, but at this point what other choice did I have. I pushed the card into the machine, typing in my code and asking for a hundred bucks. That would get us a few rooms at a shitty motel, but at least we would be warm.

I desperately wanted to take a hot shower. I couldn't remember the last time I'd had a decent shower. We always washed up in public bathrooms on the road. You didn't realize the simple luxuries you had until you didn't have them anymore.

The machine beeped, rejecting my card.

Declined.

"The fuck?"

I grabbed it, shoving it back in. Repeating the same steps.

Declined.

I shook my head, baffled. Leaving the card where it was to find the nearest payphone. I would give my parents the benefit of the doubt. Maybe they thought I would lose it and shut it off to avoid fraud and protect themselves. I could understand that. If that were the case, they would definitely wire me some money if I told them where I was and why I needed it.

No matter what they were still my parents.

"Austin," I said to the operator, calling my parents collect.

"Austin," Mom greeted after a few rings. Her voice laced with worry.

"Hey, Ma," I replied, grateful she was the one that answered.

"Where are you? Are you okay?"

"I'm in Detroit, and I'm fine. It's just—" She didn't let me finish.

"Come home. Listen, I know it's been rough for you since the accident, okay? Just come home, honey. We'll figure it out."

"Ma, there's nothing for me to come home to."

She sighed.

"I promise. I'm fine. I just need you to wire me some money. Trust me, I wouldn't be asking if I didn't really need it."

"Austin…"

"Please. I'm in Detroit, and there's no work. It's freezing out, and I have nowhere to sleep tonight."

"Oh, Austin…" She began to sob.

"Ma, I'm fine. I swear. I'll come home when I'm ready."

"Where do I wire the money to?"

"There's a Western Union in—"

"Is that Austin? Wiring what money?" I heard my dad ask in the background.

"Joseph—"

"Give me the phone. Austin?"

"Hey, Dad," I replied calmly, waiting for the wrath of my father.

"Well, look who finally decides to call. Do you have any idea what your mother has been going through? Do you have any idea what you have been putting us through?"

"I've been sending postcards, telling you I'm alive and fine."

"That makes it okay? That makes it better? You drop out of college without even discussing it with us and disappear. For months!" he argued.

I leaned my arm and forehead against the payphone. Not wanting to have this fucking conversation. I just needed money this once to survive the night.

"I knew you wouldn't approve. I knew you wouldn't understand."

"You bet your ass I don't understand! After everything we have done for you!"

"Dad, I'm fine. I'll come home when I'm ready to."

"What are you doing in the meantime, huh? Partying? Wasting your life away? Where are you?"

"I'm in Detroit. I've been working and getting by for the last eight months, Dad. Believe it or not, I'm capable of taking care of myself?"

"Then why are you calling? After all this time? Why not just send another postcard."

I took a deep breath. "It's freezing out and there's no work. I tried to use my ATM card but it was denied—"

"Of course it was. I told you. I warned you... I gave you a chance to get your shit together. I'm not going to support you wasting your life away. I cut you off the second you left. You want to fuck up your life then you do it on your own dime. I'm not paying for it."

My eyes widened, jerking my head back in shock.

"Wow… you didn't even think I could do it on my own," I stated as a question. "You've never believed in me."

"Why would I? You obviously proved my point or you wouldn't be calling asking for money. Now would you?"

I scoffed. "Do me a favor, old man, and don't worry. This won't cost you anything, except your son, which doesn't seem to matter to you anyway. The next time you wonder where I am… if I'm dead or alive? Just remember this conversation. I have no friends, and now…" I paused to let my words sink in.

"I have no parents." I hung up.

It fucking killed me to say that to him. At the end of the day they were still my parents, regardless of all the bullshit.

I love them.

I stood there feeling like a huge piece of my heart was torn out, breaking on the concrete beneath my feet. I wanted them to understand it wasn't about the money or them cutting me off. I could do this on my own. I was a grown-ass man, an adult. I guess I was just expecting unconditional love.

Isn't that what parents are supposed to do? No matter what?

The phone ringing pulled me out of my internal struggle. I debated on answering it, but my hand moved on it's own and before I knew it, the phone was against my ear.

"Austin…" Mom coaxed, her voice a soft whisper.

I leaned my head against the payphone, not caring how cold the metal was. My eyes burned so damn bad from the tears waiting to fall. I had closed my lids to keep them at bay and relieve the ache.

"Austin… please keep sending me postcards. Just tell me where to send the money, but please don't stop letting me know you're safe. I don't care where you are or what you're doing. I just need to know you're okay," she added.

I listened intently, holding back the tears that threatened to fall, one by one, right after the other.

"We love you, Austin. Your dad is just hurt. You're our baby. Austin... Austin, do you hear me? I love you."

A single tear fell from my face and I murmured, "I love you, too."

And I hung up the phone.

Briggs

"Fuck you feel good," he rasped against my ear, softly kissing down the side of my neck. His lips felt as smooth as I remembered, making their way down to my breasts. Licking and sucking my nipple into his mouth.

My breathing hitched when he cupped my pussy with his rough, calloused fingers.

"I want to fuck you with my fingers," he groaned against my mouth, biting on my lower lip.

He gripped the back of my neck with his strong, warm hand. Holding me in place, working my clit, back and forth in slow torturous movements. He deepened our kiss, pushing me to the brink of ecstasy. My legs, stomach, and body quivered, tightened, and spasmed all at once.

Our breathing escalated. My head fell back as my mouth opened wider. It was forceful, urgent, and demanding. The way his tongue sinfully played with mine. He tasted like whiskey, cigarettes, and weed, with a hint of peppermint, causing a loud, moan to escape my mouth.

My back arched off the bed when his fingers slipped inside me, angling straight for my g-spot, as if he knew my body better than I did.

"Here..." he huskily groaned, hitting my sweet spot over and over again. "You're going to come," he stated, taking me over the edge.

I panted, fisting and clawing the sheets all around us.

He kissed every last inch of my skin as he slid down my body. When he reached where I wanted him the most, I gazed down at him through hooded eyes, while he stared up at me with a piercing blue gaze that tore into my soul.

"I want to fuck you with my tongue," he rasped, slipping his tongue into my opening.

My eyes closed and head fell back against the bed. He devoured me, sucking on my clit as I rode his face, fast and hard. Coming apart yet again in a matter of seconds.

He gripped me tighter. His fingers dug into my hipbones as he thrust his tongue in and out of me. Eating all the wetness that he evoked from me, like I was his favorite fucking meal.

My body fell forward as if I was hanging off a cliff and I panted out, "Austin!"

I peered around my bedroom, shaken and confused when I should be anything but.

Alone.

"What the fuck?" I breathed out, waking up from yet another damn sex dream with the man I'd only met once.

My panties were soaked and my skin hot and tingling all over. My pussy still throbbed, mimicking the beating of my heart. I shook off the sentiment, pulling off the wrestled sheets that I was still grasping onto, throwing them to the side.

I took a deep breath, roughly yanking my hair away from my sweaty face.

"This can't be normal," I said to myself as I crawled to the end of my bed, desperately needing to get up and go take a long, cold shower.

It had been nine months since I left Miami, and I still couldn't forget about Austin. His intense blue eyes were etched in my mind.

Why couldn't I stop thinking about him?

It was like he had this hold on me. I didn't understand.

I had met him one time.

One. Fucking. Time.

It didn't make any sense.

I stepped out of the shower and changed into a tank top and some cotton shorts. Brushing my hair and teeth while I looked into the mirror.

"What is wrong with you?" I asked my reflection before spitting toothpaste into the sink.

I opened the bathroom door and made my way out into the kitchen to grab something to eat. I loved my apartment; it was my favorite place to be. It had an open floor plan, the rooms transitioning smoothly but still connecting. My stackable washer and dryer were tucked in a closet near the kitchen, keeping my laundry hidden. My windows were floor to ceiling, letting in natural light, warming up the sharp lines.

"Are you ready for your trip?" Uncle Alejandro asked.

I gasped, my hand immediately going over my heart.

"Oh my God! You scared the shit out of me! Again! Can't you knock? For once, fucking knock on the door like a normal person."

He sipped his coffee, sitting at my dining table.

"I refuse to knock in an apartment that I own."

"No shit," I murmured, walking into my kitchen to serve myself some much-needed coffee.

"I see it's your bitch-causing time."

I narrowed my eyes at him.

"I asked you a question. I don't like waiting for an answer."

"Mmm hmm," I said, sitting at the island, flipping through the latest issue of *Cosmopolitan*.

"You don't look ready."

"I have a few weeks," I said, peering away from the magazine looking into his eyes before he ordered me to.

"I give you a gift and this is the thanks I get. I'm handing you a big responsibility, peladita—"

"I'm not a little girl," I gritted out.

He grinned, folding his arms over his chest. "Then stop acting like one. You have been handed everything on a silver-fucking platter and you still act like a bitch. Throwing fits and demanding respect. You dropped out of high school and you still get to live a life of privilege." He gestured all around him. "How many other eighteen-year-olds can say that?"

"I'm not like most eighteen-year-olds, Uncle," I countered.

"I take care of you. I always have, Briggs. Since the day I picked you up from the hospital in Washington. If it wasn't for me you'd have grown up in foster care. Where do you think that would have led you, eh? *Dime?*" he asked, *"Tell me."*

"I know."

"Do you? Let me remind you. En caso de que," he said, *"Just in case."* He stood, rounding the corner to stand in front of me.

"You wouldn't have this million-dollar apartment, the name-brand closet, the fancy restaurants, the endless traveling around the world. How about the black credit card in your wallet? You know who pays for all that, Briggs? I do."

I wanted to tell him that none of that mattered to me. That I never wore half the shit in the closet. That it was there because he said I needed to wear it to the upscale parties and the fancy restaurants. Everything he does for *me*…

Was really for him.

But I didn't bat an eye. He was right about one thing. I embraced it or I had nothing.

This life was all I had.

It was all I ever had.

I smiled, big and wide. "I'm fucking thrilled. I can't wait. Thank you again, Uncle, for everything," I said in a sarcastic tone.

"Better. Next time wipe that shit-eating grin off your face."

I laughed, shaking my head.

"Why don't you go deface your body some more? Or is there no part left on your skin to ruin?"

He hated my tattoos. Every last one of them. Especially the first one I got done on my back. To say he was livid would have been an understatement. He never asked about the meaning behind it but then again, he didn't have to.

"Make sure you're ready. No fucking around. Understood?"

I nodded, ignoring him, flipping through another magazine.

With that, he turned and left my apartment.

I spent the rest of the afternoon, thinking about someone…

That I shouldn't.

CHAPTER
14

AUSTIN

Over the last two months it was only me and Mike. After Detroit, we all sort of went our separate ways. I was expecting it. I never thought I was going to make lifelong friends with the people I happened to come across. It was cool while it lasted, but everyone had to move on at some point. Mike wanted to head back to his home state, New York. He said he had a lot of friends that we could crash with. We made several stops along the way, but nothing too promising or exciting to make us stay for more than a few weeks.

We worked at a couple places in Pittsburgh to earn some cash before heading to Manhattan. We arrived in New York early one morning and managed to find a shitty motel to stay at until Mike got in touch with his friends; in the meantime, we would look for some more work. New York was expensive as shit, and I was grateful we'd made some decent money over the last two months.

I took a long, hot shower, soaking it up while it lasted. I walked out of the bathroom and Mike was lying on the bed, talking on the hotel phone.

"Yeah, I'm at Hotel Carter on West 43rd Street. Perfect, thanks." He hung up. "Feel better?"

I nodded, setting the wet clothes I washed in the shower on the air vent to dry.

"I'm going to jump in next. I ordered us some food and shit. Answer the door."

I nodded again, waving him off.

When I heard the bathroom door close behind him, I changed into my last pair of clean jeans, forgoing a shirt. Traveling was fucking exhausting. I plopped on the bed and stared up at the brown, water-stained ceiling.

I thought about how much I'd wanted to come to New York almost four years ago. How I wanted to start my life here, my career. There was still that sense of longing for something I could never have. After all this time…

I was still lost.

Still confused.

At least for now…

We'd been on a cramped train for the last few days. All I wanted to do was lay down. My back was fucking killing me. I had run out of pain pills the night before, and I was feeling the effect today. Mike said he would take care of it though.

The loud knock on the door startled me awake. I had just started dozing off. I could still hear the water running in the bathroom. Mike always took the longest damn showers. I stood, stretching my back for a second, trying to work out the knots. Rubbing my stomach as I made my way to the door, perfect timing.

I was fucking starving.

I opened the door and the first thing I saw were a pair of familiar bright blue eyes staring back at me.

Almost knocking me on my ass.

"Austin." She jerked back as stunned as I was.

"Briggs," I rasped.

We both stood there looking at each other for I don't know how long, taking one another in again as if it were the first time.

Damn, she was a sight for sore eyes.

She was wearing a white low-cut tank top that hung lose on her tiny but curvy frame. Her lacy, bright pink bra peeked out the top, revealing her ample cleavage. One of her bra straps hung low on her upper arm, the other one exposed on her shoulder. With small ripped shorts that I knew barely covered her luscious ass.

But the black combat boots, that's what really made me smile.

A dark green backpack hung low on her back. Her vibrant purple hair cascaded down her face, reaching her waist, like she hadn't cut it since the last time I saw her. Almost a year ago.

"What are you doing—"

"Was that the door?" Mike asked, walking out of the bathroom, interrupting me with a towel wrapped around his waist.

"Hey." He nodded toward her. "We met at a party a long time ago. Briggs, right?"

I glanced back at her and she nodded, her gaze settled on me. I couldn't tell if she was looking at my abs or my scars. Working in construction most of the time kept me fit as much as the gym did. I assumed it might be a bit of both by the way her cheeks turned slightly red.

"Austin, you rude fuck, let her in. She's your new best friend."

She bit her lip, not in a seductive way, but in a nervous one.

I stepped aside, opening the door wider to let her by. She walked in and my eyes went straight to her ass, as suspected the shorts barely covered her cheeks. My attention went right to the black tattooed bows on the backs of her upper thighs. Each one attached to a seam running all the way down her long legs, into her boots. They were the only tattoos she had on her legs.

God, she's beautiful.

It looked like she was wearing thigh highs and it was sexy as all hell on her.

My cock twitched, an instant fucking hard on.

I walked to the other side of the room, sitting on the couch. Trying to hide the fact that I was sporting wood like a goddamn, horny teenager.

"Just throw your shit on the table and we can decide what to buy. I'm going to throw on some clothes," Mike said, closing the bathroom door behind him.

I glanced from Mike back to her, and then it hit me like a ton of fucking bricks.

"I ordered us some food and shit. Answer the door."

"You're not here to deliver food, are you?" I whispered loud enough for her to hear, even though I already knew the answer.

She shook her head no. "I'm your new best friend, remember?"

She walked over to the beat-up coffee table in front of me, taking off her backpack and setting it on the floor beside her. She opened the top zipper, reaching in and pulled out several bags, throwing them on the table in front of me.

My eyes wandered to all the bags on the shitty table. I couldn't look away from the truth that was so blatantly staring me in the fucking face. I could feel her looking at me. I could sense she was waiting for me to say something, anything.

I couldn't.

I felt like my mind was playing tricks on me, like this was a joke and I was waiting for her to say, "Just kidding." Like she wasn't supposed to be the person who showed up at the door ready to numb my pain.

So when I heard her take a deep breath, my eyes shifted to her beautiful face. Her serious, solemn expression mirrored mine, and then she confirmed all my illusions and stated,

"I'm the drug dealer."

Briggs

And just like that...

The look he had for me seconds ago. The one I couldn't stop thinking about. The one that no one else had ever shown me...

Was gone.

Mike opened the bathroom door and walked out before I could give it anymore thought. Before I could dwell on the fact that I was his supplier and he was now my new client.

"Sweet!" he said, sitting beside Austin on the raggedy couch, eyeing the drugs spread out on the table, like a kid in a candy store.

The only response I was familiar with in the room.

"Austin, what pills do you want?" Mike asked him.

Silence.

"I'll take an eighth of weed. Two of those bad boys." He pointed to the Ecstasy. "And like ten of the Percocets."

Austin just sat there blankly staring at me, not saying a word. I reached into my backpack again, pulling out some empty plastic bags to fill Mike's order.

"What's the damage?" Mike asked, pulling out a wad of money from his pocket.

"Four hundred even," I simply stated, exchanging his bag of goodies for money.

"On that note." Mike stood, throwing some weed on the table. "I'm going to head out. Pleasure seeing you again, doll. I'm glad I kept your card. I'll be in touch."

I nodded, unable to form words, only plaguing thoughts.

"Austin, I'll see you later." With that he turned and left.

Leaving us in the silence that was deafening in the room.

Austin grabbed the cigarettes off the table in front of him, pulling one out. Looking around the room, patting his jeans for a lighter. I reached into my backpack again, throwing him some matches instead. He caught them mid-air, still not saying a word to me and lit his cigarette.

He took a drag and blew the smoke out toward his left, the furthest away from me. I never told him I hated the smell of cigarettes, but somehow he already knew that. I learned right then and there that Austin could read people as well as I could.

That wasn't an innate skill.

That was survival.

"So," I announced, breaking the uncomfortable silence that echoed all around us. "What's your poison?"

He narrowed his eyes at me before glancing back to the table, pointing to the Percocets with the cigarette in his hand.

"How many?"

"All of them."

My eyebrows raised and my mouth parted, immediately taking in his scars. Just as I predicted the night I met him, there were several scattered around his chest, and back.

In that moment, in that second, I wanted so fucking badly to ask him what had happened to him, to reach out and ease his pain.

Instead I just grabbed the bag, handing it to him.

He reached into his wallet and for some reason I couldn't explain, I looked away from him, taking in the room.

The place was a shithole. Most people rented this room by the hour. It's where whores turned tricks and junkies OD'd.

Austin wasn't one of those people. I knew that, I was sure of it.

Why was he staying here?

As I took in my surroundings, I noticed there was a dirty, tattered up duffle bag leaning up against the crumpling wallpaper in the corner of the room. The boots placed beside them looked like they had seen better days. The soles were ripping underneath them, and the shoelaces didn't match.

There were clothes scattered throughout the room, drying over the air vent like he'd just washed them in the shower with him. And the jeans he was wearing were thin, old, and had stains.

He wasn't one of those people at all.

Austin was just broke.

"How much?" he asked, pulling me away from my thoughts.

I looked deep into his vibrant blue eyes. It was then that I noticed it was like looking in a reflection of my own truths.

"It's your lucky day."

He frowned, pursing his lips, confused.

"We're best friends now, remember? I don't charge best friends," I chuckled, wanting to break the tension between us.

The truths all around us.

His.

Mine.

Ours.

"There's a shitload of pills here, Briggs."

Hearing him say my name made my belly flutter again. It had the same effect on me at the door when he first said it.

I shrugged, smiling.

Silently hoping he would catch my expression in the air and place it near his heart, like he did when we first met.

He didn't.

I shook off the sentiment, picking up all the bags and putting them away in my backpack.

"At least let me smoke you out," he offered, setting the cigarette on the corner of his lips to grab the weed Mike left behind. He started rolling up a joint.

"I don't get high off my own stash. Drug dealer 101."

He grinned, glancing over at me with mischievous eyes before returning to his task at hand.

"But… umm… I can stay… I mean for bit... you know? Hang out."

We locked eyes.

"I mean if you're not—"

"I'd like that," he interrupted, nodding toward the seat next to him.

I sat down. His fresh, clean scent assaulted my senses with a mixture of smoke, weed, and something else I couldn't quite place.

Austin.

My body instantly burned all over, remembering how in my dreams his hands, his tongue, his body were all over me. I had to look away, my face turning a deep shade of red.

He scoffed out a chuckle and I had a feeling he noticed, but he was being a gentleman and not calling me out on it.

"I went to Washington," he muffled with the cigarette still placed in the corner of his lips.

I hated smoking. I hated the smell and how the stench stuck to everything no matter how much you cleaned it. Most of all I hated the sudden taste of an ashtray assaulting your mouth when a smoker kissed you. There was nothing I liked about it.

Except, Austin…

He had a way of making it look so fucking sexy, making me wish I were the filter that was pressed against his lips.

"What?" I replied, realizing what he just said.

He chuckled, vibrating against my arm.

"Washington. I went there."

I didn't know what to say, so I didn't say anything.

"You don't talk much, do ya?"

"Seems that way, huh?" I laughed. "There's not much to see in Washington," I brushed it off.

"I know. I didn't find you," he simply stated, catching me off guard.

As if what he just shared didn't mean anything, when it meant everything.

He finished rolling the joint, took one last drag of his cigarette, stubbing it out in the ashtray in front of him.

"You looked for me?" I asked, needing to know.

He lit the joint, sitting sideways to face me. Our faces now inches apart.

"What if I did?" he blew the words out with the smoke from his lungs.

"Why?"

"Why not?"

"You only met me once. What would possess you to come looking for me?"

"I was backpacking, Briggs, and something led me to Washington when I left Miami. I didn't realize it until I got off the train." He smiled. "What can I say? When I want something, I go after it."

Leaning in close to my lips, for a second I thought he was going to kiss me. For a moment, I thought I was going to get everything I had been dreaming about for the last year.

His lips.

His tongue.

His hands.

Him.

Instead he looked deep into my eyes and spoke with conviction, "And... I want you."

CHAPTER 15

AUSTIN

Her phone rang before she could respond, breaking our connection.

I hated that she had to leave me to go deal more drugs.

I hated that she could be in situations that could quickly turn extremely dangerous.

And I fucking hated the son of a bitch who had her doing this. Not caring about her goddamn safety.

I saw the shadow of a man around the corner when she left. I assumed it was her protection in case something went wrong. I knew Briggs could take care of herself, but at the end of the day she was still just a girl. A hot-as-fuck girl. Something told me that men appreciated much more than just the drugs she was supplying. For some reason the thought of her being with another man fucking pissed me off.

She left the hotel room so damn fast. I didn't have a chance to get her number. I knew Mike had it, but I didn't want to call her on that number.

I didn't want Briggs, the drug dealer.

I wanted Briggs, the girl I met on the balcony.

The one who danced like nobody was watching, but seemed to captivate her audience with each sway of her curvy hips. The girl who was shy and timid, the girl who blushed from just a few words from my mouth. The girl who would one day rip my damn heart out.

The girl I knew was hiding behind the tattoos and purple hair.

I hadn't seen her in three days, three fucking days and it felt like an eternity. Even the pills didn't ease my anxiety. They only reminded me of her. It was Friday night and we had no plans. I sat on the bed racking my brain like I had done for the past three sleepless nights. Consumed with never-ending thoughts of her.

I lit my cigarette. The matches Briggs left behind were in my hands, I kept turning the box around.

They were taunting me.

There was a club logo on it with a website and phone number underneath.

"Mike, you know this club?"

He looked up from the TV to catch the matches I threw him, catching them in the air.

"Yeah. Everyone knows this club. Alejandro Martinez owns it."

I raised my eyebrows at him with a questioning look on my face. "And I'm supposed to know who the fuck Alejandro Martinez is?"

"He's notorious around New York. Fuck," he chuckled, "he's notorious around the world, Austin."

I cocked an eyebrow, jerking my head back, stunned. "Those matches belong to Briggs."

He shrugged. "It makes sense, bro. There is very little that Martinez doesn't have his dirty hands on. He fucking owns this entire city. He's a smart motherfucker too. The cops, the mayor... shit, you name it, he owns it. No one can touch him and nothing ever gets traced back to him. And, women, they spread their legs open for him like he's the king of the fucking universe."

"How do you know this?"

"I'm a New Yorker."

I eyed the matches that were still in his grasp.

"Austin, if you want to fuck her so bad. Call the number I have. You're a good looking guy, I'm sure she's done worse."

"Shut the fuck up," I sneered. "If I wanted to fuck her, I would have the other day. You don't know shit about shit, so watch your goddamn mouth when you talk about her."

"Jesus Christ, relax. You don't even know this girl and already you're pussy-whipped. Look," he put out his hands in a surrendering gesture, "how about we go to the club tonight? It's a few streets over on Broadway, a bit of a hike from here, but I feel like getting fucked up tonight anyway."

M. Robinson

He stood.

"Try to find something nice to wear, pretty boy. This club is dress to impress. I know the bouncer. He's been working there for years. We probably won't have to pay a cover."

We pulled up to the club around midnight.

I had brought a pair of black slacks and a few button down, collared shirts with me from Miami. I never wore them, they were the only clothes I owned that didn't look worn out and old.

Just like Mike expected, the bouncer didn't charge us. He stamped our hands, opened the velvet rope, and let us through. The people waiting in the line wrapped around the building were pissed to say the least. As soon as we walked in, I immediately realized this wasn't going to be as easy as I thought. The club was huge and packed with people. It was hard for us to even get by without having to wait a few seconds for the crowds to separate.

I was there on a whim. I knew there was a huge chance Briggs wasn't even at the club tonight, but that didn't stop me from getting dressed up and paying the sixty-dollar cab fare from our motel. The music was pounding through the speakers all around us, vibrating through my core as we tried to make our way over to the bar. The place was exceeding capacity, filled to the brim. Everyone dressed to the nines, beautiful people just getting their night started with the beat of the house music blaring above the crowds.

My eyes wandered all around the two-story building. Everything from the flashing lights to the neon strobes strumming around every corner. The plush couches and tables stacked with bottles upon bottles of Moet and other expensive alcohol. The already fucked-up people dancing their asses off with their eyes closed and their heads leaned toward the ceiling, letting the melody of the music take over them.

I instantly knew that drugs flowed in this place as much as the booze did. Which only gave me more hope that Briggs was here. Mike ordered us some drinks from the bar, while I continued to search the crowd, trying to spot the girl with bright purple hair and tattoos.

When he returned, he handed me a whiskey neat along with one of his ecstasy pills that I turned down.

I wasn't here to party.

159

He looked at me like I had grown three heads before shaking his, swallowing them both down instead. I never turned down a good time, but I didn't want to be fucked up while trying to find her. Mike found some old friends that had a table in one of the corners and they asked us to join them.

More drugs…

More booze…

No Briggs.

I was beginning to lose hope. The song changed over to '*Young and Beautiful*' by Lana Del Rey and out of nowhere, out of pure instinct, emotion, and feeling, I looked up to the second story. She appeared out of thin air, like a goddamn angel, wearing a tight white dress with red heels. She was standing in the dead center of the club, her vibrant purple hair flowing all around her with her fucking tits on full display. Her hands leaned against the railing, looking down at the crowd of people below her, swaying her body in a slow, sexy, seductive way that only Briggs could pull off.

And then… as if it was meant to be.

As if *we* were meant to be.

She found my gaze in the endless crowd of people, like she felt me too.

Briggs

I hadn't seen Austin since that night in his hotel room. Deep down, I hoped I'd hear from him with the weekend approaching, but I hadn't. I left without giving him my number, but his friend had my card and still no call.

It was Friday night and the weekends were always the best time to get fucked up. My uncle's clubs were always the place to be.

And I always brought the party.

I was sitting at my usual spot, the best table in the club with random partygoers drinking off the bottles in front of us. Nothing had changed in almost four years.

Same scene.

Different faces.

'*Young and Beautiful*' blew through the speakers and I began to let the music take over. An unexplainable desire came over me, pulling and pushing me to walk toward the balcony. I didn't know what I was looking for. An unfamiliar feeling settled in my stomach, in my heart, in my fucking soul, until I locked eyes with the man I had been losing sleep over for the last three days. For the last year.

Austin.

My lips parted and my breathing hitched. I don't know how long we stood there staring deep into each other's eyes, as if the hundreds and hundreds of people around us disappeared. Everything faded out, the music, the lights, the crowd.

It was just him and me.

No one else.

I watched him make his way toward the stairs, our connection never breaking. Each step he took brought him closer to me.

Five…

Four…

Three…

Two…

One.

The bouncer at the end of the stairs immediately put his arm out across Austin's chest, denying access. He didn't have a VIP band on.

I lunged into action. "Jon, he's fine. He's with me!" I shouted over the music.

Jon eyed me cautiously. Never in the past four years, not even once, had I ever said someone was with me. He nodded, letting Austin through and went back to standing guard.

"How did you find—"

He took my hand, interrupting me, and placed the matches I gave him the other night in my palm. Before I realized what was happening, he grabbed my wrist and pulled me toward him, engulfing me in nothing but his whiskey, cigarette, and fresh, clean scent. Wrapping his arms around me, pressing me close to his solid, muscular frame.

"Fuck… I just wanted to make sure you were real," he breathed out into my ear, causing shivers to course throughout my entire body.

My heart pounded against his chest. I knew he could feel it. I could feel his too.

"You are so goddamn beautiful, Briggs. Do you have any idea how fucking breathtaking you are?"

161

My eyes widened. No one had ever said those words to me. No one had ever held me in their arms like I was their entire world. My hands touched his back lightly.

I was feeling so much.

Yet not nearly enough.

He pulled away just enough to caress the side of my face with his calloused thumb, still holding me close with one arm. His eyes told me he wanted to say so much, though nothing came out.

The club was partying all around us. The bright lights flashing. The DJ was killing it with the music, but none of that existed to us right then.

We were too caught up in each other to care.

"What's your name?" he asked again with a knowing expression.

"I already told you. Briggs."

"No…" He shook his head. "What's your name?" he repeated, emphasizing the last three words.

I didn't know where he was going with his question, and I wasn't sure how to respond.

I licked my lips, my mouth suddenly becoming dry. His eyes gazed over as he followed the movement of my tongue. He wanted to kiss me and I so desperately wanted him to. He was causing all sorts of feelings deep within me, and the son of a bitch knew it.

"Why are you here, Austin? You know what I do. The truth's out. Why are—"

"Is that why you left that night? The night I met you on the balcony? Because you're a dealer?"

"Yes."

His hand moved to the nook of my neck, gripping it a little too hard but not hard enough.

"I'm here for you," he simply stated, not caring about what I'd just admitted. "So, I will ask you one more time. What's your name?"

"Oh shit!" a girl giggled, running into the side of us, breaking our connection.

He immediately held her up with a firm grip on her upper arm. His other arm still firmly wrapped around my waist.

"You alright?" he asked, trying to steady her.

She nodded, barely realizing she was drunk as shit. Austin glanced over at me and I knew what he was asking. I stepped aside, so he could help her sit down on the couch. He filled one of the glasses with ice water, handing it to her.

"Drink some water," he told her.

With shaky hands, she brought the glass to her lips, took a sip and gazed up at him, like she had just fallen in love. He was taking care of her like a knight in shining armor. I would be lying if I said I wasn't jealous, when I had no right to be.

At that moment I realized that Austin had a good heart. He was not only charming, but he was loving, caring, and genuine. I wanted to get to know more of him. I wanted to get to know everything.

And that scared me more than anything.

CHAPTER
16
Briggs

I leaned back against the railing and he followed suit.

"You really are a Southern gentleman, huh?"

He grinned with a mischievous gaze in his eyes.

"She will be fine. She's notorious for being a hot mess."

"I've seen worse. Shit, I've done worse," he confessed, rubbing the back of his neck.

"For some reason, I don't doubt that."

"You look beautiful by the way," he said out of nowhere.

I blushed. "Thank you, you do too."

"Beautiful? That's a new one," he chuckled, and I knew he was talking about his scars.

"Chicks dig scars. It's that whole bad boy thing," I said, trying to lighten the mood.

"So I've been told. How about you?"

I smirked, shrugging just to fuck with him. "I have purple hair and I'm covered in ink. My opinion might not hold a high regard."

"Is that right?" He pulled my hair away from my face, setting it behind my shoulder. His thumb grazed my cheek. "Your opinion is the only one that matters."

He moved his hand away but I didn't lose his warmth for long. He grabbed my hand lightly and unknowingly drew tiny circles on my skin, just to feel me.

He leaned over to ask, closer to me. "Speaking of the tattoos. How many do you have?"

I narrowed my eyes, counting in my head. "One?"

"Oh, I see what you did there." He laughed. "The sleeves." He gestured to my arms, stepping out to stand in front of me.

"Except the bows…" He leaned down to skim his fingers along the back of my thighs, pausing. "They're here." Sliding his fingers up my thighs, continuing his journey. He grazed the hem of my dress, then my panties till he reached my lower abdomen. "Then you have one here, and…." Touching along the left side of my stomach. "Another one here." Skimming his way to the right side. "And here." He lightly brushed the tips of his fingers around my stomach. "Scattered writing all along here." Moving his hand slowly up the side of my breast. "This one here," he added, rubbing the cursive writing on my clavicle bone, back and forth.

I. Stopped. Breathing.

"But my favorite," he rasped, coming close to my ear, "is the one on your back. One day you're going to tell me what all your tattoos mean, Briggs. Along… with your real name."

And with that, he pulled away from me to stand beside me and continued to softly rub my hand.

I instantly cleared my throat. "I lost count a long time ago." Trying to sound unaffected.

"How old are you?"

"I'll be nineteen in a few months. You?"

"Almost twenty-two."

He pushed off the railing, turned and caged me in, placing his hands on the bars beside my hips. Coming closer again like he suddenly changed his mind and needed to be surrounding me again.

Consuming me with his touch and presence so that when he was gone. When he wasn't around me. When we weren't together.

I would miss him.

His touch.

His presence.

The effect he had on me.

"You've gotten all that ink in a year? Damn, you must have lived at the parlor."

I shook my head. "No. This…" I gestured toward myself. "Has been over almost four years. I got my first tattoo when I was fifteen."

He jerked back, surprised. "Which one?"

165

I pointed to the one on my back.

His favorite.

"Is that how long you been..."

"Dealing?" I finished for him.

He nodded.

"Just about."

"Where's your family? Your parents?"

I looked down toward the ground. I knew this was coming and even though I expected it. I was still at a loss on how to respond and react.

"Let's not share our sad stories, Austin. Hmm..."

"Yet," he stated, making me peer back up at him. "Let's not share our sad stories, *yet.*"

There was something in his tone that made me immediately ask, "Where are you sleeping tonight, Austin?"

"Back at the motel. Mike's here too, somewhere down there." He nodded to the crowd below us.

I hated that he said the motel. He didn't belong in that shithole. No one fucking did.

So when I blurted, "Come home with me," it just felt right.

"Briggs, you—"

"We're best friends, remember?"

He scoffed out a chuckle before we made our way over to the stairs.

"Jon!" I shouted, making him look up at me. "I'm going to head out. Everything is in the office. I put it all in the safe."

He nodded, waving me off.

Austin followed close behind as I led us toward the private stairs in the back of the building. He ran into his friend Mike and told him he was coming home with me. Mike reminded him that they needed to be out of their shitty hotel room by eight in the morning. He said he would leave a note on the table letting him know where he was going.

I couldn't believe I was doing this. I never brought men back to my apartment. No one knew where I lived except my uncle. But there I was, bringing a complete stranger back to my *home*, one that took me years to build, to feel safe in my own environment, my own surroundings.

I wasn't scared that he would hurt me.

At least not in the physical sense.

I didn't know what I was expecting, what I wanted from him. Maybe I was just lonely, years of being by myself and not letting anyone in will do that to a person, and I wasn't any different. I guess, maybe I just wanted a friend.

Even though the thought alone, terrified me.

I pushed the back door open and hit the unlock button on my key fob before I stepped foot onto the pavement. The lights blinked twice.

"Damn," Austin breathed out, pulling me away from my thoughts.

"Huh?" I replied, looking to where he was staring. "Oh. Yeah," I simply stated as he continued to take in my car.

"You drive a '67 SS Chevelle?" he questioned, cocking his head to the side with an amused expression.

I bit my lip. I blew at being a girl. I just really liked muscle cars.

He softly touched along the hood of the car. "A 396 engine," he said out loud, peering only at the car. "I think I just fell in love with you."

I wasn't sure if he was talking to the car or me, but we got in before I could give it anymore thought.

"And the girl knows how to work a stick? This night just keeps getting better."

"In six-inch stilettos," I added.

He groaned and I giggled, pushing the clutch down, shifting it into first gear. The engine revved, I pushed down the clutch again and switched into second.

I could see him staring at me out of the corner of my eye. Once we got on the street, I shifted the car into third and I swear I saw him smile and shake his head.

He reached across the center console and started to lightly skim my thigh, as we drove in comfortable silence. I didn't live far from the club, so it didn't take long to get home. I made a quick left and we were pulling in and parking my car in the garage.

I quickly got out before him, needing to get some air. My decision to bring him home with me was purely based on impulse and now I wasn't sure if I made the right choice.

My heels clicked on the pavement, mimicking the pounding of my heart as we walked toward the door. I pressed the fob against the entry and the door snapped open.

My mind started running wild.

Plaguing questions assaulted every fiber of my being till we reached my apartment door. I was about to put in the key, but his hand stopped me. Placing it directly on top of mine.

We locked eyes.

"Relax, Briggs. We're best friends, remember?"

I let out a breath that I didn't realize I was holding and he gave me a comforting smile.

"How did you…" I shook my head and opened the door instead of finishing my question.

I set my keys on the island and opened the fridge, grabbing two water bottles and throwing one at him. He caught it midair, even though he was busy, taking in all my surroundings.

My home.

"Quite a place you got here. Apparently, I'm in the wrong business."

I shrugged mostly because I didn't want to explain or have to answer questions.

"There's a bathroom right there." I pointed next to the closet. "And then the rest is pretty self explanatory. I'm going to take a quick shower. There are towels in that bathroom under the sink if you'd like to take one also. I'll get you some blankets and pillows when I come out."

He nodded.

I walked away and could feel him watching my every move until I shut the bathroom door. I don't know how long I stayed in the shower lost in my own thoughts. I changed into some cotton shorts and a tank top, throwing my hair up into a messy bun on the top of my head. I didn't have a stitch of make-up on.

When I walked out of the bathroom, the smell of smoke instantly assaulted my senses. Tearing away my insecurities of having him see me without my shield of armor on.

The balcony door was open and the light breeze was blowing the curtains. I walked out there, finding Austin leaning forward against the railing, wearing just his black slacks. His shirt, shoes, and socks long gone. A cigarette placed in between his index and middle finger, staring out at the New York skyline.

He appeared as lost as I felt.

I watched from afar for a few minutes, taking in his scars, welcoming the distraction. I desperately wanted to know what happened to him, probably as much as he wanted to know my real name and the meanings of my tattoos.

He was right though.

Every last piece of ink on my body had a reason behind it. Every last piece had a sentiment attached to it. Pieces of my heart and soul were inked on my skin, etched in permanently for everyone to see, but to never know the significance, the meaning.

That was reserved just for me.

When he took a drag of his cigarette and blew it out into the air, I didn't know if it was the smoke, the fresh clean scent of his shower or just him, but I found myself reaching out to touch the scar right down the center of his back. It was the worst one I'd seen on him so far. The skin was raised and mangled as if glass had torn into him, piece by piece, settling into his skin for hours and becoming apart of him.

He immediately froze the second he felt my touch against it, my presence around him, knowing what I was doing. What I was thinking, the answers to my questions that I sought since the first time I laid my eyes on him. It was beautiful. He was beautiful.

Every last part of him.

Scars and all.

"Briggs, I—"

"I'm sorry," I interrupted not ready to hear his sad story, knowing that mine would have to follow.

I wasn't ready to divulge that information. I didn't think I ever would be. As much as he wanted the truth, I wanted to remain in the lies.

I immediately lowered my hand and turned to go back inside. Before I even saw it coming he caught my wrist, catching me off guard and tugging me towards him. I lost my footing, my hand instantly pressed against his warm, firm chest, causing heat to soar through my body, starting from my head down to my toes. The other hand still tightly locked within his grasp.

His strong arms wrapped around me, caging me against his body, his scent, his scars.

His truths...

Comforting me and tormenting me in ways I never thought possible.

His mouth collided with mine, a force I had yet to experience, only brought on by him.

Austin.

And I wasn't talking about the unexpected kiss. His lips were as smooth as they were in my dreams. He tasted exactly how I'd remembered.

Trouble.

His lips parted, beckoning me to do the same. I followed his lead, softly caressing the tip of my tongue with his. Our mouths moved against one another as if they were destined to meet and come together.

A chance, a circumstance, that's all we were to each other. We kissed and kissed until we couldn't kiss any more.

It was loud.

It was maddening.

It was everything.

He softly pecked me, slowing down the unexpected movements of our emotional, catastrophic connection. Resting his forehead on mine to stare deep into my eyes.

"Tell me you felt that..." he groaned, mimicking my panicked, heavy breathing.

"Yes," I panted, loud enough for him to hear.

He lightly smiled, like that one word, those three letters were everything he ever wanted to hear.

He pecked my lips one last time, slowly letting me go to back away from me. As if we now both needed space, to gather our life-changing emotions.

I turned without saying another word, taking relief in the escape he was offering. By the time I finished his makeshift bed, he was walking back in, closing the door behind him. He made his way over to me, rubbing the back of his head like he often did when he was lost in thought.

"The couch is really comfortable. I pass out on it all the time," I said, trying to keep my eyes from gawking at his body.

The same body I had dreamt about for almost a year, placed on top of mine. Making me come in ways I never had done with other men. The same body I had just felt beating, throbbing up against mine.

"Thank you for letting me crash," he simply stated, pulling the blankets back to lie down.

I could sense he wanted me to lie next to him. It wasn't because he wanted us to keep kissing. He wanted us to keep talking. But I knew that would only lead to more thoughts and emotions and I had enough of them already wrecking havoc on my soul.

"Don't mention it. Good night, Austin."

"Night, Briggs," he replied, failing at hiding his disappointment.

It usually took me forever to fall asleep at night, a curse that had stayed with me since childhood. I would toss and turn for hours till I was exhausted enough to pass the fuck out. But that night, sleep came immediately. I couldn't remember the last time that happened.

I had felt a sense of security with him a few feet away. Hearing his soft breathing was comforting to me. Seeing him before the darkness took over, brought me a sense of peace. I could still feel his lips pressed up against mine, our tongues tangled, and his scent surrounding me everywhere.

I could still feel him.

For the first time in forever I wasn't alone. I wasn't scared of the night and everything it had to offer. The shadows that crept in the corners were hidden.

At least that night.

I woke up the next morning. My hand immediately touched my lips, rubbing them back and forth. As if his had never left. I felt refreshed and energized. Happy even. So when I sat up and looked over toward the couch, expecting to see a sleeping Austin, all I saw were blankets and pillows placed on the corner of the sofa.

He'd left.

Without saying goodbye.

AUSTIN

She wasn't lying about her couch being comfortable as fuck. I passed out within minutes of my head hitting the pillow. I couldn't remember the last time I slept in a comfortable, clean place. Even the random couches I crashed on here and there were hard as a fucking rock. Most of the time I just ended up passing out on the damn floor instead.

I was usually an early riser, always had been. So, it didn't surprise me that she was still sleeping soundly when I woke up. I sat up, placing both feet on the floor, catching my bearings and stretching. Like every morning my back hurt like a son of a bitch.

I got up, went to the bathroom, and did my thing. When I came back out, I almost started laughing when I heard her sporadic, soft, gentle snoring.

Fuck, it was the cutest thing I had ever heard.

I couldn't help but stare at her while I was folding the blankets. Her vibrant purple hair was fanned out around her face. She was so fucking beautiful even without her make-up. More so even. It was then I wished I had a notebook to capture her beauty on paper. Make it live through the pages of my art.

I resisted the urge to crawl in bed with her to hold her in my arms. As much as I tried not to touch her last night, I couldn't fucking help myself. She was so warm, smooth, and smelled like everything I ever wanted.

I was definitely caught off guard when she offered me a place to stay. I wasn't expecting that, and I don't think she was either. I could sense her anxiety the entire drive to her apartment and even more as we made it towards her door.

Of course I wanted to have sex with her. I wasn't a fucking saint. The only time I went home with a girl was to do just that, fuck her. Briggs was different. She was the first girl I wanted to get to know inside and out. For some reason that didn't scare me. If anything, it made me happy and that was the feeling I was the most unfamiliar with.

I wasn't expecting to pull her into my arms and kiss her.

It just happened.

I kissed her because I couldn't *not* kiss her.

It was only one kiss and I already knew it wasn't nearly enough. I had kissed hundreds of girls by that point and it was the first time I actually felt like I was kissing someone.

The connection was alive and thriving all around us. The force, the pull, so fucking strong that there was no way to ever push away.

I headed to the motel room. The last thing I wanted was to get charged for another night in that piece of shit room. Mike was already gone by the time I went to go grab all my shit. He left a note on the table with an address and a phone number. I packed up all my belongings, which wasn't much and got the hell out of there. I wasn't sure if the next morning I would be at Briggs' or Mike's friends couch but one thing was for sure.

I was staying in New York.

It took me a minute to find a place to buy some breakfast for us, and I got lost trying to find my way back to her apartment. After walking around aimlessly for over an hour, I managed to find my way back. I had grabbed her key fob in case she was still sleeping when I returned since I left before the sun came up. It was already almost noon by the time I was at her door again.

I knocked instead of just walking in. I figured she was already awake maybe wondering where I went.

At least I hoped she was.

When she answered the door, I couldn't tell if she was surprised to see me again or surprised that someone had knocked on her door.

With a big grin, I raised her coffee and a bag filled with every kind of doughnut known to fucking man out in front of me.

"I got us some breakfast."

She smiled and it lit up her entire face. I caught her expression in the air and placed it on my heart, causing her to smile wider. She moved aside gesturing for me to come in. I was worried about what she would think when she saw I held all of my possessions over my shoulder, my entire world in a tattered duffle bag. The last thing I wanted was for her to think I was moving in.

I set my bag down by the sofa and made my way over to the kitchen island, where I placed her coffee and food. I was about to tell her why I had all my shit with me, but the suitcase on her bed distracted me.

Instead I turned around to face her and immediately blurted, "Where we going?"

She eyed me cautiously for several seconds, her gaze falling to my bag against the sofa.

"I can't take you with me," she replied like she didn't want to say it. "I'm leaving, and I don't know when I'll be back. I go where I'm told. I don't have any choice in the matter. And right now I'm being told to go to Colombia."

I jerked back, shocked as shit. "You're trafficking drugs?"

"I'm an exporter/importer, Austin. I'm the middle man."

"The fuck," I breathed out, instant anger taking over. "Jesus Christ. Do you have any idea how dangerous that is? Who the hell would put you in the line of fire like that?"

She reassuringly shook her head and it did nothing but piss me off further. Not at her but at the fucker that was making her do this.

"I'm fine. No one is going to fuck with me. Trust me."

"Briggs…" I coaxed, trying to calm down. The anger was overtaking me.

She wasn't to blame for this and I needed to remember that.

"There's always someone with me when I meet a new client. But it doesn't fucking matter, Austin, I've been taking care of myself for as long as I can remember."

"Then it's about fucking time that someone took care of you. Looked after you." I stepped toward her, grazing the side of her cheek. "Let me be that man, let me take care of you."

"What does that even mean?" She pulled away from my touch. "You don't even know me, Austin. We met once at a party, we talked and shared a joint, that's it. What are we doing here? What do you want from me?"

I was taken aback, knowing that deep down she felt what I did. "Don't pretend like we don't have something. I know you can feel it too, Briggs. I can see it in your damn eyes every time you look at me. I can feel it on your skin every time I touch you." I grazed her cheek again to prove my point. "Who knows where this will lead, but I sure as hell want to find out."

I stepped closer to her again, holding her face between my hands. To my surprise she let me.

"I can't stop you from doing this. It's your life but I can be apart of it. I can protect you."

She scoffed out a laugh. "You want to be my bodyguard? Austin, I haven't had one of those since I was fourteen," she revealed with pain in her eyes.

Just adding to her mysterious allure that I couldn't figure out for the life of me.

"I'll be whatever you want me to be. As long as I can keep you safe, I don't give a fuck."

"You don't know what you're saying. You don't know what you're getting yourself into." She leaned into my touch, looking deep into my eyes and whispered, "Where's your family, Austin? Where are your parents? I can't do that to you. I can't do that to *them*."

I nodded in understanding. "I don't have anything to go home to."

"You should stay away from me, Austin. I'm no good for you. This will only end badly... It always does." Her eyes glazed over, immediately filling with tears.

"Hey..." I coaxed, pulling her toward me to wrap my arms around her.

Having her in my arms felt like heaven and home. The connection we shared was like nothing I had ever experienced before. As if she was made just for me.

Only me.

"I'm going with you, Briggs. I'm not taking no for an answer."

She took a deep breath and melted into my arms like she was trying to mold us into one person and murmured,

"Okay."

CHAPTER
17
Briggs

When my phone rang, I was expecting it.

To be honest, I was expecting him to just show up at one of the places he was sending me to. He could track me down in seconds. But he didn't. He never even mentioned Austin, not once. My uncle only called me concerning important business matters and I knew this phone call would be anything but.

Austin was working again. I hated that he had to leave me to go make money. He was adamant about paying his own way and not living off of me. It didn't bother me to pay for everything, I had more money than I knew what to do with, but I understood.

The last three months were like nothing I had ever experienced before. Even though I was used to this life and it was all I'd ever known, Austin made it different for me. It changed me in ways I never thought were possible before. He made me appreciate the beauty within the darkness. The light at the end of the tunnel that I had been walking through all my life wasn't just at the end anymore.

That's what Austin showed me. He lit up my dark tunnel and brought light into my life.

Hope.

Years of being alone and only relying on myself became second nature, like a second skin. With him, with Austin, I was starting to shed through the different layers and show what lied underneath the tattoos and purple hair.

Daisy.

I laughed. I smiled, a lot. My heart felt full in ways that it hadn't since before my parents died. I was happy. And even though the feeling terrified me, I embraced it because it was just too beautiful to let go. I knew it was only three months. Three fucking months and I got attached to him. When he wasn't around, I missed him, like a part of me was missing.

The light was gone; he took it with him.

I hated that feeling more than anything in this world. He had the ability to look at me in a way that was so beautifully broken. Like two halves of a heart finally coming together and becoming one after years of being apart.

Which only added to my theory that this wasn't the first time we had been together. Our souls had met before, in another time, in another place.

We were destined.

Whether we wanted to be or not.

It was fate.

We were fate.

I had an idea to present to my uncle. I was just waiting for the phone call.

"Briggs, what the fuck do you think you're doing?" Uncle Alejandro calmly coaxed when I answered the phone.

"Hi to you too. No, how are you? What have you been up to?" I sassed. I couldn't help myself.

"I'm in no mood for your bitchiness. I have let this go on for three months without saying a word. Three fucking months, waiting for you to say something to me. Not one fucking word. So, I will ask again and it would be in your best interest to answer my fucking question. What the fuck do you think you're doing?"

"His name is Austin—"

"Taylor from Oak Island, North Carolina. Born at Dosher Memorial Hospital on June 5th. Graduated from South Brunswick High School four years ago, almost died in a car accident his senior—"

"Car accident?" I interrupted, shocked.

"Ah, so you really don't know everything about him. Would you like to know his goddamn social security number? Maybe his background? It's all sitting here in front of me. I know who the fuck he is. I want to know why the fuck he is with you?" he roared, his patience wearing thin.

"He's my friend."

Silence.

"I met him in Miami a year ago and again in New York before I left. He doesn't have anyone. He's been backpacking and pretty much homeless. He keeps me safe, Uncle. He protects me. You should see the men when I bring him—"

"Are you going to fuck him too? Seeing as that didn't work out so great for your last bodyguard," he viscously spewed.

"That's none of your fucking business. I can't believe you just brought that up. I'm a grown woman and it's none of your business who I fuck now," I sneered.

"It becomes my goddamn business when it's messing with mine, peladita."

"I thought you would be happy that I found someone who cares about me, wants to protect me, seeing that you put me in the line of fire."

"If someone fucks with you, Briggs. They fuck with me. Trust me, no one wants to fuck with me," he gritted out through the phone.

"He makes me happy. I'm happy, Uncle," I simply stated, hoping that would be enough to make him understand.

I paced around the room, trying to think of what else I could say to him to make him understand. I didn't want to lose Austin.

"You can be happy without this little fuck following you around like a lost puppy. Did you ever stop and think that maybe he's using you? How did you meet, Briggs? Hmm… at a library? I know how much you love to fucking read."

I didn't falter. If I did, I would lose him.

"He's not using me. He works. Every single place we have been to these last three months he has worked his ass off. He doesn't let me pay for anything. Trust me, I have offered. He won't let me."

"That explains the shitty places you've been staying at. How's it feel to live on the other side? Everything you thought it would be? I've given you the best and this is how you repay me?"

"Then give him a job."

"Excuse me?"

"He protects me, he looks out for me, and he's keeping me safe. It's not any different than what Esteban used to do. He keeps me calm when I meet the associates, knowing that at any point and time shit could go south. He's there to watch my back. You want me to worry about my safety?" I asked.

"So what you're saying is that you want me to pay for you to fuck the hired help again? What does that offer me?"

"Another strong person to add to your business. Your growing empire, as you call it. He's good, Uncle. He doesn't talk when I take him on runs. He just stands in the background and makes his presence known with his I'll-fuck-you-up-if-you-touch-her demeanor. He doesn't take shit from anyone. He's fucking fearless, exactly what you thrive on."

Silence.

"I'll bat for him, okay? He fucks up. Shit goes bad. It falls on me. Now those are words you understand."

"If I go down, peladita. You go down with me. Now those are words you understand," he repeated back to me, knowing he meant it.

I took a deep breath, thinking I'd lost.

"I'll play it your way for a while. I'm sending a man over. His name is Pablo. He will give your new *bodyguard* everything he needs. Including a business credit card that I will pay him on weekly. If you sleep in one more piece of shit motel, Austin will deal with me. Not you. Are we clear?"

I nodded even though he couldn't see me. "Crystal."

"Now that it's two of you traveling together, it will be easier for me to have everything ready when you get to the hotels. I see you've already been using my contacts for his fake passports behind my back. That ends now."

By easy, he meant easy to control, him, me, *us*. The situation. I didn't care as long as it kept Austin with me.

"Thank you, Uncle. I promise you—"

"Briggs, don't make promises that you have no fucking control over. Especially when it comes to that puta called love," he stated, "*bitch*" with a bitter tone I'd never heard before.

"Thank you anyway."

He hung up without saying a word. And I spent the rest of the afternoon trying to forget about the car accident that almost killed Austin.

AUSTIN

Everything happened so fucking fast.

Overnight my life changed in the blink of an eye.

Physically…

Emotionally…

Mentally…

All because of the girl covered in tattoos with purple hair.

It had been five months since I'd left with her, leaving behind the shitty life I had become accustomed to. We had traveled to so many different places after Colombia. Seen so many different things. The sky was the limit. It was a reoccurring joke between us, every new place we went we had new passports, all new identities. Sometimes we would pretend to be newlyweds, madly in love with each other.

That was my favorite.

We played the roll too well. Almost forgetting it was a ploy. I didn't fucking care, it always gave me an excuse to touch Briggs inappropriately in public. It changed everywhere we went and it was fucking hilarious coming up with new ideas with her. Never a dull moment. Not once.

But one thing was for sure.

One thing never changed…

We were friends.

Getting to know her was like waking up from a dream, like I had been sleeping my entire life. Just waiting for the moment she would come into my world and make me start living.

Which was the only way I could explain it and even that didn't do it justice.

I knew I sounded like a goddamn pussy, but nothing compared to seeing the world through Briggs' eyes. I realized pretty quickly that I hadn't even started really traveling till she was by my side. It was supposed to be for business but we were having the time of our lives, partying, getting high, and meeting new people everywhere we went. She still didn't get high off her own stash so she would buy from the suppliers before it officially became hers.

To see the world like that was surreal and it was all made possible because of her. Don't get me wrong it wasn't all fun and games. For the first three months, I worked my fucking ass off trying to make money anyway I could to support us. It was pretty easy since technically I was just a tourist passing through. Business owners loved that, being able to pay me under the table for a few days' work.

If I wasn't keeping Briggs safe with the shit she had to do, I was working on my own. There was no way in fucking hell that I was going to be dependent on her and I never wanted her to think I was using her for money.

She always told me she knew that wasn't my motive for traveling with her, but she also didn't want me to leave her side. She missed me too much when I was gone even if it was only for a few hours in the day.

She hated it.

It was unreal how fast you could become attached to a person. Which was funny because all I ever wanted was to run away from my life and everyone in it, but there I was.

Wanting to spend an eternity in hers.

Briggs didn't like to talk about the past. In fact, she refused to let me in to that part of her life, the part that led her up to this point in time. I respected her wishes but I didn't like it. I figured over time she would open up to me when she was ready. I just had to be patient.

Her future was mine.

I knew I was her first real friend. She told me that often, and I would be lying if I said that I didn't love that she chose me. Even though it made me sad for her, knowing how lonely that must had been. I was lucky in the sense that I grew up with Alex and the boys, even though we weren't on speaking terms now. I still managed to send my parents and Half-Pint a postcard every once in awhile.

I knew Briggs worked for Alejandro Martinez but not because his name came out of her mouth. The business associates, as she called them, said his name often. It was hard for me to follow since they mostly spoke in Spanish. It was a nice fucking surprise the first time I heard her speak it so damn fluently.

I jacked-off in the shower like a fucking thirteen-year-old boy when we got back to the hotel that afternoon. Remembering the sexy-as-fuck tone of her voice as she was talking to the men. I pictured her face the entire time and came so fucking hard I saw stars.

One night, two months ago, after working with a construction company for a few days, I came back to the hotel and she was smiling like a fool. Of course I walked over to her and caught her expression in the air, placing it on my heart. That had become our thing. And it always made her smile even bigger, lighting up her entire face. It was the first time I ever saw her so fucking happy, and I didn't even know the cause, but I didn't care.

The look on her face was all that mattered to me.

She pulled me on the couch next to her and told me I didn't have to leave her anymore. I was ready to tell her the same shit I had been saying for the last three months. But she interrupted me, placing her finger over my lips to silence me. She continued telling me that she got me a job with Martinez. That I was officially her bodyguard and before I had any time to react to what she just shared.

There was a knock on the door.

A man named Pablo showed up with a suitcase full of clothes, suits, shoes, everything I needed and things I most likely wouldn't ever wear. They were all packed neatly waiting to be used. He handed me an envelope with a letter from Martinez and then a briefcase. The letter stated that everything I needed was in the briefcase, including a business debit card that I had to use for everything. It already had twelve thousand dollars on it. He called it back pay for the last three months for protecting Briggs. He went on to say he would be paying me a thousand dollars a week on that card for my services of being her bodyguard.

All I kept thinking was that I would have continued doing it for free.

I opened the briefcase and found two passports, and the business credit card he mentioned before. There was some other shit in there that I wasn't sure what to do with. What caught my attention though were the two 9mm guns. One was secured in a black leather suspender holster and the other in what seemed like an ankle holster. Both guns had permits that matched the names on the passports in the briefcase. Luckily, I knew how to use a gun.

Most Southern boys do.

Everything in that briefcase was a lie. Every last document was fake but looked so fucking authentic. So fucking real. There wasn't a chance in Hell anyone would spot them as fakes.

Briggs was so fucking happy. So, I didn't think twice about it, I started working for Martinez because all I wanted to do.

Was keep her safe.

From that point on we only stayed at five-star hotels. Partying with some of the richest, most corrupt people in the world and I was having the time of my life. Working for Martinez came with instant respect, money, power, everything I never had before.

But always wanted.

All of it was new and exciting. I didn't give my new job a second thought. All the luxuries outweighed the fact that I was working for a drug lord.

Although Briggs called it organized crime, she said Martinez was involved in everything and anything. It wasn't just about the drugs. That what we worked in it was just an aspect of what he ran and controlled.

A new briefcase was waiting for me at each new location we traveled to, sometimes it would be in the limo that picked us up from the airports and other times it would be waiting for me in our room. Out with the old, in with the new every goddamn time. New clothes, new documents, new passports, new guns with permits, everything we needed without batting a fucking eye.

Each day was a new day with Briggs by my side.

Life couldn't have been better.

We were lying on the bed with our legs entwined, our bodies next to each other, watching a movie in the hotel. I kept blowing raspberries on her neck, she was thrashing around like crazy, shrieking from the pleasure and pain it brought her.

She loved it.

She just loved to pretend like she didn't.

"Austin! Stop!" She laughed uncontrollably.

Desperately trying to hold back my face, knowing it didn't matter. I would stop when I wanted to.

And I didn't want to.

She sideswiped my arms and was tickling under my chin and around my neck before I even saw it coming.

"Ohhhh, little girl, that's a way to get hurt," I threatened, grabbing her arms and locking them above her head.

I hated my neck being touched, too many years of being tortured as a child by my family members thinking it was funny to tickle my neck for entertainment.

My body was now on top of hers and I saw it immediately. Her eyes glazed over and her pupils dilated. Revealing the look of lust that I had grown so accustom to.

It had been five months since I left with her and all we did was talk, cuddle, and flirt relentlessly with each other. I couldn't remember the last time I went this long without having sex, and yet it didn't fucking bother me. Not one bit. What Briggs and I shared was deeper than any piece of pussy could ever offer me. Not that I didn't want to bury my cock deep inside her.

She was everything.

She bit her lip, waiting for what I was going to do next. I hadn't kissed her since the night on her balcony. That one kiss was all I had to hold me over.

"What's your name?" I rasped, feeling the effect she always had on me.

I'd probably asked her like fifty times up until that point and each time she changed the subject or she would blatantly lie to me and say "Briggs."

As the months went by, I learned more and more about her. How she would bite her lip when she was nervous, like she was doing right now. How she would never leave the hotel without wearing makeup, her hair was always down and flowing around her face. How the clothes she wore were always revealing, but it wasn't because she wanted to show off her body.

It was the tattoos.

For some reason she wanted them on full display. It wasn't to show off her ink. It was her way of sharing a piece of her soul with the world she tried to keep at bay.

One of the first things that caught me by surprise was how much she loved to read. Each night it was a new book. The innocence about her exposed every time she told me about the characters and the storylines, as if they were her friends or she was living vicariously through them. She beamed while she read and I could tell what was happening in the book based off her expressions.

Especially if something bad was happening, she would place her hand over her heart. Like she was trying to hold it together.

Briggs also had sad moments. Her reflect time was what I called it. The way she would get lost in her own mind when she thought I wasn't looking. How she would pretend to be sleeping when she knew I was watching her sleep.

Getting lost in her beauty.

These were just to name a few, and even though I cherished every new thing I learned about her, it wasn't what I craved.

And the crazy thing about that was she knew it.

"Austin…" she pleaded for me to stop insisting on knowing her truths.

I wouldn't until I knew them.

Every. Last. One.

"These last five months have been the best days of my life. Being with you."

She swallowed hard, her resistance wavering.

"No one has ever made me feel the way you do. You have the ability to bring me to my knees with just a look. You're my drug, my addiction. I know that Briggs is a part of you. I know she exists but I also know that she doesn't. Tell me your name. And I'll give you everything you've been dreaming about."

Her eyes widened and her mouth parted.

"You talk in your sleep. You also kind of snore."

"I don't snore." She tried to slap my chest but I caught her hand mid-swing.

"It's the sweetest sound I've ever heard."

She sighed, revealing her internal struggle. "You're my friend, Austin. My only friend. Trust me… I've let you in."

I leaned in close to her face, our mouths a few inches apart with our connection never breaking. I didn't falter and whispered, "I want to be your friend that makes you come. I want you in my bed. More than you'll ever know. Just tell me your name…"

She looked deep into my eyes and lied,

"My name is Briggs."

CHAPTER 18

AUSTIN

"Austin, why don't you ever take your shirt off unless we're in our hotel room?" Briggs asked, looking over at me from the kitchen where she was making us some food.

I could see her out of the corner of my eyes but didn't look up to acknowledge her question. I was sitting on the couch adjacent to her with my notebook in my hands.

"Hmm…" I replied, barely paying any attention.

I was too caught up, my hand bleeding against the page.

"Your shirt? You don't have a shirt on right now. You don't even take it off when we're at the beach or the pool. You barely wear one when we're in our hotel rooms. So, I'm asking you the reason for that?"

I closed my notebook and set it beside me. I hadn't shared my talent with her yet. She knew what my notebook was for. It was kind of hard to hide something from someone you have been with for seven months. But I hadn't shown her any sketches yet. I wasn't ready to let her into that part of my life, especially since she had yet to tell me her name.

She also wasn't ready to see them.

I gave up on asking her what her real name was. Mainly because I was tired of getting disappointed and having her blatantly lie to my face. A man could only take so much let down. I think it bothered her that I stopped asking. She was getting lost in thought more often than ever before.

I grinned. "Are we sharing sad stories now, baby?"

She bit her lip and narrowed her eyes at me.

"I'll tell you mine, if you tell me yours," I added.

She sighed, looking back down at the food she was preparing. Lost in thought again.

"That's what I thought," I said under my breath.

I grabbed my notebook, walking toward the bathroom to shower.

"Austin," she called out behind me, making me turn to face her.

"You can pick any tattoo on my body, except your favorite and I will tell you what it means," she said, gesturing up and down her body, wiggling her eyebrows.

I smiled, big and wide.

She was trying to make light of the serious situation. I watched her eyes go exactly where I wanted them, to the notebook in my hands. She wanted to know what I drew in there, probably as much as I wanted to know what her real name was.

I gravitated towards her like a magnet. My feet moved on their own accord, following the pounding rhythm of her heart that I knew was racing, fast and hard.

For me.

I couldn't get to her fast enough. The anticipation was alive and breathing all around me, guiding me toward a little part of her that she was finally willing to share. It wasn't what I wanted, but it was a step in the right direction. Each stride brought me closer to her before I finally broke the distance between us.

Her eyes were silently begging me to touch her.

To feel her.

My thumb swiped over her plump bottom lip and within seconds I was pulling it out from between her teeth. Taking a moment to trace along the soft, wet skin. It didn't take long for the tip of her tongue to graze against my finger.

I loved the effect I had on her.

Her eyes dilated.

My cock twitched.

I threw my notebook on the counter. Slowly gliding my thumb down to her clavicle bone, never losing contact with her skin. She stirred when she felt me caress, back and forth along the cursive writing tattooed in a language I didn't recognize.

"This one," I simply stated, eyeing her cautiously.

She blinked, her eyes immediately filling with tears.

I frowned, waiting for her to share a piece of her soul with me. It took everything inside me to tell her that she didn't have to do this.

But I needed her to.

That outweighed the turmoil it was causing her.

She shook her head, struggling to let the meaning leave her lips. "It's in Spanish. It means February 21st."

My eyebrows lowered as I stared intently into her eyes. Waiting for her to continue.

"It's the day I died, Austin. It's the day the girl you think is still inside me," she placed her hand over the tattoo, "the one you keep asking for her name. Died."

I jerked back, shocked as shit. I wasn't expecting that at all. I stepped away from her, roughly running my hands through my hair. Wanting to tear it the fuck out. I needed a second to comprehend what she just shared. It knocked the fucking wind right out of me, and I was finding it hard to breathe.

What the fuck?

Tears started to slide down her beautiful face, one right after the other. Falling onto her white shirt, leaving a trail of her pain. I used the same thumb I'd been using to stir sensations from her body a minute ago, to wipe away her tears.

They belonged to me now.

"Austin, please say something," she wept, overwhelmed by her truth and my silence.

"Jesus Christ, Briggs…" I breathed out, just as overwhelmed from her truth.

She grimaced not understanding my reaction.

"I fucking hate my scars. They're a part of me. A part that I can never get rid of, they're forever etched in my skin."

"Austin…" she coaxed, her heart breaking for me. "You're beautiful. You—"

I placed my thumb over her lips, silencing her. It was still wet from her tears. She looked up at me, her big blue eyes so full of sadness for me and I hated that even more.

I didn't want her sympathy.

I didn't fucking deserve it.

"I hate people staring at me. Asking themselves 'What happened to him?' Feeling fucking sorry for me," I paused, letting my words sink in. "I don't know how this is even fucking possible, but on the exact same date you died, Briggs. I almost died too. Except that's not the reason why I fucking hate my scars. I hate them because all they do is remind me every day that I almost killed my best friend too."

Her eyes widened.

"Oh my God," she rasped, her voice breaking as much as her resolve. Her head shook fervently.

I couldn't tell if it was from the fact that something life changing happened to both of us on the same date or the truth I just revealed.

She pressed her hand against her forehead, bowing her head. Like she had just been suddenly struck with a splitting headache.

"Briggs, I was in a car—"

She put her hand out in front of her, silencing me. " stories, Austin," she interrupted. Giving me a look I hadn't ever seen before. "I can't hear anymore."

I didn't falter. "For now, Briggs… no more sad stories, *for now*."

She peeked up at me through her lashes and spoke with conviction, "Fuck sad stories."

With that she turned away from me and went into the bathroom, closing the door behind her. I wanted to go after her, I wanted to hold her and take away her pain.

And for the first time since the car accident, I wanted her to take my pain away too.

I grabbed two pain pills, swallowing them down with no water. They burned my dry throat going down, but I welcomed the distraction. Seconds later, I heard the shower turn on and soft crying echoed through the room. It killed me that she was crying, that our sad stories could affect her that much. The tough-girl exterior gone, replacing it with the girl that I knew still lived inside her.

The same girl whose name she wouldn't tell me.

All I could do was hope that one day.

She would.

I let her have her space. Grabbing my notebook from the counter, I went back to the couch, taking out all my frustrations and sadness on blank paper. I don't know how long I sat there engrossed in my truths, when I finally heard the bathroom door open.

She walked toward me immediately and grabbed my hand. "Come on." Without another word, I set my notebook aside and followed her.

We drove in silence in the car. Both of us lost in our thoughts. I didn't even care where she was taking me, too caught up in the irony and fate of it all. She parked the car on the street, pulling up the parking brake. It was then that I looked around the building.

"Where are we?"

She opened the door and turned looking me dead in my eyes. "To make your sad story a happy one."

"What—"

She stepped out of the car before I could even finish. She was on a mission as I followed close behind her up to the door. She opened it and walked inside. I threw down my cigarette, stepping on it to put it out.

"Jose!" she called out to the guy in the back as soon as the door closed behind me.

He turned and smiled as soon as he saw her.

"Briggs! My girl!"

He was over to her in three strides, pulling her into his arms. She laughed, smiling over at me from above his shoulder. He pulled away first, peering back at me.

"Hey, man." He stuck out his hand. "I'm Jose."

I shook it. "Austin."

"You hanging out with trouble over here?" he asked, nodding toward her.

"Something like that," I chuckled.

"Hey, I bring you a new client, and you give me shit," she laughed.

"Client?" I broke in, still so fucking confused with the turn of events.

"Come on." Grabbing my hand she led me to a table.

She sat me down and it was then I realized we were in a tattoo shop. She squatted down in front of me, sitting on the balls of her feet and once again looked deep into my eyes as she spoke with conviction, "Pick a scar, Austin. Turn your pain into something fucking beautiful."

And I did.

Briggs

The second the needle touched Austin's scar, the worst one on the middle of his back, I knew he would instantly become addicted to ink. There was nothing that could ever explain the surge of adrenaline that soared through your body when you took your pain into your own hands.

Not letting it take you under. Even if it was only until the needle stopped moving against your flesh. His scar now getting covered by the outline, color, and shading.

He decided on a phoenix bird spreading its wings, flying out of the flames of Hell below.

Rising.

Reborn.

The outline took up most of his back, covering up the evidence that haunted him every day. We spent the rest of the night there, while Jose worked his magic on Austin's imperfect skin. Creating something beautiful out of something broken. He said it would take three or four sessions to finish it completely, but when it was done it'd be a pretty sick masterpiece. Austin told him he would be back the next morning, eager to get it finished.

We drove in comfortable silence on the way back to our hotel. I knew he wanted to say so much by the way he was stealing glances at me while he was smoking his cigarette. I didn't need to hear it. The happiness on his face was enough of a "thank you" for me.

Austin went right in the shower when we got back to the hotel. I cleaned up the food I left in the kitchen, deciding to order room service for us instead. I used the phone on the end table by the couch, turning on the TV after I hung up.

I would be lying if I said I hadn't been staring at Austin's notebook that was placed on the coffee table since I started cleaning up the kitchen. It was sitting right there, tempting me to open it and find out the secrets behind the cover. For whatever reason, he never left it out. I knew he drew. I just didn't know what he was actually drawing on the pages inside. I'd watch him get lost for hours with that notebook in his lap. Never finding the courage to ask him what captivated him so damn much.

I still heard the shower running. I knew it was wrong to invade his privacy without permission, but I couldn't fucking help myself.

I needed to know.

With shaky hands, I reached over to the table and picked up the notebook that held a piece of Austin's world. I wasn't worried that he could come out of the bathroom at any moment and catch me red-handed.

I was more worried about what my eyes would see.

My heart was pounding, my mind racing as if it knew that I was about to discover something that would change our friendship. Something that would change our future. Colliding us onto a path that we would never be able to veer away from.

I gasped, completely breathless from the first sketch I saw while invading his soul.

Dancing. Hair flowing wild and free. Big, bright, blue eyes piercing right at me. High cheekbones, pouty lips, long lashes, no makeup on.

I flipped the page. Wings. The left one darker, feathers misplaced, falling off, dark shading. The right one, perfect, every feather intact and immaculately placed, light shading. Bows. Skull with roses around it. Writings in different fonts scattered, flowers cascading down. Everything was so intricately drawn.

I stopped to admire each and every one of them, running my fingers over the illustrations with tears in my eyes.

I never knew what he was drawing.

Not once.

Next page. A girl sleeping, her head placed on a pillow with her mouth partly open. The sheet covering up to her stomach. Her breasts perked up. She looked so peaceful. Beautiful. I swear I could see her breathing.

More tears.

Next page. Book covers, upon book covers, upon book covers.

Next page. A girl deep in thought, her eyes so sad, so lost. So fucking captivating.

Every. Single. Page.

Every last one.

Was me.

But not me…

It wasn't Briggs staring back at me. It was Daisy. He was able to capture every detail I so desperately tried to hide. Not knowing one thing about the girl behind the purple hair and tattoos, but somehow knowing everything.

"How the hell did you do this, Austin?" I asked myself out loud.

"It was easy. I just need to look at you."

His voice startled me, making me jump. I never even heard the shower turn off. I didn't bother to look up. I was too mesmerized, caught up in the talent bleeding through the pages of a girl that I thought didn't exist anymore.

More tears filled my eyes for the second time that day. I couldn't remember the last time I cried so much. Except for the first time in I don't know how long…

They were tears of happiness.

"Why?" I found myself asking, terrified to know the answer.

I heard his footsteps coming toward me, each one louder than the last, till he sat on the edge of the coffee table in front of me. Reaching over to graze the side of my cheek with his fingers that no longer smelled like cigarettes.

A smell that I now craved.

"You're my muse," he simply stated, meaning each word.

I shut my eyes, the emotion too much for me to handle. He grabbed the notebook off my lap, throwing it on the couch beside me. Pulling me toward him effortlessly, making me straddle his lap. I could feel his arousal beneath me.

There I was wrapped in his arms, completely letting my guard down for the first time. I pressed my forehead up against his as he pulled the hair away from my face.

His eyes.

They did it to me every time.

There was so much emotion behind his gaze, and I knew it mirrored mine. There was no need for words. Our eyes spoke for themselves as his hands caressed the sides of my cheeks. Pulling my mouth toward his without any hesitation.

His lips were just as I remembered, fuck, maybe even better. He sought out my tongue before I had the opportunity to find his, moaning into his mouth the second they collided.

His lips, his tongue, his hands.

I felt him everywhere, all at once, and all we were doing was kissing. He was soft but demanding, controlling but passionate, and fucking intense as all hell.

"Austin," I erratically breathed, panting breaths on his lips.

"What, baby…" he groaned with the same sensual tone.

"I want you," I managed to speak.

My thoughts.

My words.

They all seemed to be intertwined with one another.

"I want you more than I have ever wanted anyone in my entire life," he confessed. "What's your name? Tell me your name, and I'll give you whatever the fuck you want," he replied between kisses.

I whimpered, begging, "Please."

He smiled against my lips, gliding his hands down my body until he reached the edge of my panties and reaching down between my legs. I opened them wider for him. I knew he could feel my wetness through the silk when his fingers found my folds.

I shamelessly moaned, leaning my head back. Urging him to keep going.

He slipped my panties to the side and touched my pussy for the first time. I shuddered, kissing him deeper, harder, faster. His rough fingers moved to my opening, soaking up my wetness, sliding them back and forth on my clit.

"Fuck, you're so wet," he growled, thrusting them into my opening. "Ride my fingers, baby. Fuck my hand."

No one had ever talked to me like that before. I swear to God I almost came from that alone.

He curved his fingers toward my sweet spot, pushing, pressing, and fucking me while I swayed my hips with the same momentum.

"Please make me come. Please… no one has ever made me come before."

He released a growl from deep within his chest, vibrating against my core. I opened my eyes needing to look at him even though we were still kissing. His eyes were already open, staring and taking me in.

Austin held all his secrets and told all his truths through his eyes.

He met my gaze and we moaned into each other's mouths. He pulled away to rest his forehead along mine, wanting to watch me come undone while working me with his fingers. I could only imagine what his cock felt like.

"You like that, baby? Does that feel good? Huh? Tell me, tell me it feels good," he huskily urged.

"Yes…" Was all I could manage to say as I came undone.

He fucked me faster with his fingers, and I rode him harder. I bit my bottom lip and felt my legs quiver and my pussy pulsate. I gasped, sucking in air, falling over the edge. Climaxing so fucking hard I saw stars.

We both panted into each other's mouths.

I rode the high for as long as I could, reaching for the elastic band of his gym shorts.

"No," he rasped, stopping my hand.

"What?" I asked, taken aback, trying to catch my breath.

He kissed the tip of my nose, looking deep into my eyes once again and said,

"You don't get my cock, until you give me your name."

CHAPTER
19

AUSTIN

I had been with Briggs for over a year, and she had yet to tell me her fucking name. It wasn't from lack of trying. It didn't matter what I did or said, she wouldn't share it. I didn't see the big deal. It was just a God given name for fuck's sake. It's not like I would call her by it. I just wanted to know, for her to be comfortable enough to share a piece of her past with me.

We had gotten close in other ways though. She told me more meanings of her tattoos, except my favorite. We shared a bed so I could hold her every night. We went on dates everywhere we traveled and acted like a couple, no need to pretend anymore.

We didn't talk about what we were to each other, we didn't have to, we knew. I had made her come with my mouth and fingers more times than I could fucking count. We still hadn't had sex and she hadn't touched or seen my cock. Don't get me wrong. I loved watching her come undone around my tongue and fingers, lapping up her salty sweetness that I never got enough of.

There was no sweeter taste than Briggs.

I could only imagine what her pussy would feel like around my cock. She felt my dick twitch every time I touched her, and every time she tried to touch me I stopped her.

She knew what I needed to hear.

I had the worst case of fucking blue balls known to man and my hand was getting fucking tired from jacking off so damn much. I wouldn't back down though.

Not a chance in Hell.

I wanted her.

Trust me. I never wanted anyone as much as I wanted Briggs.

I just wanted all of her.

I pulled her hair away from her face, staring down at her while she was sleeping next to me. My head leaned on my hand, propping myself up as I laid sideways taking in the beauty that was Briggs. Her purple hair was splayed all over her face and pillow, and her lips looked swollen from sleep. The camisole had risen to below her breasts and her ass was completely sticking out, I could see her hard nipples in broad daylight.

If it was even possible, she looked even more breathtaking in the morning, so peaceful, so fucking beautiful when she slept.

Mornings were always my favorite.

We had been back in New York for a few weeks now. Briggs was happy to sleep in her own bed, and I was happy to join her. I guess you could say we were living together. I was staying at her apartment instead of finding my own place. It was pointless when we traveled more than we were home. We would be hitting the road again next month, but it was nice to have some downtime and do normal shit like normal couples do.

She released a muffled breath, shaking her head and waking herself up.

I grinned, holding back my laughter.

"That wasn't a snore. My nose is clogged. It's my allergies," she justified, taking in my smartass expression.

"Whatever you have to tell yourself, baby."

She playfully slapped my chest. "Austin! I don't snore. I have allergies."

"Did I say a word?"

"You don't have to. I can tell what you're thinking," she said as she rolled away from me.

"Is that right?" I wrapped my arm around her waist, turning her and tugging her toward me.

Her body was now pressed up against mine, my leg caging hers in.

"What am I thinkin' right now?"

She slowly slid her delicate hand down my bicep and then my chest. Touching the scars that were now covered in ink. I had a tribal tattoo that started from my right chest up. The words, "Pain is temporary, pride is forever," surrounding it. The tribal extended onto my right arm, becoming a sleeve. My other arm had a sleeve as well, it was a tropical and tribal design that just went down my entire left arm.

Briggs loved the tattoos.

I got my nipple pierced along with another surprise that she didn't know about.

And fuck… I wanted to show her more than anything.

"Hmm…" she hummed, rubbing her knee on my morning wood. Playing with my nipple ring. "I could think of a few things, birthday boy."

"Does it start with your name?"

She ignored my question, leaning in to softly kiss my scar that was near my heart. She said she liked to feel it beating against her mouth, rubbing her lips back and forth over it.

"I could give you one of your presents." She softly licked in between kissing. "I'm a really good present giver. Some people have even called me a pro."

I immediately jerked her head back by her hair to look at me.

"What people?" I snapped at what she was insinuating.

She moaned, biting her bottom lip. Briggs loved to be manhandled. She also loved my dirty fucking mouth.

"I'll let you give me anything you want," I rasped, her eyes glazed over. "Just tell me your name. That's the only gift I really want from your mouth, baby."

"Really? I hadn't noticed," she sassed. "What about this gift?"

Her hands instantly ticked under my chin and around my neck. Laughing hysterically at my reaction. I grabbed her hands, locking them behind her back.

"Ah! You're hurting me," she lied so I would let go.

"You fucking love it. Don't lie, little girl."

I kissed her lips, let go, and got out of the bed.

"I'm going to go take a shower," I said without looking back.

"Wish I could help you with your problem, Austin. God knows your hand must be getting tired."

I playfully flicked her off and walked into the bathroom, chuckling to myself. "Rosie Palms is a nice lady," I said loud enough for her to hear, opening the bottle and taking two pain pills down.

She started laughing her ass off on the bed.

It was the best fucking sound ever.

We spent my birthday roaming around New York. We ended up in Central Park, where Briggs read one of her smut books and I sat drawing inappropriate pictures of her. A few weeks ago while walking past an art gallery that had always caught my attention since I first got to New York, she asked me why I never pursued a career in art. I just told her that it had always been a dream of mine, but it wasn't in the cards. She dropped it after that, which I was grateful for.

We went back to the apartment to get ready for dinner. Briggs made reservations at some fancy place on Fifth Avenue. I would have been happy staying in and ordering pizza, but she insisted. When she walked out of the bathroom wearing a black, tight, short dress with red fuck-me heels, we were late for her reservations.

I decided to eat her instead.

After dinner we walked around, holding hands, talking about nothing in particular, just laughing and enjoying each other's company. I couldn't have asked for a better birthday. The last few had been pretty shitty, spending them by myself.

We passed my favorite art gallery, the one that had always caught my eye. The glass windows displayed the room full of different artists. Everything from sculptures to abstract paintings, to sketches and photography.

"Come on." She nodded toward the door, leading the way inside.

"You want to buy some art, baby?"

"Maybe."

"Is that right? Mine not good enough anymore?"

She shrugged, grinning at me as we made our way to one of the other rooms.

"Way to crush a man's dream. You going to kick me in the balls next?" I said, holding my heart, forging hurt.

"There's actually this really hot new artist that I have been dying to show you."

"The fuck?" I breathed out.

"Briggs," the owner walked over to us, interrupting our conversation. "Is this him?" he asked, looking only at me.

She beamed.

"Austin, right?"

I nodded.

"Rafael."

We shook hands.

"I told Briggs I had been dying to meet the man behind the sketches she showed me. They make a great addition to my collection," he informed, catching me completely off guard.

"Excuse me?"

Briggs cleared her throat, stepping in between us.

"I'm going to go give him his present now. We will be right back."

Rafael nodded in understanding.

"Baby, what's going—"

"Close your eyes."

I arched an eyebrow, cocking my head to the side.

"Don't you trust me?" She smiled, blowing me a kiss.

I caught it in the air and placed it near my heart.

"With my life," I simply stated, closing my eyes.

It didn't take long to walk through the small crowd, reaching our destination.

"Keep them closed, okay?"

"Yes, ma'am."

She let go of my hand and turned my body in the direction she wanted me to face. Standing behind me, she placed her hands over my eyes.

"Happy birthday, Austin," she murmured into my ear, taking her hands away.

I blinked my eyes open, trying to get rid of the haze. I stood face to face with the picture I drew of Briggs the day she told me about the meaning of her first tattoo. Except, it didn't have the date written over her clavicle bone anymore, it had been replaced with…

Daisy.

Briggs

I wanted to tell him what my name was for the last four months. I was just waiting for the right time. When he told me about his dream of going to art school and it not being possible, I immediately got an idea for his birthday that was coming up.

There were very few people in New York that my uncle didn't know. When I asked him if he could pull a few strings and get me a meeting with the owner of the art gallery, the same one that Austin had been eyeing for several months, I was expecting an interrogation of why from my uncle.

He didn't.

He hung up, and an hour later he texted me the date and time.

Austin turned around to face me with a look I had never seen before. He smiled at me, and it melted my heart. His fingers found my cheeks, brushing them lightly up and down. I leaned into his embrace, loving the feeling of his warm hands on me with the familiar, comforting smell of cigarettes.

He brought my lips close to his, softly kissing me a few times and murmured, "Nice to finally meet you, Daisy."

His bright blue eyes weren't telling me what he wanted to say like they normally do. I waited on pins and needles.

"Daisy, I'm in—"

"Daisy," I heard a voice call out, pulling my attention from Austin.

I grimaced, recognizing the voice immediately. My heart fucking dropped. Austin frowned, taking in my sudden change. My face paled like I had just seen a ghost. And in a way I had, the reaction from hearing a voice, a voice that I thought no longer existed. Austin followed the voice from behind me.

My two worlds were about to collide.

"Daisy, is that you?" he added, coming closer.

I shut my eyes, needing a minute to gather my emotions that were running wild. Taking over, wreaking havoc on my soul. I opened my eyes to gaze into my future, Austin, with a concerned expression on his handsome face.

Taking a deep breath, I turned to peer into my past and said, "Esteban."

CHAPTER
20
Briggs

I nervously fidgeted, unsure of what to say or what to do.

He looked older. No longer the man I remembered from five years ago. His once blue, familiar, warm eyes were cold and dark. Sad even.

"Wow... you look. Different," he laughed.

I looked down at myself. "Yeah, you could say that. I'm glad to see you... alive," I blurted.

I never knew what happened to him after my uncle's men dragged his bloody body from my room. The last time I saw him was my fifteenth birthday. I never gathered enough courage to ask my uncle what happened to him after that tragic night. To be honest, I didn't think he would ever tell me the truth anyway.

Austin stepped beside me. His questions and confusion were radiating off of him and searing into my skin.

I reached over and held his hand, trying to ease his answers.

"Aren't you going to introduce me to your friend here?" Esteban asked, nodding toward Austin.

"Right. Esteban this is my umm..." I frowned not sure how to introduce him. I could feel Austin's stare burning a hole in the side of my face. Waiting to hear how I would respond.

"Umm... Austin. This is Austin," I stated, tightening my hold on his hand to reassure him.

"I'm Esteban." He reached out his hand and Austin shook it. "I used to be Daisy's bodyguard."

Austin nodded, unsure of how to proceed with the man that knew my real name.

"Look at you all grown up now," he said, turning back to me. Gesturing up and down my body, his eyes wandering to my chest and staying there a little too long for my liking.

Austin twitched beside me. I could see his expression changing. The hold he had on my hand increased a little too hard. I turned slightly toward him to cover up my cleavage.

"How long has it been now?" Esteban asked, cocking his head to the side, looking only at me now.

"Umm…" I looked up at Austin. "Five years, right?"

"Too long. I'm glad to see you're okay."

We stood there in awkward silence. Austin wouldn't look at me, but he had no problem staring at Esteban.

"Well, I will let you two get back to your evening. It was nice to see you again, Daisy," Esteban acknowledged, leaning in and kissing my cheek.

I nervously smiled.

"Take care, Austin," he added with a nod.

Esteban looked at me one more time with an expression I couldn't quite place before he turned and left.

I glanced at Austin who was still intently looking at Esteban.

"Austin—"

"Not here."

"I know, but—"

"Not. Here," he gritted out.

We walked back toward Rafael and Austin thanked him for the opportunity to show off his art in his gallery. Rafael told him it was a pleasure and that he had my number and would call as soon as any of his pieces sold.

We took a cab back to my apartment. Austin still hadn't said a word to me, but I knew he was bothered by the handful of cigarettes he smoked on the ride back.

The door closed behind me as we walked into my apartment.

"Austin, I—"

He immediately turned around, stepping in front of me, causing my back to hit the door from the impact of his built frame that suddenly loomed over mine. I winced from the sting. He glared at me with a predatory regard, caging me with his arms. Our faces a few inches apart and our bodies maybe a foot.

Both our chests heaved profusely.

Our emotions running wild.

His eyes were dark and daunting with an intense, crazed stare as he looked me up and down. It was the first time I had ever felt him in that way. The first time I had ever seen him lose his cool. The man in front of me wasn't the Austin that I knew, the one that I'd spent over a year with.

The one I had fallen head over heels in love with but hadn't voiced my feelings yet.

The man in front of me thrilled me and excited me in ways I never thought possible.

I had nowhere to go.

I could barely move.

But my body felt on fire.

"What are—"

He cocked his head to the side and raised an eyebrow, causing me to stop what I was going to ask. He moved his face a little closer, barely a centimeter setting us apart now. I was engulfed in nothing but the dominance that he displayed over me in that minute, and I swear he could smell my arousal from it.

I was at his mercy.

Exactly where he wanted me.

"So, tell me, Daisy? What the fuck was that back there?"

I lowered my eyebrows, overwhelmed and confused by his question. He had never spoken to me that way. It was then that I realized I had also never pissed him off. He suddenly seemed taller, looming over me, ready to snap.

"What are you talking about?" I shook my head in confusion.

Was he angry at me for taking his sketches or about the unexpected visitor?

There was a hint of sadness that passed through his eyes that made me question what he was really asking me.

"He was my bodyguard," I stated out of pure impulse.

"A bodyguard doesn't look at your tits like that. He also doesn't look at you like he knows you. *In.* And. *out.*"

My breathing hitched, my eyes widened.

"How old is he, Daisy? Because five years ago, you were fucking fifteen."

"It's not what you think," I pleaded.

"Is that right?" he breathed out against my lips. "Tell me what I think then?"

There wasn't an inch of me that didn't ache for him, that didn't want him. I craved his touch now more than ever before. I licked my lips needing the moisture to soothe the burn of his mere words and breath against my mouth. His eyes followed the simple gesture of my tongue.

"I think you're reading too much into it. Men look at me all the time. It's never bothered you before. Hell, you're my bodyguard and you look at my tits and know me *in* and out, too," I argued.

He pulled back a little, narrowing his eyes at me.

"First, watch your fucking tone. That's different and you know it. Second, it doesn't bother me now. What's pissing me the fuck off, baby... is that you stumble around not knowing how to fucking introduce me."

"That's not fair. You can't—"

"I can't? Tell me, Briggs, what can't I fucking do?"

"I was just as caught off guard back there as you were."

"Was that before or after he called you Daisy? Seeing as it's taken me over a goddamn year to learn that bit of information."

He roughly smacked my ass, causing me to yelp, and not giving me a chance to answer. He picked me up off my feet as if I weighed nothing and wrapped my legs around his waist. Carrying me into the bedroom where he laid me down on the bed, hovering his huge frame over mine.

My dress was off of me before I even saw it coming, my bra and panties within seconds right after.

The heels stayed on.

He had seen me naked several times, but it was the first time I felt so fucking exposed to him.

In a way I never had before.

Maybe it was the predatory look on his face.

Maybe it was the fact that I had just seen another side to him.

Or maybe it was just because I knew I was going to touch him, feel him, and see him in ways I hadn't yet.

"You're so goddamn beautiful," he praised with a sincere tone, standing above me at the edge of the bed.

Taking in every last inch of my body as if it was the first time he was really looking at me.

"Spread your legs for me, baby."

I did, running my hands down my thighs and slowly parting them. Opening them in a V with my knees bent outward. He made a noise that came from the back of his throat, adding fuel to the flames burning inside me. Pulling me to the edge of the mattress by my legs, he got on his knees.

My pussy throbbed.

He kissed and licked his way down my thigh. Grinning when my pussy was directly in front of his face.

He inhaled my scent, softly kissing around my folds.

"Everything about you is fucking addicting. From your smile, to your smell, to your sinful fucking body. Especially…" He licked at my opening, pushing his tongue into my pussy. "Your goddamn taste," he growled, pushing it in again.

My head fell back as he fucked me with his tongue.

No one had ever made me feel worshipped like Austin could. The closeness of his mouth to my most private area was a feeling that had me grabbing the sheets in a frenzy, and he had barely even started touching me.

I expected him to be rough, but he was being gentle, taking his time to devour me, making me wet for him.

"Oh God," I whimpered in pleasure.

He licked me one last time and then stopped, peering up at me with hooded eyes.

"Tell me what you want. Beg me for it," he huskily urged.

"Please…" I responded on edge.

He always did this to me. Making me beg to come.

"Please… what, baby?"

"Please make me come."

He growled and returned to lapping at my pussy, eating me like I was his favorite fucking meal. Making me go crazy with passion and desire.

Feelings that only he could ever produce.

I screamed out in ecstasy and it made him suck my clit harder, side-to-side, forcefully, urgently. Austin knew my body better than I did. Within seconds he was making me come, hard. I shook the entire time as he let me ride out my orgasm against his lips, releasing me with a pop. My legs fell forward from weakness, still shaking when he dove forward, attacking my mouth.

I tasted every last bit of myself that was still all over his lips, with one hand at the back of my neck keeping me close to him exactly where he wanted me. I moaned, moving my hips to get him to give me what I'd wanted for so damn long. I could feel him smiling at the recognition of my subtle request.

He suddenly grabbed a fistful of my hair, and I yelped at the sudden intrusion on my scalp.

"I'm only going to say this one time. You're fucking mine. Do you understand me? Mine. Briggs… Daisy… every last inch of you belongs to me."

AUSTIN

I hated the way that fucker was looking at her. With longing, lust, like he knew her. Like he *really* knew her.

"Yes," she panted, affected by my words as much as my touch.

I kissed her long and deep one last time.

"I want to fuck you raw," I whispered against her ear. "I want to feel all of you, Daisy. Nothing between us. I've never done that with anyone."

"Then it's a good thing I'm on the pill because I want that more than anything."

Her delicate hands moved to my belt, undoing it. She unbuttoned my slacks and slid them down with my boxers. My hard cock jutted out. Her eyes immediately widened, taking my dick in for the first time.

"You're pierced?" she asked, completely caught off guard.

I chuckled, taking in the expression on her face that still hadn't left the piercing through the head of my cock. I moved to lie on top of her, caging her in with my arms around her face. Gripping the back of her neck not wanting to lose our connection.

We both wanted to get lost in the moment.

Lost in each other.

The love that lived in our souls.

The only place she ever existed.

"Could that piercing get lost inside me? Because that would really—"

"The only thing that's going to get lost inside you is my cock, and it's going to feel fucking amazing for you."

"Oh… other girls have liked it then?" she asked in a sad voice.

"No, baby. I got this done for you," I rasped, kissing her.

She beamed, closing her eyes.

"Don't close your eyes. I want to look into your eyes as I make love to you."

She immediately opened them and I tightened the grip at the back of her neck. Angling my cock into her opening with my other hand.

I slowly thrust inside her, our foreheads rested on each other, our mouths parted open. She was so fucking wet and felt so fucking good.

"Oh my God," she moaned when I was balls deep inside her.

I stopped, just wanting a moment to peer into her eyes. They had so many emotions that I couldn't even begin to describe. Her arms went around my neck as I slowly thrust in and out of her, making me feel whole and complete for the first time in my life.

My place was right beside her.

It's where I belonged.

"Fuck, you feel good," I groaned, thrusting harder. "You're so fucking tight."

I grabbed her leg, angling it higher. It was much deeper that way, my piercing hitting her g-spot effortlessly and her pussy tightened around my shaft, which earned her a growl. I never once let up on holding the back of her neck.

I continued to move at a hard and fast pace that had her weakening beneath me. Making love to her in a way I never had with anyone else. It wasn't just about the movements or touches, it was about the feelings and emotions that came along with finally fucking being inside her. Feeling every last inch of her wrapped around me, our bodies tangled together on the white sheets.

I cherished every sound, touch, expression that radiated off of her. We kissed, savoring the new sensation of our skin-on-skin contact. She moved her hips forward as I thrust in. Our bodies moved in sync with one another as we made slow and passionate love.

It was everything I ever wanted.

And didn't know I could ever have.

"Fuck," I grunted, rotating my hips, harder, faster and more demanding.

I wanted to love her so damn hard that she would still feel me in the morning.

I was close and so was she. We were both on the verge of going over, and I wanted to do it together.

"I'm going to come," she panted against my mouth.

I gripped the back of her neck, looking deep in her eyes. Kissing her passionately.

"You're. Fucking. Mine."

And I meant every word.

CHAPTER
21

AUSTIN

"Fuck!" Briggs yelled, jumping out of bed in a panic.

My head was pounding and my back was fucking throbbing. I felt like a semi-truck ran me over, threw it in reverse, and ran me the fuck over again.

The goddamn pain was crippling.

We had been up partying with business associates in Colombia for last two days straight with no sleep. The drugs finally wore off enough a few hours ago to where we could shut our eyes and catch some Z's.

Briggs had another important meeting with some new associates that morning and she wanted to stay up, but I convinced her that we needed to get some sleep for at least a few hours.

"Austin! Get up! We're so fucking late!" she screamed, running around the room gathering up her clothes.

Our hotel room was a disaster. Things got a little hazy toward the end for me, and I guess we'd brought the party back to our room.

"Baby, relax," I coaxed, sitting up on the edge of the bed, trying to open my eyes.

I leaned forward, placing my elbows up on my thighs, cradling my head that felt like it weighed a thousand pounds in my hands.

"Relax? Are you for real right now? Get your ass up, now! We're over an hour late and we still have to drive there and that's another thirty minutes!"

"Babe, it's fine. Just explain—"

"Explain what, Austin? That we've been getting fucked up on X and blow for the last forty-eight hours? Jesus Christ! These are drug lords not fucking PTA members. Get up!" She threw some clothes at me.

"I'm up, I'm up! Jesus, stop fucking screaming at me, Briggs. I'll be ready in ten minutes. Let me jump in the shower."

She sighed in frustration, hurrying out of the room to go find God knows what, but at least that meant she had stopped yelling at me. I walked into the bathroom, turning on the shower to let the water run for a minute so it could get warm. The pipes in Colombia fucking sucked. It didn't matter how much you paid for your five-star suite. In the last year, we had been back there three times since that night in New York. I learned fast that this country was definitely where most of the deals went down.

I inspected my face in the mirror. I looked like dog shit, my eyes were bloodshot red, and my pupils were still so fucking dilated. The pain in my back got worse as time went on, especially since I never got therapy for it. The Percocets stopped working over a year ago, I became immune to them or some shit. I started taking Oxys instead. I didn't have to take as many and it numbed the pain, but that was like a double-edged sword. Being numb allowed me to do things I probably shouldn't have, only fucking up my back more.

I downed two of them on my way to the shower, doing a quick rinse just to wake up. I threw on some jeans and a black t-shirt.

"Fuck," I breathed out to myself, sinking into the chair, trying to put some shoes on.

I was still so damn tired and out of it. I could hardly fucking see straight. My mind was shot to shit, and I could barely form a coherent thought. All I wanted to do was crash and sleep away the shitty feeling. There wasn't a chance in Hell I'd let Briggs go by herself. If something happened to her, I'd kill the motherfucker responsible and then myself.

She was my everything. We hadn't said I love you to each other, but we didn't need to.

We knew.

Actions would always speak louder than words.

I shook my head, looking at the blow that was still sitting on the dining table.

"Briggs?"

Silence.

We never did drugs before a meeting. Not even weed. In the last two years that I had been with her it was one line we never crossed. We always went in with a clear head, just in case shit went down. But the way I was feeling at that moment, trust me…

She wanted me to snort some cocaine.

At least then I would be lucid.

I did a line up each nostril before deciding to do two more. The effects not as potent as they were a day ago, but it immediately took the edge off and I grabbed a Red Bull from the fridge.

"You ready?" Briggs asked, opening the door peeking her head in.

Even ate up as shit with two days of partying and barely three hours of sleep, she still took my goddamn breath away.

"Yeah." I raised my drink. "Want one?"

"I have one already in the car."

I grabbed my gun, placing it in the holster on my back. "I'll drive," I said, grabbing the keys out of her hands.

"You sure?"

"Yeah. I feel better now." I kissed her, and she smiled.

"I'm sorry I yelled at you. I just can't believe we slept through the alarms."

"Shit happens. Come on."

I sped the entire way there, knocking off fifteen minutes of our drive time. By the look on Briggs' face, she was grateful for the small miracle I just pulled off. I opened the door stepping out of the car, but she caught my arm stopping me.

"What?" I asked, taken aback.

"The man we're about to see, Austin, he's different, okay? He's not like what you're used to seeing."

"What the hell is that supposed to mean?"

"Just that, I've met him a few times. Which is why he won't have his bodyguards beside him. So… keep that in mind, okay?"

"Baby, I don't know what you're trying to imply, but I'm not going to let any motherfucker talk—"

"I know, Austin. That's why I'm telling you all this. He's not just anyone. He's a friend, okay? Behave yourself and keep your emotions in check."

"I thought you didn't have any friends besides me."

"Not mine," she simply stated.

I nodded, understanding. She meant it was Martinez's friend. She kissed me, giving me a loving look before exiting the car.

I lit a cigarette, suddenly fucking pissed that I didn't know what I was walking into.

Over the last two years, we had been all over South America. We never stayed in one-place longer than two weeks tops. Briggs said it was safer that way. She literally sat down and met with the business associates, while I stood in the back watching. Always with one hand behind my back on my gun, prepared and waiting for one of these fuckers to make a wrong move.

Sometimes it was one guy, sometimes up to four.

I had gotten used to standing in the background, watching their mannerisms, looking for anything out of the ordinary. Picking up sentences here and there, since they usually spoke Spanish. I hadn't met or talked to Martinez yet. Briggs said that was a good thing, it meant we were doing a good job. She barely even talked to him herself, so I guess it wasn't just me. Briggs really did know how to take care of herself and handle business. None of the men she encountered ever disrespected her either.

At first it was surprising, especially since she was a woman. It was almost like they were scared of her because they had to be. I just summed it up to them fearing Martinez and they knew she worked for him.

Don't fuck with the hand that feeds you and all that bullshit.

"You're late," a man dressed in a pinstripe suit announced when we walked into the warehouse.

He was a fat fuck with balding gray hair and wrinkled skin. If I had to guess, I'd say he was in his late fifties or early sixties.

There was a long narrow table in the middle of the room. Chairs surrounded each edge even though it was only him in the vacant, empty building. Though I was more caught off guard that he was speaking English. That rarely happened in these meetings.

"I know... I'm sorry. We got—"

"Y este pendejo quien es?" He nodded toward me. I think he was asking Briggs who I was as soon as she sat down.

She didn't turn around to follow his gaze. She knew he was referring to me.

Already I didn't fucking like him.

213

"He's my bodyguard."

"Bodyguard?" he scoffed out the word, leaning back against his chair. His hands firmly placed on the table in front of him.

"Martinez is having a woman shuffling his deals now? I guess it does make sense that you would have a strong man behind you," he sneered with a strong Spanish accent.

I resisted the urge to tell him to go fuck himself. Instead, I stood there with one hand on my gun and the other clenched in a fist at my side.

Briggs smiled, leaning back in her own chair. "Says the man who has four."

He cocked an eyebrow, and I recognized the predatory look on his face. He wanted to fuck her, and I wanted to make him eat his own goddamn cock.

"You're lucky you're pretty, peladita."

"I'm not here for you to whisper sweet nothings in my ear."

"Just like Martinez. All work and no play. Must run in the family."

Family?

She sidestepped his comment not paying it any mind.

"My bodyguards aren't here. Mira?" he said in Spanish, looking all around the warehouse, gesturing with his hands. "Your superman can leave now."

"Hector—"

"There's not a chance in Hell I'm fucking leaving her alone with you," I interrupted, unable to control myself.

I hated the way he was looking at her, and I hated it even more that she was letting it happen.

"Pretty boy, can talk too? If he knows what's good for him, he'll shut his goddamn mouth and let us handle some business. That's why we are here, right?"

I stepped toward him. Briggs immediately put her hand out in the air stopping me, even though she was several feet away. Her eyes never shifted from his face.

"I'm here to handle business. He's not leaving. You want to make a deal? You make it with him in the room, or I walk too."

He cocked an eyebrow, challenging me.

"Martinez wouldn't be happy about that. Trust me. I would know more than anyone what makes him happy," Briggs warned.

My eyes immediately went from him to her, confused with what she just shared. She sounded like she had been his fucking whore.

I took a deep breath, willing my emotions in check, but she wasn't making it easy on me by any means.

His glare met hers and he specified, "Forty thousand dollars a kilo."

She laughed even though there wasn't anything fucking funny about the situation.

"Jesus Christ, Hector, take a girl to dinner before you try to fuck her up the ass."

"If that's all it takes, I'll make reservations for you and I tonight."

"Twenty-eight thousand and not a dollar over," she ignored his comment, and all I saw was fucking red.

He stood, his hands still firmly placed on the table in front of him, now hovering above it.

"The only way I'll settle for twenty-eight thousand," he murmured loud enough for me to hear, "is if it includes your pussy and your mouth wrapped around my cock. I'll even let that little cocksucker over there watch."

"AUSTIN, NO!"

Before Briggs even got the last word out, I was charging and roughly body checking the motherfucker over the chair and onto the concrete floor. We both hit it hard, rolling away from the table.

My body on top of his.

"YOU PIECE OF FUCKING SHIT!" I roared, gripping his head and slamming it onto the ground.

His body immediately went lax. I didn't falter, I straddled his waist, punching him in the face repeatedly. One fist after the other connected with his mangled face.

"AUSTIN, NO! STOP!" Briggs screamed, bloody murder.

I ignored her and continued my assault on the fat fuck's face and body. Beating him within inch of his life. Showing him no fucking mercy.

I felt Briggs' hands, ripping at my shirt trying to pry me off of him. I could hear her screaming, but the rage was too strong. The fat fuck wanted her to show up alone because he wanted to fucking rape her. He wanted to hurt what was mine. That's why he wanted me to leave.

"AUSTIN, STOP! PLEASE!"

I don't know if it was the drugs that were coursing through my system or the fact that she didn't give a fuck that he was disrespecting her in front of me. Or it may have been that Martinez put her in this goddamn situation in the first place. Where she could have ended up raped or so help me God something fucking worse.

But I stopped and stood up.

"Who's the cocksucker now, motherfucker?"

Pulling out my gun, I aimed it directly in front of his fucking face.

Briggs

It was like Deja vu.

For a second I thought I was fifteen years old and back in my room. Witnessing that hell all over again. Except this time it wasn't my ruthless, corrupt, murdering uncle.

This was Austin.

My Austin.

He looked fucking crazed. I had never seen him like that before, and it was scary as hell.

"Austin…" I coaxed, gently settling my hand over his that was still placed on the gun. "Give me the gun. You're not a murderer. Now, give me the gun."

"What do you think he was going to fucking do if you had shown up by yourself? Why do you think he wanted me to leave? Huh?" he argued with a dark tone in his voice I'd never heard before.

"It doesn't matter. You were here. Now, put the gun away or give it to me."

He peered back and forth between us.

"Austin, we have like five minutes to get the fuck out of here before this place is swarming with cops or worse, his men. I guarantee you there are cameras in this fucking warehouse. We need to go," I ordered. "Now get your shit together and put away your damn gun. You already did plenty of damage."

He took a deep breath and placed the gun back in his holster. I breathed a sigh of relief.

"Come on." I grabbed his hand, pulling him with me. Austin spit in his face before he came with me.

We ran out to the car. He put it in drive before I even had a chance to close my door.

"Jesus Christ, Austin!" I screamed, smacking my hands on the dashboard. "You have no fucking idea what you've just done. You don't know who you just fucked with."

And I wasn't talking about Hector.

He just drove ignoring my statement, white knuckling the steering wheel. His hands were still bloody from the brutal assault, and I resisted the urge to ask him if he was okay.

We got stuck in over an hour-and-a-half of traffic, a horrible car accident blocking up all the roads. Which only made me dwell more on the fact of what I knew would come of this. By the time we made it back to the hotel room I had the worst feeling in the pit of my stomach. I knew the worst was still yet to come, and his name was Alejandro Martinez. And that scared me more than anything. I wasn't ready for any of it.

How the fuck could Austin do this?

"We got to go," I rambled, running inside, grabbing as many clothes as I saw lying around our disaster of a room. "You have no idea what shit storm you just created."

He gripped my arm, stopping me.

"Are you fucking kidding me, Briggs? Do you honestly think I would ever let someone talk to you like that? In front of me! What the fuck were you doing provoking him like that? What kind of man do you think I am? I would never fucking let anything happen to you! What the fuck do you think was going to happen had I not been there?"

I shook my head, ignoring his question about provoking Hector. That's just the way it was with my uncle's friends. It was meaningless bullshit banter.

"No, Austin. My unc—" I stopped myself from revealing the truth.

He cocked his head to the side with a glare in his eyes that said he already knew something was up.

"Your what, Briggs? Finish that fucking sentence," he gritted out.

217

"Her uncle."

I immediately shut my eyes, hearing my uncle's voice as he walked into the living room from the balcony in the other room. Stopping when he was standing right next to us.

"I suggest you let go of my niece's arm before I remove it for you."

"Uncle," I murmured, opening my eyes to look deep into his.

His cold, dark eyes didn't waver from Austin's. And Austin didn't cower down either, but he let go of my arm.

"Your uncle?" Austin roared in a tone that I knew my uncle wouldn't appreciate. "He's your fucking uncle? Oh my God... I'm such a fucking idiot."

He backed away from me, immediately taking his warmth, his comfort, his love with him.

The air was so thick between us I could hardly breathe. My heart was pounding and my mind was spinning.

"No shit," Uncle spewed. "What the fuck was that back there?"

Austin was over to him in three strides, getting right in front of my uncle's face. I stood back and watched in terror. No one stood up to him and if they did, they were now six feet under.

No one crossed him.

Period.

My uncle didn't even blink. Remaining the solid man he always was behind the expensive suit.

Austin sized him up and down with an intense look like he had lost his goddamn mind.

I swallowed, hard.

Waiting.

"I was doing my job. Protecting *your* niece, seeing as you don't give a fuck about her safety."

There was no reaction from my uncle.

Not one.

It was then that I saw it... there was a war raging in his eyes.

I just didn't know if it was in our favor.

Uncle suddenly cocked his head to the side, taking Austin in for the first time.

"You want to step up to me, Austin Taylor?" Uncle coaxed in a calm tone, like right before a snake kills. "I protect what's mine.

You want to question that? Then I'll be sure to send you Hector's cock on a silver fucking platter."

My eyes widened not expecting his response.

He killed Hector?

"It was my warehouse. Next time you decide to pull this shit. Finish the fucking job. I don't like wiping up shit, especially if it didn't come out of my own fucking ass," Uncle warned.

I looked back and forth between them. My eyes couldn't focus on either one of them for very long.

"No one fucks with me, Austin. And if you don't step the fuck back, you will find out why."

"Austin…" I grabbed his arm, hoping it would help.

It took him a second to gain control. He slowly backed away not taking his stare off my uncle.

"Briggs, next time you want to be a cock tease, make sure it's not with someone who actually wants to fuck you. I've taught you better than that," he warned, stepping toward me until he was right in front of my face. Narrowing his eyes at me.

"Judging from this filthy fucking room and the amount of drugs spread out on the table," he paused, letting his words linger. "I'm going to assume that neither one of you were in the right state of mind today. Which tells me I need to re-evaluate your place in my fucking business. Pack your shit. You're coming home with me."

He looked over at Austin and sneered, "You're not fucking invited."

Austin opened his mouth to say something, but I interrupted him, "I'm not going anywhere without him. He goes where I go and vice versa, Uncle."

I could see it in his eyes, he wanted to tell me no. He wanted to order me around like I was still the little girl that lived under his penthouse roof.

"We're going back to my apartment. I'm not going back to *your* home," I simply stated.

I fucking hated that penthouse.

It wasn't my home.

It never was.

He leaned in close to my face. "We're done playing it your way, peladita," he breathed out. Turning around he left.

219

Crave Me

Leaving me to wonder what the hell he just meant by that.

CHAPTER 22

AUSTIN

It had been three days since we flew back to New York and we had yet to talk about what happened in Colombia. To be completely honest, we barely talked at all. I was still pissed about the situation and how everything went down. The fact that she never fucking told me that Martinez was her uncle. Not that I ever asked, but who the hell would ask something like that. It never even crossed my mind to find out anything about him.

He was irrelevant.

The signs were all there. I just didn't pick up on them. That pissed me off more than anything.

I was too caught up trying to find out her real name.

As luck would have it Martinez was in Colombia because Hector had personally asked for Briggs to take the meeting. Which had never happened before. Martinez had a feeling and that was why he set it up in his warehouse. If shit went down, he would know about it. Briggs was never in danger.

I wanted to ask her all sorts of damn questions, but she seemed so fucking lost in her own head. As if she didn't know what to do with her life now. Like her uncle had taken everything away from her. I finally realized that this wasn't just a job for her.

This was her life.

It was all she'd ever known.

She barely talked to me other than small banter about what I wanted to eat for dinner and meaningless conversations, never addressing the elephant in the room. She hadn't smiled or laughed once since we arrived back in New York.

It was killing me not seeing her face light up. The only time I felt close to her in the last few days was when we were in bed. She still let me hold her every night.

I woke up from a bad dream about my family. I never dreamt about them. It was the worst feeling, the worst fucking anxiety and I didn't know why. I summed it up to being worried about Briggs and overwhelmed with everything that had gone down recently.

When Briggs left the apartment that morning to go grab the mail from the mailroom, I found myself grabbing her computer. Every once in a while I would check the online Oak Island newspaper and something told me that I needed to.

I clicked it.

After three years of being gone, there before my very own eyes was the headline news.

Savannah Ryder, beloved wife of Dr. Robert Ryder, esteemed member of the community dies at age forty-nine, losing her four-year long battle to breast cancer.

My heart dropped.

I couldn't fucking breathe.

The ground beneath me swallowed my body whole.

She will be laid to rest at noon today at the...

I immediately shut the laptop unable to keep staring at the truth that was blatantly in front of my eyes. I don't know how long I stood there with my emotions bleeding out of me. Trying to come to terms with the fact that I didn't get to say goodbye to a woman who had raised me like her own.

A woman I was proud to call a second mom.

I wished I had kept in touch with her. I hadn't felt homesick up to that point, but the news hit me hard. It was a reality slap that made me doubt some of my choices.

I couldn't stop the tears that formed in my eyes. The pain in my heart was ripping at my soul and eating me alive.

I faintly heard Briggs open the door and walk in with the mail, it was like I was there but I wasn't. The emotions crippling me in ways I had never experienced before, not even after the accident. The guilt was too much to bear.

"Hey, I'm going to make some food. Did you want—" She stopped dead in her tracks, taking in my appearance. "Austin..." she coaxed, walking toward me. "What's wrong? Are you okay?"

Our eyes locked.

I didn't have a chance to register her face. I just pushed off the island and walked past her to grab my suitcase. Throwing it on the bed, grabbing random shit from my closet.

"Austin, are you leaving me?"

Her worried tone snapped me out of the chaos surrounding me that was taking me under.

"Never," I simply stated. "Baby, grab some shit. We got to go."

"Go? Go where? What are you talking about? You're scaring me, Austin."

I didn't falter. "Home. I got to go home."

Her head jerked back, stunned by my revelation. I told her I had no one to go home to, and I knew that was one of the reasons she agreed to let me come with her in the first place.

We never talked about my past.

Not my parents.

Not the boys.

Not even Alex.

They didn't exist in my new life. Out of sight, out of mind for the most part. Which was about to come back and bite me in the fucking ass.

There I was about to take her home to my truths, the ones I had been running away from for the last three years. At that moment, in that second, I didn't care about the repercussions that would follow from her learning my reality.

I needed her.

More now than I ever had before. She was my rock, my reason. The one thing that was constant in my life.

There was no way in hell I could do this without her.

She was all that mattered to me.

"Home? I thought—"

"Baby, we don't have time for this. We need to go if we're going to make it."

"Make it? What exactly are we making? Are you on something right now? You're not making any sense," she asked even more confused.

"The funeral."

Her eyes widened.

I shook my head, walking back to the closet to change into some black slacks and a black collared, button-down shirt.

"Baby, please…" I urged as I was throwing my slacks on, not looking at her but feeling her stare.

There would be too much hurt evident on her face, and I was already feeling that enough deep within my core. I watched her finally move, going into the closet to change and pack some clothes.

It didn't take us long to get to the airport. I broke so many traffic laws on our way there, I just wanted to board that plane and get there. I was lucky enough to find us tickets on a flight departing within the hour. I wasn't taking any chances. We didn't talk the entire two-hour flight, but at one point she reached over and held my hand. Still intently staring out the window from her seat. As soon as the seat belt light turned off, I got up to use the bathroom on the plane. Feeling sick to my fucking stomach with what I was about to walk into.

I grabbed the Oxy's from my pocket crushing them up on the small metal counter with a credit card. I didn't want to feel any of the shit that was going on around me.

It was like I was drowning in the deep end of a pool that had no water.

I. Couldn't. Fucking. Breathe.

The agony I felt was more severe than any pain in my back could ever be. I rolled up a bill and snorted the contents up my nose, not wanting to wait more than I had to for them to kick in and numb the pain.

It was alive and thriving all around me.

We landed at ten-thirty, getting to the hotel by almost eleven-thirty where we checked in and left our luggage to be taken up to our room. By the time we hailed a cab, it was well after noon.

We were late.

"Daisy," I murmured, staring out the window of the taxi.

I never called her that. I could see her glancing at me in the reflection on the glass. Worry written clear across her beautiful face.

"I would never intentionally hurt you. Please remember that."

She opened her mouth to say something but quickly shut it, looking back out her window. We weren't more than a foot apart in the backseat, but it felt like miles of distance were placed between us.

Physically and mentally.

We pulled up to the cemetery around one. I paid the driver, and we got out of the car. It was the moment of truth. My heart was pounding out of my fucking chest. I grabbed Briggs' hand, needing to feel her.

The funeral was over but there were still people scattered around. I didn't pay attention to anyone, too focused on the grave that we were walking toward. Grabbing a single rose from one of the several floral arrangements, I finally made my way to her grave.

I bowed my head, closing my eyes. The pills weren't working. I don't think the strongest drugs in the world could touch the pain in my heart at that moment. I still felt everything.

I hunched over, my legs unable to support my crumbling body. I delicately placed the rose above the engraved beloved mother, burying my face in my hands. I had no idea how long I stayed like that with my grief spilling out of me. Briggs' hands placed on my back, gently rubbing back and forth trying to comfort me.

Not saying a word, not asking any questions, just being there for me in my time of need.

I could have been kneeling there for a minute or an hour. Time seemed to standstill but the pain seemed to keep going on all around me.

I wiped my face before I stood. Briggs grabbed my hand as I locked eyes with Lucas who was maybe thirty feet away. His gaze took me in, no longer the boy I was when I left. Now a man covered in tattoos with more guilt to add to his never-ending list.

"Austin," Alex called out, running towards me.

I smiled for the first time in three fucking days, turning toward her voice. I let go of Briggs hand, catching Alex in my arms.

"Half-Pint," I greeted, immediately picking her up off her feet, swinging her side-to-side.

It felt so damn good to hold her.

"It's so good to see you," she wept, still hugging me tight.

"Shhh… don't cry," I whispered in her ear.

"I know it's just been a really rough few weeks."

I nodded, feeling even more like a piece of shit for not being here for her.

I placed her back down on the ground, wrapping my arm around Briggs' waist, who suddenly seemed frozen in place. I was sure this was all too overwhelming for her.

"Alex, this is my girlfriend Briggs. Briggs this is one of my best friends, Alex."

Half-Pint smiled, shaking Briggs' hand who still hadn't said a word.

"Everyone is going to be so happy to see you," Alex said.

"Everyone?" Briggs chimed in, talking for the first time since I told her we were going to a funeral.

"Of course. His family and friends have missed him all these years," Alex unknowingly added.

I kissed Briggs' cheek and tried to turn her chin towards me, but she snapped her head back. She wouldn't look at me, and that hurt more than anything.

We made our way toward Lucas when I realized that he still fucking hated me, maybe even more than ever before. I couldn't blame him.

I hated myself more now too.

I still hadn't seen my parents.

We went back to Alex's parents' restaurant. It was so fucking surreal. I never thought I'd be back here, at least not anytime soon. I exchanged hugs with Jacob and Dylan, catching up on random bullshit, almost like I had never left. We didn't talk about the past or the last time we saw each other.

It was pointless. Too much had happened. In all of our lives.

I introduced them to Briggs, but she didn't say much, just nodded and shook the boy's hands. She had barely said more than a handful of words the entire day, and I knew why. As much as I wanted to work it out with her right then and there, I couldn't. She went to get us some food while everyone was sharing memories of Lucas' mom on the stage where they usually had a live band playing.

The boys were all standing by the stage about to take their seats to listen to the rest of the eulogies. I was up next. I needed to say my peace and my official goodbye. I would forever regret not being able to give her a proper goodbye, I wish I could have seen her face one more time.

"You probably think this is my fucking karma, huh?" Lucas asked, when he saw me walking up to them.

"You gotta be shittin' me right?" I replied, taken aback.

"Lucas, relax, it's not the time—"

"What the fuck do you know, McGraw? Your mom's not the one that's six feet under," Lucas interrupted with a look of disgust.

"She was a mom to us all," I reminded.

"So much of a fucking mom to you that you're just now showing up, right? Makes sense. Go up there, Austin. Make your speech. Should help with the guilt." Lucas scoffed out.

"That's enough," Jacob ordered, only peering at him.

"Speaking of guilt. How's your kid Lucas?" I blurted, regretting it immediately. I shook my head disappointed in myself. "Fuck, man, I didn't—"

He left, not giving me a chance to apologize.

"I didn't mean that," I informed, needing them to hear it anyway.

"We're all hurting, Austin. You take it out on the ones you care about the most. He knows that," Jacob said, patting my back.

I nodded, making my way to the stage. Everyone turned to look at me.

Briggs had already been staring at us for a while. Her eyes went from me to them, back to me again. I took a deep breath, trying to focus on why I was really there.

"I knew that she was sick, and I wish I could have been back sooner. I would give anything right now to talk to her one last time. It's no one's fault but my own. I found out this morning that she had lost her battle with cancer. I never thought she wouldn't make it." I cleared my throat, rubbing the back of my neck before putting my hands in my pockets, trying to keep my voice from breaking. "She was one of the strongest women I have ever known. I grew up with Lucas and the rest of the boys, including our Half-Pint."

Alex smiled at me, her eyes gathering with tears.

"Savannah was like a mom to us all. It's just who she was." I shrugged. "One of the best memories I have with her was when I was eight. Savannah made all of our Teenage Mutant Ninja Turtle costumes for Halloween. Alex was Splinter, our sensei." I chuckled, nodding to her. "Savannah had spent over a week making those costumes. They were all sold out at the stores by the time we stopped arguing who would be what Ninja Turtle. I was Leonardo. You know, the coolest one... he had swords."

Everyone laughed. The boys sat there shaking their heads at me. I smiled, remembering the memory as if it happened yesterday.

"It was Halloween, and we were playing in the lake. Jumping off the trees to land in the water. I always had to one up the boys. I was the youngest and the smallest back then. Alex begged me not to do it. She said she had a bad feeling, but I didn't listen. I climbed the highest tree and ended up breaking my leg from landing wrong in a shallow area and hitting the bottom hard. After getting yelled at by Alex first, of course. Then the boys. Then my parents. Then the boy's parents..." I scoffed out a chuckle.

"I had to go to the emergency room, where we spent most of the night. The boys and Alex ended up going out trick or treating without me. Being eight years old, it was devastating that I missed it. The turtles weren't complete without the coolest one. When everyone came to visit me the next day to sign my cast, all they talked about was how much of a hit their costumes were and how much candy they got because of it. Except for Alex, she knew I was pretending like it didn't bother me. That I wasn't upset that I missed out on it. Half-Pint always knows everything."

The boys and I peered over at her. They all knew I was right.

"They went downstairs to eat lunch that my mom made for us. Savannah brought mine up to my room for me. When she came in, I was upset. I was just so sad that I didn't get to go trick or treating with everyone. When I told her that, she promised she wouldn't tell the boys. I remember clear as day as if she was standing right in front of me, right now... She said, 'We will go trick or treating tonight.' I looked at her like she had five heads explaining to her that it was yesterday and it was a once a year thing. I don't know how she did it but she managed to pull it off. She made some phone calls and ended up cutting a slit in the pants of my costume so my cast could fit."

Everyone was crying including Briggs. I was holding back tears as well, bowing my head to keep them from coming out.

"That's just the kind of woman she was. And I'm going to miss her very much. I loved her like she was my second mother, and I will regret for the rest of my life... that I didn't get to say goodbye." I steadied my composure before I looked back up.

Locking eyes with my parents.

Briggs

He lied to me.

He fucking lied to me.

I cried along with everyone else when he was making his speech. My heart broke for him, but that didn't change the fact that he lied to me.

He had a family...

He had friends...

I watched them from the corner of the room before Austin gave his speech. It looked like they were exchanging heated words, but that didn't even matter. I could still see the love behind their eyes. The brotherhood they had.

The more he told his story, his memory, his love for a woman who wasn't even his real mother. The more I realized how much he really did have waiting back at home for him.

He had the childhood I dreamt about, the friendships that I craved, the parents I cried for.

The love I never had.

I left our plates filled with food by the trays not bothering to take it back to our table. I went to the bathroom, pacing back and forth. There was no place for me to go to be alone. The restaurant was packed with people that loved him. He had so much love out there, yet he ran away from it all.

I wanted to fucking scream.

At him.

At myself.

I would have never taken him with me two years ago. I would have never introduced him to this life if I knew he had a home. People who fucking loved him. The guilt was eating me alive and swallowing me whole with no remorse or absolution.

I took a few deep breaths, splashed some water on my face, patted it dry and glanced at myself one last time before walking back into his life.

A life that I didn't belong in.

"Oh, Austin. It's so good to see my boy."

I stopped dead in my tracks, staying behind the wall.

"It's good to see you too, Ma," Austin replied.

I placed my hand on my forehead, leaning my head against the wall. I wasn't ready to listen to this conversation, but it was as if my feet were glued to the goddamn floor.

"Hey, Pop," Austin added in a strained tone.

He had parents that loved him too.

We were nothing alike. I thought he was an orphan like me. I thought we were one in the same. He had everything I always wanted.

"Look at you. Where's my blue-eyed boy?" his mom asked, her voice laced with nothing but love for him.

"He's behind all the tattoos that have now ruined his life even more."

I winced with his dad's response. I was to blame for that too. I couldn't stand around and listen any longer. I pushed off the wall and walked out to the patio, finding a secluded spot toward the side. If it were up to me, I would stay there until we left. I couldn't stand being around his truths any longer. All it did was add to the lie that he told me.

The lie he made me believe.

Two years, two fucking years I'd been with him. Not once had he mentioned a home. The family who loved him. Waiting for him to come back home instead of wasting his life away with me.

His future.

I watched Austin's friend Lucas walk out onto the beach. I could see him, but he couldn't see me. It was his mom that passed away. He stared out at the ocean like he wanted to disappear into the night. Let the waves take him under instead of his emotions. He looked so broken and lost. I remembered feeling that exact same way at my parents' funeral.

It was like your mind and heart were running away but your body was standing in place.

With nowhere to go.

"God, when was the last time we were all together like this?" the girl, Alex asked, pulling me away from my thoughts as she walked out onto the beach to stand next to Lucas.

"Three years," Austin answered, walking up behind her, gently tugging her hair.

The other two boys, Dylan and Jacob quickly followed. They all stood together, each one of them appeared as if they were fighting their own demons. Their own plaguing thoughts.

Especially Austin.

"It's been too fucking long," Jacob chimed in, pulling Alex to his side.

"Jesus… look at those kids surfing. It seems like just yesterday that was us out there," Dylan reminisced, looking at the water with the same sense of longing I felt for Austin, even though he was only a few feet away from me.

"How have we let three years go by without all of us being together? We used to spend every second together," Dylan added.

"I know," Alex breathed out. "I can't tell you how much I miss you boys. God… Austin, it's so good to freaking see you." She strolled from Jacob to him, wrapping her arms around his waist.

Austin kissed the top of her head. "It's nice to be home."

Hearing Austin say those words was like taking a knife to the heart. *Home.* I thought I was his home. The longer I sat there out of sight, the more I realized I didn't know Austin at all. Not like his friends did. It was like he was living a double life.

And I was the outsider looking in.

The boys left, leaving just him and Alex alone together. They sat on the beach in easy silence for a few minutes. Austin pulled her to his side with his arm wrapped around her as she laid her head on his shoulder. Exactly the way he had done to me so many damn times I'd lost count.

I loved being wrapped in his arms. I'd never felt so safe. Alex looked so comfortable, so at ease in his arms. As if she spent most of her childhood there.

The way they looked at each other.

The way they talked to each other.

There was familiarity in his gaze when he peered at her. As if he was staring at me. I recognized it immediately.

At that exact moment I realized why Austin hadn't ever said I love you to me. The truth was playing out in front of me, unfolding

231

before my very own eyes. The home that I built with him out of a deck of cards was crumbling down on me.

He didn't love me...

He. Loved. Her.

I got up.

And left.

CHAPTER
23

AUSTIN

After talking to Alex on the beach, catching up on the last three years, I walked back into the restaurant looking for Briggs. She was nowhere to be found. I checked everywhere, even leaning my head into the women's bathroom calling her name.

I walked back out into the main dining area.

"Austin," Mom coaxed, grabbing my arm to stop me. "Please, honey, don't listen to your father. You look good." She placed her hand on the side of my face. "Handsome. Very handsome. You've done a lot of growing up, haven't you?"

After my dad spewed his venom, I walked away from them. The last thing I wanted to do was start a fight at Savannah's funeral. It wasn't the time or place.

"How are you? From your postcards it seems like you have been all over the world traveling."

I nodded, searching the room for Briggs again.

"With that girl?"

Mom pulled my attention back to her. "Her name is Briggs, Ma."

She lovingly smiled. "I'm so happy you're home. We can—" I put my hand up, stopping her.

"I'm only here for the funeral. My home is in New York now. With Briggs."

She raised her eyebrows. "New York? Are you going to—"

I shook my head no, knowing what she was about to say. "I'm not going to college. I work. I make good money. You don't have to worry about me. I'm happy. Happier than I've ever been."

"As long as you're happy. That's all that has ever mattered to me. Your father—"

"I don't want to talk about him, Ma. I'll try to keep in touch more, I promise. It's good to see you. I've missed you."

"I love you, Austin. No matter what."

"I love you, too."

She kissed my cheek and made her way back to my father's side. We locked eyes from across the room for a few seconds before he shook his head and continued his conversation with Dylan's dad.

I couldn't find Briggs anywhere. I pulled out my cell phone, calling her number. It went straight to voicemail.

"The fuck?" I said to myself.

I looked out at the patio and around the beach. Going back into the restaurant to look around one last time. I told Dylan, Jacob, and Alex I was heading out. Dylan asked me if I was staying around for a bit, and I told him probably not. He nodded in understanding and Half-Pint hugged me again, whispering in my ear not to be a stranger. I nodded.

I called Briggs again while I was in the cab and it went straight to voicemail again. Which only added to my frustration on where the fuck she went.

I walked into our hotel room, starting to panic.

"Briggs?" I yelled out to no avail, looking around the room.

That's when I noticed the sliding glass door to the balcony was cracked open. I found her sitting out there, blankly staring at the ocean.

"What the fuck, babe? I've been looking all over for you. Your phone is going straight to fuckin' voicemail. Why would you leave me like that?"

She didn't even look up at me when she whispered, "You looked fine to me, Austin. I left you with your friends and family. Where you belong."

"Baby…" I coaxed, moving her chair that she was sitting in to crouch down in front of her on the balls of my feet. "Let me explain."

She cocked her head to the side. "Explain what? That you're a fucking liar. That you have lied to me for over two years now."

"I would never lie to you," I simply stated.

She looked me dead in the eyes. "I recall you saying 'I don't have anything to go home to.' Sound familiar?"

"I don't."

"Then we have two very different definitions to that statement, Austin."

"Briggs, listen to me. My family, my friends and I... fuck... it's complicated. What you saw today... There's a lot you don't know."

"No shit."

I jerked back. "It's not like you've been a patent of fucking honesty, Briggs. Or should I call you Daisy Martinez. Your uncle might appreciate that," I snapped.

"My name is Daisy Mitchell. Not Martinez. He was my mom's brother."

"Was?"

She scoffed. "Yeah, Austin. Was... You want to share sad stories? I'll go first. I'm a fucking orphan. The only reason I didn't tell you Martinez was my uncle is because I didn't want you to stop looking at me the way you do. You haven't looked at me the same since you found out. You don't know this life. You don't know what I've seen. What he's capable of. When people realize that I'm related to him, it changes the way they look at me. The way they treat me. The way they act around me. You really think a woman would have been respected the way I was if they didn't know I was his niece."

I took a deep breath, knowing she was right.

"I've lived a very fucked up life. My parents were killed in a car accident when I was six. I still dream about their dead bodies in the car. I still see all the blood, their bodies mangled, glass shattered everywhere. I still remember the last thing I told them, telling them I hated them."

A single tear fell down her face. I just sat there shocked as shit with what she had just revealed, knowing she wasn't even done yet. Never in a million years did I expect her to say those things.

She held it together, never once making me think she was that broken over the last two years.

"I still hear my own voice, yelling at them, begging them to hold me. To comfort me. Pleading with them to wake up. Not understanding why they wouldn't. I still remember waking up in a hospital next to me a man I'd never met before. A man with cold, dark eyes and no soul with an expensive suit. A man who never held me, never told me he loved me, never consoled me when I woke up screaming in the middle of the night."

Her tears fell freely now, one right after the other.

"The first time I saw someone murdered, it was on my fifteenth birthday. It was my uncle's gift to me. What a sick fuck right? He killed the driver of the car that took away my life. Right in front of my eyes. His blood is on my hands now. To this day I still feel his brains and skull all over me," she wept, her breathing becoming erratic.

"Baby." I reached out for her, and she harshly pushed me away.

"Oh come on, Austin... I'm just sharing my sad story. It's what you've always wanted, right? For me to tell you my truths," she bellowed, her voice breaking with each word.

"Esteban was my only friend, and he wasn't even a friend. He was paid to protect me. He took my virginity, the same night my uncle took the little bit of innocence I had left."

"Jesus Christ," I breathed out.

"My uncle found us. He beat him within an inch of his life. His men dragged him out of the room. For the last five years I didn't even know if he was dead or alive. I've been a Martinez since that night. Daisy Mitchell died with her parents in the car."

She shook her head, willing away the memories. Knowing it was no use. They were etched in her soul as much as my scars were carved on my skin.

"Your favorite tattoo, Austin... I got it done a month after I became a Martinez. I dropped out of school and started dealing drugs. I saw the world through his eyes. And I fucking hated it. I walked into the parlor already knowing what I wanted. I had it all drawn out. The pin up girl, Austin, it's me. I have an angel and devil on my shoulders. My uncle and my mom," she bawled.

I couldn't take it anymore. I immediately pulled her into my arms, holding her as tight as I could. Trying to keep her heart from breaking into pieces right in front of me.

"Shhh..." I murmured. "Shhh... You will never be alone again. You won't ever be scared again. I'm here, baby, and I'm not going anywhere. We're best friends, remember?" I added, trying to lighten the mood.

She shook her head, pulling away from me. Looking deep in my eyes.

"You have enough best friends, Austin. I witnessed your relationships today. So don't make promises you can't keep."

"Briggs, I—"

"How long, Austin?"

I frowned, not understanding what she was implying.

She didn't falter.

"How long have you been in love with your best friend? How long have you been in love with Alex?"

Briggs

"Is that why? Is she why you left Oak Island? What am I, the rebound girl?" I asked, needing to know.

"No, baby. You're the only fucking girl for me."

"Don't lie to me again. That's bullshit."

"I'm not lying to you. I don't have anything here for me. I never did. That's the reason why I left. My relationship with my parents... with my dad, with the boys... it's... I love them, don't get me wrong. I would be there for them at the drop of a dime. Even Lucas, and he fucking hates me. I left because I almost killed Alex in a car accident. I drove drunk and raced a friend through the fucking woods. We hit a tree, Briggs. I was in a coma for a week. Alex was in a coma for a few days too. You've seen my scars. I had to have brain surgery. I suffered several broken bones and was in physical therapy for months. Shit went downhill fast after that. Especially my friendship with the boys."

I took in every word he was saying. Finally hearing his truths, his sad story.

"My parents want me to be something I'm not. They always have. They have never accepted me for who I wanted to be, and it's a big part of why it took me so long to figure out who that person was. I've always felt like I wasn't good enough, I wasn't smart enough, I just wasn't enough. Alex and I have always been the closest. I think it's because we're really similar in the sense that we have always just wanted to be one of the good ol' boys. She didn't even start wearing girl clothes till she was almost eleven. Thinking she was one of us since the day she could fucking crawl. She's always been there for me. No matter what. She was there. Somewhere along the way I confused that relationship, and I thought I loved her. I thought she was the one. Up until I met you... I still thought that."

He kissed the tip of my nose, hugging me closer to his body.

"And you're right, she's part of the reason I left. Lucas and Alex are meant to be together. I've always known that. I think a huge part of me just wanted a connection with someone. To feel loved and accepted. I never had that before you. From the second I laid eyes on you, I wanted to know every last thing about you. Everything I thought I felt for Alex didn't even come close to what I feel for you. The night we met, the night I had my first conversation with the girl who had purple hair and tattoos, I realized how wrong I was, how I had misinterpreted my feelings for Alex.

"You know why, Daisy? Because the day you walked into my life I started living again. *You* gave me a reason to start living again instead of just surviving."

I smiled.

And it felt like forever since I had last done it. He grabbed my expression in the air and placed it near his heart. Grabbing the sides of my face, looking deep into my eyes.

"I love you. Daisy Mitchell. Briggs Martinez. I'm so fucking in love with you."

I bit my lip, my eyes filling with tears again.

"You will never be alone again."

I nodded, fresh tears falling down my face. He kissed them all, wiping them away with his lips. Then he kissed me again.

"I fucking love you," he repeated against my mouth.

He picked me up off the chair, grabbing me by my ass. I wrapped my legs around his waist. We kissed fervently as he carried me to the bed. Gently placing me on top of the mattress, with his body lying on top of mine. He took his time savoring me, making slow, passionate love to me all night long.

There wasn't an inch of my skin that he didn't touch, kiss, or lick. There wasn't a moan or pant left for me to voice after he thoroughly made love to me the way we wanted.

The way we both needed.

I was lying in his arms, kissing the scar near his heart. He was covered in ink now, but it was the only one I wouldn't let him get a tattoo over.

It was my scar.

It belonged to me.

I peered up at him with loving eyes and whispered,

"I love you, too."

CHAPTER
24

AUSTIN

We decided to stay around Oak Island for a few more days.

I showed her all the spots the boys, Alex, and I used to go and cause trouble at. Sharing a part of my world with her. I even took her to the dock where I used to go to be alone and draw. By the time we made it there, it was already nightfall. We sat at the edge of the wooden planks with our feet splashing in the water, like I had done so many damn times as a kid, getting lost in my own thoughts.

Something came over me and I pulled Briggs in front of me to straddle my lap. It was hotter than Hell out, and she was wearing a dress. I slipped my cock through the zipper of my jeans and slid her panties over. Lifting her just enough to thrust my dick inside of her. She let out a loud moan that echoed off the water.

We made love just like that. I wanted nothing more than to make new memories with her there. To replace all the sad ones from my childhood.

We didn't hangout with the boys, Alex, or my parents. I had enough emotional bullshit to last me a lifetime. I didn't need them causing more drama around Briggs. I just wanted to make new memories with her in a town I'd spent the last three years running away from.

I loved every second of it.

I even tried to show her how to surf, but the second she saw a shark she flew the fuck off the board and said there was no way in hell she was getting back on it. She laid out on the beach reading instead, while I surfed the entire day.

It was like I was reliving the best parts of my childhood all over again. Except the love of my life was right there with me. The way it was always supposed to be.

I was paying for it though. By the time we got back to the hotel my back was fucking killing me. I took down two more Oxy's and smoked a joint with Briggs on the balcony. How the girl found a drug dealer in Oak Island while I was out surfing was beyond me.

We landed back in New York the next evening.

"It's good to be home. I miss my bed," Briggs said, putting the key into the lock of her apartment.

"I miss fucking you in your bed."

She grinned, turning to face me.

"Our bed," she simply stated with a huge smile on her face.

I leaned in and kissed her lips.

"Our bed," I repeated, pushing her back against the door, kissing her hard and deep as she fumbled to get the door open.

I heard the lock release. I walked forward not breaking our connection as she walked backwards into the apartment. My hand immediately went to her panties, reaching inside to touch her pussy.

"Jesus Christ, you can't even keep your fingers off my niece's pussy long enough to walk through the goddamn door!"

"Uncle!" Briggs shrieked, shoving me away to pull down her dress.

"You're lucky it was my fingers and not my tongue. Knock on the fucking door next time before you make yourself at home in our apartment," I spewed, pissed that he was there unannounced and uninvited.

He cocked his head to the side, arching an eyebrow. "Our?"

"Did I stutter?"

"Austin…" Briggs coaxed, gently placing her hand on my chest, trying to get me to back down.

Martinez didn't scare me.

"This isn't even her apartment. It's mine. I pay for it. Briggs, how about the next time you ask someone to move in, they are aware of who fucking owns it first."

"There won't be a next time. I'll start paying for it. Just tell me who to make the check out to," I said, not cowering down.

I really hated this fucker and everything he stood for, including all the shit Briggs told me she went through because of him. How the man couldn't fucking hug her or console her as a child. Why he couldn't tell her that he loved her was beyond me. I couldn't imagine being a child raised in the middle of this lifestyle.

It was something I couldn't fucking fathom.

He grinned, narrowing his eyes at me. Contemplating what he was about to say. He looked back and forth between us before his stare settled on Briggs.

"I've decided to make some changes. You want him involved in every aspect of your life, peladita? I can't stop you… but I'm personally over the fact that you're spreading your legs for the goddamn help again."

I stepped toward him, and Briggs held me back.

He scoffed, standing. Placing his hands in the pockets of his slacks. He rounded the corner of the island unfazed. Stopping about a foot away from us. Briggs stood right in the middle, waiting to intervene if needed.

"Since you're so fucking involved in my business and what's mine," he paused, looking at Briggs, "including this apartment, I've decided to promote you."

"No!" Briggs yelled, stepping toward him between us. "You can't fucking do this, Uncle! I won't let you. He's not—"

"Baby, I don't need you to answer for me," I sneered, pulling her aside to stand in front of Martinez.

Man to fucking man.

His eyes glazed over. It was quick, but I saw it.

"What you did in Colombia took some fucking balls. I can appreciate a man that protects what he thinks is his. You would have shot Hector in the fucking face had Briggs not stopped you. Without even batting an eye, I know you would have pulled the fucking trigger. I was ten when I had my first taste of blood. I murdered a man point blank, protecting what I thought was also mine."

"Uncle, please… don't do this," Briggs whispered, her head bowed with an expression I couldn't see.

"I don't need both of you. Austin here," he nodded toward me, "is now in charge."

"What?" I replied, confused.

"You want to be boss man? Well then here's your fucking chance."

Briggs

I knew my uncle was going to do this.

The second he told me that he was done playing it my way…

From the moment Austin put the goddamn gun to Hector's head, I fucking knew my uncle's dark cold eyes would dilate. He would see an investment, something of value to him.

Something that was mine.

He would see a different side of the man that I had been trying so desperately not to change. Not to let this life take over. The man that would do anything to protect me, the man that if given the chance would thrive on the power, the respect, the goddamn lifestyle that I hated with everything inside of me.

The man that he could control.

I would have never brought him into this life if I'd known he had a home to go back to. I should have left him back in Oak Island where he belonged. I should have saved him from my uncle. Protected him like he protected me.

But leaving him wasn't an option.

I love him.

The mere thought of not being with him every day was too much to bear. I knew I was being selfish, but I was finally happy for the first time in my life since... At the end of the day Austin was a grown ass man, and all I could do was standby and watch it happen.

Praying to God that it wouldn't change him. That he wouldn't turn into what my uncle wanted me to become.

My worst nightmare.

"You want me to take over Briggs' job? I can't do that to her," Austin stated with a sincere tone, shaking his head.

My eyes lit up, glancing over at him, thinking I won. That this may lean in my favor.

"I could never take this away from her. It's—"

"She will be right there with you. Won't you, Briggs?"

My uncle locked eyes with me.

I spoke too soon. I glared at him. I loved Austin too much to ever leave his side. Especially when it came to this life. Uncle knew I wouldn't say no. He knew he had me right where he wanted me. Austin was his ticket to my soul.

"He doesn't know what—"

"And that's why you'll teach him. I'll have someone else take over the traveling for the time being. He will run New York with you. Look at it this way, he will have plenty of time to fuck you in your own bed," he mocked, interrupting me from the pitiful excuses I had.

It was the first time in over fifteen years, after everything he had put me through, made me see, made me experience, that I wanted to tell him that I...

Fucking. Hated. Him.

Uncle's phone rang, breaking through my plaguing thoughts. He grabbed it out of his suit pocket. Putting a finger out in front of him before he turned answering the phone.

"Habla," he ordered, "*Talk*," walking out onto the balcony, shutting the door behind him.

Austin grabbed my chin, making me look up at him instead.

"I don't want you to do this," I blurted, unable to hold back my emotions.

He jerked back, offended. "What? You don't think I can do it?"

"I don't want you to do it," I repeated with a stern tone that time.

"So, it's good enough for you but not for me? Is that what you're saying?"

"I don't want you in this life." I roughly pulled my face out of his grasp.

"Look at me. It's a little too late for that, Briggs. It's your life, and now I'm a part of it. At least this way I won't have to worry about your safety anymore."

"What about yours?" I countered.

"You don't think I can handle myself, baby?"

"There's a lot more that goes into this lifestyle than what I've been showing you. I've kept you in the dark for a reason. You don't know what the fuck you're getting involved in. You're signing your life away to the devil, and you don't even fucking realize it."

"As long as it keeps you by my side. I don't give a flying fuck where my life goes."

"You don't know what you're saying. You have a family and friends back home. What about them?"

I was trying anything and everything to get him to open his eyes and see the picture clearly.

"I don't give a fuck about anyone but you, Briggs. All I know is this gig makes a shit ton of money. I know that it keeps you in the lifestyle that you're used to. I can't give you this life without him, do you understand?"

I shook my head. "I don't care about any of that. Fuck the money, fuck this apartment, and fuck him," I viciously spewed, pointing to the balcony.

"I care!" he argued. "None of this belongs to you, Briggs. I can do this for a few years, and I can set us up. We can get married, get a house, have you barefoot and pregnant in our kitchen." He grinned and my heart melted.

He was saying everything I wanted to hear. Everything I ever wanted.

A home.

A life.

A family.

Us.

He stepped toward me, grabbing my chin again to look deep into my eyes.

"I love you. Trust me. I know what I'm doing. Let me take care of you. That's all I've ever wanted to do."

I took a deep breath. My resolve fading.

"Austin... I don't—"

"I would never lie to you. I promise it will only be for a few years, baby. That's all I need to give you your dream. To give you a happy life." He grabbed the sides of my face, caressing my cheeks with his thumbs. "I want to marry you, Daisy. I want the white picket fence. The three kids I plan to knock you up with. The dog. The cat. The whole nine yards, baby. I want to give you the life that you deserve. No more sad stories. Only happy ones from here on out."

"I want all that too," I whispered.

My uncle walked back in from the balcony. Austin kissed the tip of my nose, murmuring, "You're my girl." Then he turned to face him.

I would forever remember this moment for the rest of my life. Two words. Two simple words.

"I'm in."

Since the death of my parents…

Austin was the first place I ever called home.

He was also the first person to ever destroy it.

CHAPTER 25

AUSTIN

"I'm in."

Two words that changed my entire life two and a half years ago, Briggs was right. I had no fucking idea what I was getting myself into. There was so much that happened behind closed doors that she never introduced me to. That she never told me about for whatever reason. I was her bodyguard for over two years before I took over and became boss man. After being in this lifestyle you would think I'd have experience, but I felt like I hadn't learned one fucking thing. That I was seeing everything for the first time through new eyes, a completely different outlook on life and everything it had to offer.

The power. The respect. The money.

The drugs...

Jesus Christ, the fucking drugs.

When Briggs was in charge and we were traveling it was all about the meetings, the locations, the shipments, the costs, the quantities, and how to import it into the US. It was very rare that we saw or handled the actual drugs that she was trafficking. Unless we were partying, they weren't really around. Except the pain pills and weed I had on me constantly.

But now...

They weren't ever *not* around.

Briggs walked in with groceries in her hands. My girl had become domesticated since she had all the time in the world to do what she wanted. She hadn't gone on runs with me in well over a year. It was better to have her stay home. I didn't have to worry about her safety that way. I could handle my business and come home to her.

The best part of my day was coming to home to her.

Even after almost five years of being together, she still took my goddamn breath away. On several occasions I would come home and she would have Spanish music blaring through the speakers. Her hips and body swayed to the beat while she cooked our dinner. She looked sexy as fuck. I would stand there and watch her move in a way only Briggs could. So addicted to the sight of her dancing that I knew no one else had ever seen. I'd stand out of view, waiting until the song was over before I'd carry her to the closest place, where I would have my way with her. Ordering her to say dirty things to me in Spanish before I'd make her come with my tongue, my fingers, and my fucking cock.

"Baby, come try this shit," I stated, snorting another line from the new shipment of blow we received that morning.

My boys Jon and Mitch were sitting on the couch across from me, smoking a blunt. They worked for Martinez too, and we became friends about a year ago. It was easier to have friends that lived in this lifestyle. I didn't have to hide what I did or who I was.

It made things simple.

Briggs walked into the living room, cocking her head to the side. "How many times do I have to tell you? I don't get high off my own stash."

"Technically, it's mine," I replied, leaning back into the couch letting the blow take over me.

The distinct taste of the drip running down the back of my throat was the best fucking part. She shook her head in disappointment, walking out onto the balcony.

I sighed, getting up to go follow her out there.

"Go show her who's boss," Jon laughed.

I flipped him off, grabbing her birthday present that I'd hid under the bed. She was turning twenty-four the next day, and I wanted it to be perfect. I put a lot of thought into my gift. I planned on spending the entire day with her, but that wouldn't happen if I didn't straighten this shit out now.

I knew why she was pissed.

Briggs was leaning against the railing, already lost in thought. Even though she had just stepped out there not even a minute ago. It was happening a lot more lately, which only meant I had to work extra hard to make her smile for me. She didn't really acknowledge me when I walked out, shutting the double doors behind me.

I lit a cigarette, making my way over to her. Sliding her hair to the side to kiss the back of her neck like I knew she loved.

"Austin…"

"What, baby?" I rasped, turning her to face me.

"You said you weren't going to get high today. Remember last night you said—"

"Was that before or after I made you come on my cock?" I asked, kissing along her neck.

"That's not fair," she replied, pushing me off.

I took a drag of my cigarette, blowing it out to the side. I caged her in with my arms, placing my hands on the railing. She still hadn't noticed the gift in my hands, she was obviously too pissed off at me to care.

"Hey." I kissed the tip of her nose. "I love you." I kissed her cheeks and all over her face. "Where's my girl? Hmm… where's my Daisy?"

On her birthday last year, I tattooed a key over my heart with the name Daisy engraved on it. I surprised her with it later that night in bed when she was touching the scar near my heart like she did every night.

I kissed her lips, beckoning her to open them for me. When she finally did, I groaned into her mouth, and she smiled against mine. Her resolve was breaking. She could never stay mad at me.

We loved each other too much.

"I got you something, birthday girl."

She smirked. "My birthday's tomorrow. You trying to butter me up, Austin?"

"Depends. Is it working?"

I stepped back, taking another drag off my cigarette before snubbing it out in the ashtray. Then handing her the gift.

"I see you wrapped it yourself," she teased, making fun of my shitty attempt.

She tore open the package. Her eyes widening once she pulled out the blanket.

"Oh my God," she whispered, her eyes immediately filling with tears.

She took in every last square of the memory blanket that I'd had specially made for her. There was a picture of her mom, her dad, and her as a baby. A few family shots scattered around. There was a photo of us that was taken in Oak Island and daisies to fill in the spaces between. The rest were my sketches, her favorite pictures that I drew. She ran her fingers over all the pictures, tears falling down on them.

"It's for when I work late and you're alone. I know you hate it. I know you worry, even though you have nothing to be scared about. But now, you can wait for me wrapped up in this blanket and feel safe and secure until I come home to you."

She peered up at me with her big, bright, blue eyes, tears falling down her beautiful face.

"How did you do this?"

"Believe it or not... Your uncle."

Briggs

I jerked back, stunned. "What? My uncle helped you?"

"I told him that I wanted to give you a piece of your childhood for your birthday. He gave me an address and a key. He said everything I needed would be in there. It was a storage unit that didn't have much, just some boxes. There were photo albums, clothes, and some jewelry. He told me to keep the key. In case you wanted—"

"My uncle? He's kept all this. Why didn't he ever tell—" I shook my head, wiping away my tears.

I gave up trying to understand Uncle Alejandro years ago. I took in every last picture, especially the one of my mom and dad. They were kissing. They looked so happy, so in love. I couldn't believe Austin did this. It was the most thoughtful thing anyone could have given me.

A piece of my happiness before the darkness set in.

"You look like her. But you have your dad's blue eyes," he chimed in, pointing to my dad in the picture.

I smiled, more tears spilled over. "My dad used to travel a lot. My mom would let me sleep with her in their bed when he was gone.

She'd tell me that she didn't miss him as much when I was lying next to her. That all she had to do was look into my eyes and she would see my dad's staring back at her."

Austin grabbed my chin, making me look at him. Wiping away my tears with his thumb. The smell of cigarettes along with his touch comforting me the way it always did.

"I didn't have this made to make you cry, baby."

"They're happy tears," I reassured him.

"Anytime you want to talk about your parents. I'm here to listen. I wish I could have met them, so I could tell them how amazing their daughter is and how much I'm in love with her."

"I love you too. Thank—"

"Austin!" Mitch called out, peeking his head through the door, interrupting our special moment.

I had forgotten that they were here. Which was surprising since they were here more often than not. I didn't get fucked up with Austin nearly as much as I used to. I thought if I stopped partying, if I led by example, then he would follow in my footsteps.

I was wrong.

He just got new friends to party and get fucked up with.

"Your phone is ringing off the damn hook in here. Either answer it or turn it the fuck off," he said, holding Austin's ringing phone out in front of him.

Austin glanced over at me silently asking my consent, and I nodded. He walked away from me to grab the phone. I stayed by the railing, admiring my blanket.

He was so fucking sweet when he wanted to be.

"Yeah," he answered, his tone and demeanor quickly changing. "No shit, motherfucker, it was supposed to be here last week. You either make it happen or I'll find someone who will!" he snapped, making me jump.

I stopped going on runs with him a long time ago. He didn't need me with him anymore. I was just another thing for him to worry about during deals. I hated the person he would turn into. He wasn't my Austin when he was working. He was a complete stranger. The power, the money, and the drugs took over. It didn't happen overnight. But as weeks turned into months, and months turned into years, the more I started to see him become someone I didn't recognize anymore.

Someone that scared me.

Someone that reminded me of my uncle.

I just stopped going, and he never asked why. I think a part of him knew. It was easier for him to be that person if I wasn't around. To let the darkness take over. He loved the power and the respect. The money was just an added bonus because what he really loved.

Were the drugs.

It was no longer about the pain in his back. For years I justified him popping pain pills like they were fucking candy. That he was actually in agony from the muscle spasms, to have to take the Percocets, the Vicodins, the Oxys that I supplied him with. Anything I could get my hands on to help him get through the day. That wasn't the case anymore.

There were days that I couldn't tell if he was high or sober. Sometimes it all blended together, and that terrified me. I lay awake waiting for him, not caring if he came home high, just as long as he came home to me.

Wrapped his arms around me.

Told me he loved me.

That I was his girl.

That I was his everything.

Promising me a future that I desperately wanted to believe in, but as the years went on, the more it became a dream than a reality. At times I felt like an outsider looking into the life I caused. The life that I brought him into, the life that he had because of me.

No one else but *me*.

There were days that I felt so lost, not knowing what happened to my life. The life that I hated was now replaced with a life I didn't recognize.

The irony was not lost on me.

I was home alone one day a few months ago. Austin had gone on a run. He had been drawing all morning, still pictures of me, of us. Always capturing the happy memories, never the sad ones. For some reason I went into the closet and grabbed his old notebook, the one that I had opened for the first time years go, wanting to finally see a part of his life. I sat on our bed, my favorite place in the entire apartment, smelling him all around me.

Craving him to be there holding me.

Feeling like I was found in a moment where I felt so lost. My fingers turned to the very first sketch he ever drew of me. The drawing where I was dancing, so free not knowing that my life was about to change forever. Taking a drastic detour to the love I'd always wanted.

I tore the picture out of the notebook, instantly turning it over. I started writing. After years of reading books, I began writing the story of my life. Starting from the day Daisy Mitchell died. I transferred the few paragraphs to a Word document on my computer. Every so often I would pick up my laptop and write a few more paragraphs, a few more sentences, a few more pages. Usually when I felt lost again, which seemed to be happening a lot more lately.

"You have two days, do you hear me? If it's not fucking done, you'll have to answer to me, and trust me, you don't want to fuck with me." Austin hung up the phone, bringing me back to the present.

"Sorry about that, baby."

He was like night and day with a flick of a switch. Like Dr. Jekyll and Mr. Hyde in a blink of an eye. But the man I loved was back. He kissed my face and pulled me into his arms. As if he knew what I was thinking, what I was feeling, what I needed that only he could ever give me. And just like that. He made everything...

Go away.

CHAPTER
26
Briggs

I needed a break.

I needed to step back and look at the whole picture, not just what was in front of me from day to day. My mixed emotions caused chaos all around my mind. Wreaking havoc all around my life and what it had become.

I felt like I was a hamster on a spinning wheel, running in circles with no end in sight. Our relationship had always been intense and still was to that day. From the second we laid eyes on each other in Miami, the whole world disappeared and we started to live in our own little bubble. Our own little creation where nothing else existed or mattered, only each other. I went from being alone, from having no one, hating my life and where it was going till, him.

Till Austin.

He became my everything. My best friend. My only friend. My lover. My partner. My confidant. I was happy, for the first time in my life, I was really truly happy to have found someone that was just as alone as I was. Someone who needed me as much as I needed them.

Love was blinding and at times cruel. You only saw what you wanted to see, what you so desperately desired. Only picturing the good, never the bad.

I didn't realize that Austin had demons that lurked within him, or maybe I did and ignored the signs. Maybe it had always been just waiting around the corner.

For the taking.

His bright blue eyes that I loved for so many years were dull and void now. I couldn't remember the last time I saw them shining bright, full of life. They had been replaced with a dilated gaze. The darkness out-weighed the light and the life that I once cherished.

I could still see his love for me. Even behind the lies I told myself everyday.

He knew me inside and out. I used to love that he was the only person that had ever touched my heart, my soul. It built the bond we shared. Now it just felt like a double-edged sword, placed directly in my heart. There were days I saw him. *My* Austin peeking back at me through the drug-induced haze, the haze that seemed to always surround him.

I didn't want to believe what was so blatantly in front of my face. It was easier to live in denial instead of admitting the truth that I knew in my heart.

I walked around New York aimlessly the entire day, lost in my thoughts. The city was alive all around me, yet I still felt like I was walking the streets in slow motion. Strangers were passing me by in a blur. I lied and told Austin I was going to the spa. That I needed a girl day and I was finally using the gift certificate he had given me to spoil myself for the day.

Truth was, I wanted out of my fucking apartment. I needed out. The walls were caving in on me the more I was around the truth. It was easier to live in the lies than the reality. There were always people around, hanging out, drinking, doing drugs. We were rarely alone anymore. Drugs were everywhere all the time. Spread around the apartment, on the kitchen island, on the coffee table, on the dining room table. With the open floor plan, I had nowhere I could escape it.

My safe haven had become my Hell.

Austin and I fought about it often and his answer was always the same. He would say he understood. That it wouldn't happen again. That he loved me. That I was his girl. That he was sorry.

He was always, always fucking sorry…

When I made it back to the apartment it was already nighttime. I heard the loud music blaring the second I opened my car door in the parking garage. It vibrated against the walls of my small building. I was instantly thankful I only had three other people that lived on my floor and most of the time they weren't even home. I knew security wouldn't do a damn thing about the noise. My uncle had everyone on his fucking payroll. Even the cops would look the other way.

I pushed open the door on my floor. My heart mimicked the beat of the music. I deliberately walked slower down the hallway, not wanting to witness the shit show I knew I was about to walk into. Taking a deep, calm, soothing breath, I grabbed the knob and pushed the door open to the place I used to call my home.

"What the fuck?" I said to myself, taking in the crowd of people.

The billowing smoke from weed and cigarettes and God knows what the hell else hung heavy in the air. I couldn't see over the strangers who were making themselves at home in my personal space.

"Where the fuck is Austin?" I whispered again to myself, getting more and more frustrated as the seconds passed.

I pushed through the people, not caring who I knocked the fuck over, looking for Austin among the madness. I rose up on my tippy toes searching the unfamiliar faces, when my eyes focused on what I thought was a little person's hand.

My worst fucking nightmare played out right in front of me. A kid exposed to this life.

My dining room table was covered in drugs. So much so, I couldn't see the glass anymore.

"Oh my God!" I shouted.

No one turned to look my way.

Panic coursed through my body as I put my hand over my mouth, watching in complete horror and disbelief. The little girl, I had never seen before, played with the pills like they were toy cars. Sliding all the different colors and tablets through the white powder on the table. She reached for a needle and I lunged into action, roughly pushing my way through the crowd. Hurrying to the little girl before she grabbed the syringe.

"No! No! No!" I yelled over the music once I got to her, but it still sounded muffled.

She jerked back, frightened that someone was suddenly in her face. Her little lip jutted out and tears filled her eyes. I crouched down in front of her seat, wanting to be on her level.

"It's okay, sweetie, don't cry. I'm Briggs. What's your name?"

I rubbed her back and she bowed her head. "Molly," she whispered so low I could barely hear her.

"How old are you, Molly?" I coaxed, trying to get her to trust me.

She put her hand out in front of her, holding up four fingers.

"Wow. You're a big girl."

She nodded, smiling. Her guard coming down. I looked up at the table in front of her and noticed a My Little Pony coloring book beneath the pills and blow that she had just been playing with.

"Can I carry you? We can go outside, it's so loud in here. Have you been outside? There's a balcony and there's a whole bunch of buildings and bright lights," I said, excitedly. "And sometimes birds come and they sit right on the railing, or even better, at the table with you."

Her face lit up. Nodding her head fervently. "Like Cinderella?"

"Yes. Exactly like Cinderella. Okay, come on," I said, picking her up under her arms and placing her on my hip.

Not one person was paying attention to me. No one was watching her, taking care of her, looking after her. No one fucking cared. They just left her with a coloring book and crayons at a table full of drugs.

Why would someone bring a kid here?

I couldn't imagine what would have happened if I didn't see her reaching for a fucking needle of all things. If I hadn't come home when I did. I shook away the thoughts, taking her in my bathroom first. I lifted her up on the sink to wash her hands of the drugs that she was just playing with, thinking they were toys. I asked her repeatedly if she put anything in her mouth, if she ate anything and each time she shook her head no. I didn't know whether to believe her or not, but she looked fine.

If she took anything it would have already had an effect on her. I was there now. If she started acting funny, I wouldn't hesitate to call 911. I didn't give a shit what the repercussions could be. It made me sick to my fucking stomach that some asshole would bring their baby here and that Austin would let it happen.

I picked her back up on my hip, grabbing Austin's notebook from his nightstand with a few colored pencils since her coloring book was covered in cocaine.

At the last second, I grabbed my memory blanket, hoping that it would give her the same security it always gave me. I made my way through the crowd out to the balcony. Finally finding Austin out there, smoking a cigarette with Jon and a few other random people.

"Baby," Austin greeted as soon as I opened the doors. "There's my girl… I was starting to worry about you," he slurred.

He took a drag of his cigarette as he walked toward me, blowing the smoke to the side, before pulling me into his arm, trying to kiss me. I shoved him away, and he stumbled back. He still hadn't even realized I was holding a kid in my arms.

"The fuck?" he muffled out, gripping my arm. "What's your problem?"

"You! You're my problem. Whose kid is this, Austin?" I asked, nodding toward her.

He blinked a few times, trying to focus on the little girl but failing miserably in doing so.

I sighed, disappointed, furious, and annoyed.

"Everyone go inside!" I roared.

They all looked back at Austin as if it didn't matter what I said. Like it didn't matter that this was my damn apartment, my space they were all invading. He nodded towards the balcony doors.

I sat Molly on a wrought iron chair, throwing all the shit that was on the table onto the floor. Not giving a fuck what it was. I placed Austin's notebook in front of her, opening it up to a blank page and handing her the colored pencils.

She beamed, sitting up on her chubby little thighs to see and reach the notebook better.

"Will you draw me a picture? Maybe Twilight Sparkle? I love her purple hair," I stated, pulling back her soft brown hair away from her round baby face.

"Yes. She has purple hair like you," she said in the cutest little voice.

My heart was breaking for her and we'd only just met. I smiled, and she went right to work. It was starting to get cold out and she was dressed in summer clothes, so I placed the blanket over her shoulders and she snuggled right into it.

I took another deep breath before turning to face Austin. He was intently staring at us. As if everything he ever wanted was a few feet away from him.

I saw it.

For a moment, *my* Austin was peeking through the haze.

I walked toward him, dragging him to the furthest spot on the balcony, away from her, so she wouldn't hear us.

I didn't falter. I couldn't. If I did, the love I had for him would win and that wasn't going to happen tonight. Not after all this.

"Did you know she was here?" I gritted out, pointing at Molly.

He looked back over at the little girl who was happy as could be and then immediately peered down at the ground, rubbing the back of his neck.

I scoffed, shaking my head in pure utter disbelief.

"You knew she was fucking here? You knew someone brought a child? And you still let it happen? What the fuck is wrong with you?" I shoved his chest.

"Baby..." He stepped toward me and I instantly stepped back, placing my hand out in front of me.

"How fucked up are you right now? She was playing with drugs, Austin. Reaching for a fucking needle when I found her," I snapped, trying to keep my voice at bay. Even though all I wanted to do was scream at him.

He winced before I had the last word out, it was quick but I saw it.

"Who are you?" I breathed out unable to control my emotions.

His dilated eyes widened and mine filled with tears. I turned to look out over the city. Instead of the man I barely recognized anymore.

"Who the fuck are you right now? I don't even know you anymore," I bellowed with tears streaming down my face. I looked back at him. "*My* Austin... the man I love, would have never let a kid come into this apartment tonight. He would have never put a little girl's life in danger. What if I didn't find her when I did? What if she took a hand full of fucking pills, Austin?"

He just stood there with a confused look on his face, not understanding the severity of the situation.

"The man you were a few years ago, would have never been so fucked up not to care," I cried, sucking in air that wasn't available for the taking.

His hands reached out for me again, but I slapped them away.

"Daisy, I love you. I'm sor—"

"Yeah." I nodded not allowing him to finish. "You're always fucking sorry. How about this, Austin? How about try to not have to be sorry for anything, how about that? Huh?"

He rubbed the back of his head again. He was so fucked up he couldn't even come up with a string of excuses. His mind not catching up with his bullshit justifications.

I wiped away all my tears, but it was no use. They were coming down hard and unforgiving.

"Just go. Just go back inside. Go to your junkie friends. Go back to your drugs. Because that's all that matters to you anymore," I viscously spewed even though it killed me.

Even though I didn't want it to be true. Even though I prayed every night that he would come back to me.

That our love would prevail over his demons.

"That's not true. You're all that matters to me," he argued with a stern tone, pushing through the emotionless state. "I fucking love you. I made a mistake, okay? I'm not perfect, and I never claimed to be. I'm sorry. I'll make it right," he pleaded with sincerity laced in his voice.

"It's too late. You're too late. Just fucking go. Get out of my damn face. I can't look at you when you're like this anymore. You make me sick. Get those people out of my fucking apartment. Now!" I yelled, letting my anger take over.

I looked back at the little girl. She didn't seem fazed. Which only made me realize she was around this a lot. My heart broke for her even more.

"Our apartment, Briggs. Our fucking apartment," he stated, making me peer back at him.

He had an expression I couldn't read. He tried to reach for me again, but I just turned around not saying another word. It was pointless to talk to him right now. I walked toward the little girl, turning my back on the one person I had ever loved.

I heard him take a deep long breath before he walked back inside, shutting the doors behind him. I wiped away the tears on my face that seemed to keep falling, absentmindedly rubbing my stomach. I couldn't remember if I had eaten at all that day. I sat down next to her, grabbing a color pencil to help.

"This is beautiful, Molly."

She smiled and it lit up her entire face. I didn't understand how someone wasn't taking care of her. She was such an innocent little girl.

"Where are your parents?"

She shrugged.

"So, who did you come here with?"

"My daddy."

"Where's your mommy?"

She bit her lip, grabbing another color pencil.

"Maybe we can call your mommy to come get you, do you know her number?" I coaxed, pulling out my cell phone.

She peered up at me with sad eyes, and I swear on everything that was holy I thought I was looking in the goddamn mirror. Like it was me as the little girl, staring back at me as the woman.

"My mommy died. She's with the angels now. It's just me and my daddy. He will find me." She smiled. "He always does."

I jerked back like she had slapped me across the face.

My life flashed before my eyes, the past, the present. She went back to her drawing as if what she had just told me didn't change my entire future.

Everything that I so desperately wanted, now becoming everything I could never have.

I gently rubbed the back of her head, wanting to touch her soft hair, to look at her baby face, to take in the little girl that I would never have.

At least not...

In this life.

CHAPTER 27
AUSTIN

It had been well over a month since the party. Since the night I royally fucked up. Briggs still wasn't talking to me. She barely fucking looked at me anymore. It was like I disgusted her. Every time I tried to reach for her in bed and pull her into me, she would move away. I would try again, hoping she would give into me, but she would just get up and go sleep on the couch.

I didn't stop trying though.

I never would.

It didn't matter what I said or what I did. I failed at every attempt to get my girl back. Every last one of my efforts were shot down.

I hated that she was so pissed at me. It was the worst fucking feeling in the world not being able to make things right. I hated seeing her so depressed and not being able to bring her back to the light.

Bring her back to me.

I should have never caused her darkness in the first place. I knew the kid was there, but I was so fucked up, it just didn't register. I wasn't proud of it by any means, but shit happens. I would think she would have been a little more understanding. She used to do all these drugs with me. It was never a fucking problem until it was. I couldn't even remember the last time she actually partied with me. She didn't even smoke weed anymore.

I went out with the boys one night, hoping that if I gave her the space that she obviously wanted, she would maybe miss me. We could work this out and have things go back to the way they used to be. I was so fucking depressed because my girl wouldn't even fucking glance at me, let alone talk to me. I just wanted to forget the hurt I felt in my heart from the dagger she was fucking stabbing me with.

I wanted to get away for a few hours, just kick back and have a few beers. I promised myself that I wouldn't get high.

I would be better for her.

Instead I found myself at Jon's place and one thing led to another and I ended up trying crack for the first time. I had no excuse for it... other than for a few short hours it took away the pain. The hurt I felt deep within my soul was numbed. I was able to forget that she was upset with me.

That I may have lost a piece of her heart.

At first I turned it down when Mitch said he had some rock on him. I wasn't much for uppers, I mean I did blow and shit, but that was only to wake up and come off the downers. Oxys were still my drug of choice. The boys started smoking it and it smelled so fucking good. I couldn't say no. Before I knew it the pipe was in my hand and not even three seconds later I felt like I was the king of the goddamn world. But it wasn't my cup of tea, like I said I wasn't a fan of stimulants.

I got home late as shit that night, but I always went home to Briggs.

No matter what.

She was waiting up for me, lying on the couch, wrapped in the blanket that I had made for her. As soon as she saw me walk through the door she released a visible breath, shut off the light, and turned her back to me to go to sleep.

Not uttering a word.

As much as I hated that she did that, it was better than having her see what state of mind I was in. I thought I was in the clear, but drugs make you do very stupid fucking things. I would never lie to her.

I was just omitting the truth.

When I came home the next day after doing a few runs, she was sitting in bed with my jeans in her hands. The same jeans I wore out the night before.

I knew what was coming next. I knew what she found, but it still didn't prepare me for the hurt I felt in disappointing her yet again. The girl that meant everything to me.

Absolutely everything.

"I thought I would do something nice for you today," she said in a desolate tone, breaking my goddamn heart even more.

"Baby… let me—"

"Let you what? Explain? Apologize? Lie—"

"I don't lie to you," I stated, grabbing the back of my neck. Looking down at the floor, feeling guilty as hell.

"Right," she sarcastically laughed. "You only lie to yourself."

I was over to her in three strides, sitting in front of her on the balls of my feet. I grabbed her chin and she tried to pull away from me, but I gripped it harder. Making her look at me.

We finally locked eyes after what felt like fucking forever. For the first time her eyes weren't a bright shining, color of blue. They looked sad. Swollen from crying and sleepless nights. They were hollow, even though I could still see the love she had for me hidden behind the emptiness.

"You haven't said one word to me, Briggs. Not one fucking word in over a month," I stated the truth.

"And that's supposed to make this okay?" She held up the pipe she found in my jeans.

I must have placed it in there after we stopped smoking. I didn't even remember doing it.

"All I'm trying to say is that I fucking miss you, baby. I miss you so much that I can't breathe. I can't function without you."

"I miss you too, Austin. I miss you more than you'll ever know."

"Then why are you doing this to us? *Us.* Briggs."

"How do you not see it? How can you be so fucking blind? You're always fucked up, Austin. I don't remember the last time I saw you sober, that's how bad this is."

"That's not true," I said, shaking my head.

"Really? What are you on right now?"

My eyes widened. "Pain pills. What I'm always fucking on. What I've been on—"

"For pain! For fucking pain! How many have you taken today? Ten, fifteen, maybe twenty? What does it take for you to not feel pain anymore? It's not about the pain!"

She roughly tore her chin away from my grasp, looking deep into my eyes.

"It hasn't been about the pain in years! It's about you being high now. It's about you being fucked up! How you can't see that is beyond me!"

"Jesus Christ." I stood, peering down at her. "Do I not function? Do I not fuck you good anymore? Do I not make you come enough? Am I not bringing in the money? Huh? What am I not doing? I take care of you! I'm not sitting around just doing fucking drugs, Briggs! I'm not a fucking junkie!"

She stood up, right in front of my face, pointing her finger into my chest and spoke with conviction, "No, Austin. You're just a fucking addict."

She turned around to leave before I had a chance to respond to her allegations.

"Baby." I grabbed her arm, turning her to face me.

She immediately shut her eyes as if it pained her to look at me. I reached up instead, holding onto the sides of her face, willing her to open her eyes for me.

"Daisy," I lovingly coaxed.

I only ever called her that when I really needed her...

To look at me.

To talk to me.

To listen to me.

To feel me...

"I love you. I love you so fucking much. I'm so sorry. I'm sorry for everything. I fucked up. I know that. But baby, I'm not an addict. I don't have a problem. I can stop whenever I want. I just got caught up for a minute okay? That's it," I explained, caressing her cheeks with my thumbs.

Praying that she would believe me.

"Almost four years, Austin," she murmured loud enough for me to hear. "Your minute has turned into almost four years, babe."

I grimaced, backing away from her.

Had it really been that long? No, she's wrong.

My mind was spiraling, trying to find some clarity. Some truth within the haze.

She opened her eyes and they mirrored more fear, more worry, and more love than I had seen in forever, like she was answering the questions that immediately plagued my mind.

When did she start looking at me like that?

Neither one of us said anything. We said it all. The silence was deafening all around us. The air was so fucking thick between us. That I couldn't breathe.

She was the first to break our connection, as if she could no longer bear to see the man staring back at her. I didn't stop her when she turned to leave this time. I stood there and watched the love of my life walk out the door, terrified that she wouldn't ever come back. I couldn't will myself to move, my feet were glued to the goddamn floor, the ground swallowing me whole.

I collapsed onto the edge of the bed, my legs no longer able to support my weight. My inner demons were taking over.

My worst fears coming to life.

I cradled my head in my hands. My mind was racing, my head was throbbing, and my heart was breaking. Every last part of me left with Briggs through that door.

The picture frame of us on the nightstand caught my attention. I reached over and grabbed it, remembering the day we took it. She was so happy, so beautiful. She had so much life in her eyes. So much light that I put there.

"When did we lose our way, baby?" I whispered to her face in the picture.

My fingers skimmed along the glass, all around her beautiful face. My eyes blurred and sobs tore through my entire body. The truths crippling me in ways I never thought possible. Before I knew what I was doing, I had my hand in the air, chucking the frame against the wall in front of me. Shards of glass crashed to the ground in an instant.

Mimicking my soul.

A separate small square picture caught my eye. I got up, my feet moving on their own accord toward the shattered frame on the wooden floor. I pushed away the broken glass holding up a black and white picture.

It was then I understood.

It was then I realized.

A sense of calm instantly came over me.

M. Robinson

I held my entire future in the palm of my hand.

Briggs

I felt as lost as I did back before Austin came into my life. I almost found myself driving to the Brooklyn Bridge to seek solace, clarity or something, anything but the pain and sadness that had taken over and made itself home in my heart. Instead I just drove around aimlessly, hiding underneath the hoodie of my sweatshirt, leaning my head against the window. I was locked away in my own thoughts, my mind held captive by the feelings and emotions that were spilling out of my soul.

Out of the little voice in the back my head.

The one I had been trying to ignore for the last four years. The one that wouldn't fucking go away no matter what I did or told myself.

I was a prisoner to the memories of the man that made me fall in love with him. The one that protected me, made me laugh, made me smile.

My friend.

My everything.

No longer the carefree girl that lived and thrived with all of her heart. That smiled and laughed all the time. The girl that was alive and not dead inside.

I no longer felt whole, complete, or safe.

I didn't want those memories to be just a time in my life where I lived in a fantasy because now...

Now this was my reality.

I hated that feeling more than anything.

Loving Austin had always consumed my every thought, my every desire, my every want and need. None of that changed, it was just in a very different way now. Ways that I barely understood, ways that scared the hell out of me and made me feel alone and lost. I was beginning to hate life again, and I had no one to blame but myself. I let him in, I let him love me, and I also let him destroy my heart. I didn't know how to find my way without him. He was the reason I found it in the first place.

It physically pained me to watch the emotional detachment of everything I said to him. All the facts within the lies he was telling himself. Like time got lost for him. The days. The months.

The years.

As if the drugs had taken control of his very being. Including his heart.

My Austin disappeared more and more as time went on.

I couldn't find him through the haze. Not yesterday. Not today. I could only pray for tomorrow. A new day may bring back the old Austin. All I had left was wishful thinking.

I parked my car in the parking garage, noticing that his hadn't moved from the spot he left it. I would be lying if I said I wasn't nervous about what I would be walking into. Which Austin would be there... the good or the bad?

The one I loved with all of my heart. The one I still saw behind all the lies.

Or the addict that I loved though wanted to hate. The addict I just wanted to save.

I opened the door and was immediately assaulted with a fresh clean scent. I peered around the open space with wide eyes and a confused expression. The apartment was spotless, not a thing out of place. The bed was nicely made, complete with the throw pillows Austin hated.

What shocked me more than anything was there were no drugs in sight. All the usual places cleared off and wiped down. My hand went to my mouth in complete and utter shock. This must have taken him forever.

How long was I lost for?

I continued to take in what appeared to be a dream before settling my gaze on Austin, who was dressed in black slacks and a blue, collared button-down shirt. His sleeves rolled up, showing off his tattoos.

But it was his eyes that caught my immediate attention.

They were bright blue again. I couldn't remember the last time I saw that color. No longer tainted by the dark, dilated glare.

By the haze.

By the drugs.

My heart instantly leapt out of my chest, profusely pounding against my ribs. Crippling me as I made my way over to him.

There were candles lit on the dining table, trays of covered food waiting to be eaten with champagne chilling in a bucket of ice.

"What's all this?" I asked, taken aback. My hand now placed over my heart, trying to hold it together.

He stood, rounding the corner of the table, stopping with only a few inches of space between us.

I smiled. I couldn't help it. He looked like everything I ever wanted. Breaking through my resolve and hatred.

Austin.

He placed his hand on the side of my face, using his thumb to caress my cheek, as he had done so many times before. I could smell the lingering scent of cigarettes that I had come to love over all these years.

I got lost in his eyes, in his gaze, in the way he was looking at me. Devouring me with his stare as if it were the first time he ever laid eyes on me. With the same depth he showed when I was dancing in Miami six years ago. It was the look that melted my heart and made me weak in the knees. The same look that brought my walls crumbling down.

"I'm so sorry, Daisy."

"Austin—" He placed his finger on my lips, silencing me.

"I know I keep apologizing to you time and time again. I know I may sound like a broken fuckin' record at this point. But I swear to you on our love, on the love that I have for you so deep within my bones, that I've always, always meant it. That it's always been true."

My lips parted, trying to steady the beating of my heart that I swear he could hear.

"I don't know what happened, baby. I wish I had a better reason for you. A better explanation after all this time, after everything you've been going through. What I've put you through. I'll never forgive myself for that. I've been racking my brain the entire day trying to figure it out."

He took a deep breath, trying to gather his thoughts. His emotions.

"I got lost. I got so fucking lost with the lifestyle. The drugs. The parties. I don't know how I lost my way. It just took over. It was almost as if I was an outsider looking in. Every time I told myself I'm not going to get fucked up tomorrow, I'm not going to give in, I

269

was doing the drugs before I even realized it was already the next day. It took control."

"I know," I breathed out.

He shut his eyes, the pain of my words too much for him to hear.

"It's why I didn't want you to take over in the first place. I've seen what happens, I've seen it my entire life. Men come and go in this business, some are lucky enough to walk out the door."

He opened his eyes when he realized what I implied.

"I thought I lost you, Austin. I thought you weren't going to come back to me. That the drugs, money, and power replaced what we had. I thought everything we shared was—"

"Shhh…" he whispered against my lips, gripping the sides of my face tight.

I leaned into the warmth that I'd missed so damn much.

"That won't ever happen. I promise you that I won't ever, ever make you feel that way again. I will never let you feel alone again. Nothing can take me away from you. I swear to you. You're my home, Daisy. You've always been my home, my heart, and my soul. I didn't start living until I met you. I'm so fucking sorry, baby."

I took in every last emotion he was giving me. Letting his words that I so desperately wanted to be true, take over.

He kissed me, lightly beckoning my lips to open for him. They did.

Feeling him.

Loving him.

Needing him.

"Everything is going to be different from now on. I promise, baby. We can go. We have more than enough money. Let's escape this life, escape the sadness that this life has brought on. Make new memories. We can start our life together. The one you've always wanted and the one I've never stopped wanting to give you."

Tears streamed down my face. I wanted to believe everything he was saying.

No more lies.

"What? You mean it? We can go? We can start over? Somewhere else… somewhere far away from here?" I asked, question after question not knowing which one I wanted answered the most.

"I'll go wherever you want. As long as we're together, that's all that's ever mattered to me," he rasped in between kissing me.

He rested his forehead on top of mine. Never breaking our connection.

Our love.

He looked deep into my eyes with more sincerity than I had ever seen before, like his soul was staring back at me.

"Marry me."

I tried to jerk back, but he held me in place by his grasp.

"What? What did you just say?"

He rubbed his nose back and forth over mine and spoke with conviction, "Marry me, Daisy."

I released the breath I didn't realize I held, my hesitation bringing me back.

"Are you serious? Are you being serious right now?" I wept, my tears covering his hands.

"I've never been more serious about anything in all of my life. I love you more then anything on this earth. Marry me."

I wanted to say yes so fucking badly… but so much had happened between us.

He smiled, kissing me all over my face, wiping my tears with his lips. Taking away all the pain that had lived inside them for so many years. He stopped and my body slowly slid down his until my feet touched the floor.

"You're my girl. You'll always be my fucking girl," he stated with his own voice breaking.

He kissed me passionately, our tongues taking what the other needed. His grasp still tightly placed on the sides of my face. We kissed one last time, long and true before he pulled back to look deep into my eyes again and said,

"You're going to be the best mama to our baby, Briggs."

My. Heart. Broke.

Again.

CHAPTER
28

AUSTIN

I felt her immediately tense in my arms, going rigid like someone just knocked the wind out of her.

"Why would you say that?" she asked, searching my face for an answer. Worry evident in her tone.

I kissed the tip of her nose and let go of her face. I grabbed the flutes, pouring some champagne in each one. I handed her a glass and picked up mine clinking it against hers.

I smiled. "I found the ultrasound picture in the frame on our nightstand," I said, taking in her distress. "I know you can't drink, but I got us sparkling cider to celebrate the news," I added, placing my hand over her stomach, over our future.

She instantly stepped back away from my touch as if it burned her. I shook my head in confusion, not understanding what I had done.

"What's wro—"

"That's why you did all of this." She frantically looked around the apartment, her gaze not settling on one place for very long. "The clean apartment, the dinner?" She stared down at the table and then back up at me. "The realization, the future, the proposal, that's the only reason you did all—"

I stepped toward her, and she stepped back again. I cocked my head to the side, taken aback.

"Baby, I've always wanted to marry you. What are you talking about? You're not making any sense right now. I know the timing may seem wrong, but you know that's not true. I love you, Briggs. Finding the ultrasound picture of our baby made me realize what the fuck I was doing. Knowing that a part of me is growing inside of you. Brought me clarity. Made me see what I needed to do. To stop fucking up. I would never put your life or our child's in danger. You know that? You. Know. Me."

"No!" she yelled out, chucking the glass of sparkling cider that was in her hand at the wall behind me.

Liquid and glass flew everywhere.

"The fuck? Jesus Christ! You can't be this upset that I found the ultras—"

"No! Are you fucking blind? This is about you, not me! I don't know you! I don't know the man you have become, Austin! I've been living with a complete stranger for almost four years! *My* Austin is gone! The drugs took him away from me!" she screamed, shaking to the core with anger.

I set my glass down on the table, putting my hands out in a surrendering gesture. I knew her emotions were running wild, that I had hurt her and she was just lashing out.

"I know. Calm down. This isn't good for the bab—"

"THERE IS NO FUCKING BABY!" she screamed at the top of her lungs, falling to the floor, burying her head in her hands.

Sobs consuming her entire body.

I instantly stepped back, blown away by her words. A sense of loss settled over me. I didn't know what she was talking about. I saw the ultrasound. I saw our baby with my own two fucked up eyes. I didn't go to her. I didn't comfort her. I started to pace back and forth, my hands roughly pulling at my hair, knowing that she was about to rip my fucking heart out.

"What are you—"

"Jesus, Austin… haven't you seen me? When was the last time you really looked at me before today? I've barely been able to get off the couch because I've been recovering."

I grimaced, locking eyes with her. "Recovering? Recovering from what, Briggs? What the fuck have you been recovering from?"

She placed her hand over her mouth, holding the truth in.

"ANSWER ME!"

She just sat there on the floor in front of me, drowning in her own misery and shook her head no. Not wanting to tell me, as if she didn't tell me, if she didn't say it out loud then it wasn't true.

She didn't do it.

"You killed my baby. Didn't you?" I spewed, saying it for her. "Is that what you're recovering from, Briggs? Killing our fucking child?!" I seethed, beyond livid, beyond reason or doubt.

I couldn't see straight. I wanted to scream. I wanted to punch something.

How could she have done this to me?

To us?

She shook her head, getting up on her feet and narrowing her eyes at me.

"NO! You don't get to be the victim here, Austin! Have you seen our home? Have you seen what you've done to our goddamn home? What you've let inside our house? I would never bring a child into this world! Not in a million fucking years! You're never fucking sober! What do you think would have happened to Molly? That little girl at the party if I hadn't walked in here when I did? Huh? Tell me!"

I scoffed. "That's why you killed our baby? That's your justification for killing my child? Without fucking telling me!" I violently roared.

My fists clenched at my sides. My anger taking control, seeping out of my blood onto the woman that I thought I knew.

"What about you, Briggs? Hmmm… even if I fucked up, you couldn't have raised our kid? Are you that fucking cruel? You didn't have to fucking kill it!"

"Stop saying that," she gritted out.

"Stop saying what? The truth? What would you like me to stop saying? Because trust me, baby. I'm not even close to saying what I really fucking want right now."

"You want to talk about truths. How about this one? My parents died. Were killed in a car accident. Were taken away from me in the blink of an eye, and I had no control over it. Not one. Who took me in, Austin? Who raised me? In this life. In this godforsaken life! That little girl, Molly … her mom died too. You know who she was here with? You know who brought her to your party? Sat her down at a table full of drugs with junkies all around. Leaving her to fend for her goddamn self! HER FATHER! And you know who let it happen? YOU! Why? Because you were too fucked up to even care. That's why! That's fucking selfish! I would never be able to live with myself knowing that if anything were to happen to me, my child would be raised in this life by you! Or by my uncle! Do you understand me?" she paused to let her words sink in, raking me up and down with a look of disgust.

"That's why I did it. And it almost fucking killed me. I fucking hate myself for it. But where have you been, Austin? Because the man I fell in love with would have known that something was wrong with me! The second I walked through the fucking door. You would still be oblivious to my pain had you not found the ultrasound picture that I placed behind that picture. That picture is not us anymore, we are not that couple anymore. I've been living in hell, mourning the life I took away for six goddamn weeks, Austin, while you've been lost in your hazed world."

I took in everything she was saying.

Every. Last. Word.

"You say you don't know me, Briggs. That I'm not the same man you fell in love with. Well, then, baby, that fucking makes two of us. I have no idea who you are either because the woman I love would have never killed our baby. I may be an addict, but at least I'm not a murderer," I viciously spewed, regretting it immediately.

Words could cut you open like knives, and I knew I just sliced away a huge part of her heart with what I said. I couldn't take it back. As much as I wanted to, the damage was already done. I knew she would never forget my words, but I prayed to God that one day she would forgive them.

Her hand was up in the air before I got the last word out. I caught it mid-air, tugging her toward me. She tried to break free, roughly pulling her arm away from my grasp. I grabbed her other arm, the momentum of her trying to fight me off made me unintentionally slam her against the wall.

She winced but didn't stop struggling.

"Get the fuck out! Leave!" she yelled, whipping around.

"Stop!" I argued. "Fucking stop! I don't want to hurt you! Calm down! Calm the fuck down!" I ordered through a clenched jaw, trying to control her thrashing body.

She slowly gave up, panting profusely. Her chest rising and falling with each second that passed between us. I leaned forward, our lips almost touching.

"Why, Briggs? Why didn't you fucking tell me? Why didn't you give me a choice in the matter? It was my baby, too. I should have had a say. Why didn't you give me that right? Why did you take that away from me?" I asked, needing to know.

She opened her mouth to say something, but nothing came out.

"As much as it kills me to have said all those things to you, I won't apologize for it, because at the end of the day our baby is gone. No excuses will take away the fact that you didn't have the common decency to tell me. You made the decision for both of us. Like I didn't even matter. Were you ever planning on telling me?"

Her breathing hitched. By the look on her face, the answer was no.

I peered deep into her eyes and breathed out, "You just killed a part of me that you will NEVER get back. That *I* will never get back."

I let her go, stepping away from her.

She swallowed hard, her eyes watering, her lips quivering as if she knew what I just said was true. For the first time I didn't want to comfort her, to hold her, tell her she was my girl, and that I loved her. Because for the first time...

I was staring at a stranger and not the woman that I knew and loved. I finally understood what she meant when she said she didn't know me. For years she kept saying that I had changed, that I had become another person, which only made me hate myself more because I knew I brought this on myself. I was the reason that she felt like she had no other choice. No other decision to be made.

I. Did. This.

That realization was my rock bottom...

Or so I thought.

"Austin..." she coaxed, reaching out for me.

It was like she knew what I was going to do even before I did.

I turned around and left.

"Austin, please don't do this. Please, don't lose yourself again." she begged as I opened the door, walking out of the apartment, not bothering to shut it.

I wanted her to watch me walk out of her life. Two wrongs don't make a right, but a part of me wanted to hurt her as much as she just hurt me.

I drove around New York City for I don't know how long. Time just seemed to standstill as the pain in my heart took over. There wasn't one ounce of my body that didn't yearn. That didn't feel like it was dying. I had never felt so empty and hollow in all my life. But the underlying demons were waiting, always my companions, always sitting right next to me, waiting for the emotional devastation to take over.

So they could come out and play.

I blinked and I was sitting on Jon's couch, snorting line after fucking line. Trying to forget, trying to go numb, trying to block out the last twenty-four hours. But it wasn't working. The pain was still alive and bleeding out of me, leaving nothing but destruction in its wake.

"You want to forget, bro?" Jon asked, sensing my distress.

My bloodshot eyes settled on the needle in his hand and then back up to his face. He was tightening the belt around my upper arm before I could even answer. Telling me to make a fist.

I did.

The second I felt the needle poke through my skin, I watched my despair fill the syringe with blood. And then... Jon pushed down the plunger.

I kissed goodbye our baby.

I kissed goodbye Briggs.

I kissed goodbye Austin.

Leaning my head back against the couch, letting the crave take over.

The worst part was that I just kissed goodbye my future and everything I believed in.

Briggs

I went to the storage unit. Austin had left the key for me if I ever wanted to go there. I did. For the first time I came face to face with all my parents' belongings. Trying to seek comfort and guidance. There was none to be found there. I decided to stop at a church on the way to the clinic, needing some sort of peace of mind. I'd never been in a church before, too afraid that all my sins would make the roof cave in on me. I didn't even know if I was Catholic. At that point I didn't care and it didn't matter. I dipped one finger into the cold holy water, hoping it wouldn't burn me and made the sign of the cross, like I'd seen in movies. One foot in front of the other, I walked toward the first pew of the empty cathedral, right before God. A man I didn't even believe existed until that very second as I made my way into his house. The echo from my feet mimicked the sound of my heart beating against my ribs.

I got down on my knees, crying, and praying for forgiveness for what I was about to do.

"Please God... Please forgive me," I pleaded with every last fiber of my being. "Please grant me forgiveness... I have no other choice... Please you have to believe me, just please show me some mercy. Please guide me."

I sat there pleading with someone I wasn't sure existed, but I had to try and believe. Try to make this right, when all of it was so wrong. I don't know how long I was there on my knees waiting for I don't know what.

A sign?

I got to my feet, looking at Jesus on the cross and whispered, "I'm so sorry."

Before turning to leave.

I cruised through the streets of New York fighting the urge to drive back home, tears still streaming down my face. I turned around several times and headed to my safe place, trying to block out the girl's voice on the GPS telling me I was going the wrong way. But she was right. Home was the wrong way and I had to stop running.

I pulled up to the clinic just after one and sat there looking at the sign through blurred eyes. My thoughts raging a war in my head. I closed my eyes, leaning my head on the cool steering wheel, trying to catch my breath. Breathing in and out. Telling myself that this was the right decision, pleading for my mind to console my heart.

Before I knew it, I was out of the car and walking in. The door binged as I opened it, startling me out of my hazy state. I walked up to the receptionist, gave her my name and was told to take a seat.

I sat in the lobby of the doctor's office, waiting for my name to be called. It broke my heart to see all the women awaiting the same fate.

Words couldn't describe the emotions coursing through my body, the turmoil and doubt that had taken residence inside of me.

The last two weeks weren't like anything I had ever experienced before. I would hate myself for the rest of my life for going through with this. But I would hate myself even more, if Heaven forbid, something happened to me and my child would be left to an addict and the god of organized crime.

As each patient was called back, my heart sped up more and more. Another piece of me dying little by little. I knew it would be my turn soon and as much as I wanted to get this over with, I was also terrified. My legs were bouncing nervously, the anticipation killing me. I got out of my seat to grab another magazine that I was blankly looking through.

There were no words to describe the pain I felt in my heart at that moment. What I had been going through alone.

Always alone.

Bing.

I walked out of the office, needing some air. I crouched down near the curb, all of a sudden feeling like I was going to be sick. I clenched my only lifeline in my hand, contemplating calling Austin. My heart was pounding out of my chest, there was a ringing in my ears and the world in front of me began to spin. I dry heaved a few times, only then remembering I hadn't had breakfast that morning. I slid my phone open and pressed recent calls. Austin's name was the first on the list, staring at me, judging me. I was just about to press send when the door behind me binged again, making me jump and drop my phone onto the sidewalk.

I'd known I was pregnant for a week the day of the party. I wasn't feeling well for a few days, but I honestly thought it was from everything that was going on with Austin. I blamed it on the stress, the nerves, and the emotional mayhem causing my body to shut down. I didn't want to eat. I was always nauseous and just felt like shit in general. I went to the doctor hoping she could prescribe me some antibiotics or something to make me feel better.

When I told her my symptoms, she immediately asked me when my last period was. That's when it hit me that I was late. Right then and there I knew the cause of my sudden illness.

She gave me a cup to pee in and a few minutes later, the test confirmed that I was pregnant. She told me how far along I was but honestly, I checked out. Everything faded as she did the ultrasound and handed me the photo when she was done. All that mattered was that I was pregnant. Any other person would be happy with this news, but I was torn. I spent the rest of the day at home by myself just lying around. Rubbing my belly, fantasizing about life with a baby. Looking at the ultrasound photo for hours. Austin was working or getting high or whatever the fuck he was doing at that point.

He came home later that night with Jon right by his side. They smoked and did some blow. I sat out on the balcony with my memory blanket wrapped around me, gazing at the buildings, at all the lights and sounds of the city that never slept.

Allowing the chaos to take control over what had become my life.

The day of the party I spent walking around the city, lost, confused, and overwhelmed. I wanted to tell Austin I was pregnant. I wanted to share the news with him, hoping that maybe it was what he needed, the push to come back to me. I was scared, terrified that even if I told him, nothing would change. He would be happy and want to celebrate by getting high or partying. But then I walked by the art gallery I took him to for his birthday, and his sketch of me was now sitting dead center in the window.

For all to see.

That was when I realized he needed to know, that I needed to tell him. If he still didn't change, if it still didn't help him find his way then I would raise the baby by myself. There wasn't a chance in Hell that I would ever let my child step foot anywhere near this life.

The second I got home and parked my car in the garage, a sick, disturbing feeling manifested deep within my core. I walked to my door with my heart heavy and full, filled with nothing but worry, concern, and anxiety. Coming home to a party was nothing new, but when I saw that little girl my heart dropped. Molly playing with drugs, nobody watching over her, nobody protecting her, nobody taking care of her. My heart shattered along with the fantasy of the life I thought I could have.

It was Austin that drove the dagger into my heart even further when he confirmed that he knew she was there. That he was just too fucked up to care. Reality set in, and it was then that I grasped I would be raising our baby by myself. I didn't even contemplate getting an abortion. It wasn't even on my spectrum of thinking.

"Daisy Mitchell," the nurse announced, saying my real name.

This wasn't Briggs who was doing this. This wasn't me hiding behind someone I created to survive.

This. Was. Me.

The girl that died in the car with her parents was now alive and killing someone else in her life.

The irony was not lost on me.

When Molly, the little girl, said her mom had died and that she was there with her dad. That her father brought her to this hellhole and that he would find her. That he always found her.

It hit me like a ton of fucking bricks. My parents had died too, and I didn't have a choice in how my life turned out. I couldn't do that to another innocent life.

Especially my baby.

What kind of mother would that make me?

I couldn't be that selfish, even though I wanted this baby more than anything in this world. What if something happened to me? I'd leave it with their drug-addicted father or even fucking worse, my uncle.

My child would become Molly.

My child would become me...

I contemplated adoption, but there was no way in Hell that I could have this baby, our baby growing inside me for nine months. The baby that I already loved with all my heart just to give it away to someone. I would end up keeping it.

The vicious cycle would never end.

There was no way out of it. I struggled with my emotions, with my choice, with my decision for over a week. There was no other choice to be had. I made the appointment, and I've hated myself ever since.

"Are you Daisy Mitchell? We're ready for you," the nurse announced again, holding the door open, waiting for me to come back in.

I grabbed my phone and walked back in. I followed her through a long corridor. Feeling as if I was being taken to my execution.

And in a way, I was.

Crave Me

She took me into a room that had an examination table. The nurse asked questions about my medical history and other personal questions that I imagined were standard.

The doctor came in followed by the nurse. She explained to me the steps of the procedure. I lay back on the table with my feet in stirrups. The uncontrollable tears slid down my face and the nurse grabbed my hand in sympathy.

"Honey, you don't have to do this. Do you want us to call someone for you?" the same nurse asked.

I shook my head no and spoke through the tears, "There is no one."

I couldn't be selfish. This wasn't about me. It was about destroying another life.

More blood on my hands.

They were extremely understanding and reassuring, telling me over and over again that there was no judgment. She explained the aftercare. I nodded the entire time, feigning attention. It happened in less than five minutes.

The last piece of my heart was taken away from me.

A part I knew I would never get back. No matter how much I wanted to. No matter how many times I'd pray. I did this, and I had no one to blame but myself.

The burden was mine to carry.

All I knew was that I cried the entire time. When it was done, they took me into a comfortable room with leather recliners and I curled up in one for a few hours wrapped up in some warm blankets.

Cradling my stomach, mourning the loss of something I wanted so desperately, so fucking badly. Something I had never even held in my arms.

I didn't just kill my baby that day.

I. Killed. Me.

I ended up slipping out without being noticed because I didn't have anyone to pick me up. I probably shouldn't have driven in my condition, but all I wanted to do was go home.

Once again it was a reminder that I really was alone in this cruel world.

I took a shower the next day, wanting to wash away the misery. I curled up in a little ball, letting the hot water run over my broken body. The tears wouldn't stop, and my body was shaking to the core. I couldn't breathe.

I kept repeating over and over again, "What have I become? I'm so fucking sorry, baby. I didn't have a choice, I'm so so sorry. You're with grandma and grandpa now, they will take care of you,"

I cried harder, talking to a life that didn't exist anymore, thinking about my parents and everything that had ever been taken from me. I stayed there till the water was too cold to bear. I grabbed my blanket then buried myself in my bed and sobbed the entire day, so alone. No one to comfort me, hold me, no one to tell me they loved me. That everything was going to be okay. It was like I was that little girl. The one that had no friends, no family, no love.

As if Austin never existed.

But he did and that only made it worse. Because I knew what it was like to have that. To have him. To have everything I ever wanted only for it to be taken from me. Without my say or consent.

My uncle took yet another thing from me.

Adding to the endless pile of things I didn't have anymore. Things I could never get back.

I placed the ultrasound picture behind my favorite picture in the frame by our bed. That was all I had left.

My memories…

It started to get late after Austin left me pleading for him to stay. I just didn't want him to go get fucked up. I didn't want him to go numb his pain and drown his sorrows with drugs. I wanted him to stay with me and mourn the loss of our baby together. To help each other through it, like a normal loving couple.

What we used to be.

I was so conflicted I couldn't even fucking see straight. I knew I should have packed up my shit and left, but I couldn't. I loved him. After everything he had put us through, I still loved him so goddamn much. He was all I'd ever known. I didn't know how to be without him.

There was no *Daisy* without Austin.

I felt so much guilt for the man he had become. I brought him into this lifestyle when I already knew he was popping pain pills like candy. I knew he had an addictive personality. I knew he loved to numb his pain so he didn't have to feel anything. It was like he had a death wish, and I put a loaded gun in his hand.

I blamed myself.

I wanted to save him.

To save one fucking person in my life.

I knew what he said was out of anger. That he didn't mean it. I could see that he regretted saying those hateful things to me immediately. I knew he was hurting. I knew he was sick and maybe I was sick too.

I had become as co-dependent on him as he did with his drugs.

At the end of the day, I didn't know if that was right or if it was wrong, all I knew was that I fucking loved him.

I was honestly just so fucking devastated that he let that little girl come into the party. It burned into all my insecurities of what I didn't want to be true. As all the lies I told myself for years came tumbling down on me. Suffocating me in ways I never thought possible.

When one a.m. turned into three a.m. and three a.m. turned to four a.m. and four a.m. turned into the next afternoon, and the next evening, and then the next day…

No Austin.

He had never, not come back to me. It didn't matter how late it was, how fucked up he was. I always went to sleep with him in our apartment. For five days, five fucking days I didn't see him. I didn't hear from him.

I didn't know if he was dead or alive.

I wanted to call my uncle to ask him if maybe he sent him somewhere or Austin requested to be sent somewhere. But I didn't. The last thing I needed was to bring my uncle into this fucking havoc. I called local hospitals instead. I drove and walked around places I thought he could be. I left voicemail after voicemail on his phone. I was so desperate to find him I even called Jon and Mitch's phones as well.

I didn't sleep fearing I'd miss his call. I sat up waiting for the call or the knock on the door that thankfully never came.

After five days. I finally heard the lock on the door turn at almost eleven at night. I wanted to run to him, to hold him, to have him hold me. To have him kiss me, call me his girl, and tell me that he loved me. I was just so fucking thankful he was alive and had come home to me.

I didn't.

I stayed seated on the couch, watching the doorknob turn and him walk in. Almost expecting what I was about to see but even that didn't prepare me. He looked like he hadn't slept or showered since he'd left. His eyes were bloodshot, and his pupils were non-existent in a way I'd never seen before. Dull blue eyes stared back at me with no familiarity behind them.

No Austin.

He walked toward me, wearing the same clothes he had left in. The sleeves now rolled down his arms but not buttoned.

My heart dropped.

It was loud.

It was clear.

It was everything that was left of me.

Of us.

Tears instantly pooled in my eyes. I couldn't believe I still had some left after all the crying I had done since he left me. Begging him not to go. Not to do what I knew he was going to.

He stood right in front of me, peering down with dead, glassy, soulless eyes. The haze clouding all around us, he was still clearly high as fuck.

My eyes fell on the blood seeping through the forearm of his dress shirt.

"What did you do, Austin? What did you fucking do?" I whispered so low, scared that if I said it any louder then it would be true.

His head leaned back a little, barely able to hold himself up.

"Let me see your arms. Roll up your sleeves."

He followed my gaze down to the blood, blinking a few times before he realized what I meant. I already knew what was lying beneath the stained fabric, but I needed to see it with my own eyes, if I saw it I couldn't make excuses anymore.

He cocked his head to the side, slowly starting to unbutton his shirt. He let it slide down his shoulders, to his hands and threw it on my lap. I held his blood-stained shirt in my hands and saw the dried red marks on his veins.

Tears slid down my face, one right after the other.

"Why? Why would you do this?" I cried, not understanding.

He narrowed his eyes at me and spoke with more conviction than I had ever heard before, slaying the last bit of will I had left.

"You decided to kill a part of me, baby, without even telling me… so I'm just finishing what you started."

CHAPTER
29

AUSTIN

My body felt like it weighed two hundred pounds, sinking into the mattress. My head was fucking throbbing. All I could hear was a wah wah sound echoing all around me.

"Daddy! Daddy! Wake up! Please wake up!"

I felt little hands poking me, opening my eyes to a beautiful baby girl with a halo of light shining behind her long brown hair. Bright blue eyes that mirrored Briggs'.

"Austin! Austin! Wake up! Please wake up!"

"Daddy, you need to wake up. Mommy needs you now. Come on, sleepy head, get out of bed. Go back to Mommy. She needs you more than I do. I'm fine. We will meet one day. I promise."

I tried to talk to her, to reach for her, but every time I did my baby girl would move further and further back into the light. Away from me. Always leaving me without my consent, without my approval.

This was the closest I had ever been to her. Usually I just saw her bright blue eyes staring back at me. Sometimes she would be twirling around, playing, laughing, and smiling.

I didn't want her to leave me. I wanted to take her in my arms and never let her go.

"Come on, Austin, don't do this to me!" Briggs yelled from above me, clapping her hands in my face.

Slapping my cheeks.

Shaking my body.

"Daddy, I love you. Wake up. Wake up. Wake up."

I reached for her again when she appeared right next to me. She didn't leave me that time. For the first time since I started seeing her a year ago after the night I started my own demise. She let me hold her. I held her so fucking tight. I felt her soft baby skin against my arms. The smell of her baby scent surrounded me. I wanted to tell her I loved her, I loved her more than anything but my mouth wouldn't move.

I couldn't get it to fucking move.

"I know, Daddy. I love you, too," she said as if she read my mind. *"But it's not your time yet. Mommy needs you now. Okay? So you need to wake up now. Do it for me, Daddy. Wake up for me…"*

Her last words faded into the distance and she was gone. Torn out of my grasp.

I screamed, "NO!"

Over and over again but no sound came out.

My lips were moving to no avail.

"No, baby, don't leave me again. No, no, no, come back to me, baby girl. I'll change. I swear I'll change. Just come back to me. I don't want to live in a world without my baby. God, fucking take me now. I've been punished enough. I'm so fucking sorry…"

"AUSTIN! Please don't do this to me! Wake up!" Briggs screamed.

I slightly opened my eyes, the light blinding me immediately. My baby girl was gone. But the same pair of bright blue eyes were now staring down at me.

"Babe, what the fuck?" I groaned out, my mouth dry as fuck.

"Oh my God! You stopped breathing! You fucking stopped breathing!" she shouted too close to my face.

Almost to the point of hysterics.

"What? No… I just closed my eyes for a second. I must have fallen asleep. Where is she?" I whispered, my throat burned.

"Are you fucking kidding me? I went to take a shower and when I came out, you weren't fucking breathing, Austin! What did you take? What the fuck did you take? And who the hell are you talking about?"

I shook my head, squeezing my temples.

"Baby, my head is pounding, please stop screaming. I'm fine, okay? Look." I opened my eyes, blinking away the fogginess to focus on her face. "See. I'm fine," I repeated, closing my eyes again, unable to see her clearly.

Hoping she would come back.

My daughter.

Our baby girl.

"Jesus Christ, Austin. I think you just OD'd. What if I hadn't been here? What if—"

"Briggs, I didn't OD. Stop. I'm fine. I must have fallen into a deep sleep or something," I reasoned, rubbing her leg as she sat next to me on the bed. "Relax," I coaxed.

"A deep sleep where you stop fucking breathing? Really? What the fuck kind of sleep is that?"

"Oh my God, Briggs! Fuck! Cut this bullshit. I'm fucking fine. I'm breathing. I'm awake. My head is fucking pounding, so please just leave me alone." I rolled away from her.

I knew she was glaring at me even though my eyes were closed. She was overreacting. I was fine. I didn't do anymore dope than I usually did. I just wanted to go to sleep.

Our relationship had become strained over the last year or so. I was barely working anymore. Just disappearing more often than not. I didn't know how hours turned into days, shit blended together more frequently. I loved Briggs but I couldn't forgive her for what she had done, as much as I wanted to forget, as much as I tried to, and yet I couldn't let her go. Feeling miserable with her was better than enduring life without her.

"Baby, come here. I'm sorry. I'm just tired. Okay? I'm sorry… come here. I love you. Where's my girl? Come here," I coaxed, pulling her into my arms.

She came effortlessly, she always did. It was like we both needed it, I needed to hold her as much as she needed to be held.

I rolled to my side, tucking her against my body, pulling her in tight so we were one. She curled up in the nook of my arm, her face pressed against her favorite scar near my heart. I felt her softly kiss it as I kissed the top of her head.

"I love you, Briggs. I love you more than anything. I would never intentionally hurt you. Tell me you know that."

I held her closer, tighter, wrapping her up with my legs, not just my arms. Coming in and out of consciousness, I was still so fucking tired, so fucking out of it. I thought I felt her crying or maybe I heard her, fuck... maybe I was imagining that too.

I couldn't tell the difference from reality or a dream anymore.

"You're my girl. You'll always be my girl. No matter what," I softly murmured, letting sleep and darkness take over.

I dreamt all night of bright blue eyes, of our baby, of Briggs. Being happy, laughing, her smiling beautiful face as she held our daughter.

Holding onto the illusion that it was real, that it wasn't just a dream. That was the best part of my day, when I was high, lost in the fog where my mind would play tricks, showing me the life I wanted. The life I could have had. The one I promised Briggs. It was the only time I was happy. The only time I felt whole, the only time I was sober.

The dreams in which I was a father, Briggs was my wife, we had a family...

Those were the best dreams I ever had.

I wasn't spinning out of control, fading in and out of love again, broken beyond repair.

I inhaled the smell of Briggs as I fell deeper into the spaces in between my drug-induced slumber and dreams. Feeling her run through my veins, my bloodstream, mixing with the demons that had taken over my body. She was floating inside me, etched so far into my soul.

I woke up the next morning, immediately reaching for Briggs, patting the empty space beside me. She wasn't there and my heart dropped, panic set in. My eyes instantly opened, sitting up looking for her.

I breathed a sigh of relief when I saw her, sitting on the couch watching me.

Our eyes locked.

She looked like she hadn't slept all night. Her memory blanket wrapped securely around her shoulders, her knees pressed against her chest with her arms wrapped tightly around them. Holding the blanket in place, like she was barricading herself in to feel safe.

She looked so tiny.

So scared.

Her eyes were bloodshot red, tears streaming down her face. Like she hadn't stopped crying all night.

"Baby... come here—"

She shook her head slowly, not breaking our eye contact.

"You almost died last night. You OD'd, Austin."

"I didn't OD—"

"How would you know? You were practically dead. You stopped fucking breathing."

"Briggs, stop. I'm fine. Look." I lifted my hands in the air. "I'm alive. Nothing happened," I reasoned with her, pulling the covers off of me.

Her eyes widened with a crazed expression I'd never seen before. I got out of bed, walking over to her.

She put her hands out in the air stopping me. "Get dressed."

I cocked my head to the side. "What?"

"Get dressed, Austin. I'll be waiting in the car."

With that she got up and left. It was almost as if she needed to leave or else she wouldn't go through with what the hell she was thinking.

"The fuck?" I said out loud as I watched her walk out the door.

It wasn't like I could have gone after her. I was in my damn boxers.

My head was still fucking throbbing. No matter how many times I rolled my head around, popping my neck, it still fucking hurt. I made my way into the bathroom. Taking down four Oxys to help with the splitting pain. I threw on a pair of jeans and a black t-shirt. Grabbing a Red Bull from the fridge on my way out the door.

She was sitting in the driver seat, staring blankly out in front of her. Lost in thought. Not even acknowledging me as I got in the car. I lit up a cigarette and downed the drink in my hands in one gulp. I was finally starting to feel somewhat fucking normal.

The pills were finally kicking in.

"Baby, where are—"

She reached for my hand, holding it tightly in her grasp before placing it on her lap. As if she needed to feel my touch.

My warmth.

I'd never seen her like that. She was starting to scare me. I wanted to talk to her, to ask what was going on, but something told me she wouldn't have answered. There was no getting through to her. She had fallen down a hole that I had never been down before.

I chain-smoked the entire drive to God knows where. When she got off at the Brooklyn Bridge exit, I really didn't know where the fuck we were going. She parked the car on the side of the road once we hit the bridge. Swinging her door open and getting out of the car before I even said a word.

I followed close behind her as we walked up the pathway. She stopped when we reached the arches and it hit me. I had passed this bridge hundreds of times and never noticed what those arches symbolized. But seeing Briggs stand under them, it was the first fucking time I saw the angel wings within the arches above her head, mimicking the angel wings on her back.

"Baby, what the fuck is—"

Her intense glare over the edge of the railing made me stop talking. I watched with a captivated stare, wanting to know what the hell she was thinking. What the hell was going on in her mind...

I watched in horror as she stepped up onto the railing. I lunged into action, roughly grabbing her around the waist, spinning her to the ground in front of me.

I immediately pulled away needing to look at her.

"What the fuck are you doing? Are you on—"

She pushed me away from her. I stumbled back more from the unexpected shove than the force of her moving me.

She looked back over the edge and I swear to God I was ready to tackle her to the goddamn ground if she tried to step on the railing again. Instead, she peered back at me with a penetrating glare that resonated deep within my bones.

"What is going on in that beautiful mind of yours?" I asked, needing to know before she hurt herself.

She slowly stepped back and I quickly stepped forward, gripping onto her waist, tugging her toward me. Our faces were now a foot apart. I could feel her rapid heart beating against my chest, vibrating against my entire body.

Shaking me to my core.

She looked deep into my eyes and asked, "You want to die, Austin?"

My eyes widened in shock. Hers filled up with fresh tears as she continued, "Well then, here's your chance. Jump. Stand on the ledge and fucking jump."

She shook her head. Tears now falling down her devastated face.

"I won't stop you," she added.

I jerked back from the impact of her words, from what she was saying to me.

Letting her go.

She didn't falter, stepping toward me.

Roaring with execution, "Fucking jump, Austin, if you want to die. Because I can't watch you kill yourself slowly anymore."

Briggs

We stood on the bridge staring at each other for a second, possibly a few minutes, maybe several hours. Time seemed to blend together as much as his drugs did.

I was the first to break the silence.

"Austin, I'm fucking exhausted. You have no idea what I go through every single day in this life with you. I don't remember when I had a good night's sleep. You disappear for days at a time. I don't know whether you're alive or dead in an alley somewhere. Every bad thought runs through my head. I question everything. Especially, what the fuck I'm still doing here trying to save a man that obviously doesn't want to be saved. I sit here putting my life on hold, waiting for you to walk through that damn door or worse, the cops knocking to tell me you're dead," I paused to let my words sink in.

"But you know what I keep telling myself... the man that's standing in front of me right now is already dead, so why should I fucking worry myself sick."

"Briggs—"

"I'm tired of you punishing me, Austin, for making the only choice I could."

"I would have straightened out if you would have given me the chance. You saw me after I found the ultrasound photo. I would have stopped using the moment you told me. I would have been the man that you fell in love with. I would have—"

"For how long, Austin? How long until things got scary and you found solace in your drugs again?"

His eyes glazed over, understanding what I said.

"And what if I died, Austin? It happens everyday, all around us. What if something happened to me? Would you relapse or would you stay clean for our baby? Would you be the man that takes our child to a drug party? Huh? Leaving him or her at a table to fend for herself? Tell me, since you have clearly proven that you can't handle emotional distress. You numb—"

"That's not true," he said through a clenched jaw.

"Really? What part? What happened after you found out about what I did? Is that not enough proof for you? You ran straight for the drugs, only this time it was the worst kind. How about Savannah's funeral? How fucked up were you for that? Hmm? Want more? How about since your car accident?"

"I was taking pain pills for my back," he gritted out.

I scoffed, "Ten to what? Thirty a day? How many do you have to take for your back not to hurt, Austin?"

His eyes widened, taken aback.

"You've been numbing your pain since you were eighteen. It's been ten years. Ten fucking years, Austin! It's all that you know anymore. Now, tell me... how would you deal with something happening to me? What is the first thing you would do? What is the first thing you would turn to?"

He opened his mouth to say something but nothing came out. Not one word. He reached his hand up to rub the back of his neck, looking away from me.

"Exactly. Let me see how accurately my guess is. I think you'd let our kid stay with my uncle when you decided you needed to go on a binge. He'd be the perfect babysitter, seeing as you don't talk to your friends or family at all. Or you'd skip the babysitter all together and be like Molly's dad. Subjecting our child to drugs. You're still dealing. Working for my uncle. Not as much because you've become a goddamn junkie. The life you promised me, the reason that you started doing this in the first place... is long gone. So, you tell me? What fucking choice did I have?"

His chest was rising and falling with every word that left my mouth, battling against his own reality. The wind picked up at that moment, causing chills to run throughout my body.

"I'm done having you punish me. The burden I'm already carrying is more than I will ever be able to bear. Ever," I stated, accenting the last word. "I love you, Austin, but I can't watch you kill yourself. It's the drugs or it's me. You can't have both anymore. It's your choice. Your only choice. But if you don't choose me, then fucking jump off this ledge because all you're doing is prolonging the inevitable."

It literally killed me to say that to him. I stood there on pins and needles, waiting for my entire life that was standing before my eyes, to choose me.

To choose his girl.

His Heaven instead of his Hell.

His internal struggle was written clear across his tormented expression. He swallowed hard turning to walk over to the railing, and for a split second I thought I was going to watch the love of my life jump to his fate. His hands tightly gripped the wires as if they had all the answers for him.

"You don't fucking get it, Daisy. It's the only time I see *her*," he rasped.

He hadn't called me that since he learned the truth of what I did. My heart soared for the first time in a year.

"See who, Austin?"

"Our baby."

"What are—"

"When I found out… that night…" he stuttered, not being able to say it. "I saw her. Through the haze. She was there. She has your eyes, Briggs. Your dad's eyes. The only time I see her is when I stick a needle in my arm," he scoffed out.

"Oh my God," I breathed out.

He bowed his head, releasing a deep sigh. "I'm scared, baby. I'm so fucking scared," he confessed, looking at the traffic below us.

I immediately went to him, turning his body around to face me. Grabbing the sides of his face so he would look at me, like he had done so many times to me.

"I don't know how to not be high anymore. It's who I am now, Daisy. I don't want to stop seeing our baby girl either."

"I'll be there every step of the way. We will do this together. I promise I won't leave your side."

"When I'm high I get to see the life we could have had. The life I promised you. It's the only time I'm happy. It's the only time I don't feel the guilt over everything that's become of *us*. Everything I've done. The hurt and pain I've caused you."

"I know. I'm scared too, Austin. But I know in my heart." I placed my hand over the scar near his heart. "I know you're still in here. Buried deep within the pain that you keep masking with the drugs. The excuses you're making to continue on your downward spiral, that's only going to lead you nowhere but six feet under. I don't want that. Please... don't make me bury someone else I love. Please... don't leave me alone. I need..." I said, my voice breaking. "We can make that dream a reality without the drugs... We can still have that life."

"What if I'm not that person anymore? What if the man that you love so fucking much is gone, baby? What if I can't reach deep enough to find him anymore?"

"I love every single part of you. The good and the bad. Do you hear me?"

"I'm sorry, Daisy. I know I say it all the fucking time. But I'm so fucking sorry. For everything I have put you through. You're still the only thing that matters to me."

"No. I'm not. Your drugs are, but that's why I brought you here. To save you."

"I hate myself. I hate what I've done to us. To you. To our love. I hate that I made you feel like you didn't have a choice when you got pregnant. Having a baby, a family, a life with you... it's all I've ever wanted. I don't know how I lost my way. I don't know how the drugs took over. I ask myself that every single day with no answers, with no excuses. I have nothing but the syringe that I keep injecting into my arms. Chasing the dragon down the rabbit hole that only takes me further and further away from you. It just takes away the pain."

"Austin, I can't help you unless you want to be helped. I can't do this for you."

"I can't lose you. I'm nothing without you." He caressed the side of my cheek, and I leaned into his embrace.

Soaking up his warmth.

His love.

His truth.

That I hadn't felt in so long.

"I don't want to go to rehab. I just need you. That's all. I can do this at home with you by my side."

I nodded, smiling.

He caught my expression in the air and placed it near his heart. He hadn't done that in years.

And for the first time, it gave me hope that everything was going to be okay.

CHAPTER
30
Briggs

"Please... please... please... baby... just give me one hit to take the edge off... just one fucking hit... I'm dying, Briggs... I feel like I'm fucking dying..." Austin wailed.

Two days went by, but it felt more like an eternity. I hated seeing him in so much pain. The withdrawals crippling him in ways I never thought were possible.

"Baby... just let me have a taste... just a taste... it hurts... it fucking hurts..." he slurred, grinding his teeth and shaking to the core.

It didn't matter if I put three layers of blankets on him, he couldn't stop shivering. His body was convulsing and he was in and out between hot and cold sweats.

I was sitting on the bed with my back against the headboard. Austin's head was on my lap, his arms securely wrapped around my waist. He was sweating profusely as if he had just stood in the pouring rain. His body trembling so hard that it vibrated the entire bed.

I was lightly rubbing his head, trying my best to ease his discomfort. Anytime I touched any other place on his body he said my skin felt like daggers against his sensitive flesh.

That stung my heart, but I knew it was the withdrawals talking.

"Baby! Please, please! I'm fucking dying! It hurts... everything fucking hurts... please, just a taste," he groaned in pure agony, punching his legs from the intense muscle spasms.

Arching his back then contracting into a ball like a possessed man.

"Austin... shhh... you're okay... you're okay... come on... I know... baby..." I soothed the best I could, knowing it didn't mean anything.

"I'm going to get a cold rag, okay? I'll be right—"

"No! Don't leave me!" he panicked.

He wouldn't let me out of his sight, no matter what I said. We had moved from the couch to the bathroom where he laid with his head on my lap on the tile floor for the first few hours, throwing up constantly once the drugs wore off. At one point I just sat him against the bathtub to let him puke in there. His body was so weak he couldn't crawl to the toilet. I don't know how he still had shit coming up.

I was in and out of consciousness, not wanting to leave him alone, although his physical distress wouldn't allow me to anyway.

I used to lie awake counting the freckles and scars on his arms that he always laid across me. Holding me tight against his body. Now I counted the tracks on them, which were almost physically impossible to see under his tattooed sleeves. All the colors, shadings, and inks covering what our reality had become for the last year.

Austin hadn't slept at all, the extreme pain keeping him from being able to drift off. Insomnia set in fast and with no remorse, keeping him wide awake to feel every ounce of withdrawal. His body was craving the drugs that it had been living on for years. I knew opiate and heroin were the worst withdrawals. I just never imagined that watching it would kill me as much as the drugs were killing him.

Terrified he wouldn't make it through the night.

And the addiction would win.

It was like that for two more days. Same old shit just a different day. Both of us were so fucking exhausted. I was able to get him to eat some crackers and drink some water, and for the most part it stayed down. He had no energy. Even when I would help him walk around our apartment for a few minutes every few hours just to get his muscles to move. It seemed to help with the cramping and spasms.

By the fifth day it looked like we were passed the worst. I saw light at the end of the tunnel again.

At least physically.

Mentally he was so out of it, but I knew a big part of it was from him not sleeping. I crushed up two sleeping pills in his water without him knowing and even that took several hours to finally kick in.

I took a hot shower for the first time since we got home from the bridge. I stayed in there letting the hot water drown out my sorrows. Trying to cling on to hope, praying to God we would make it through this.

That *he* would make it through this.

Austin took the first step by flushing every last drug we had in the apartment down the toilet. He was fine for like twelve hours before the withdrawal crept in slowly then it just took the fuck over.

I had never seen that many emotions take over a person's body before. Why anyone would do this to themselves was beyond me. I just prayed that the pain was enough to keep Austin sober.

Enough to keep his demons at bay.

One thing was for sure, there was no way we could stay in this apartment, possibly even New York. There was no way we could continue this lifestyle and Austin make it out alive. At that point in time, my uncle never questioned what the fuck was going on, but he had to assume. Austin hadn't been around or answering his phone. I would be lying if I said it didn't shock me that he just didn't show up at our apartment demanding to know what was going on.

I placed my memory blanket on top of Austin, careful not to wake him. I grabbed my phone from the nightstand and went outside, leaving the balcony door cracked in case he woke up.

It rang two times before he answered.

"I've been expecting your call," Uncle answered.

I took a deep breath. "Hello to you too, Uncle."

"How is he?"

Shaking my head in disgust. I scoffed out, "You knew?"

"Briggs, there's very little I don't know when it comes to my fucking business, and even then, I always find out."

"And you still had him dealing? Even though you knew? What the fuck is wrong with you? When are you going to start—?"

He completely ignored my questions. "He's a grown-ass man. I'm not his keeper—"

"You were mine. But seeing as you did such an amazing job of raising me, I guess I couldn't expect any less."

I shook my head, once again disappointed by the turn in events.

"Tell me, Uncle… if you didn't want me, then why did you take me in? Why not just leave me in foster care? My parents didn't have a will. It's not like you were obligated. So, why? Why go through all the trouble and burden to raise me if you didn't want me?" I asked for the first time, needing the answer to the question that consumed my very being since the day he brought me back to his penthouse.

"We're family, Briggs. You're my niece whether you want to be or not. No matter what you think of me, I would never turn my back on my family. Ever," he spoke with conviction.

"You have a very deluded sense of the word family, Uncle."

"I raised you the only way I knew how," he rasped out almost in a sad tone I'd never heard before, causing me to jerk back from the sudden emotion in his voice.

"Do you even love me?" I blurted, raising my eyebrows as soon as the question left my mouth.

He didn't falter. "I loved your mother, and you're a part of her," he simply stated.

"I stopped trying to understand you fucking decades ago. But if you want to finally do something for me, then you'll let us go. If he has any chance of living a normal life, I need to get him out of here. Away from you."

Silence.

"Please… please… Uncle."

I would beg him on my hands and knees if I needed to.

"You will always be my niece, Briggs, and I will always be your uncle… in any life you choose," he forewarned and immediately hung up before I had the chance to say anything.

I didn't give it anymore thought, walking back into the apartment I looked over at a sleeping Austin.

Finally feeling hopeful.

AUSTIN

I woke up at the crack of dawn with a sleeping Briggs in my arms. I couldn't remember the last time I watched her sleep. She was usually out of bed before me and that was if she even slept at all. She was lying on my arm, curled around it like a stuffed animal. Her memory blanket placed on top of both of us.

She was a sight for sore fucking eyes.

She looked like an angel with her hair spread out on the pillow and her pink pouty lip that she loved to bite was sticking out.

Damn, I was a lucky son of a bitch.

It had been over two weeks since I stopped using. I wasn't even taking pain pills. And I owed it all to the woman in my arms. For the first time in over a decade I was completely sober.

It was the craziest fucking feeling. Ever.

It was like I had been on a roller coaster for years and it finally came to a halt. Except I couldn't find my balance no matter where or how I stood, and I would be lying if I said it didn't scare me. There were triggers all around me.

Fuck, this apartment alone was a trigger.

A part of me felt like I was just living in the gray area, hoping that I would soon find the black or white. I didn't want to relapse. I swear on my love for Briggs that I wanted to stay sober, but it was such unfamiliar territory for me.

As if it were a new world, one that I hadn't existed in since before my car accident. Somewhere along the way I let the darkness and the demons, creep in through the cracks.

I never thought people could become so weak to the point of letting anything control their lives. Never in my wildest dreams did I think I would ever become one of them. I knew I was slowly killing myself from the first time that needle went into my arm. There was no going back for me. There was no going forward either. I was at a standstill with no place to go but down into the dark abyss of addiction.

Being able to see our baby girl didn't help, all it did was add fuel to my already burning fire. Taking down everything in its wake.

Including Briggs.

She was burning alive because I was already dead.

I couldn't even remember the last time I touched her, the last time I fucking tasted her, or the last time we fucked. Let alone made love. I used to pretty much live inside her, day in and day out. It was my favorite place to be. Buried balls deep inside her.

I could see her nipples through the cream color satin of her tank top that had rose up while she slept. I softly caressed her stomach with my knuckles, leaving goosebumps in their wake. She felt like silk against my fingers as I slowly made my way down to the edge of her panties, slipping my fingers into her warm welcoming heat.

She stirred, and her body told me to keep going even though her eyes were still closed. My fingers moved slowly at first, and with each elevated breath that escaped from her lips, I moved them faster and more precise.

She moaned, fluttering her eyes open.

"What's going—"

I pushed my fingers into her opening. Her head rolled back against the pillow, and her back arched off the bed.

"You're so fucking beautiful," I groaned, watching her come undone time and time again. My thumb played with her clit while I continued to fuck her with my fingers, wanting nothing more than to make her come for me. I intercepted her hand and placed it above her head when it moved toward my cock.

"No, baby. Let me take care of you," I murmured.

"I want to take care of you too," she panted.

"All you do is take care of me."

"Austin," she whimpered as I thrust my fingers in again.

"Open your eyes, baby. Let me see those blue eyes."

She did just as I hit her g-spot harder and with more determination. I let go of her hand to grab onto her hip for leverage. Thrusting harder and harder.

"I love you, Daisy. I love you so fucking much."

That was her undoing. Her pussy clamped down, riding out her orgasm against my fingers. And I loved every last second of it.

"We need to talk, babe," I coaxed before I lost the nerve. "We need to go. We need a fresh start. I can't stay—"

"I know. No more running away, Austin. I think it's time that you went back home."

I frowned, lowering my eyebrows in confusion.

"What do you mean I need to go back home? I'm not fucking living without you, Daisy. You are my home."

"Calm down. I meant with me. I think we could make a really nice life in Oak Island. I loved it there, and it's where your family and friends are. I want that. I want that more than anything else. To be apart of the place you used to call home."

Crave Me

I took a deep breath, contemplating what she said. I could see it in her eyes. Everything she just shared was something that she really wanted.

After all those years, after everything I put her through, put us through.

I would give her the world if I could.

Even if it meant going back home.

CHAPTER
31

AUSTIN

We moved back to Oak Island a few days ago, and I was still unsure about being back in the place I tried so hard to forget. We didn't exactly have a welcoming committee either. I'd been sober for a little over two months and I wasn't going to lie, it was a daily struggle. My back pain was still alive and fucking thriving. I ignored it. I just tried to stay busy, and with Briggs by my side it was fairly easy to do.

Briggs said she settled everything with her uncle before we left. I was stunned when she told me that he was just letting us go with no repercussions, but she said it was behind us and that was the end of the conversation. We left all our belongings in New York besides some of our clothes. She didn't even take most of her wardrobe with us, saying that her uncle was the reason she bought half that shit anyway. I took some of my clothes but not much either.

We both wanted a fresh start.

We found a furnished apartment on the beach to rent in the meantime. She said she wanted to find us the perfect house and that would take us some time. I honestly didn't give a fuck where we lived as long as it kept that smile on her face.

I wish I could tell you that I was miraculously cured and that the craving to use had gone away.

It didn't.

Oak Island was a living and breathing trigger by itself for me. When I called my mom to tell her we were moving back home, to say that she was excited would have been an understatement. She was actually the one who picked us up from the airport and drove us to our apartment. My dad was nowhere to be seen, but she said he was working. I knew in my heart that was just a bullshit excuse. He was the boss, he could come and go as he pleased.

He just didn't care to see me.

My mom and Briggs seemed to hit it off. Talking about random shit and laughing like they were old friends catching up. Briggs looked happy for the first time in years, and that's all that mattered to me.

We'd been getting everything situated to begin our new lives. We bought a car, groceries, and little things we needed for our apartment.

Normal daily life kind of stuff and the concept still seemed so fucking foreign to me.

We hadn't seen the boys or Alex yet but that was about to change. Lucas and Alex found their way back to each other and the inevitable happened. They had gotten married a few years back. Half-Pint gave birth to their first baby three months ago. A little boy they named Bo. They were throwing a party at their house for their son and for Jacob and I moving back to Oak Island.

The good ol' boys would be together again.

A part of me missed them, the bond and brotherhood we had. Lucas was the first one to call me after I told my mom we were moving back. She gave him my number. Neither one of us mentioned what happened in the past as if the memories stayed there. Buried. Thank fucking God. I didn't think I could live near him if he still hated me.

"What if they don't like me?" Briggs asked for the tenth time on our way to the party, looking at herself again in the visor mirror.

"Baby, they already know you," I chuckled, grabbing her hand and placing it on my lap as I drove.

"I know but that was under a really sad circumstance. We exchanged maybe five words the entire time, so that doesn't count. They really know nothing about me at all."

"They're going to love you. I love you, so there is that."

"Maybe I should dye my hair? Like a normal color now."

I glanced over at her. "You're not touching one hair on your goddamn head, baby."

She beamed. "I just look so different from everyone around here. Did you see the way the cashier looked at me this morning?"

"Yes. And if he looks at you like that again, I'll break his fucking face."

"Austin! He thought I was weird looking!"

"He thought you were something alright, and trust me 'weird looking' wasn't it."

She sighed, leaning back into her seat.

"I'm covered in tattoos, and in New York I blended in. I feel like I stick out like a sore thumb here."

"You never blend in anywhere, Briggs." I grinned at her. "Besides I'm covered in tattoos, too. You're beautiful. I love that you don't look like anyone here. My friends and family are going to love you. I mean, my mom already does."

She smiled. "I like her too. She emailed me all these recipes that you used to love as a kid. I'm going to make them for you."

I kissed her hand.

We were the last ones to arrive at Lucas and Alex's house that was right on the water. Everyone welcomed Briggs with open arms, making her feel like she was part of the family. I knew that meant a lot to her since she always felt like she didn't belong anywhere.

"Baby, I'm going to get some food," I told her, standing up.

She nodded, talking to Alex. I kissed her cheek and walked inside from the lanai.

"So, how are you doing, bro?" Jacob asked, grabbing some food beside me.

"Never better. You?"

I caught him staring right at Lily, completely ignoring my question. It was quick but I saw it.

"Is that right?" I asked, bringing his attention back to me.

"What?"

"At least she's legal now," I joked with a shit-eating grin on my face.

"Fuck you," he scoffed out, smiling.

"Does Lucas know?"

He shook his head no.

"At least I won't be the only one he's ever hated."

307

He stopped scooping food on his plate to look at me with a questioning stare and replied, "You think he will hate me?"

"You think he won't?" I countered with a cocked eyebrow.

"I don't fucking know… I love her. I've always loved her."

I knew he was telling the truth. The way he looked at her spoke volumes.

"Lily has always had that effect on people. It doesn't surprise me, man."

"So, Briggs, huh?" he asked, changing the subject. "You next? Marriage and a baby carriage and all that shit?"

I winced. I couldn't help it.

"Shit… did I—"

"I'm going to take this food to Briggs," I cut him off.

Making my way back toward Briggs with my demons sitting right on my fucking shoulders. The craving to use was so goddamn intense. I thought I had a pretty good handle on my sobriety, but the mere mention of what started my demise had me crumbling in minutes. My heart was beating out of my chest and sweat began to pool at my temples.

I was jonesing.

I stopped in the hallway, realizing that I had gotten lost dealing with my internal struggle.

And the irony was not lost on me.

I closed my eyes, needing to get a hold of my emotions. My desire to relapse was running deep, taunting me with each step that I took in the wrong direction. All I saw was Briggs' beautiful happy face, smiling, laughing for me.

I took a deep breath, turning around. Once again gaining control over my turmoil and plaguing thoughts.

Was it always going to be like this?

"Oh my God, Alex, he's gorgeous."

I stopped dead in my tracks, recognizing Briggs' voice instantly. I stood there frozen, listening to what sounded like a baby cooing.

"He is pretty perfect, but I'm biased," Alex replied, laughing. "Would you like to hold him?"

"Oh… umm… are you sure? I have zero experience with babies, Alex. Is that okay?" She let out a nervous laugh.

"Of course, you have to start somewhere. Here, put your arms in a cradle position and just support his head and you're good."

My feet started to move forward through the narrow hallway as if a goddamn rope was pulling them. I found myself following their voices, fighting against the current every step of the way. I knew I should have turned around.

I knew what I was about to witness.

But I couldn't stop. The gravitational pull was too strong. The force too powerful to fight against it.

"Awe, you look really good holding him, Briggs. It suits you. He's usually fussy around new people, and he doesn't even seem fazed by you. That's a good sign, it means you're going to be a great mom someday," Alex said, ripping my heart out of my fucking chest with her words.

"Bo, you are so precious. Look at these chubby cheeks. Alex, he is going to be a heart breaker."

The dagger that was already lodged in my heart, twisted a little more.

"God help me if he's anything like his daddy," Alex laughed.

"I can't wait. I want to be a mom so bad. To wake up and see a face like this everyday would melt my heart. I'd love to have a family since I didn't really have one growing up. Holding him right now is making me wish I had one of my own."

I willed my body to walk the fuck away. To walk back in the other direction. I didn't need to hear this, not now when I was struggling to stay clean. But I stopped when I heard my name.

"Austin would make an amazing dad, Briggs. He's always liked kids. Even when we were younger and the other boys didn't want anything to do with them."

"Yeah…" Briggs replied in a sad tone. "I'd love that. To have a family with him. It's all I've ever wanted," she added her voice breaking. "I'm sorry, I don't know why I'm getting so emotional."

"It's okay. Baby Bo has that effect on women, he gets it from his dad."

They laughed.

Before I knew it, I was standing in front of the room. Watching Briggs cradle and rock Bo as if he were her own.

As if he was *ours*.

She leaned her lips against his face and kissed his cheeks, looking at him adoringly, loving him immediately.

"Austin," Alex announced, looking up.

Briggs grimaced, shutting her eyes almost instantly.

"Come meet Bo. Although, I don't know if Briggs is going to give him up. I think she has baby fever. Maybe it's time you—"

Briggs interrupted, "Alex."

Locking eyes with me.

There was so much sorrow behind them. She held everything she ever wanted in her arms. It was like my best dream and my worst nightmare right in front of my eyes.

Except there was no waking up.

This was my reality.

And that…

Was my biggest fucking demon.

Briggs

Call it intuition if you would, but the second I saw Austin coming out of the bathroom later that evening, I knew. Clear as fucking day he had just used. I wanted to call him out on it and yell at him for going back down this road again.

"What the hell are you doin', man?" I overheard Dylan ask as I walked toward them.

"Not this shit again. Give me a fucking break," Austin roared, raking him up and down.

"Wipe your nose a little better next time and maybe I won't ask you."

Austin immediately bowed his head, sniffling, cleaning his nose.

"Get out of my fucking sight before I search you," Dylan warned.

Austin took a deep breath like he wanted to say something, but at the last second changed his mind, turned and left. I didn't have to wonder what he was going to say.

I knew the chance of relapse would be high. I just didn't think it would happen that fast. Which I guess made me really naive.

"How long has it been this fucking bad?" Dylan asked me, pulling me away from my thoughts.

I didn't know what to say, so I didn't say anything. I stood there dumbfounded as much as he was.

"Jesus Christ," Dylan whispered, tugging his long hair back at the nook of his neck. That's when I noticed he was strapped and right next to that on his holster was a shiny badge.

"You're a cop?"

"Detective," he corrected me.

I had no idea. Austin never talked about his friends.

"Well, thanks for not searching him."

"He's my fuckin' brother, Briggs. I love him."

"I know," I whispered, lowering my head, defeated.

He sighed. "I know he went through some shit after the car accident, but I thought... shit... I hoped he had worked it out. Especially having you by his side now. He fuckin' adores you, that's not hard to see." He shook his head. "I've never seen him look at anyone like he looks at you."

"I love him more than anything in this fucked up world. I'm trying, Dylan. I swear to God I'm trying. He's been clean up until now."

"Try harder," he simply stated and left.

I didn't give our conversation too much thought. I needed to find Austin. After searching the house and asking if anyone had seen him, I found him. He was down at the beach, sitting in front of the shoreline with his arms draped over his knees. A cigarette in one hand.

I stopped when I was a few feet behind him, taking in how handsome he looked with the full moon shining down on him. The soft lighting was all around us with the gentle breeze blowing by. I wrapped my arms around my waist in a comforting gesture, needing any solace I could find.

"I used to come here as a kid. Watch the waves roll in, smell the saltwater in the air. It used to be my favorite place to not feel so fucking lost. And here I am sitting in the same exact spot, more fucking lost than I've ever been."

"So those two weeks of Hell that we both went through to get you clean." I paused, trying to fight back tears. "They were for nothing? Why do you need drugs to escape, Austin? Why can't you just face life like everyone else?"

A single tear slid down my face onto the sand between us.

"I'm sorry, baby."

"You know what the worst part is? I knew the second I held Bo that you would relapse. I didn't want you to see me with him. It's why I went with Alex into his room. The second I heard her say your name, I knew it was too late. I knew with every fiber of my being you would be fucking weak, that you would betray me and use again. Just tell me one thing... did you already have them on you?"

"No. I've lived in Oak Island all my life, Briggs. It just took a phone call."

"Do you have more?"

"I did but I threw it in the ocean."

"And I'm suppose to believe you? I can't do this anymore. I can't—"

He was up and over to me in three strides.

"I won't do it again. I promise. It was a one-time thing. I swear—"

"I don't believe you."

"I don't lie to you. I've never lied to you."

"Omitting the truth is lying. Jesus Christ, Austin, you don't have to say it for it to be a lie."

"Baby..." He reached for me, and I stepped back, even though all I wanted was for him to hold me.

"Don't fucking 'baby' me right now. I can't go through watching you suffer again. I can't keep going through this. Either you go to rehab or I'm gone. It's your choice."

"I don't need rehab. All I need is you."

"If that were true, you wouldn't have just used."

AUSTIN

I bowed my head, rubbing the back of my neck like I always did when I was pissed. I had no one to blame but myself.

"Fuck," I groaned, kicking at the sand. "Fuck," I said a little louder. "FUUUUCK!" I finally screamed out, grabbing a rock from the sand. "Goddamn it, fuck you!" I chucked it as hard as I could in front of me, cursing myself for being such a fuck-up.

Breathing heavily, heart pounding, mind battling. Fighting all my thoughts, all my emotions, every last sentiment pulling me deeper and deeper until I didn't know which way was up or down. Knowing the difference between what was right and what was wrong didn't matter. All of it consumed me as if I were drowning in the waves of the ocean.

Taking me further down the path of destruction.

My body was shaking.

My heart was breaking.

I couldn't take it anymore, it was too much, and it was too fucking real. I peered back up at Briggs with my arms out in the air beside me.

Defeated.

Once again, fucking defeated.

With nothing but my remorse, my shame, my guilt.

"Do you think I want to be like this? Do you think I like being this fucking weak? This big of a goddamn pussy? Do you think I want to fucking live like this, Briggs? I hate myself right now! I hate that just watching you hold a baby in your arms can do this to me! Can make me run back to the one thing that will take you away from me! The one thing that fucking matters the most in my life! I don't know how to be any other way! I don't know how to feel, to cope and be fucking normal! Even though it's all I want! I want that more than anything!" I yelled, struggling to keep it together.

"I can't do this anymore, Briggs! I can't fucking live like this! I feel like I'm dying, baby. I feel like I'm fucking dying! Every time you look at me the way you are right now. Every time I know that I have hurt you again! Fucking disappointed you! I didn't think I could hate myself as much as I do right now! And I don't know what to do! To make it better for me... for you!" I cried, broken, fucked-up tears falling down the sides of my face.

"Please... please... fucking help me. I don't want to lose you, baby. I can't live without you. I fucking love you! But I know..." I sobbed so hard my body shuddered to the core.

Taking down the last bit of strength I had. The last bit of courage that was left in me.

The last part of Austin.

I fell to my knees in pain. I couldn't take it anymore and started bawling harder. I sobbed for the first time in front of Briggs, in front of the woman who was trying to save my life, while I just kept trying to destroy it.

Crave Me

My resolve broke like a chain that had been stretched to the max. I heard it snap loud and clear. Shattering into a million pieces, blending into the sand along with my demons. Except the shackles that were tied around my soul, my heart, and my mind were now secured tighter, restraining, pressing in so fucking deep. So fucking intensely, to the point of blinding agony. Dragging Briggs right along with me.

I was killing her as much as I was killing myself.

Our love was bleeding, oozing from the shackles, hammering out of me with each passing second placed between us. I could physically feel it deteriorating away, piece by piece.

I placed my hand over my heart desperately trying to keep it together. To keep our love where it's supposed to stay forever, but it was too late. I couldn't stop it, and for the first time I was terrified that it would never let me go.

"I know that if I keep using, if I keep going down this road, I'm going to die, and I don't want to fucking die," I bellowed, shaking my head. "That's not an option. I'm not trying to die. But I don't know how to fucking break free from the demon that lurks in my shadow. Seeing what I saw tonight, you with baby Bo, broke my heart again. I needed to numb the pain, even if it was only for a few minutes." I looked up at her with a trembling lip, struggling to continue. "I saw her again. Our daughter standing right in front of me with so much sadness in her eyes. Not smiling like all the times before. She took one look at me and shook her head, Briggs. My own drug-infected illusion was disappointed in me. Then she was gone, she vanished."

My body fell forward burying my face in my hands letting everything out.

Every last part of me.

"I don't know what to do, Briggs! I wish I could be stronger for you. For us! I wish I could be the man you fell in love with. But I don't know how! Every single day is a struggle for me to stay sober, and I don't think it's ever going away. As much as I want it to... as much as I pray... it's apart of me now. AND IT WON'T LET ME GO! I thought leaving New York and coming here would eliminate the triggers, but it hasn't. Please God! Please... fucking help me!"

She didn't waver, getting down on her knees to hold my crumbling body in her arms. I went willingly, needing comfort, needing solace.

Needing her.

"I'm sorry, I'm so sorry. Please help me, Daisy... please God help me. Please, please.... Take away this fucking pain in my heart. I need you, baby, I need you like I need fucking air to breath. I'm nothing without you! NOTHING! Please... just fucking help me!"

"It's going to be okay, Austin. I'm here," she wallowed, her heart breaking for me.

I sobbed harder, my face tucked in to her chest with my arms wrapped tightly around her. She was the only thing keeping me together, even though there wasn't much left of my hollow existence.

Everything changed that night on the beach.

Briggs took me home, and I slept in her arms all night. Knowing that after tonight I wouldn't get to hold her for a while. She woke up early the next morning, and I stayed in bed for as long as I could. Battling between my craving to go use and my desire to stay with her. Thank God...

My love for her won.

She checked me into rehab.

And *I* went willingly.

CHAPTER
32

AUSTIN

Four years later

"Go fuck yourself," Briggs sassed.

"Why would I do that? When I could just fuck you."

She immediately got up from her chair to run away.

"Where do you think you're going?" I laughed, grabbing her around the waist.

She shrieked, doubling over as I tickled her.

"You're supposed to let me run first. It takes all the fun out of it if you catch me before I get a chance to run, Austin!" she giggled, gasping for air.

It was still the sweetest sound I'd ever heard.

"Why would I have to chase you if you're already in my arms?"

"Because I run and you chase! That's the game we play," she playfully teased.

I loved these moments with her. She was so carefree and happy again.

My girl.

"Is that right?"

I tickled her one last time before turning her around to face me, roughly smacking her luscious ass and giving it a squeeze. She let out a yelp and squirmed in my arms, trying to break free.

Her mouth parted and she bit her lower lip, making my cock twitch. I picked her up to straddle my waist, rubbing her up and down my hard dick.

"I like this game better," I rasped, carrying her over to the front counter of my tattoo shop.

Positioning her ass on the edge.

It had been four years since my relapse that night on the beach. Each day was a struggle, but it was getting better and easier as more time went by. Briggs dropped me off at rehab the morning after I used. I checked myself into the ninety-day program. We only told Dylan what was going on. She told everyone else that I had to finish up some work stuff in New York.

No one asked after that.

During that time Briggs got really close to my family and friends, including my dad, which shocked me more than anything did. But then again, she always had that effect on people. She was hard not to love. I knew having a family was what Briggs had always wanted, and I was thrilled that they were able to offer her that.

Rehab fucking sucked.

But I stayed and did what I was supposed to.

For her.

Anything for *her*...

I tried exercises and stretches, but my back pain was still there. Mostly, I just kept ignoring it. It became a part of me like my addiction. I went to my classes, I did my therapy, I found a sponsor, and I worked through my steps to achieve my ultimate goal.

To stay in recovery.

I was scared shitless the last day of my program, even though I wanted nothing more than to go home to Briggs. To sleep in our bed together. To hold her anytime I wanted or needed. My counselor said that was normal for everyone to feel scared to enter the real world again. That it would have been weird if I didn't feel that way. It was easier to stay clean in a controlled environment.

Briggs found us a four-bedroom, three-bath house with a pool and a huge backyard. She had it fully decorated by the time I came home. The house was beautiful but not nearly as beautiful as the smile on her face when she jumped into my arms the day I was discharged with a treatment plan that I kept everyday for the last four years.

We christened every corner of our new home, making up for lost time.

Twice.

We had more money than we knew what to do with, but I was getting restless needing to do something. I started sketching again, after years of being so fucking high, and numb. It not only affected my body but also my creativity. One day out of nowhere, I was drawing a sleeping Daisy on the couch beside me and for some reason her tattoos were my main focus in the sketch.

When she woke up I asked her what she thought about me getting my license to become a tattoo artist. She smiled, replying by kissing all over my face and sucking my cock like a goddamn pro in approval.

We opened a shop not long after. I tattooed and she handled all the managerial, customer service bullshit that I didn't give a fuck about.

Her uncle had come to visit us a few times, checking in and keeping tabs on us I imagined. They still had a weird dynamic, but at least he was trying to be around in the only way he knew how. During his visits, we never talked about the past, but it was always lurking just around the corner. I would be lying if I said that seeing him didn't trigger the demons that I had managed to keep at bay. I think a part of him knew that too.

"What's your favorite thing to do, Austin?" Briggs whispered, looking deep into my eyes as she wrapped her arms around my neck.

Bringing me closer to her.

I immediately caged her in with my arms around her pretty little face. Slightly pulling back her hair at the nook of her neck just like she loved. I leaned in close to her mouth, biting her bottom lip and huskily rasped, "Fucking you, baby. That's my favorite thing to do."

We were happy again.

And more in love than ever.

"Prove it," she challenged.

I didn't have to be told twice. It was after hours, and we owned the fucking place. She was counting inventory and decided to sass me with her smart-ass mouth.

Her body was perfectly proportionate with mine as I stood in between her legs. She looked up at me with adoration and yearning. The heady expression that I could never get enough of had me losing control. I roughly grabbed the back of her neck and plunged my tongue into her eager and awaiting mouth. It went back and forth between us, each giving the other what we craved. She clutched on to my hair and I pulled on hers, beckoning her head to fall back and give me the liberty to assault her neck.

I ran my nose from her chin to her collarbone, kissing all over her breasts.

"Who's my girl?" I baited, knowing she loved it when I asked.

Her nipples were already hard when I pulled down the front of her dress, waiting for me to take them into my mouth. I sucked and gently bit one while my hand caressed and fondled the other. Her breathing escalated and both of her soft, delicate hands gripped my hair as her hips gyrated forward on the edge of the counter, on the brink of falling.

I heard the rustling of my jeans as she unbuckled my belt, pulling out my hard cock. My hands went around to her ass, as I effortlessly picked her up off the counter. Sliding her panties to the side and slamming her right down onto my cock before she even saw it coming.

In one thrust, I was balls deep inside her.

Home.

We moaned in unison, both appreciating what the other was giving. She fit like a fucking glove, tightly wrapped around my cock. My arms leveled her up and down, thrusting her onto my shaft.

"Fuck… you feel good."

Her g-spot was hitting the tip of my cock ring so perfectly and precise.

"Let go a little, look at me, I got you, you're not going anywhere."

She loosened her hold and hitched in a breath when she looked into my eyes. I braced my forehead on hers and we never once took our eyes off each other. I knew it took all her willpower to not let her eyes roll to the back of her head.

Within seconds, we were both gasping and breathless for air. Her moans were getting louder and heavier. I could feel her come dripping down my ass. I fucked her harder and with more determination. Wanting to feel her sweet pussy come on my cock. Within minutes, neither one of us could take it anymore.

We both came together.

Hard.

I kissed her one last time before placing her back down on her feet. Holding her upright till she balanced on trembling legs.

"I want you to give me a tattoo," she said out of nowhere, looking sincerely into my eyes.

"Right now?" I replied, tucking my cock back into my jeans.

"It won't take long."

I walked toward my chair, patting for her to sit.

"Where and what would you like, pretty lady?"

She grinned, grabbing a piece of paper from her purse, sitting in the chair, lifting up her dress to point on her lower abdomen.

"I want these dates in numerical numbers."

She handed me the piece of paper with a serious face.

"You want this date from a week ago and this one from almost a year from now?" I asked, confused. "Why?"

"It's the day I found out I'm pregnant and the day the baby is born."

I jerked back. "What did you say?"

"Your baby is in my belly." She smiled.

"How?"

She cocked her head to the side with a snide smirk. "Well… when a man and woman really love each other they—"

I laughed, "You're on the pill."

She shrugged. "Sometimes it doesn't work. This is one of those times."

"You're sure? Like positive? One hundred percent?"

"I went to the doctor and she confirmed it. I've just been trying to find the right time to tell you."

"We're going to have a baby?" I questioned again, needing more confirmation.

She enthusiastically nodded with tears in her eyes.

"I can't tattoo you, Briggs. You're pregnant… But you're going to have my baby?"

She beamed, and I pulled her into my arms.

Finally holding everything we ever wanted.

Briggs

"I love this room," I said, lying down in the guest bedroom with Austin's head on my stomach, looking around the space. "I actually thought this would be our first baby's room when I bought this house," I added, scratching his back.

"First?" he replied, peering up at me.

"I want four or five kids, Austin. So we will probably have to be buy a new house, but we're good here for at least another two."

"Is that right? Do you hear your mama? Already talking about giving you siblings. What do you think about that?" he asked my stomach, kissing it.

He started having conversations with the baby growing inside me since the day he found out I was pregnant, two months ago. Everyday he talked to my belly, it didn't matter what it was about. He said the baby needed to learn his voice so it would know who its daddy was. Every night he sat with his head on my stomach, just to feel close to our child. It was the sweetest thing I had ever witnessed.

My heart was so full on most days. I could hardly take it.

When Austin first got out of rehab, I was scared that he was going to relapse again, but to my surprise every month it got a little easier. He never missed his weekly meetings, and he talked to his sponsor often. He told me his triggers were always there, but as the years went by it was easier to ignore them and take them for what they were.

The past.

His future was with me.

End. Of. Story.

We hadn't told anyone I was pregnant yet. I think we both wanted to enjoy it being just ours for as long as we could, knowing that his family and friends would soon want to be involved in everything they could. They had become like my own, taking me in and treating me like one of the family.

"That reminds me." He got up. "I'll be right back."

I rubbed my belly while he was gone, loving the feel of something growing inside me.

Our love.

"I got you something," Austin said, lying in the same position he was in before he left.

He handed me a box with baby animals and balloons decorated on it. I opened the lid and there was a soft pink baby blanket, a few pink, purple, and white baby onesies, all with sayings on them. I held up the pink one, it said, "Daddy's baby girl." The purple one said, "My other girl." The white one made me laugh, it said, "Party at my crib 2 a.m. B.Y.O.B." There were a few bibs with similar sayings on them. But it was the photo album that brought me to tears. It said, "You're all we ever wanted."

"Austin," I wept, unable to form words with all the emotions coursing through me.

"I drove by a baby store the other day, and I couldn't help myself. Don't cry, babe." He wiped away my tears. "I know she's a girl. I feel it."

I sniffled. "This is the worst thing you could do to a pregnant woman. I'm going to be crying for days."

"Then I'll be wiping away your tears for days."

"I never thought..." I expressed, getting choked up. "I mean I hoped, I prayed... I just never thought you would make it back to me." I started crying harder, imagining life without him.

My biggest fear.

Losing him again.

"I'll never leave you again, baby. I'm not going anywhere. I owe my life to you. In every sense of the meaning. I love you."

He kissed me, grabbing the onesie that said, "My other girl." Placing it on my belly.

We sat there for the rest of the day, planning the rest of our lives. That finally included.

A family.

CHAPTER
33
Briggs

A piercing pain in my stomach woke me out of a dead sleep. I immediately placed my hand on where the pain was radiating from.

"Austin," I whimpered, recoiling into a fetal position.

He stirred, his arm that was draped over me slightly moving.

"Hmm…" he groaned still sleeping.

"Austin, I can't… oh my God… Austin," I stammered, the pain unbearable.

"Baby?" He sat up instantly, blinking away the sleep. "You okay? What's wron—"

"Ah!" I moaned out in excruciating pain, tightening the hold on my stomach.

He pulled the sheet off us.

"Fuck! Baby, don't move. You're bleeding. Fuck! There's blood everywhere."

I heard him fumbling in the linen closet for towels as I lay there in a pool of my own blood and worst nightmare.

"No!" I cried, already knowing what was happening. "No! Please, no!"

"Shh… it's okay." He took a towel and wiped the blood off between my legs. "Baby, we need to get you to the hospital right now. You have lost a lot of blood. Hang on, okay. I love you."

He picked me up off the bed in a cradle position, and I instantly curled into his chest.

"It's okay, baby. You're fine," he reassured, kissing my head as he carried me to the car.

He sat me in the passenger seat and leaned it back for me to lie down. He didn't let go of my hand the entire time he drove. I not only cried out from the pain but for the news we were about to receive. It didn't matter what comforting words Austin kept saying to me.

It wouldn't change the truth.

They immediately wheeled me back into the ER where the doctor did an examination and an ultrasound to confirm what was going on. One minute we had all the happiness in the world, and the next it was ripped away from us without so much as a goodbye.

I wanted nothing more than to block out the next few hours of our lives.

"Is it something that I did?" I asked the doctor, only looking at Austin who appeared as broken as I felt.

There was a familiar gaze in his eyes, one that I hadn't seen in years.

Lost.

Devastated that our baby was no longer with us.

"No. Sometimes these things just happen. But the good news in this situation is that you got pregnant without a problem and you're still young. In a few months, you can definitely try again. I'm going to keep you here for a couple hours just to monitor the bleeding and if all goes well, you will be able to go home soon."

The good news... I wanted to tell him that there was no good news at this moment.

Only tragedy.

He left the room, leaving Austin and I to grieve over what we just lost. What we both wanted so badly.

Our baby.

I was discharged mid-morning, scheduling an appointment with my OBGYN for the next day.

"Are you okay, Austin?" I whispered loud enough for him to hear.

The silence was deafening in the car on the way home. Both of us consumed with the dark state of our thoughts. He barely said more than a few words the entire time at the hospital.

He nodded, reaching for my hand. "Are you okay?" His intense stare remained on the road ahead as if it pained him to look at me.

I didn't know what was the right or wrong answer so I went for the safe one.

"They said we could try again in a few months. I don't have to go back on the pill. We could try—"

He squeezed my hand stopping me from continuing.

"Yeah…" I breathed out, leaning my pounding head back on the headrest to aimlessly look out the window.

Watching the streetlights and trees blur by.

Home was the last place I wanted to be, but we ended up going there anyway. Austin made me some tea and grabbed a beer from the fridge. Sitting beside me on the couch, he pulled me into his arms. I leaned into his embrace, fighting back my tears and the emotions threatening to surface. All his warmth was replaced by an unfamiliar frigidness.

I didn't want to cry. I knew he was hurting, and the last thing I wanted to do was light the match to the fire that I could already smell burning. I laid my head on his shoulder, his tense arm tightly wrapped around me.

He kissed the top of my head. "I'm sorry, Daisy," he murmured, letting his lips linger there.

I didn't know what he was apologizing for, and I was too scared to ask.

"It's not your fault. It's no one's fault."

My resolve was starting to break the tighter he held me against his cold body. It felt like all his warmth left with our baby. As if he was waiting for me to breakdown, waiting for me to lash out, waiting for something that maybe didn't have anything to do with me. I was so worried about him that I couldn't even contemplate what just happened. I couldn't mourn the loss of our baby because I was terrified that I would soon mourn the loss of the man sitting beside me.

The one that took years to make it back to me.

Loving an addict was like being on a roller coaster with no seat belt on. You had no idea when it was going to turn. You're just confused, disoriented, fearful, praying...

All you could do was hang on for dear life and hope that it didn't kill you.

"Do you think—" He stopped himself, leaning over me to grab his beer from the table.

"What?" I peered up at him. "What were you going to say?"

He wouldn't look at me. Not for one second. He shook his head, taking a swig of his beer. Polishing it off with one gulp.

He didn't need to say it. I knew what he was thinking.

"It's no one's fault, Austin. You heard the doctor. He said these things just happen, usually for no reason at all. Please don't blame yourself."

"It's not me I'm blaming."

I tried to jerk free, but he held me tighter into his chest.

"Baby, I didn't mean it to come out like that. I just... I love you... we can do whatever you want. You want to try for another baby, I'll give you whatever you want," he said with a tone void of any emotion, still blankly staring at the wall in front of us.

It hurt immensely that he couldn't even look at me. He wasn't able to look me in the eyes and tell me what he really meant by that.

"Austin—"

"Briggs, stop. I'll hold you for as long as you need. I'm not going anywhere. I can promise you that. I just can't talk right now, okay? I just want to sit here with you in my arms. I just want to feel you. That's all."

Tears threatened to surface as I bowed my head in defeat. He lightly skimmed his fingers through my hair. I closed my eyes holding onto the love we shared, the last four years, the first four of our relationship, the memories, anything I could cling onto for hope.

Exhaustion won the battle I was fighting. I fell asleep silently crying in Austin's arms on the couch. I woke up from a dream, except before I even opened my eyes I realized I was alone. My memory blanket securely placed on top of me. The darkness from the outside world was shadowing in through the sliding glass doors.

Revealing the truths I already knew.

I whipped the blanket off of me, needing to find him. My feet moved on their own accord to the room that was going to be our baby's. I just had a feeling that I would find him there.

As soon as I walked in I saw him, his demons prevailed. My fears went unheard. He didn't even try to hide it. I don't know if that was better or worse. He peered up at me with his vacant constricted pupils.

His blue eyes so illuminated.
So hollow.
So. Fucking. High.

AUSTIN

I tried.

I swear to God on our love. On Briggs' life. On our unborn babies.

I. Fucking. Tried.

I sat there for hours holding her, praying that it would be enough to keep me strong. To hold me together. To hold me back from what was calling for me, what my mind and body craved. After she passed out, I still sat there not wanting to let her go. Letting the night's events play out in my head, trying to understand what it all meant.

When I saw the blood in between her legs, it didn't even register in my mind what was going on. I just wanted to get her to the emergency room to make sure she was okay. Not once did I think that it could be our baby. The thought never crossed my fucking mind. When the doctor confirmed it was a miscarriage, my whole life flashed before my eyes.

In seconds.

And I'm not talking about the life I was currently leading. From that moment I felt it.

My sobriety.

My recovery.

My demons were emerging from the darkness, sitting right on my goddamn shoulder, whispering, lurking, and fucking waiting.

I ignored it. Almost like you did to an itch that needed to be scratched.

I thought if I held her. If I had her in my arms, I'd be able to fight off the demons. Knowing that if I relapsed, I could lose her. I could lose everything I ever wanted. But it didn't matter because I already felt like I lost another part of me. Of us, and nothing was bringing our baby back.

I felt guilty for not sharing my many emotions and thoughts, things that I didn't want to say out loud, not wanting them to be true. That was my first mistake.

In the end.

The craving won.

There I was lying in the same bed where we spent almost three months talking about the future. Planning our lives. The very life that included our baby. I didn't get to say goodbye. I didn't get a choice. A say.

Again.

I turned my head and came face to face with an angel. My whole life was standing in the doorway with nothing but disgust and disappointment in her eyes. Then it hit me…

The cause was lying in bed limply holding a needle in his hand.

Me.

Again.

Briggs didn't have to look down at my arm to know, my eyes always told her the truth.

"Four years, Austin. Four fucking years," she said her voice breaking. "Why? Of all things why did you have to use that one? Or any of them?"

I took in her distress before I simply stated, "I wanted to see her."

She immediately put her hand over her mouth, fervently shaking her head back and forth.

"That's not fair! You cannot play that card every goddamn time life throws you a fucking curve ball."

"It's the truth."

Tears streamed down her beautiful face, and I resisted the urge to comfort her. Too caught up in my own misery.

"I'm hurting too, Austin. You know the real fucked-up part is that I knew this was going to happen. The minute you lifted the sheets and saw the blood. I couldn't contemplate what was going on because I was too fucking worried about you. How is that fair to me? I can't mourn the death of our baby because of you!"

I watched each one of her tears fall down the sides of her face, one right after the other. Playing out in slow motion, absorbing into the wooden floor below.

"I'm sorr—"

"Stop, right there. I know exactly what you're going to say. 'I'm sorry, Briggs, I'm so fucking sorry.' Am I right? Did I hit the nail on the head, Austin?"

"Baby, I really am so fucking sorry."

She visibly cringed at my apology, and I knew why. I hadn't said that to her in so damn long. It even felt foreign coming from my lips.

"I promise I won't do it again. I swear to you. I just needed something to take away the pain. Something to cloud my mind from what was going on. It was a one-time thing. Look." I showed her the needle in my hand. "No more left. I only got enough for one time. I won't put you through this again. I can't."

"Austin, this is the same story, just a different time. How can I—"

"I don't lie to you. I've never lied to you."

She took a deep breath unsure with how to respond. I got up and went to her. Backing her against the wall, caging her in with my arms. Her eyes instantly went to my forearm where I had used. I lowered it, grabbing her chin to look at me instead.

We locked eyes even though I knew it was the last place she wanted to focus on right now.

"Four years, Briggs. Four fucking years. Trust me. I made a mistake. I know that. You know that..." I let go of her chin and kissed along her face. "Where's my girl? Where's my Daisy? Hmm..."

I could feel her melting against my touch.

"I love you more than anything. I'm sorry. I won't do it again. I promise."

I kissed along her lips, beckoning them to open for me.

They did.

She let me in just like I knew she would. I kissed her with everything I had, wanting her to feel my apology. To feel my undying love for her. My hand went to the nook of her neck pulling her closer as my tongue assaulted hers. She let out a soft moan and pulled away, breaking our connection. I pecked her lips a few more times, moving down her neck and back up to her lips, kissing her one last time.

"You can't do this to me again," she murmured against my lips. "Please, I can't—"

I gazed deep into her eyes. "Shhh... I'm sorry. I love you. I made a mistake. I promise I'll call my sponsor. I'll tell him what happened. I'll go to more meetings. I won't do this to you again. Please believe me."

Without a word she looked at me one last time, turned and left. I let her go because it was the right thing to do. Even though it felt so fucking wrong. The damage was already done. There was no going back.

Only forward.

CHAPTER 34

AUSTIN

It had been a year since Briggs miscarried our baby. So much had fucking changed, nothing in our lives was the same after that day. I worked all the time, leaving Briggs alone a lot. It was easier to get lost in my art than it was to face reality. At first she used to come in with me and work, both of us needing the distraction, but as the months passed, the less frequent her hours became.

She usually just worked a few hours a week and hired Mason, Lucas' son and Alex's stepson to work the front desk on the weekends and after school. He was fifteen and a punk ass kid who reminded me a lot of Lucas at that age. A smartass mouth that would get him in trouble one day and stubborn as shit.

"Hey, Mom," Mason announced as Alex walked through the door.

"Mason… your dad is going to kill you. Your report card—"

"Because he loved school so much? I want to go into the military. I don't need school to be a Marine."

She sighed, and I resisted the urge to chuckle. Instead I just smiled and shook my head.

"What's so amusing over there?" Alex called out, catching me.

I shrugged, sitting in my chair sketching up some designs for clients.

"The kid wants to fight for our country, Half-Pint. It's not like he's saying he wants to join the circus."

"Mason, can you go get me a coffee next door please?" Alex ordered.

331

"Mom, I'm not eight anymore. I know you're going to sit here and talk about me. I don't need to leave. At least this way I can defend myself. Am I wrong?"

"Mason…" she warned in her Half-Pint/mom way.

Mason was well over six feet tall already, towering over Alex.

"This is bullshit," he murmured under his breath, grabbing her money and walking to the door.

"Mason Ryder!"

"Love you, Mom," he said over his shoulder, walking out of the shop.

I started laughing my ass off. I couldn't help it. Lucas to a fucking T right there.

"What am I going to do with that kid? Lucas is seriously ready to strangle him," she stated, turning her attention back to me.

"Look, Half-Pint, his balls dropped. He's going to step up to Lucas eventually. It's a right of passage for every boy." I couldn't stop laughing. "And… karma is a fucking bitch."

"God and I still have to go through this with Bo?"

"At least you have your baby girl." I looked over to her with a smirk.

"Who is five, going on eighteen. She will not leave her brothers alone. All she does is follow them around and nags them."

"Sounds familiar." I smiled.

"I was never that annoying though."

"Debatable," I chuckled.

Her eyes widened. "At least it's good to see you smiling and laughing, Austin. Even if it's at my expense, I'll take it."

I looked back down at my drawings, the smile fading fast. She was right. I couldn't even remember the last time I truly smiled or laughed for that matter.

"What's going on with you? Are you and Briggs okay? You didn't seem okay at the barbeque a few weeks ago."

I ignored her, continuing to draw as she made her way over to me. Pulling up a chair beside mine.

"Hey…" She placed her hand on top of mine, stopping me. "What's up?"

"Alex, what do you want me to say?"

"I love Briggs, and she won't tell me anything either. She's actually much harder to get something out of than you are. Which is hard to believe, the way you keep your feelings bottled up."

"We're just going through some shit. You wouldn't understand."

"Try me."

I cocked my head to the side.

"Oh, come on. I can keep a secret. You should know that more than anyone. I never told a soul that you kissed me. Not even Lucas knows. It's no one's business, but ours."

"Half-Pint, you know why you didn't tell him and that's not the reason."

"It was part of it. It didn't mean anything, and you knew that when it happened."

We locked eyes.

"You know?"

She smiled. "You've always been the rebel, Austin. It's who you are. And because of that you isolate yourself a lot. You still do. It's the way you cope with things, and it's never been healthy. To keep that all bottled up inside, waiting for it to erupt like a volcano. I think that's why you confused your love and our friendship for something you've always wanted. But you and I both know it was never me. I was just the only girl in your life that made sense. That's why I never told Lucas or anyone else."

I narrowed my eyes at her, taking in what she was saying and knowing that it was the truth. Every last word of it, I remembered when I told Briggs that exact same thing.

"The way you look at Briggs is so devastatingly beautiful. I've never seen anyone look at someone the way you look at her. I know that you've gone through a lot by yourself, and I'm sure even more with her. But you can't just shutdown, Austin. It will only—"

The bell from the door rang. Mason walked back in with the coffee, and I couldn't have been more grateful for the distraction. I had no desire to continue this fucking conversation.

There wasn't anything left for me to say. I had used my excuses all up. It was easier this way. To pretend like everything was okay rather than face the reality of what happened to our relationship since the miscarriage.

The guilt alone was too much to bear.

"Austin." Alex stopped on her way out the door, pulling me away from my plaguing thoughts and feelings. "We all lost you once. I believe in my heart that she helped you find your way back. You need to remember that when you feel lost again." She turned and left.

I spent the rest of the afternoon thinking of what she said. Silently praying that when I realized that.

It wouldn't be too late.

Briggs

The more Austin pulled away from me, the worse I felt. The more I died inside. It had been a year and a half since my miscarriage, and I asked him at least twice a month if he was using again. That's what our relationship had come to. He swore on everything that he had ever loved and promised me that he wasn't using, that he hadn't relapsed since that night. The only problem was he acted like he was.

The sad thing about it, I couldn't tell if he was using or not. It had been too long or maybe I was just too blind. Too emotionally exhausted to think otherwise. The tattooed sleeves on his arms made it nearly impossible to see any track marks.

He was still going to his NA meetings and talking to his sponsor often. Doing everything he did before he relapsed, maybe even more so now. But the way he acted. It wasn't *my* Austin, and that's what confused me the most.

The air was so thick between us that some days he would hide out in the room that was supposed to be our baby's. I hated going in there, and I think he knew that. It was his safe place to get away from me, away from real life.

Away from us.

I found some support groups online with women who had miscarriages, and a lot of them said that their relationships with their husbands or boyfriends suffered because of the tragic loss. That sometimes their partners blamed them, causing an even bigger rift and turmoil in their already shattered relationship from the miscarriage itself.

"It's not me I'm blaming."

Those five words haunted me everyday.

Which was why I let him be. I believed every word that came out of his mouth because he'd never lied to me. I trusted him because I loved him. I lost myself more and more every day during that year-and-a-half, the reason being that. I didn't recognize the woman staring back at me in the mirror. Most days I tried avoiding my reflection, not wanting to accept what was happening.

Austin was all I'd ever known. I went from my uncle's fucked up grasp, to his. There was no middle ground. I didn't know how to be anyone else but his girl.

And that scared me more than anything.

I started going to some NA meetings without him knowing about it. Trying to understand the way his mind worked. How an addict's mind worked. Hoping that I could gain some insight on how to proceed, how to help him. I learned that addicts are very selfish people and that their addiction becomes so consuming that they don't even realize it. I heard the words "rock bottom" come out of so many damn stories, and it made me question if Austin had truly hit his.

Enough for him to change.

I wondered if he ever stood up and told his story to a bunch of strangers that were all united and tied together by drugs. Their addiction. I wondered if his story included me, what he said, what he feared. What he wanted out of life. I used to think it was me. Love. Happiness. A family.

I didn't know that anymore.

I began to question if I ever knew it at all.

"Baby..." Austin groaned from behind me, pulling me into his embrace.

He kissed all along the back of my neck, and I leaned into his affection. There were times like this where he would show me the love that I knew was still in there, even though we were both hurting. We would make love for hours, and he would hold me and tell me he loved me. He would call me his girl. With the snap of a finger, the next day he would go back to ignoring me.

Pushing me away.

I couldn't keep up anymore. His emotions were causing me whiplash, and after all these years, I finally felt the havoc it brought upon me. We never discussed trying for another baby. It wasn't an option. I went back on the pill and that was the end of it. Austin all of a sudden started to pull out when we had sex. There were very few times he actually came inside me anymore.

He didn't want to try again, and I guess I couldn't blame him. Neither one of us could survive the heartbreak of losing another life.

There was so much blood on my hands that I could barely see them.

The entire time I was pregnant, all we talked about was our wedding, marriage, and our future together. I knew he was going to ask me to marry him, I just didn't know when. Now, I couldn't tell you if that was even in the cards anymore.

One thing was for sure. We couldn't go on like this.

I couldn't go on like this.

"You smell so fucking good, Daisy."

I loved it when he was this way with me.

Mine.

"I have to go in to the shop for a few hours. I have a client I have to finish up. I'll stop by Half-Pint's restaurant on the way home to get some dinner and that chocolate cake you love. I'll bring you home the whole fucking cake, baby. You just have to smile for me." He turned me around to look deep into my eyes. "Just give me that goddamn smile."

I did. He caught it and placed it near his heart. Kissing me. Long, hard, and deep.

"I love you, baby. I know it's been a cluster fuck lately, and I've been an asshole. I just…" he breathed out, peering down at the ground while rubbing the back of his head. "I would never intentionally hurt you, Briggs. Please, tell me you still believe that. Tell me you still know that."

"Yes," I honestly spoke, making him immediately look back up at me. Surprised by my answer.

"Everything is going to be different from now on. I swear. You're all I need. We will get through this and be stronger because of it. I promise you."

I nodded with every fiber of my being. Wanting to believe him, needing to believe him.

"I'll see you soon." He kissed me one last time and walked out the door.

I spent the rest of that afternoon happy. At peace even. Which should have been the best feeling in the world, but it wasn't. Not even close. After it got dark out and the night took over, I couldn't calm the anxiety that I felt so deep in my fucking bones. Etching and burrowing in, making itself at home. There wasn't a damn thing I could do to get it to go away.

I paced the hallway nervously twirling my hair around my fingers. My heart was pounding, echoing off the narrow walls. My head was reeling with what ifs. What if he's lying? What if he's using?

What if...

What if...

What if...

Over and over again, playing out in my mind.

Something else I learned from the meetings. Addicts lied. They lied so much they couldn't tell the difference between the two anymore.

Austin was different, right?

I walked past the room that was going to be our baby's, probably a hundred times in a few hours. Debating on going in there, the intuition to walk into the bedroom along with the voice in the back of my head hammering at me to go in there wouldn't stop.

As much as I wanted it to.

As much as I tried.

I opened the door and turned on the lamp that was sitting on the nightstand. Taking in everything immediately as if it were about to disappear any second. Everything appeared the way it should be. Nothing seemed out of place even though Austin spent a lot of time in there.

I walked around the room. My fingers lightly touched along the walls.

"I think we should do a soft yellow color on the walls in this room."

"A soft pink. It's a girl, Briggs, I know it."

My feet softly skimmed the wooden floors.

"We need to have Lucas install carpet in here."

"Austin, the floor doesn't need to get replaced."

He kissed the tip of my nose. "I protect what's mine."

I looked around the closet, still picturing the baby clothes that Austin surprised me with that I had to hang up the same afternoon he gave them to me.

"Not that one, baby." He grabbed the *"You're all we ever wanted" onesie out of my hands. "This is the one we will take her home in,"* he rasped, *getting down on his knees to kiss my belly.*

A few weeks after the miscarriage, I'd found myself in the baby's room, crying for what felt like the millionth time. Skimming my fingers over the onesies that Austin was so excited to show me. All of it was just a painful reminder of what we would never be bringing home. I decided it was best for the both of us if I took all the baby stuff and store it back in the same box Austin had given me. Placing it back on the exact shelf where it was in the closet. Except this time, it wasn't empty anymore. It now held all of our hopes and dreams inside of it.

All of our sadness and despair.

It was one of the last times I ever stepped foot back into that room. I held the box firmly in my sweaty hands, slowly walking toward the bed, each step bringing me closer to our truths. I sat down on the soft place that contained all our happy memories of the baby we lost.

My heart was pounding out of my chest, my ears ringing, echoing all around the room. I placed the box in my lap and closed my eyes, taking a deep breath. Preparing myself for I don't know what or maybe I did know and didn't want to come to grips with it. I removed the lid off the box and placed it beside me. Trying like hell to ease the fear I felt in my heart. The anxiety I couldn't ignore for the last year and a half. Something led me there, and I had a feeling I knew exactly what that something was.

"He doesn't lie to you, Briggs, he has never lied to you," I reassured myself, opening my eyes.

Seeing for the first time, exactly how many fucking lies he told me, and I believed him.

Every. Last. One.

CHAPTER
35

AUSTIN

"Hey, man," Dylan called out, bringing my attention over to him.

I placed the order for our dinner and made my way over to the boy's table.

"Have a beer with us," Lucas said, pulling out the chair next to him. "Barely seen you around lately, brother. Everything alright?"

Jacob handed me a beer and I took a swig, placing it down on the table.

"Just working," I simply stated.

"Bullshit. We're all fucking working," Jacob chuckled. "And we all have kids. Try again, motherfucker."

Dylan narrowed his eyes at me, and I played it off like I didn't see it.

"We're all fuckin' adults now. We're not kids, and we've all gone through shit," Dylan added only looking at me. "Fuckin' talk. No judgments here."

I took another swig of my beer, leaning back into my chair, resting the bottle in my lap.

"There's so much shit you don't know," I scoffed out, shaking my head. "I wouldn't even know where to start."

"How about from the beginning," Jacob suggested.

All eyes were on me.

"No one has time for my life story."

"Good, we don't want to hear how fuckin' borin' you are. What's been going on with Briggs?" Dylan asked.

"She was pregnant."

They all jerked back, stunned. Dylan followed, "Was?"

"She woke up in a pool of her own blood one night. The doctor said it happens a lot I guess. I don't fucking know."

I shrugged like it was no big deal, when it was really tearing at my heart again. I took another swig of my beer, avoiding their stares.

"Fuck…" Jacob breathed out. "That's rough to come back from. How is she?"

"I don't even know."

Lucas frowned. "What the fuck does that mean?"

"It means I'm a fucking asshole. From the second the doctor told us it was a miscarriage, I blamed her. I blamed the woman who has done anything and everything for me. The same woman that has saved my sorry ass more fucking times than I care to count," I admitted out loud for the first time.

Immediately feeling like the piece of shit I knew I was.

"There's got to be a reason you feel that way, Austin. We're all fucking assholes. Especially that son of a bitch right there." Lucas grinned, angling his beer toward Dylan. "We know you love her. You're just as pussy-whipped as we all are."

"Speak for yourself," Dylan chimed in.

"You may not be with Aubrey, but that doesn't mean you don't want to be. Play that card somewhere else, McGraw," Jacob called him out. "But this isn't about you—"

"Listen, guys, I really appreciate this, but I don't want to—"

"No shit, Austin. You never want to talk about it. It's who you've always been. How far has that gotten you, huh?" Lucas countered, interrupting me.

The words were spilling out of my mouth before I even knew it.

"Briggs had a fucking abortion, alright? Happy now? Years ago. For reasons I don't want to get into with you assholes. I think a part of me has never forgiven her for it. I love her more than anything and I don't blame her for her choices, but I can't help the way I feel. Her miscarrying just brings all that shit back up for me. I question whether the miscarriage had something to do with the abortion even though I don't think that's even physically possible. All my thoughts and feelings are irrational and fucking selfish, but there isn't anything I can do to make them go away. So there…"

I drank the rest of my beer, placing it on the table. I stood shocked as shit that I had just shared that. I'd never told anyone.

"The fact that I even just admitted all of this to you makes me hate myself even more than I have since the miscarriage. I'm fucked up. I'm so fucked up in my head that it's just a cluster of bullshit in a hollow place. I love her more than anything. I couldn't imagine my life without her. She's my reason. For everything."

I took a deep breath, rubbing the back of my neck.

"Austin, we've all fucked up. Especially with our girls. You're human, bro. You need to stop punishin' yourself and just fuckin' talk to her. I know that's hard for any man, but fuck it," Dylan advised.

"Have you talked to Aubrey? Huh? You forgiven her?" I threw back at him.

He winced. It was quick, but I saw it.

"Exactly." With that I turned and left.

I grabbed our dinner order from the counter and got my sorry ass in the fucking car. Needing to get away from them. To get away from this fucking hell that has lived inside of me for God knows how long. I felt every minute of that drive home, down to every last second.

My mind raced.

My body craved.

My heart shattered.

By the time I made it home, I was running out of the car. Throwing the food on the island table, heading straight for the stairs. Taking them three at a time. My body came to an immediate stop, the force alone almost knocking me the fuck over.

The bedroom door was open. The room that was going to be our baby's. The room that Briggs never went in.

The room I used for the sole purpose to betray her.

I couldn't move. My feet were glued to the goddamn floor. The only light shining in our dark house came from the same place I let my darkness take over me. My heart was pounding out of my chest. My palms became clammy and sweat pooled at my temples. The walls of the hallway were closing in on me.

The fucked up voices already screaming, "No! No! No!" In my mind. I gripped the back of my head, wanting to rip my goddamn hair out. Trying to decide if I should leave or face what might be waiting for me on the other side of that door. I took a deep breath and made myself walk forward, each stride brought me closer to my own demise.

No more excuses.

No more lies.

No more I'm sorry.

I pushed the partially closed door open and walked into the room. Briggs' head was bowed, her body slumped over with her purple hair slightly hiding her face. She looked so broken. So defeated. So fucking sad. As if every last part of her had died. My closed box was securely placed in her hands, her grasp so tight that her knuckles had turned white.

She knew.

She finally peered up at me after what felt like maybe a few minutes, hours, days... everything blended together now. Nothing made sense in my life anymore. All I knew was my whole world was sitting on that bed.

The good and the bad.

My angel and my devil.

With a solemn expression she asked, "This what you're looking for, Austin?" She held up the box, finally looking me in the face.

I swallowed hard. It felt like knives going down my throat, directly toward my heart. Just from the look on her tear-stained face. It was always the same goddamn look.

Hurt, disgust, disappointment.

Making me feel like a worthless piece of shit.

"How long?" she said barely above a whisper.

My eyes shifted back and forth between her and the box. Battling between the woman I loved most in the world and the box that held the things I hated the most but craved.

"How long have you been fucking lying to me?!" she screamed loud enough to shatter glass.

I didn't even bat an eye as I replied, "Since the night I relapsed."

She grimaced, the impact of the truth crashing into her. She stood from the bed with the box still in her grasp. Walking over to the furthest corner of the room, away from me.

"I don't even get high anymore, baby. It's not even about that. I need it to take the edge off. I swear to you that's all," I rasped out, trying like hell to keep it together.

Tears slid down her face onto the box in her hands.

Our baby.

My lies.

The truth.

"You need this shit," she said, lifting the box up. "To be with me," she wept her voice breaking. "That's why? Because of me, right? That's what you're taking the edge off of?"

I shook my head no, grabbing the back of my neck.

"Then what? What excuse do you have now? What lie are you going to tell me? Do you even know anymore, Austin? The truth from the fucked-up fiction you created in your head to justify why you're an addict."

"Briggs." I stepped toward her, but she put her hand up in the air stopping me dead in my tracks.

"I'm just as fucked up as you are! I'm your fucking enabler! I make excuses and lies for you because I love you! Because it kills me to think that you're not the man I fell in love with! The man that protected me from every bad thing in this world! The man who was my first friend! The one that made me feel safe and loved for the first time since my parents died! The same man that's looking at the box with all his fucking drugs in it, rather than looking at me!"

My body was physically starting to cave in on me. Pushing me further and deeper into the black abyss of an addict. I hadn't used since I found Briggs in the kitchen that afternoon, before I left to go to the shop. My head was throbbing, my body clawing at itself, and the ache spreading through me was so fucking crippling. I blamed my relapse on the pain that the miscarriage caused.

I kept using because the guilt I felt from blaming her was unforgiving. It didn't help that I kept seeing our babies when I was high.

Everything about it was so fucked up.

Every time I used, I told myself I wasn't going to do it again, that this was the last time. I couldn't bear the pain of her knowing, of her finding out that I fucked up once again. I was a fucking coward. I couldn't have her see me get sick and know the reason behind it. I honestly used to take the edge off, but today was the first time that I wanted to use to cope with all the emotional bullshit.

I wanted her to know the truth. I wanted to say all of this to her. To know every last secret, every last lie, every last demon in my

343

fucked up existence. To finally be honest with her like I should have done before I relapsed following the miscarriage. But I couldn't get the words to come out of my mouth. I could barely form any coherent thoughts, the overpowering crave to use took over my mind, body and soul.

My nose started running, my teeth chattered, my body locked up. The hot and cold sweats were kicking in, creeping upon my skin. It wouldn't take long for the nausea and the cramping to hit either. Turning me into the man with no desire for anything, other than taking away the pain from my body betraying me.

As I betrayed her.

The irony was not lost on me.

"Baby, please…" I begged not knowing what for, as I leaned over, placing my hand on my stomach.

There were so many tears coming down Briggs' face that I could barely see her eyes anymore. Her beautiful smile replaced with nothing but agonizing pain and despair.

"Please what, Austin? What are you jonesing for? What can I enable you with now?"

"Briggs…" I rasped, clearing my throat that felt like it was closing up on me.

Fighting back the ache in my bones. Willing my body not to betray me any further.

Betray *her*.

"For the longest fucking time I blamed myself for doing this to you. For bringing you into this lifestyle, practically shoving drugs at you," she admitted with her head bowed.

The hurt from withdrawing and seeing her like this was causing me to die a little more inside. She slowly looked up at me, her hair falling away from her tear-streaked face.

With nothing, but emptiness in her eyes.

"I kept telling myself that you would have never become an addict if I wasn't there to enable you. That I am truly the cause of your demise. This is one of my biggest excuses I use to forgive you over and over again. It's one that I'm battling with right now as I sit here looking at the man that is supposed to love me, trying to find him under all his cluster fuck of lies. All I see is the man that has been lying to me for the last year and a half! I don't know who you are anymore, and I'm starting to think I never did."

"Jesus Christ, Briggs…"

I was starting to see spots, my vision coming in and out of clarity. I blinked a few times to no avail. I leaned up against the wall for stability. The last thing I needed right now was to give her another reason to fucking hate me.

"I fell in love with you when I was seventeen years old on a balcony without even knowing your name. I loved you then, did you know that? Now I can't even fucking look at you. It kills me to fucking look at you! Do you have any idea how much I hate you for that! You were the only good thing in my life, Austin! The only fucking happiness I'd ever had! How could you do this to me! How could you make me hate you! I fucking hate you! I hate you so damn much! I hate your apologies! I hate your excuses! Your lies! Your fucking love! Especially because I can't stop loving you! And I want to… I want to stop loving you so fucking bad it hurts everywhere inside of me. Especially here." She put her hand against her heart. "But I can't! I love you still and I fucking hate you for that!" she bawled, her body shaking so fucking hard it mirrored mine.

My girl stood there breaking in front of me and all I could do was stand there and watch her go down. I couldn't comfort her. I couldn't lie to her. I couldn't do one damn thing but watch.

My body wouldn't let me. It was dying right along with hers.

"Do you hear me?! Do you understand me?! I fucking hate you! I HATE YOU! Do you even care?! Am I even important to you?! Do I even matter to you anymore? Or have I been replaced by your demons, Austin? By your fucking drugs!"

"I love you more than anything," I let out in one breath.

"LIAR! You're such a fucking liar!" she screamed out so damn loud.

Her body gave out on her and she crumbled to the ground, rocking back and forth on her knees. I shuddered. It reminded me of a waterfall, she was a pile of nothing at the bottom. Clutching the box tight against her chest. Wanting to feel closer to our baby. Wanting to keep my stash that I so desperately needed right now to survive, away from me.

"Why do you keep doing this to me? Why can't you just stop? Why do you keep hurting me? After everything we have been through! Everything you have put me through! Why can't you just love me? Me, Austin. *Your* girl. Why am I not enough for you, like you are for me! Why?" she bellowed, question after question with no pauses in between.

Not giving me a chance to speak, even though I couldn't get my goddamn mouth to move.

I fell to the ground in pure agony for her.

For how I was feeling right that moment.

Pain.

Sliding against the wall, inch-by-inch, feeling every word she said to me, piercing my soul. Feeling every sensation that coursed through my veins, breaking my heart and will to keep going. I needed to make this better, but I couldn't get the fucking words out to talk to her.

My body wouldn't let me.

The drugs had taken over.

It was like I was there, but I wasn't. My body was in the room, but my mind was lost. I got on my hands and knees, and slowly crawled to her. Trying to reach for my angel as the devil clawed at my feet. Each movement made my sore muscles ache in ways I had never experienced before.

"Daisy…" I murmured so low, my voice sounding so distant.

I knew she couldn't hear me over her sobs of despair. I watched the scene from above us as if I was having an out of body experience. Her sobs would forever haunt me. I would remember her like this, always. A curled up, broken woman tucked away in the corner, waiting for someone to heal her.

"Baby…" I whispered against her tear-stained face.

Her cheek felt so warm against my cold skin.

"I'm sorry… I'm so fucking sorry…" I managed to say, kissing all over her face, soaking up her tears that were still falling from her torn eyes. "I love you… where's my girl? Hmm… where's my Daisy?" I whispered close to her ear so she could hear my sincerity.

She shook her head, closing her eyes, leaning away from me. At least that time she didn't push me away.

"I'm sorry… I love you… please… baby… I love you…"

I sensed her resolve breaking. Her body betraying her like I had by giving into my embrace.

"I would never intentionally hurt you," I reassured her, pulling her a little closer, feeling her warmth against my clammy exterior.

"I love you, Daisy. I love you more than anything. You know that. We're best friends, remember?"

She winced still keeping her eyes shut. I pulled her hair back away from her face, grazing her cheeks with my trembling thumbs.

"You're so fucking beautiful. I'm so lucky to have you, baby. You're all I ever wanted. All I ever needed. I'm sorry... I'm so fucking sorry... you know I would die before hurting you. You know that. You're my whole world."

I shut my eyes, swallowing the bile that was rising in my throat. Leaning my forehead on her shoulder for support. I turned my face, laying soft kisses down her neck.

"Please... please... baby... I fucking love you..."

I kissed all along her cheeks again, savoring the feel of her against me. All while battling the urge to tear the box out of her hands. My eye's fixated on it.

"Why do you keep doing this to me?" she wept, breaking down against my lips when I reached hers.

"Shhh... Shhh..."

I wrapped my arms around her, wanting her to seek the comfort she needed in my arms. Return the love that I always received from hers. I knew that I didn't deserve it, but I was a selfish son of a bitch, I needed it. I held her shattering body in my trembling arms, physically feeling her soul breaking piece by piece. Every last part of her slipped through my hold. My limbs locked up on me from the slightest movements.

"Oh fuck... Daisy..." I groaned out in pure agony from everything.

Her swollen eyes suddenly opened, looking at me in a new light. We locked gazes for a second, taking each other in. As she reached up to wrap her arms around my neck, the box simultaneously fell from her grasp to the hard wood floor between us. The slow motion boom, echoed all around us. My mind was telling me no, but my body didn't give it a second thought.

The ache won.

Betraying both of us.

I grabbed the box, and stood, my body moving on its own accord. Her arms slipped away from my neck, and I instantly missed her warmth.

Her love.

My Daisy.

My mind was raging war with my body, battling not to leave her there, broken. Struggling to not use again. Fighting for my life that was still sitting on the floor, realizing what I just did to her.

It wasn't enough. It never was. I walked to the door without a second glance.

And left.

CHAPTER
36
Briggs

"Rock bottom."

Two words I'd heard mentioned countless times in stories at the NA meetings. Every last addict repeating those two words, I never realized that I could have one too, not until that day. I thought after finding the drugs in the room that was supposed to be our baby's and coming to the realization that he'd lied to me for the first time in over a year and a half, was my rock bottom.

Except it wasn't.

He'd never chosen drugs over me.

I always came first.

No matter what, I was the most important thing. His demons, his struggles, his addiction were always secondary. Our love was number one, primary in all aspects of our fucked up lives.

I lost.

That was my rock bottom, and I couldn't do it anymore.

I don't know how long I sat there stunned by the turn of events. Crying my eyes out for what felt like the millionth time. The slamming of the front door jerked me away from my thoughts. There wasn't an emotion left in my body for me to feel.

I raged with fury.

A decade of solitude and years spent void of any emotion. No love, an endless stream of hurt, pain, and emptiness always in my shadows. The barricade that surrounded my heart, never allowing me to leave, was a ticking time bomb that waited, had now exploded.

It was loud, disastrous, and chaotic.

Crave Me

It was going to take everything around me with it, like a tornado spinning around in circles. No one stood a chance, especially me. It elicited feelings I never thought would be possible, emotions that one should never have to experience.

I felt every loss of breath. It cluttered my mind willing me to keep going, to push through. I couldn't keep up with the agony that grasped onto me like a fucking vice. Taking me deeper under the ground where there was no one, but... me.

Alone.

Forever destined to be alone.

Life was cruel like that.

I hated him...

I hated myself.

I crept up off the floor, my skin itching and my mind burning. My reflection in the mirror made me sick.

My misery.

My hand caught my mouth as I ran into the bathroom, hurling my head over to the toilet. I heaved over and over again.

Getting rid of the toxic poison inside of me. Our love.

I spit out the rest of it, wiping my lips with the back of my hand. I rinsed my mouth out with water and fervently shook my head side-to-side, trying to block out the last several hours of my life.

His lies.

His touch.

My memories.

Austin.

They were forever seared in my soul. It was now a piece of me, something that I would never be able to detach myself from. I screamed out my frustration, unleashing the rage, the wrath I no longer had any control over. It pounded into me as furiously as the truth did minutes ago. I walked out of the bathroom, slowly walking toward our bedroom. Remembering how many times he made love to me when he was high. When he was fucked up, fucking me. Lying to me, saying he wasn't using. That he loved me. That I was his girl.

His Daisy.

I took one last look around the room before I grabbed my suitcase from the closet and threw it on the bed. Grabbing everything I could from my drawers. I scurried around the closet, my feet stomping everywhere I stepped, leaving a path of destruction in its wake. I packed everything I could find not caring what it was. My eyes blurred with tears every time I shoved a piece of me into my bag. My body twisted with the desire to fall apart. To crumble to pieces right then and there.

"I fucking hate you! I fucking hate you so much!" I yelled, talking to myself.

I repeated it over and over again to let it sink into my pores, wanting it to become a part of me. To fuel my determination to leave him and not look back. I grabbed a few things from the bathroom, brushing my teeth and washing my face. I hurried, rushing as fast as I could to get my shit together and leave. Praying that I could get the hell out of there before he got back. I didn't want to hear his lies. His excuses. His manipulations.

Luring me into his spider web of deceit.

I packed enough things to get me through the next few days, not knowing where the fuck I was going. Just knowing that I needed to get out of there. I zipped the suitcase and grabbed it off the bed, dashing out of the bedroom that I made out of nothing but love and devotion.

For him.

My heart pounded, and my ears rang as I raced down the stairs with my suitcase in tow. Rounding the corner so fast I almost tripped over my own two feet, catching myself on the wall before I fell over. I made it another ten steps before hearing the front door click, seeing the knob turn over, all playing out in slow motion in front of me. Stopping me dead in my tracks.

We locked eyes for only a few seconds when he opened the door. His drug-induced gaze going from my face to the suitcase I was firmly holding. The realization hitting him like a ton of fucking bricks.

We both heard it loud and clear.

"What the fuck are you doing?" He closed the door behind him. "Where the hell do you think you're going?" he snapped, stepping toward me.

Causing me to take a step back.

He wavered, standing still.

"Daisy…" he coaxed, still peering back and forth between my face and the suitcase I was holding so fucking hard to the point of pain.

"I love you," he said with so much sincerity in his tone.

That it nearly killed me to hear him say it.

"Get the fuck out of my way," I roared, trying to side step him to no avail.

"Not a chance in fucking Hell, Briggs. Let's talk, okay?" He put his arms out blocking my escape. "Talk to me—"

"Oh! Now you want to talk! Now that you're high, Austin! Now that you chose your drugs over me—"

"I didn't choose drugs over you. I would never do that and you fucking know it! I was seconds from having a goddamn seizure up there," he spewed, roughly jabbing his finger in the direction of the bedroom. "I was fucking dying! You know what withdrawal is! You have witnessed it firsthand! The last thing I wanted was to have you see me like that again! I left so you wouldn't have to—"

"Oh my God!" I blurted, accenting every word with wide eyes. "In your own fucked up head, you actually think that's fucking true! You actually think that you did that for me! That you didn't just chose your precious drugs over me! Are you fucking kidding me? It doesn't matter what excuses you tell yourself, Austin! The truth is blatantly fucking there!"

"Stop fucking saying that, Briggs! I would never choose drugs over you! I would have fucking used in front of you if that were true! I wouldn't have given a flying fuck if you saw me. I wouldn't—"

"Have left the love of your life breaking down! Sobbing! Desperately trying to keep it together! Drowning in a sea of your fucking lies! Tell me, Austin! What wouldn't you have done?! Lie to me some more?! Since you're so fucking good at it! Take a bow, asshole, that was the performance of a lifetime."

I immediately grabbed the vase of flowers off the counter that he brought home for me a few days ago and threw them directly at him.

"You selfish son of a bitch!" I screamed.

He ducked as the glass vase hit the door behind him, shattering into thousands of pieces. Mirroring my heart.

"Fuck you! Now get the hell out of my way!" I yelled as loud as I could.

My hands fisted at my sides. Traitorous waves of anger rolled off me. My body shook, vibrating down to my core. He was over to me before I even saw him coming. Reaching for my chin, forcing me to look at the disgrace of a man in front of me. I jerked my face out of his grasp.

"Baby, just let me explain. Please, just give me a chance to—"

"No! Not going to happen this time! You've had plenty of chances. You blew what was left. You did this to us, not me! You!"

As soon as I felt his strong arms wrap around my waist, I pushed him away as if his touch burned me.

"Don't fucking touch me!" I shouted bloody murder, pushing him again as hard as I could.

His back hit the column, and I didn't falter.

"You liar! You're nothing but a fucking liar!" I repeated, hitting him all over his face and his body. Anywhere I could.

He tried to block each and every advance, so I pushed him and hit him harder. Taking out every ounce of frustration and hatred on him.

"Briggs, calm the fuck down," he ordered, trying to grip onto my wrists.

"All you do is lie to me! That's all you fucking do! I don't even know who you are anymore! Maybe I never fucking did," I cried, hitting and shoving him the closer he tried to come toward me.

I wasn't strong enough to hold him back any longer. My attempts became weaker and weaker. My eyes blurred with nothing but tears. My body giving out on me with each second that passed between us.

"I hate you! I hate you!" I screamed, beating my fists on his chest.

Emotionally and physically drained.

Mentally spent.

I brought my hand up and slapped him across the face as hard as I could. Ready to slap him again when he shoved me against the wall.

"Do your best, baby," he snidely rasped against my lips. Locking my wrists above my head. "We both know this is only foreplay for you," he added, kissing me so damn hard I didn't have a chance to reply.

I bit down on his lip till I tasted blood. He immediately jerked back, pulling my hair by the nook of my neck. I panted, frantically trying to gather my bearings. My body shaking, every part of my resolve was hammering all around me. I could hear it at my temples. I swear every part of my nervous system was breaking, shutting down, making it hard to see, let alone stand.

All I could do was feel and I didn't want to fucking feel. It brought me nothing but turmoil and distress.

I weakly thrashed around some more, ignoring the pain in my head. The hurt in my heart. The sorrow in the depths of my soul. He held me tighter against his chest, both of us gasping for air. Adrenaline coursed through our veins.

"Stop! Fucking stop! I don't want to hurt you!" he shouted, tightening his grasp on me.

I frustratingly screamed out, knowing that I wasn't going anywhere unless he wanted me to. Closing my eyes, I tried to govern my breathing, my thoughts.

My fucking heart.

His grip loosened, and I felt his face brush against mine. The smell of cigarettes assaulted my senses. Memories instantly attacked my mind at rapid speed.

"Fuck you, Austin!"

"I'd rather fuck you, baby," he rasped along my lips. "I'm sorry. I love you. You know that. You fucking know that… where's my girl? Huh? Where's my Daisy?"

I turned my face away from his, but he gripped my chin making me peer back up at him again. There was no fight left in me. I leaned my head back against the wall, glaring deep into his constricted pupils. We stared at each other for what felt like hours, both of us lost in our own darkness.

He rubbed my bottom lip with his thumb, licking away the blood from his own lips. For a moment, it felt good that I could cause him any pain. Even as minuscule as that for the suffering he put me through.

"I blamed you, Briggs," he said out of nowhere, breaking my goddamn heart even more.

AUSTIN

I wanted one minute to touch her, to look at her, to feel her, to hold her.

My other hand moved to the side of her face, lightly caressing her cheek. Slowly bringing down her walls. I angled my head to the side to take in her beauty as I placed some of the damp pieces of her hair that had fallen, behind her ears. Her eyes were immense. I had never seen them so big.

So soft…

So warm…

So smooth…

She remained still the entire time, giving up on her assault. Her arms fell slack to her sides, and her back was placed firmly against the wall. She didn't move or speak, as if she was taking me in as well.

"From the second I heard the doctor say it was a miscarriage, I blamed you. I should have told you that day, but I didn't want to hurt you any more than you already were. I knew you were hurting too. That's the reason why I kept using. I felt so fucking guilty for feeling that way toward you. Baby, you don't deserve that. I'm sorry. I love you more than anything in this world. You know that, Briggs."

Her chest rose and descended with each second that passed. Tsunamis of emotions raged in her eyes, and with each stroke of my fingers against her sensitive skin, I got to see each one unfold.

I leaned in and caressed her cheek with mine, still running my finger along the crevices of her lips.

"I fucking love you. I'm sorry. Let me make it up to you. Let me make it all better," I whispered, clutching onto the back of her neck, needing her closer to my chest.

To my heart.

I trailed my fingers from her lips to her chin, and down to her neck, moving them to the sides of her body. I wanted to look into her eyes like nothing else existed but her. She seemed so fragile in my arms, vulnerable and broken. The pain I caused was all-consuming, burning into my skin. She stared up at me, her eyes never strayed from my face the entire time I spoke. I felt them stabbing me everywhere.

I roughly clung onto the back of her neck again and brought her to me. She came without a fight, letting me hug her tight to my body.

She fit me like a glove, made only for me. With my face on the side of hers, I glided my cheek along the crevice of her jaw, making my way along the side of her neck.

"Please, baby… please forgive me…"

I moved my lips to her mouth and kissed her. She didn't push me away. Kissing me back softly. I had touched every last part of her, but in that moment, it felt like the first time. It was different.

We were different.

"I need to be inside you," I whispered in between kisses.

I unbuckled my jeans, and pushed up her skirt, slowly pulling her panties down. I gripped onto the back of her thigh, placing it on my hip. My pants fell to the ground effortlessly, my hard cock sprung free. She still didn't say a word.

"I love you… I love you so much. I'll fix this. Us. I promise. I'll go back to rehab. Whatever it takes, baby."

Caging her in with my arms, I aligned my cock at her opening before plunging into her pussy. In one swift movement, I was deep inside her. Her breathing hitched.

She cried out not saying a word.

I gripped onto her thigh again, lifting it higher to hold her in place. I thrust in and out, groaning in approval. Fucking her slow like she loved.

"Does that feel good, baby?"

Every thrust inside her, she felt the mass of my body movement, inching her a little higher each time. I softly kissed her, taking my time with each stroke of my tongue as it entwined with hers. Savoring the velvety feel of my mouth claiming hers. I pushed in and out of her before I pulled away needing to look into her eyes.

I knew Briggs' body better than she did. My fingers moved to her clit and she let out a soft moan, her resolve breaking with each stroke. Her pussy clamped down onto my cock, and I knew she was close. Her head fell back against the wall and her arms wrapped around my neck. I lifted her up, wanting her legs wrapped around my torso.

I fucked her harder and with more determination. Her heart was beating as fast as mine. I kissed her passionately with everything that was left inside of me. Needing her to understand my shame and remorse.

"Fuck, you feel good," I growled out. "Come on my cock, baby. Please let me feel you come for me."

She moaned, squeezing her thighs with her release. Taking me right along with her. I held her in my arms for what felt like hours, but I knew it had only been minutes. When I placed her back onto the ground, she immediately backed away from me. Her body trembling like she was in shock or something.

"Daisy?" I grabbed her chin and she roughly jerked it away from me. "Shit. Are you okay? Was I too rough? Did I hurt you?"

She shut her eyes, letting tears stream down her face. I didn't even realize she had been crying while we were making love.

"Fuck... baby. I'm sorry. I would never fucking hurt you."

She instantly opened her eyes, and for the first time, I didn't recognize the woman staring back at me.

My girl was gone.

She narrowed her eyes at me, shaking her head she scoffed out, "All you do is hurt me, Austin. That's all you fucking do."

I jerked back from the impact of her words.

"Congratulations, you got what you wanted. I gave into you. Your touch. Your lies. Your manipulation. Your love. Again. You know how to work me like I'm your favorite fucking toy. I'm done being played with. I can't do this anymore with you. That right there... what just happened is how easily I lose all my sense of reasoning when it comes to you."

I watched her grab her suitcase off the floor and walk to the door, taking my goddamn heart with her. She bowed her head, leaning it against the door like it killed her to be leaving me.

As much as it was killing me to watch.

At the last second she turned around and for a second, I thought my whole world was coming back to me.

"You're addicted to drugs, Austin." She shrugged, her voice breaking. "And I'm addicted to you."

Looking deep into my eyes she spoke with conviction,

"And our love is just as fucking toxic."

CHAPTER
37
Briggs

"How does that make you feel?"

"I hate it when you say that, Dr. Holden."

"And yet after six months of coming to see me, you still know I have to say it," my therapist chuckled.

Two days a week I sat on a comfortable leather sofa and poured my heart out to a complete stranger. We talked about anything and everything. Sometimes she just listened, and other times she asked questions. Trying to figure out the root of my problems and how to help me move on.

It had been six months since I left Austin. Six painful months since I ended up back in New York, knocking on my uncle's penthouse door in the middle of the night. I had nowhere else to go. Before I even realized what I was doing and where I was, a woman answered the door. A young woman I had never seen before now.

"Jesus Christ, how many fucking times do I have to tell you not to answer the fucking door," Uncle Alejandro roared.

"How many times do I have to tell you that I don't care what you fucking want?" she snapped back.

My eyes widened in disbelief that someone spoke to him that way and they were still standing. I'd never once seen a woman around my uncle, let alone in his penthouse. Even though I knew he went through pussy like they were nothing. I'd heard enough stories, but I'd never witnessed that side of him.

The door opened wider. He cocked his head to the side when he saw me, taking in my appearance. I could only imagine what he thought.

"Hey," I greeted, fumbling with the strap of my bag. Not knowing what else to say.

He turned back toward the girl, who looked like she could be younger than me.

"Leave us," he simply ordered.

She frowned, peering back and forth between us, even more confused than I was. She left.

"You're kind of a dick."

"So I've been told, but I'm not the one standing at your doorstep at five in the morning."

"You know why I'm here. Let's not pretend you don't know everything that has been going on in my life. And I'll pretend that you've been keeping tabs on me because you actually fucking care." *I walked past him. "I just need a place to crash for a few days until I figure out what I'm going to do. I'll sleep in your guest bedroom, okay? You won't even know I'm here. It will be like old times. You remember, right? You were hardly there for that too."*

He arched an eyebrow. "So this is a pleasant visit, I see. Perhaps we can blame your foul mood on your bitch-causing time."

I rolled my eyes at his asshole remarks.

"You know where your bedroom is. I don't think I need to remind you, seeing as you're sharing such fond fucking memories from your childhood."

"My bedroom? You kept my room?" I asked, shocked as shit. "Who are you?"

"Your uncle. The only family you have, peladita."

"It makes me feel confused. Austin is the only man I've ever known outside of my uncle. He was my family. My heart. My reason. I miss him every single day, but I have so much hatred for him. I also still love him, which outweighs that hatred some days. I don't blame him for my abortion. I did what I thought was the right thing to do at that time."

"Do you think he would have stayed in recovery if you had kept the baby?"

I shook my head no. "If you would have asked me that back then I probably would have said yes, but now after everything that's happened. I don't think he would have stayed in recovery.

Something would have happened to make him relapse. There was always something happening."

"Do you think the abortion played as a downfall in his addiction?"

"I know it did." I bowed my head, playing with the seam of my shirt. "I think that's another reason I stayed so long. I felt responsible for some of his demons. The choices I made that not only affected me but him too."

"That's normal, Briggs. To feel the way you do. Have you spoken to him?"

"You know I haven't."

"Do you know how he's doing?"

"See, that's the worst part. I lost his friends and family too. I haven't been back to Oak Island since I left. I don't know if he's in recovery. I don't know anything anymore."

"Is he still calling you?"

"Every day."

"Are you still listening to the messages? Reading the texts?"

"Not as much as I used to. I'm trying to be strong, but I can't help the guilt I feel. I know you keep telling me that it wasn't my fault that he became an addict. In my mind that makes sense, but in my heart, Doctor," I placed my hand on my chest, "it doesn't feel that way."

"Austin is an addict, Briggs. He would have become one with or without you. Do you understand that?"

I nodded.

"Family members, especially partners, they always feel responsible no matter what. His problems became your problems, his demons became your demons, and his addiction became your burden. It would have killed you, had you stayed. You made the right choice by leaving him, Briggs. He wasn't going to get any better with you there. Addicts need consequences. If they don't have any then why would they change? I'm not saying that you leaving was his rock bottom, but eventually, he will find one. They always do. It's just whether he will be alive when it happens."

I grimaced. I couldn't help it.

"I know that's hard for you to hear. But in situations like these, it becomes about their lives. Only them. Killing yours in the process.

Addicts die every day, Briggs. It's the nature of the beast. If he doesn't want to stay clean, then he won't. Bottom line."

"It was already killing me. I don't understand why I stayed for as long as I did. I should have left years ago, but I couldn't."

"You loved him. You still love him. He's a very sick man. Addiction is a disease, Briggs. It's contagious in the sense that it overpowers everyone involved, including the non-addicts. You're sick too. Which is why you're here. Austin won't get better until he wants to. You can't want it for him. You stayed because you remembered the man he was. Not the man he became. They're two different people. You can't continue to blame yourself for that."

I nodded again.

"Let me ask you this. If it weren't for the guilt you have from him becoming an addict, bringing him into that life and then the abortion being another catalyst. Would you have stayed as long?"

I looked around the room, trying to seek the answer out like it was written somewhere on the walls.

"I wanted to save him," I finally admitted out loud for the first time. "I wanted to save one person in my life."

"Your parents," she simply stated already understanding.

"I know it was just a coincidence that I had a temper tantrum when the car hit us. I do know that *now*. I spent most of my childhood and adolescence thinking I killed my parents', Doctor. You know my uncle. Everything I've seen and lived through. I wanted to save someone. I didn't want another person that I love to die. Not at my hands."

Her eyebrows raised, surprised by my revelation.

"If you hated that life so much, Briggs, why did you stay? Why not leave when you turned eighteen?"

I nervously chuckled. "I spent years upon years asking myself that same question. Especially, when I first started working for him," I paused to gather my thoughts. "My uncle is the only family I have. I was scared to be alone, plain and simple. I didn't have any friends or role models in my life. Even though I hated what I was doing, it was the only life I'd ever known."

She nodded, understanding. "How do you feel about your uncle?"

"I stopped trying to understand him decades ago. That man is a mystery."

"Do you think he loves you?"

"I don't think he knows the meaning of the word, Doctor," I honestly spoke.

"He's the reason you're here, isn't he?"

"He is, yes. I was still living with him at the time. A few days after I ended up at his penthouse, he woke me up and told me he scheduled an appointment with you. He said I needed to talk to someone who gave a fuck about what I was going through. I guess that was his way of showing me he cared, right?"

She smiled.

"I've wanted a family my entire life. I think a part of me thought that if I worked for my uncle that maybe he would be proud of me or something. That it would miraculously change our relationship."

She cocked her head to the side.

"It's stupid, I know."

"That's not stupid. You lost your parents at a very young age. It's normal to want to find a home. You found that with Austin. It's one of the reasons you fought so hard for him. You didn't want to lose another person over life's unpredictable circumstances."

"It's why I didn't want him to start working for my uncle in the first place. I couldn't stop that, so I thought that if I quit partying and doing drugs recreationally with him, he would stop too. But I know... he has to want to, I can't want it for him," I repeated the same phrase she had been telling me for months.

"Exactly."

"One day at a time, right?"

She nodded. "You did good today, Briggs. It will get easier. Learning to love yourself is one of the hardest things for a person to do. Especially for the first time in their life."

"Yeah," I shyly smiled and nodded.

"Same next time week?"

"Yes. Thank you, Doctor."

"Keep writing, okay?"

"It's the only thing keeping me sane at the moment."

And it was.

AUSTIN

"You know what I did today, baby? I went to the dock with my notebook, and I drew you. I sat there for hours with my feet in the water, drawing. Do you remember the dock? How many times we made love there? It was one of your favorite places to go together. Except this time you weren't there. I was so fucking alone. I'm always alone. I keep seeing you everywhere, Briggs… You're standing in front of me right now. Your purple hair is spread perfectly all around your face. I keep catching your smile and placing it on my heart. I haven't done that to you in years. Do you remember that, baby? I have the perfect view of the sun right now. It's overlooking the harbor from the warehouse I'm at. I hate this fucking place, but it's making you glow… you look beautiful, baby. Always so fucking beautiful. I only wish I could still see our babies. I never see them anymore. All I see is you… They left with you, Daisy. They left with their mama."

I shook away the thoughts.

"Baby… Briggs… Daisy, pick up the phone. I miss you so fucking much. Come home… I'm your home. I need you… where's my girl? Where's my Daisy?"

Beep, beep, beep. The line went dead.

"Motherfucker."

I immediately debated on calling her back, leaving her another message, but I couldn't remember how many I had already left that day. I was beyond fucked up. My eyes were fluttering to stay open. The drug-induced haze trying to take me down the rabbit hole, but Briggs wasn't down there. I didn't want to go where she didn't exist. She was smiling in front of me. I saw her all the time now, always through the haze of my darkness. She was my only angel among the demons that were around me all the time.

My only light.

My only hope.

She left me over a year ago. I hadn't seen her, spoken to her, found her… It wasn't from the lack of trying. I looked for her everywhere, even went as far as going to her uncle's penthouse. No one answered, though. It was like Miami all over again. I searched to no avail. She was a figment of my imagination. A ghost. All I had were the memories of her, and with each passing day, I went further down the black abyss because it was the only time I saw her. I craved that time with her.

I got to hold her.

I got to touch her.

Love her.

I drowned myself in work, and when I wasn't working, I was high. Six months after she disappeared, I sold our house. I couldn't be there anymore. It was too painful to walk past the room that held so many memories. Good and fucking bad. I was renting a small apartment closer to my shop that consisted of a couch and a bed. Everything else went to storage, with the hope that Briggs would come back to me. I barely saw the boys or Alex. It was easier that way, to just be alone. No one knew what I was going through. No one knew about my demons. They all had their perfect fucking lives, with babies and white picket fences and shit.

The haze won out and I shut my eyes, my head falling back against the dirty, mold-infested couch. My spot. Briggs was there though. She was laughing, and dancing around in front of me. Damn I missed that sound. I reached out to touch her and she leaned into my embrace.

"I'm sorry, baby. I'm so fucking sorry," I said, struggling to get the words out.

"I love you, Briggs. I'll always fucking love you. No matter what. Dead or alive. You're mine."

I stayed in that shithole for the rest of the evening.

Lost.

CHAPTER
38

AUSTIN

"Get up!" someone yelled from above me.

"Mmm…" I stirred, grabbing my head. "The fuck," I slurred.

I hadn't even opened my eyes yet and my head was already fucking pounding.

"Carajo! Get the fuck up!" He kicked my bed, making it shake.

"Jesus Christ," I groaned out, sitting up, and placing my feet on the floor.

Hunched over, I held my throbbing head in between my hands.

"It's three o'clock in the fucking afternoon," he roared, too close to my face.

I peered up, narrowing my eyes at him. It was so damn bright, I could barely make out his figure.

"How the fuck did you get inside my apartment? And what the fuck are you doing here, Martinez?"

I hadn't seen Briggs' uncle since before she left me. I couldn't even tell you when that was, everything fucking blended together. Years, months, days.

Especially the goddamn days.

"Two and a half years."

I cocked my head to the side.

"That's how long I've been fucking waiting for you to get your shit together!" he yelled, making me wince.

"What?" I replied, confused.

"Jesus Christ. Take a cold fucking shower. We need to talk. I'll be waiting in your sorry excuse of a fucking living room."

Two and a half years? Is that really how long it's been?

I wiped the sleep from my face, and grabbed the t-shirt I had worn the night before off the ground, pulling it over my head. I took some pain pills from my nightstand, swallowing them down whole with no water. Once they kicked in, it didn't take me long to get ready.

"You should really consider moving into a nicer apartment complex. All it took to persuade your landlord to let me in was a hundred dollar bill," Martinez informed as I grabbed a Red Bull from the fridge.

Drinking it down in three swigs, I crushed the can then threw it on the counter.

"I'm surprised he didn't take a twenty, you got ripped off. I apologize if my accommodations aren't what you're used to. I could meet you at the fucking country club up the road. That's where your breed goes to hang around these parts. You can talk to my parents. I'm sure they would love you," I sarcastically remarked.

"I'm not here for pleasant conversation, Austin."

"Then why the fuck are you here?"

"To save your sorry excuse of a life."

"A little late for that," I scoffed out.

He eyed me up and down from where he stood against my wall, before pulling something out from the inside of his suit jacket. He threw an envelope on the counter in front of us. The contents slipped out just enough to see. It took me a second to realize that they were pictures. Some were from the club when I first saw Briggs again. After I found out she was a drug dealer. Others were from our trips around the world.

"Briggs is very special to me. I love her very fucking much."

We locked eyes and I jerked back, stunned. He folded his arms over his chest, cocking his head to the side with a snide smile.

"Don't look so fucking surprised. She's hard not to love. As you well know. I watched you and kept tabs on you because I didn't fucking trust you. As far as I knew, you were some punk-ass motherfucker, taking advantage of my niece. I tolerated you because it made her happy. Then you proved yourself worthy of her love with the incident in Colombia. You would kill for her, and a man like me can respect that about a man like you. A man who knew nothing about what he was getting himself into. But you stayed just to protect her."

"I love her," I simply stated.

"You need to get your shit together. You're a fucking junkie. Look around." He gestured to the shithole I called home. "Is this how you want to live or is this where you plan to die? You would think losing the one thing that mattered to you the most would straighten your ass out, but all its done is the fucking opposite. You're a goddamn fuck-up, Austin."

"Oh, I'm the fuck-up? What about you, Martinez? Do you know how fucked up you made Briggs?" I paused, waiting for him to say something, but he didn't.

He just stood there with a knowing expression.

"That's what I thought. You're nothing but a fucking pussy behind expensive suits."

Before I knew what was happening, he was over to me in three strides, grabbing me by the shirt.

"You cocky son of a bitch, you have no idea who the fuck you're talking to," he gritted out, practically spitting in my face.

He slammed my back into the wall. I hit it with a hard thud.

"You're lucky I'm even here. The only reason I am is because I fucking owe you. You brought life into Briggs again. Something I had never known how to do. Her mother would want me to at least try to help you, motherfucker. Now, get your shit together before it's too late."

With that he let me go, stepping away from me. I slid down the wall, crouching over and rubbing the back of my neck. I hated to admit it, but he was right. It was also easier said than done.

"Where is she? I've been—"

"You've been what? Not doing a damn thing, but drowning in your own fucking shit that you created by getting high! You think she deserves a man like that? You think your children, your babies would? I'm only going to tell you this once. One. Fucking. Time. She's moving to Myrtle Beach because for some reason that I can't fucking fathom, she loves the Carolinas. Get your life in order before it's too late and there is no life to fucking save."

He threw a piece of paper on the counter, turning around to leave.

"Do you know?" I asked, stopping him dead in his tracks.

Needing confirmation. He spun to face me again. Looking me dead in the eyes. He didn't falter.

"Kids aren't in the cards for me, but I can only imagine what it would feel like to lose one. With or without my consent."

He turned around and left without so much as a second glance. I immediately grabbed the paper, realizing he left me with her address. I grabbed my phone and keys, mentally preparing for whatever the fuck I had to do to get her back. I was in my car and driving to her house with hope in my heart that the reason she was moving to Myrtle Beach was to be close to me. It was only an hour away.

I couldn't live without her any longer. I'd barely been living since she left me. Slowly killing myself with thoughts of her through a needle in my vein. I would do anything it took to be with her again. I'd go to rehab, live in a sober living community, fuck even just be her goddamn friend if that's what it took for her to trust me again.

I knew she still loved me as much as I loved her. She was mine. End of story.

I sped the entire way there with a heavy heart and a guilty conscience. Ready to beg for her forgiveness, her mercy.

Her fucking love.

I followed a car into her gated community. She lived in the suburbs of Myrtle Beach. One of those neighborhoods that looked like it came straight out of one of her books that she *use to* read. There were kids playing outside everywhere, laughing and smiling. Not a care in this corrupted world. It calmed the anxiety I felt all around me.

"One-zero-six Oak Field Drive on the right in one-hundred feet," the GPS informed.

I decided to leave my car at the park down the street. I didn't want her to see me coming. I thought it would be better to surprise her. Not allowing her to have time to not answer the door. I grabbed my burgundy beanie off the seat, taking one last look at myself in the visor mirror. I looked like I hadn't slept in months, but she used to love this beanie on me.

My mind raced with thoughts of what to say to her, with each step that brought me closer to her house. Praying that she would at least talk to me. After all this time she would give me a chance to make things right again.

I saw the moving trucks in her driveway and on the street before I found her. My eyes wandered everywhere trying to spot her amongst the workers.

Waiting to see my girl.

My Daisy.

And just like that she appeared, my angel walked down the ramp of the moving truck with a few small boxes in her arms. My eyes widened and my breathing hitched, staring at a woman that I didn't recognize. That I didn't know. I shook my head and blinked a few times, thinking it was my fucked up mind playing tricks on me.

It wasn't.

Her hair was a deep shade of brown. Like the vibrant purple that I'd loved had never existed. The new color made her blue eyes stand out more, but they weren't bright and shining or full of life. I couldn't see any of her tattoos. They were all covered up by one of those prissy fucking sweaters she always hated. She wore it over a buttoned-up blouse and black slacks. She was still breathtakingly beautiful, but she was no longer *my* girl. No remnants of the woman I had spent years with existed anymore.

"The fuck?" I whispered to myself, trying to figure out what the hell was going on.

Did Martinez send me here to rip my fucking heart out all over again? Did he do this on purpose?

She smiled, big and wide. I didn't have to follow her gaze to figure out what was causing her to smile. The same smile that would make me catch her expression in the air and place it near my heart.

My heart fucking dropped.

I stopped breathing.

Everything played out in slow motion as if I were in one of those black and white movies. My whole world and everything I so desperately wanted to believe in came tumbling down on me with no remorse or compassion.

He grabbed the back of her neck, bringing her lips to kiss his. She went effortlessly, kissing him with the same love she once kissed me with.

She smiled against his lips, as he softly pecked hers again, grabbing the boxes out of her hands. He said something that made her laugh. Her head fell back, making her body shake. I could hear her laughter in my head from all the times I made her come undone.

My feet moved of their own accord to hide behind the moving truck. Needing to hear what they were saying as if seeing her with another man wasn't enough for me to realize the truth of what Martinez was trying to warn me about.

"So that was your fee for helping me with the boxes, wasn't it?"

"Of course. Men need to be rewarded, Daisy."

I immediately shut my eyes, leaning my forehead and hands against the side of the truck for support. Trying to reel in my fury. Feeling like I just took a goddamn bullet to my fucking heart. Nothing could ever compare to the hurt I was drowning in right at that moment. The hole in the ground that was swallowing me alive.

"Well..."

I opened my eyes when I heard her voice again, continuing to watch my nightmare unfold before me.

"There's still a shit-ton of boxes left in the truck. I might run out of rewards for you," she flirted, twirling her now brown hair around her finger.

"I'm sure I can come up with other ways for you to repay me, baby. One that requires you to get down on your knees."

She giggled like a fucking schoolgirl.

I resisted the urge to lay the motherfucker out right then and there. Fighting back the compelling need to hit something. It took everything in me not to blow my cover and punch a hole in the side of the fucking truck. My teeth clenched and my fists tightened at my sides. My chest heaved as rage coursed through my body, causing me to see nothing but red.

"Oh, really? Is that all I am to you? A piece of ass?"

She softly smiled as he caressed the side of her cheek like I had done a million times. Nothing could have prepared me for what happened next.

Not one damn thing.

My. Rock. Bottom.

"You know what you mean to me, Daisy."

And just like that...

"I love you," he sincerely added.

My. Life. Ended.

When hers was just beginning...

With Esteban.

Briggs

I sat in the emergency room waiting area with my screen-shattered phone clutched tightly in my grasp. My knee nervously bounced with anticipation, unable to sit still. It felt like I'd been sitting there for days, but in reality it was only a few hours. I got out of my chair a few times, pacing the room, looking out in the hallway at the double doors where Austin was taken back.

Nothing.

Waiting.

My mind raced with thoughts, with guilt, with shame from everything that Dylan had just reminded me of. Bringing back everything that I had worked so hard to push to the back of my conscience. Every last feeling made its presence known. I spent the last two and a half years in therapy with Dr. Holden. Having several breakthroughs in my sessions. Finally believing that his addiction wasn't my fault. When I saw my phone light up with Dylan's name, I knew if he was calling me after all this time, something bad had happened. I didn't answer, I was too terrified. I listened to the voicemail he'd left, asking me if I had talked to or seen Austin. The panic in his tone immediately brought up red flags. Then Austin called a few minutes after and all it took was one fucking phone call to send me spiraling out of control once again.

I hadn't talked to him since I left Oak Island. I knew if I had, I would have gone back to him and died a little more inside. I needed to heal. I needed to find myself. I needed to learn how to love myself before loving somebody else. He still called me and left voicemails all the time. The text messages were endless. All went unanswered. I started to delete them without hearing or reading a single message. My therapist asked me why I wouldn't change my phone number and put an end to the problem.

Out of sight, out of mind.

I had yet to give her an honest answer to that question. Deep down, I knew I couldn't let go. He had a hold on my soul. Something made me answer that particular call tonight. It hit me like a ton of fucking bricks. I finally realized that all I'd been doing was waiting.

Knowing that eventually I would answer the phone. I would pick up his call, and he would be on the other end…

Dying.

"Briggs!" Dylan called out, making me look up from my chair.

I stood, swallowing hard as everyone came barreling in through the automatic emergency room doors. The boys, Alex, Lily, and Aubrey came toward me while his parents went straight to the nurse's station.

"Is it true?" Lucas snapped a few feet away from me.

Alex instantly caught his arm, holding him back.

"I… I… I'm sorry…" I nervously breathed out.

"You're sorry? That's your fucking response?" Jacob argued, standing in front of me with an anxious Lily on his arm.

"How long? How long has this been fucking going on?" Lucas roared, bringing my attention back to him.

I shook my head unable to form words. Overwhelmed by all their questions and accusations that were running wild in their heads.

I was to blame here.

I was the outsider.

The enabler.

"Unbelievable. Are you a junkie too? Did you do this to him? Did you make him this way?" he added.

"No! I swear! I tried. I tried every day! I promise you that! I never wanted this. I never wanted to see him like this!" I sincerely replied, my eyes filling with tears.

"Why didn't you tell us? We could have helped him. We're his fucking family," Jacob chimed in.

"He didn't want anyone to know. He was in recovery for four years, I didn't think he would relapse and when he did, I didn't know. The day I found out, I left. Okay? He was lying to me too. I haven't spoken to him in two-and-a-half years. I swear I didn't know it was this bad."

They all jerked back, stunned by my revelation.

"He didn't tell you? That we weren't together?"

"He works all the time, Briggs. We knew you guys were having problems, and he told us you went back to New York for a while, but we figured you still spoke and were trying to work things out. You never answered or returned any of my calls. Austin never specified and we just figured…" Alex paused, frowning. "Oh my God. How did I not know this?"

"Austin is really good at making you believe what you want to see," I simply stated.

"You!" Austin's dad yelled over everyone, pointing a finger at me. "Did you do this to my son?! Is he in there because of you?! Why didn't you tell us?! Who the hell do you think you are to hide something like this?! We're his parents! We deserved to know what was going on!"

"I know I—"

"We treated you like you were our own, like family. How dare you lie to us?" he added with the same fierce tone.

"I'm sorry. I'm so sorry," I wallowed, my heart pounding out of my chest.

I didn't know what to say to them, which only pissed me off further that Austin never told anyone. The shit-storm was falling all on me. Once again his poor decisions were all my fault.

"Get out," his dad gritted through clenched teeth, aggressively pointing to the emergency room doors.

"Joseph," his mom coaxed, looking up at his face and then back at me with sympathy in her eyes.

"You don't belong here. You never did," he ordered not paying his wife any mind. "My son is fighting for his life because of you. Now leave before I have you escorted out," he heaved with anger.

"Me?! How about you?! For always treating Austin like he was never good enough. For being a piece of shit father, and not wanting to accept your son for who he wanted to be. Everyone in this room, including myself, is partially responsible for him being in there," I honestly spoke, unable to control the truth.

His grimaced. It was quick, but I saw it. "I won't tell you again. Get the—"

"That's enough," Dylan interrupted me, speaking up for the first time since they all arrived.

All eyes were on him, including mine. Realizing quickly that this wasn't going to end in my favor. I shook my head, turning to leave, defeated.

"I knew," Dylan declared, making me stop dead in my tracks.

I winced, knowing the truth he was about to share with everyone.

"I've always known. He's been struggling with addiction since the car accident."

I shut my eyes, taking a deep breath, slowly letting the air escape from my lips.

"Briggs is right. She saved his life more times than any of you could ever possibly know. She deserves to be here more than any of us. I'm sorry, Briggs. I spoke out of anger on the phone. If it wasn't for you, we would be planning a funeral."

I spun around to face them once again. Each one of them looked at me. Hatred was replaced with shame and remorse. I was so grateful for Dylan coming to my defense. He could have let them continue to rip me to shreds, but he stepped up, throwing himself under the bus. Aubrey kissed him, pulling him into her arms.

No one spoke after that. No more questions, accusations, anger. We all took a seat awaiting the doctor. They all had someone with them, except me. My someone was lying in a hospital bed, possibly dying.

Even though there was so much to say, it took a backseat.

All we could do now was wait.

CHAPTER 39

AUSTIN

I was in ICU for twenty-four hours before they transferred me to the detox unit, where I went through being medically withdrawn from the drugs. If there was anything to be thankful for, it would be for not dying and not having to experience the withdrawals awake. Since I OD'd and technically died for a split-second, I had to have a sitter with me twenty-four/seven. It was hospital protocol, to make sure I wasn't suicidal. I was mostly in and out of consciousness for the majority of my stay. They kept me sedated enough to where I barely felt any discomfort, just exhaustion.

I dreamt about Briggs mostly, except she wasn't how I remembered her.

My girl.

She looked like the woman that now belonged to Esteban. Smiling, laughing, loving him, as if I never existed. Even in my dreams I was still haunted, tormented by the truth of my reality.

By the third day they allowed immediate family to visit with me. My parents were beyond disappointed and furious but relieved that I was still alive. I immediately admitted that I needed help that I couldn't do this on my own. Realizing for the first time that I couldn't do it alone. I needed my family, and my friends. The people that loved me, to help in my recovery.

I didn't want to die, again. That was never my intention in the first place. I just didn't want to feel pain anymore. Dying once was enough for me to come to terms with the fact that if I continued this lifestyle, I would end up being a part of a goddamn statistic with a sad fucking story.

My parents set me up with the best rehab facility in North Carolina, my treatment plan was going to be intense and I would be transferred into it in the next few days. It would become my new home for the next six months. My parents didn't ask many questions, but I knew it was only a matter of time before everything was laid out on the table.

My demons were emerging from the darkness, coming into the light.

Over the last two days, they allowed the boys and Alex to visit. They were on the same page as my parents. I think everyone was just fucking relieved that I was still here and had a second chance at life. I hadn't asked for Briggs. I knew now more than ever that she fucking hated me. My mom told me she was the one that found me and she was the reason I was alive.

She saved my life.

Again.

The last thing I remembered was seeing her with Esteban. The image would be forever ingrained in my mind. Burned into my soul.

My mistakes. My choices. My weaknesses.

Cost me the love of my life.

She unknowingly slipped through my grasps. That was the hardest pill for me to swallow. Seeing her move on was my rock bottom.

She was now the one that got away.

It was the last day of my hospital stay before I was discharged to the rehab facility. I would be lying if I said I wasn't scared of my future and everything it had in store for me.

A life without Briggs.

I shut my eyes, needing a moment of clarity. A few seconds to calm my plaguing thoughts.

"I love you, Daisy. I'll always love you. No matter what."

She smiled. "I know. I'm yours."

I immediately opened my eyes sensing her presence. There she was, standing by the open door, her dark brown hair flowing all around her face. She was a sight for sore eyes, wearing jeans with a sweater and her favorite tattered Chucks. She looked so tired like she hadn't slept in days. Once again I was the reason for her discomfort and pain. Dark circles were prominent under her swollen eyes.

She was still so fucking beautiful.

Beautifully broken.

"Hey," she announced, barely above a whisper.

I smiled. I couldn't help it. "Hey," I rasped.

We both stared at each other, lost in our own thoughts. I looked over at my sitter with a pleading expression. I couldn't be left alone. They even had cameras set up in my room, watching my every move. The nurse was in there with all my visitors, overhearing every private conversation. I silently prayed she would grant my request this one time.

She met my eyes, and then peered back at Briggs.

"You're Briggs?" she stated, raising her eyebrows.

"Yes."

"He owes you his life, young lady." She nodded toward me.

"In a way, I owe him my life, too. So I guess we're even," Briggs said out of nowhere, bringing my attention back to her.

"You have twenty minutes. I'm going to get some coffee, and I will be standing right outside that door. No funny business, okay?"

I held up three fingers. "Scouts honor."

She left, closing the door behind her. Briggs didn't move from where she was standing against the wall. The craving to hold her was as powerful as the craving to use had been.

Both were deadly for me.

"Your hair," I coaxed, nodding to her, breaking the silence between us.

She smiled, grabbing the ends and looking down at them.

"Yeah," she simply stated not elaborating any further.

Awkward silence filled the space between us.

"You still have your tattoos, right?" I chuckled.

She nodded never breaking eye contact, finally asking, "So, how do you feel?" Like she'd been waiting to ask since she found me in the warehouse.

I shrugged. "Like shit. Which is better than I deserve. You're looking at me like I'm going to break or something, Briggs."

She shook her head, looking down at the ground. I immediately regretted saying something.

"You weren't breathing, Austin. I couldn't feel your heart, your pulse. You died right in front of me." She rubbed her forehead, deeply sighing as if she was reliving it all over again in her mind.

"Are you okay?" I asked, pulling her away from her thoughts.

She eyed me cautiously. "I was. I think. I don't even know anymore." She pushed off the wall and walked over to sit in the chair by the side of my bed. "I left the hospital when they told us you were going to be okay. I had every intention of not coming back. But my mind has stayed with your unconscious body in the warehouse, Austin. I see you lying there on that filthy floor, unresponsive every time I close my damn eyes. I haven't been able to sleep since that night. I keep thinking that if Dylan hadn't called me first, I wouldn't have answered your call. Or what if I hadn't been in Oak Island when I answered you. You would have died. My therapist—"

"Therapist?" I frowned.

"I've been seeing her since I left you. She's been helping me understand everything. My childhood, my uncle, you, me, *us*... fuck, my life, I guess. She told me that I was the one that ran away from you. I would never be able to move on until we had closure or some sense of peace. It was then that I realized I never changed my phone number even after she told me I needed to. I knew... I knew in my heart that this was going to happen. Subconsciously, I had been waiting for it," she paused to let her words sink in.

Peering around the room for a few seconds, battling a visible internal struggle in her mind. She didn't have to tell me what she was about to say. I knew it from the moment I opened my eyes and saw her standing in front of me.

I said it for her instead, "You're here to say goodbye."

Briggs

We locked eyes.

Seeing each other's truths for the first time in two and a half years.

"Yes." I nodded. "I can't run away from you again. It almost killed me as much as it did you, the last time. I need to say my peace and walk away this time."

"I'm going to rehab tomorrow. For the next six months. I'll be there getting my shit together. Getting my head out of my ass and back in the real world. I guess both of us have some healing to do," he stated, grabbing the cup of water on his bedside table and taking a drink.

I didn't falter. "Why are you going to rehab?"

He narrowed his eyes at me, confused.

"Is it for your parents? Your friends? *Me?* At the end of the day you need to go there for you, Austin. Your recovery, your sobriety. It needs to be something that you want, not what everyone else wants for you. If you don't want it, if your head isn't in the right place, all you're doing is wasting everyone's time. Especially your own. See, I learned that was the biggest problem in our relationship. You always got better for me, for us. Never for you. As much as I hoped and prayed that it would be enough, it wasn't. It never was. I can't want it for you. Your parents and friends can't want it for you. No one can. You have to want it for yourself."

He took in every single word that came out of my mouth. Listening intently. I could see it in his eyes, he knew I was right, and that gave me hope for him.

"I saw you."

I lowered my eyebrows, cocking my head to the side. Not understanding what he was talking about.

"With Esteban."

I grimaced, jerking back stunned. "What? How?"

"Do you love him, Daisy?" he asked not answering my questions.

Staring deep into my eyes, willing me to answer him truthfully. Now was as good a time as any to get out what I've been holding in for so long.

"I went back to New York after I left our home. I lived with my uncle in the same penthouse I hated growing up in. I stayed there for a little over a month, trying to stand on my own two feet but still stumbling every time I stood. When I was ready to be on my own again, I moved into another condo he owned in Manhattan. I ran into Esteban at the park one afternoon, a little over a year and a half ago. It was nice to see a familiar face when I still felt so fucking lost. We went and grabbed some coffee together, and I ended up pouring my heart out to him. He sat there and listened to our sad story for three hours."

379

I shook my head, remembering that day as if it happened yesterday.

"He was different but still the same, if that makes any sense. We exchanged numbers and said our goodbyes. For the first time in my life I had a friend that wasn't you. One night a year ago we drank a little too much, and one thing led to another."

He immediately shut his eyes, the hurt evident all around him. Radiating deep into my core. I hated knowing that I was hurting him. I hated knowing that he was probably craving to use. But I needed to tell him this. He needed to know.

As much as it killed me inside.

"I'm not saying this to hurt you. I swear the last thing I want is for you to leave here and go use, Austin."

"Do you love him, Briggs?" he repeated with a hard edge to his tone.

"Does it really matter?"

He immediately opened his eyes with a pained look in his glare like I had never seen before.

"Is he the cause of your makeover?" he accused, taking in my new appearance. "You're not mine anymore. You're his."

I bowed my head not knowing how to reply. What was the right or wrong answer? I just shook my head, looking everywhere but at him.

"Did you hear any of my messages? Did you know how much I was hurting? How much I looked for you, like I did the first time you left me in Miami? I saw you everyday, Daisy. You may have not been real, but I still saw *my* girl. My Daisy. It was the main reason I used so fucking much. I stayed high to be near you."

Tears streamed down my face, the ones I had been trying so hard to keep at bay.

"When I saw you with Esteban, it literally almost killed me. I died standing there watching him touch my girl, kissing the lips that I claimed as mine a long time ago. I'm not blaming you for my piss-poor decisions. I never meant for any of this to happen to us. I wanted to give you the world, Briggs. Everything you never had. The house, the white picket fence, a million shitlins running around the yard," he chuckled, leaning forward to catch one of my tears.

"I love you more than anything in this world, baby. I lost sight of what was important. I fucked up, and I can't take that back," he paused, his voice breaking. "I'm no good for you. At least not right now. I can't keep doing this to you. I love you too fucking much to not let you be happy. That's why I OD'd. You deserve to be happy with or without me. I have to let you go even though it's the last thing I want to fucking do right now."

I wiped away the tears from my face, feeling like he just ripped out my heart and stomped all over it. I couldn't fucking breathe.

"But none of that matters now. I have to let you go. Set you free. I love you. I'll always fucking love you," he added, making my heart explode.

I nodded unable to form words, but it didn't matter because there was nothing left to say. We said everything that mattered.

I stood, turning to leave. He instantly grabbed my hand, pulling me into his arms. Before I even realized what was happening, I was sobbing against his chest with his strong arms wrapped around me, feeling him cry too.

"I'm sorry, baby. I know you hate those words, but I'm so fucking sorry for everything I put you through. I put us through. I ruined us when all you did was try to save us. Losing you will be my biggest regret in life. I love you so much, and I need you to please never ever forget that. Please…" he begged in a tone I had never heard from him before.

"I love you too, Austin," I bellowed as he held me tighter.

I stayed there in his arms, both of us knowing this was our end. This was goodbye. I pulled away first, and he wiped away all my tears, kissing all along my face for the last time. I sucked in air that wasn't available for the taking, standing to leave. His arms falling to his sides, empty. I made my way toward the door, trying like hell not to look back at his broken expression.

I didn't want to remember him like that.

"Daisy," he called out as I walked out the door.

I stopped, waiting on pins and needles for what he was going to say.

"Where did the name Briggs come from?"

I chuckled, grateful that he was trying to end this on a good note. For the both of us. I spun to face him.

"She's Twilight Sparkle. It was a doll with bright purple hair that my parents wouldn't buy for me. I was holding her at the grocery store the night they died. Her name was Briggs," I said, for the first time.

I had never told anyone where the name came from.

"It was the last time I was happy, so I took her name."

He smiled, taking me in.

Every last expression.

Every last movement.

Every last word.

Wanting to remember me anyway he could. I did the same. Giving him one last, beautiful smile. He caught it in the air and placed it near his heart. Exactly how I knew he would.

I turned back around.

And left.

CHAPTER
40

AUSTIN

"Hi, my name is Austin Taylor, and I'm a drug addict," I announced like I had done at every NA meeting I attended.

Except this one was different.

"It's been six months since I took my last hit in a warehouse downtown, where I OD'd. I actually died that night." I let out a nervous chuckle, rubbing the back of my neck. "This is my last day in the facility, and I'm receiving my six-month sobriety chip tonight," I paused, while everyone around me applauded.

"I can't say this has been the hardest thing I've ever had to do. This time it's been different in every aspect. The first time I was in recovery for four years. Trying to find solid ground when everything was shaking around me. I got sober for my girl. I stayed sober for her. I went to therapy for her. I worked through my steps for her. I went to meetings, and talked to my sponsor, I did everything for *her*. Not me. I was a ticking time bomb during those four years, waiting to fucking explode. Until one day I did. Spiraling out of control."

I peered around the room, gazing from the boys, to Alex, to my parents. Everyone who loved me was there, hearing my story for the first time.

Except, the one person who mattered.

The one person I wanted.

"In the end, I lost my girl. I hit rock bottom the day I figured that out. My therapist tells me that I have never been able to talk about my emotions, and that has been the cause of most of my problems. Here's the thing, I've always wanted to fit in. With my family, with my friends, with the people that have always mattered the most to me. Never realizing that I was slowly causing my own demise. Tearing rifts between the people I loved. When you're young, you think that you know everything, and that was one of my biggest downfalls," I paused to let my words sink in.

My mom smiled and winked at me, giving me the courage to keep going.

"I'm scared every morning when I wake up. I have feelings, emotions, and memories that I struggle with on a daily basis. I'd self-medicated to numb the pain, to not feel anything anymore. Look at it this way, I was a human garbage disposal. Blaming my problems on everyone, but myself. I'm not proud of the things I've done. I'm more ashamed than anyone could possibly ever know. I'm learning to forgive myself. I'm learning to love myself. And for the first time I'm here, wanting to get better for me. I want it. I need it. I deserve it."

Alex wiped a tear from her face, smiling at me.

"All I can do is take it one day at a time, and ask for help. Thank you," I smiled, stepping off the podium.

Everyone stood up and applauded as I made my way down the aisle, toward my family and friends.

My mom was the first to hug me. "I am so proud of you, baby."

My dad shook my hand. "You did good, Son."

"Bro, that was some deep shit," Dylan praised, patting my back.

"You really did amazing, Austin. We're very proud of you," Aubrey added, pulling me into a hug.

Lucas, Jacob, and Lily were next. They all congratulated me, and headed to the refreshment table, leaving Alex and I alone. I pulled up a chair next to her, flipping it around to sit on it backwards.

"That was amazing. You're an inspiration," she stated, smiling.

"I didn't sound like too much of a pussy, huh?" I laughed, trying to get a rise out of her.

"I always knew you were the strongest among the boys, Austin." She nudged my shoulder.

"I don't know about all that, Half-Pint. None of them are fucked up."

"I do. To come back from everything you have been through, and admit your defeat. That takes more courage than anyone could ever imagine."

"You sound like my therapist. I should just hire you, instead of paying out my ass for the one I have," I said jokingly, making her laugh.

"I have something for you." She reached into her bag, pulling out what looked like a book. "I met Briggs for lunch a few days ago. She's doing great, Austin. She looks healthy and happy."

I nodded. "That's good to hear, Alex. Thanks for telling me."

"That's not all."

I cocked my head to the side, arching an eyebrow.

"She told me everything."

"Everything?" I replied, caught off guard.

"You protected her, Austin. From day one, she was all that ever mattered to you."

I rubbed the back of my neck. "I guess she did tell you everything then. I'm going to tell them all eventually. My therapist and sponsor know already, but I'm not ready to remember all that yet."

"I understand. You can tell everyone when you're good and ready to. I won't say a word. I promise."

"Thank you." I said, feeling more at ease.

"Did you know that she liked to write?"

I took a deep breath in and slowly blew it out. I hadn't really talked about Briggs with anyone other than my therapist.

"She loves to read, Half-Pint. I honestly think she's read every romance book out there, twice. She loved living in the fantasies, experiencing what she never had. I knew she liked to journal and stuff. What's this about?"

"After you took over for her uncle, she started writing one day. As things progressed with you over the years, she started writing down memories and her feelings. She said it was her way to cope with what was happening to you. It helped her, Austin."

"Why are you telling me this?"

Alex looked down at the book in her lap, handing it to me a few seconds later. It was a black hardback with the words "Crave Me" written in silver lettering. I glanced back at Alex still confused.

"It's your story."

I jerked back. "What? You fucking with me?" I shook my head in disbelief.

"She told me that after she'd left you, her therapist recommended for her to put all the entries together from over the years and add to it. It was a way to realize her growth and how far she's come. It started off like her therapist suggested, but it took a life of it's own. She ended up writing your love story."

My eyes widened. Shocked to the core from what she was telling me.

"She thought reading it, might help you heal like it helped her. She wanted me to tell you that you don't have to read it, but she wanted you to have the very first manuscript. It's been picked up by a publisher, Austin, Briggs is an author."

My hands started shaking, knowing that I was holding Briggs' soul under my fingertips. Alex stood up and I followed suit.

"She also wanted me to tell you that she was proud of you," she relayed, pulling me into a tight hug.

I kissed the top of her head, held up the book, and told her thank you, smiling at her as she walked away. I wanted to leave. I wanted to go lock myself in my new room and read Briggs' book from start to finish. Anxiously waiting for when I would be alone to do just that, but my parents were walking towards me. They were taking me to dinner, and then dropping me off at my new "sober living" facility. I told them I wanted to continue living in a controlled environment. I wasn't ready to be on my own yet. Not ready to step out into the world where temptation and triggers were all around me. I'd be staying there for another six to eight months, more or less.

"You did so great, honey. We are so proud of you," Mom praised again, kissing my cheek. "You've come such a long way, but you still have a long road ahead of you. We will be by your side every step of the way."

"I know, Mom. Thank you."

And I did; I wasn't cured by any means. She lovingly nodded, excusing herself to go use the restroom.

"Your mother is right, Austin. We will always be here for you," Dad agreed, bringing my attention back to him. "I've made so many mistakes, Son. More than I care to remember. I keep telling myself that if I would have let you go to art school, if I'd let you become the man you wanted to be, if I hadn't—"

"You can't do that, Pop. I'm the only one that's to blame for my choices. No one else. You did what you thought was best for me, like I imagine any parent would. I may have not seen it that way back then, but I know that now."

"Briggs made me realize at the hospital how much of a shitty father I was. I'm sorry if I ever made you feel like you weren't good enough, Austin. You're my greatest accomplishment," he confessed with tears in his eyes.

I'd never seen my dad be anything but the solid man he always was. I wasn't surprised in the least that Briggs spoke her mind. She always did. It was one of things I loved the most about her.

"I love you no matter what, Son. If I could go back, I would change a lot of things, but you're right, I can't. I can only move forward and I want nothing more than to build a relationship with the man standing in front of me."

"I would really love that, Dad."

He pulled me into a hug, and I actually felt my father's sincerity and love. For the first time in I don't know how long, I felt like everything was going to be okay. That my life was going to get better. That I was going to get better.

Even though my future didn't include Briggs.

Briggs

"Jesus Christ!" I placed my hand over my chest when I walked into my house. "Why can't you just fucking knock on the door like a normal fucking person?!" I yelled at my uncle, shutting the door behind me. "You don't own this house. I do. So fucking knock on the door," I ordered, setting my groceries on the kitchen island.

He just sat on the barstool without a care in the world, not paying me any mind at all. Holding his head up high in his I'm-Alejandro-Martinez-and-I-don't-give-a-fuck kind of way.

"To what do I owe the honor of your unexpected appearance, Uncle? You must know Esteban is out of town or you wouldn't be here."

"Oh, I missed him? What a goddamn shame. By all means, give that motherfucker my regards."

I rolled my eyes. It had been a year since Esteban and I moved in together. He hated the Carolinas, and wanted to move back to New

York. It was one of our biggest arguments. He was actually there right now, traveling on business.

"Can't an uncle just want to visit his favorite niece?"

"Your only niece, and an uncle, yes. You, no," I declared, peeking my head out of the fridge to look at him.

He grinned, amused with my banter. I continued to put away the rest of my groceries.

"I hear your book is the talk of the town. You're all over the bookstores in New York City."

"Are you scared the FBI is going to knock on your door, Uncle? Don't worry I changed your name."

"I've read it, Briggs."

My eyes widened as I breathed out, "You lie."

"*Antonio*, never lies," he chuckled, using his name from my book. "I was there the day you were born, *Daisy*. I was one of the first people to hold you. Your mom named you Daisy because—"

"It was her favorite flower," I interrupted.

He smiled, peering around the room as if he was recalling something from his past. He was a dangerous, mysterious man, but he loved my mom. There was no doubt about that.

"Yes. It was her favorite flower," he repeated with sad eyes and a solemn expression. "You look like her. That's the first thing I thought when I saw you in the damn hospital bed when you were six. I couldn't believe how much you fucking looked like her. You were a spitting image of her as a child, and are even more now as a woman."

I took in every word he was saying. Scared that if I interrupted him, he would stop talking about my mother. Stop sharing memories that pained him for some reason. A reason beyond my understanding, and I knew he'd never tell me if I asked.

"Ask," he ordered, reading my mind.

I looked him in the eyes and asked the one question that had always plagued me.

"Why did you take me in?"

"I promised your mother that if anything ever happened to them, I would take care of you."

I frowned. "You were there when I was born, but I never remember seeing you around after."

"I never forgot any of your birthday's or holiday's. You received my gifts, I made sure of it."

I opened my mouth to say something, but quickly shut it.

"She took you away from this life, Daisy. The life you hate so fucking much. Only for me to bring you back in it."

He stood and I immediately thought our conversation was over. I was beyond disappointed. I had so many questions that had gone unanswered. He walked over to the screen door, his hands placed firmly in the pockets of his slacks. Peering out the window, like his life was flashing before his eyes.

"I raised you the only way I knew how. Putting a roof over your head, making sure you were alive and fed."

"What about affection, Uncle? What about love? Did you not think I needed that? Wouldn't any little girl need to be held? To be told that everything was going to be okay? That they were loved?"

He turned away from the window, narrowing his cold, soulless eyes at me.

"Mistakes are what run this world, Daisy. The past cannot be changed as much as we may want it to. I am no different. I have always been there for you, despite what you think. I still am."

"Why did you read my book?" I blurted, needing to know.

"I wanted confirmation," he simply stated, making his way back to the kitchen island.

"On what?"

"I let you both go, didn't I?" He ignored my question.

I don't know what came over me. I slammed the cabinet door, and made my way over to stand in front of him. Looking deep into his eyes.

I didn't falter. "Do you love me, Uncle?"

"I raised you, didn't I? I protect you. I'm here for you. No matter what."

I shook my head no. "That doesn't answer my question. Do you love me?"

"Daisy, I'd kill for you. I'd take a bullet for you, and I can't say that about anyone else."

My eyes widened, realizing that would be the best answer he would ever give me.

"If you could go back, would you still raise me the same way?"

"Yes," he answered without any hesitation.

I bowed my head, disappointed. He grabbed my chin, making me look at him again.

"This is the man that I am, Daisy. I won't make any excuses for that. What you see," he paused, "is what you get. I made you strong and resilient. I gave you the tools to survive, and I showed you the reality of the world. I wouldn't change that for a goddamn thing. Tough love is the only way I know."

I stood there in disbelief. He released my chin, and took a seat on the barstool.

"As much as I'd love to keep going down memory lane. This visit isn't about me. That's not why I'm here. Have you talked to Austin?"

I jerked back. "No. Have you? Wait... do you talk to him?"

"What I do is not your concern, peladita. You're not happy."

"I'm happy."

"Being content is not happiness," he simply stated.

"And you're the expert on what happiness is?" I scoffed out. "I'll take my chances."

"Don't confuse things. I live the life I fucking want. I don't give a fuck what anyone thinks about that."

"I live the—"

"You live the life you think you need to be living. You always have. Aren't you tired of being someone you're not?" He held up my brown hair, twirling it around his finger, taking in my appearance. "You're scared to be alone, Briggs. Waiting for happiness to come to you. You want something then go after it, and if you can't get it, you fucking fight for it. Why are you with Esteban? I remember very clearly asking you if you loved him. I'm fucking certain you said no. Tell me, are you with him because he stole your goddamn virtue?"

"He didn't steal it. I gave it to him."

"And here you are... still giving it to him. What about you? What can he give you?"

"I... well, there's..."

He snidely grinned. "People make mistakes, peladita. No one is perfect, and sometimes it takes someone to get lost, to finally find their fucking way back. From what I hear, absence makes the heart grow fonder, Daisy," he said, walking to the front door.

"I'll make sure to tell Esteban you said hello."

"And I'll make sure not to accidentally shoot the motherfucker in the goddamn face. Then we both can pretend that we fucking love him."

Without another word, he left me there with thoughts of a love I once had.

Austin.

CHAPTER
41

AUSTIN

"Half-Pint, I'm not going to tell you again. Stop setting me up on these fucking dates! I don't want to date anyone. This may come as a shock to you, but I actually want to be single. I don't need a girl. I'm happy being by myself."

She sighed. "She was a nice girl, Austin."

"I wouldn't know. I spent the entire fucking time counting down the minutes before I could pay the bill and leave."

"You're so frustrating!"

"Mind your own damn business."

"I don't know how to do that," she gritted out, making me laugh. "It's been almost three years, Austin. Three years."

"I can read a calendar, Alex. I'm fully fucking aware of how many years have gone by."

She rolled her eyes, placing her hands on her hips.

"Baby, give Austin a break," Lucas said, coming to my defense. Slapping her ass for good measure.

"Half-Pint, he's still getting fuckin' pussy, and he doesn't have to deal with the emotional bullshit. Man's onto somethin'," Dylan added, making Aubrey reach over and slap him on the back of the head. "Suga', you have a wonder pussy, and I fuckin' love you."

"You're so romantic," Aubrey sarcastically stated, shaking her head.

"It's a known fact that women are crazy. I'm only speaking the truth here. Austin has always been a master of getting laid. I taught him everything he knows. Alex, leave the man be."

Alex threw her hands in the air, giving up.

"Austin, make sure you make up for the lack of sex Dylan won't be getting until further notice," Aubrey chastised, only looking at him.

"Until further notice? You mean until tonight when I put my tongue up your pus—"

Aubrey immediately placed her hand over his mouth. I laughed so hard that my head fell back. He was such a fucking asshole, but it felt good to laugh with all of them again.

"Oh my God, Dylan." She let go of his mouth. "I'm sorry my husband has no filter."

"It's part of my fuckin' charm, and you fuckin' love it," Dylan reminded, pulling her to him by the nook of her neck, kissing her lips.

That was my cue to get up and man the food on the barbeque.

We were all hanging out at Lucas and Alex's house. Shooting the shit like old times, grilling out with all the boys and their wives. I had become the seventh wheel. Which was what gave Half-Pint so much initiative to try to find me a girl. It didn't matter how many times I told her I didn't want one. She was a persistent little shit.

I already had my girl.

My soul mate.

I hadn't been with anyone since. I'd fucked enough girls to last me a lifetime. None of them would have been Briggs, so it didn't matter anymore.

It had been almost three years since I last saw Briggs. Almost three years since I OD'd. Almost three years since my life started over, and I was in recovery. I was given the greatest gift.

Life.

My second chance.

I lived at the sober living facility for over a year, attending a NA meeting at least two to three times a day while I stayed there. My sponsor and therapist became my new fucking best friends. I was fortunate enough that I didn't have to work, and could concentrate solely on my recovery. I was working through my twelve steps of sobriety, currently on step number nine.

Making amends with everyone that I had hurt during my addiction. Of course, Briggs was the first person on the list. My therapist scheduled sessions with everyone that I had hurt, my parents, the boys, and Alex. I told them everything. They knew every lie, every memory, and every single truth. Including the shame and remorse I felt about all the things I'd done. Especially being a drug dealer. It was like a weight had been lifted off my shoulders. For the first time in forever, my demons were dormant. But that didn't mean they weren't still there. They would always be apart of me.

I was still an addict.

I was just an addict in recovery.

I still went to my therapist regularly and met with my sponsor a few times a week, and attended daily meetings. Finally admitting defeat. I couldn't do this by myself, and as hard as it was for me to ask for help, it was getting a little easier every time I did.

Which was often.

The boys and my parents, especially my father, took responsibility for their part in my addiction. My dad actually broke down, and had a few times since. Our relationship wasn't fixed by any means, but it was getting better. Same with all the boys, they were my fucking brothers. They always would be.

We were family no matter what life threw at us.

When I was ready to be discharged from the sober living facility, I started looking around for a house to move in to. I ended up buying the home that belonged to the dock that held so many memories from my past.

The good and the bad.

My therapist didn't agree with the choice I made, saying that it could present itself as a trigger for me to relapse. When I did my final walk-through before signing the papers, I quickly realized that I didn't belong anywhere else, but there.

I was finally happy to be home.

I couldn't live anywhere else.

It had been almost a year-and-a-half since I'd moved in there. Lucas' company remodeled the six-bedroom, four-bathroom house. I added a pool to the huge backyard. My realtor said I was buying it for the family I wanted, and maybe in a way I was. I had people over often. It was rare for me to be alone anymore. I preferred it that way. I spent way too many years being alone.

I opened my tattoo shop back up, and had more clients than I knew what to do with. The place was booming, and I was scheduled out a few months in advance.

I even started sketching again.

I had yet to read Briggs' book. Our love story. As much I wanted to, I couldn't bring myself to turn the pages. It sat on my nightstand next to my NA book. I would stare at it for hours, but at the end of the day, I always choose to read the NA book instead. Every time. I had that book memorized, and I still managed to learn something new every time I re-read it.

"I'm going to head out, guys," I announced, standing up after finishing my plate.

"Come by the restaurant tomorrow," Lily said. "Jacob is working late and you can have dinner with me and the kids. Riley wants to show her Uncle Austin how she can write her name now."

I nodded. "Can't wait," I said, giving her a wink.

We said our usual goodbyes and I left.

"Austin!" Alex called out, making me look up from my car door.

I closed the door, rounding the corner of the hood, as she came running towards me.

"Did I forget something?" I asked, patting my jeans.

"No, I wanted to give you something." She handed me a white envelope.

"What's this?" I looked at her.

"It's from Lucas' mom, Savannah."

I peered up. "What? How?" Jerking back, stunned.

"She gave it to me a few days before she passed away. She said that I couldn't give it to you until you were ready. Until you were in a good place again. I didn't understand what she meant by that at the time. I held onto it all these years, hoping that one day it would make sense. To be completely honest, over the last few years I'd forgotten about it. When you were in rehab, I found it in my old art notebook my mom kept. I was looking for my book to come draw with you. I thought you could use some good memories right about then. I was going to give it to you the day you received your six-month chip, but Briggs gave me her book. I realized it wasn't the right time yet."

"Why now?"

"You're happy, Austin. I don't remember the last time I saw you this happy. You're in a good place, and I firmly believe in my heart that you're going to stay there. I'm not saying it's ever going to get easy for you, but I can see it in your eyes. You're Austin again. My good ol' boy is back."

I brought her in for a big hug. Even though she was a pain in my ass, she always knew the right things to say. I took a deep breath, appreciating everything she had just said.

"I talk to Briggs sometimes. She's doing great, Austin. She's touring around the world with her books. Attending signings everywhere. She's really taken off. She's happy."

"Thanks for telling me that, Half-Pint. It's always good to hear. As long as she's happy, that's all that matters to me. All I ever wanted was for her to be happy. I just wish it could have been with me."

"Life is very unpredictable, as you well know. I ended up with Lucas. Aubrey's with Dylan. Even Lily ended up with Jacob, and I didn't think that would ever happen. So crazier things have happened in our lives."

I nodded.

"I love you, Austin, and I'm so proud of you."

I kissed her head, giving her a loving smile, and she left. I drove home, listening to "Mad World," thinking about everything I'd been through in life. I pulled into my driveway, got out, and headed straight for the dock. I slipped my shoes off and sat with my feet in the water like I had countless times before. I lit a cigarette, letting the nicotine work it's way into my lungs, and opened the letter that I couldn't stop thinking about the entire drive home. Bringing the cigarette to the corner of my lips, I started reading.

Austin,
My rebel boy.
From the second you could crawl, you never looked back. You were the most independent boy I had ever seen before. You were so quiet; we never knew if you were up to something. Always needing to learn everything on your own. There was no holding you back. Your mom had to put a lock on your window, because you would open it at night and climb up the banister to sit on the roof. You were four. I remember the first time your mom caught you. She almost had a

heart attack. The next day she had installed a state-of-the-art lock to keep you from hurting yourself. You saw her lock it one time, and you figured out how to unlock it to continue sneaking out. There was no telling you that you couldn't do something when you put your mind to it.

That's just the boy you were. So curious about the world, and every last thing it had to offer. But you were the sweetest boy ever, the most loving of all the good ol' boys. You didn't care. You did your own thing, often ending up alone. I worried about you a lot. Your parents worked all the time, and it was hard for them to keep up with you because you were so damn quiet. We all assumed everything was okay, since we never saw otherwise.

I caught you drawing on the dock a few times while I was looking for Lucas. You seemed so lost and alone. Even at that young of an age. The car accident changed you, Austin. It sucked the life right out of you. The guilt and shame came tumbling down on you. You weren't the same boy. There were days I barely recognized you. It scared all of us.

When you took off, I would be lying if I said I wasn't expecting it. You needed to leave. You needed to find yourself. Most importantly you needed to forgive yourself. Love yourself in a way you probably never have before. I know you have gone through more stuff than I could ever imagine, and one of my saddest regrets is that I'm not going to be there to help you find your way.

But I know it wouldn't matter anyway because you need to find it on our own. It's who you are. I knew one day it would happen. The demons that haunted you would be at bay, and you'd fight for your life again. If you're reading this then I know that day has come.

You're happy.

And I'm smiling down on you. Proud that you made it back home.

I don't have to tell you to take care of each other, your brothers and your Half-Pint. There's nothing that could come in between a bond like that, ever. No matter what life throws at you, your family will always be there to catch you when you fall.

I love you, Austin. I'm here if you ever need to talk. I always will be.

Your second Mom,
Savannah

I folded the letter, and placed it back into the envelope. Inhaling a puff of my cigarette, remembering how many times I'd sat on this dock. Feeling as lost as she said I appeared.

I smiled.

Taking one last puff of my cigarette, stubbing it out on the side of the dock. I stood, walking back inside.

Knowing that I wasn't lost anymore.

CHAPTER 42

Briggs

"You ready?" my assistant asked, grabbing the last few things off my table at the signing.

"Yeah, give me a second," I replied, grabbing my bag from under the table. "Shit. It's stuck on something. You can go, Avery. I can catch a cab. Thanks so much for all your help today. I'll call you tomorrow."

"Okay. Everything is set with the bookstore, you're free to go."

"Awesome. Thanks again."

She waved, turned, and left. I looked under the table, not seeing what my bag was actually stuck on. I crouched down and crawled under the cloth, until I was fully underneath.

"There! You stupid dick of a table leg," I grunted, pulling as hard as I could to no avail. "Damn it!"

I tried to scoot the leg over, but it was no use, the damn thing was too heavy. I pulled on my bag some more, cussing up a storm, getting pissed it wouldn't budge. All of the sudden it lifted on it's own, and I quickly pulled out the strap that was stuck.

"Finally!"

The leg was set back down, and I immediately heard something placed on top of the table above me. I shimmied backwards, trying to get the chair beneath my ass, to sit back up. I ended up hitting my head in the process.

"Shit! Ow!" I yelped, scooting some more to clear the edge of the table. "Motherfucker, that hurt."

I rubbed the bump on my head, still peering down at my lap as I sat back on the chair. The object that was set on the table caught my eye. It was then that I remembered somebody helped me by lifting the table, so I could get my bag out.

I turned my head slightly. "Thank you so—" I stopped breathing.

Sitting on the table was the original hardback copy of *Crave Me*. My book. There was only one person that would have that copy. I didn't have to look up to know who was standing in front of me. My heart pounded out of my chest, and I swear it echoed in the corner of the room.

How after all these years did he still have this effect on me?

I took a few deep breaths, trying to steady my thoughts. I felt him place his hand on top of mine. Soothing the bump on my head that suddenly seemed miniscule, compared to the emotions that were coursing through me.

"You alright?" he said with the same southern drawl that I still dreamt about after all this time.

He haunted my dreams almost every night.

"I don't know," I blurted.

He chuckled, moving my hand, and leaning over the table.

"Let me take a look."

I shut my eyes, feeling the simple touch of his hands on my head. Everywhere. All consuming. He let his hands linger for what felt like forever, but I knew it was only seconds. I instantly missed his touch, his warmth when he backed away.

"You're going to have a nasty bump. Best if you get some ice on that when you get home."

I nodded not being able to form words. I was as nervous as I was the first time I met him. For some reason, it felt like I was about to see him for the first time, and that confused the hell out of me. I knew everything about this man.

I had seen him at his best, and at his worst.

I took a deep breath, opening my eyes and locking gazes with him for the first time in over three years. He looked better than I remembered. He was definitely one of those men that got better with age. He was wearing a white tight shirt that emphasized every last muscle on his solid chest and firm arms, like he lived at the gym again. His tattoos only accenting his bad boy facade, I-don't-give-a-fuck kind of look that only Austin could ever pull off.

"Hey, Daisy," he greeted, bringing me back to the present.

Taking me in as much as I was taking him in.

His blue eyes that I hadn't seen in God knows how long were bright and shining. With a hint of mischievousness in them, gazing at my once again vibrant purple hair. With a predatory regard, he eyed me everywhere, as if he couldn't decide where he wanted to look at me the most.

"You still take my goddamn breath away," he rasped, barely above a whisper.

I blushed, peering back down at the book. Breaking our heated connection.

"I see you read it," I spoke, looking at the worn binding and pages.

"I more than read it. I lived it."

We locked eyes again.

"Seeing it through your eyes though," he paused, slightly shaking his head, "was like experiencing it for the first time," he admitted with so much sadness in his tone.

My eyes began to fill with tears.

"It was a long time ago, Austin. I'm not that person anymore, and from the looks of it... you're not either."

"You'll always be my Daisy. My girl with the tattoos and purple hair," he said, reaching for a lose strand, twirling it around.

I smiled. I couldn't help it.

"You look good."

"You look beautiful."

I chuckled, smiling wider. He immediately caught my expression in the air and placed it near his heart. Causing my stomach to flutter.

"Why are you here, Austin?"

"For you," he simply stated.

I swallowed hard. Trying like hell to govern my breathing.

"I'd love for you to sign my book. In fact, it would mean the world to me."

I smirked, grabbing a pen from my bag. He handed me the book, holding onto it for a second longer, grinning.

I opened it up to the title page and signed, "Your best friend, Daisy."

He laughed as I handed it back to him.

"Can I buy you lunch?"

I hesitated, and he noticed.

"We're best friends, remember?"

I scoffed out a laugh. "Only if I get to choose the place."

"Baby, I'd follow you anywhere."

"Still quite the charmer I see."

"Only with you." He grabbed the heavy bag off my shoulder. "Lead the way."

"I actually came with my assistant. I was going to take a cab home. I don't live far from here."

"You're in Oak Island," he stated, confused.

I nodded, not elaborating.

"Well then I guess I'll be driving, Miss Daisy."

I laughed again. Damn I missed him. I hadn't laughed or smiled this much in years. He always brought out the best in me.

We drove in silence on the way to the restaurant up the road. Music played just above a whisper. It was a small diner but it was on the beach, and I loved going there with my computer to write. Something about the sound of the waves and the ocean breeze, took me away to another place and time.

I could sense that Austin wanted to reach over and grab my hand like he used to every time we were in the car together. His thumb tapped on the steering wheel instead, while a cigarette was placed in his other hand that was hanging out the window.

His eyes remained on the road ahead, blowing out the smoke from his lungs through the corner of his mouth. The furthest away from me.

Making me smile from the memory of it all.

Him.

Before I knew it we were being seated out on the beach patio of the restaurant. The sun was shining bright, highlighting the red in Austin's hair.

"Thank you," I told the waitress after ordering my food.

She nodded and left.

"How have you been?" He was the first to break the silence.

"Really good, Austin. The best I've been in a long time, actually."

He sadly smiled, looking out toward the water.

Not faltering, he stated, "I'm glad Esteban makes you so happy, Briggs. Even if it's at my expense. You deserve all the happiness in the world. To be treated the way you always deserved."

It broke my heart a little to hear him say that.

I cleared my throat, bringing his sudden solemn expression back to me.

"I'm not with Esteban."

His eyebrows rose, taking in what I just shared.

"I haven't been with him in almost a year-and-a-half. We're still good friends. It was a mutual decision. It seemed like a good idea in theory, you know trying something else. After Esteban and I ran into each other, I changed my hair back to its original color. I covered my tattoos with clothing I would have never worn before. A part of me wanted to try to be the girl I was before my parents died. The Daisy I thought I was supposed to be. I thought I was happy, and in a way I was. But being comfortable isn't being happy. I confused the two. He was good to me, and I knew him. I was hurting, and he was the perfect distraction. As much as I hate to admit it, I didn't want to be alone."

"Did you love him?" he asked, his stare not wavering from mine.

"No, Austin. Don't get me wrong, I love him, but I was never in love with him. He knew it. It's probably why he traveled so much. It was easier that way. He will find the right girl one day. It's just not me. We sold the house after we broke up, and I started traveling all over for signings. I lived in and out of hotels for a good year, finding my independence for the first time in my life. It was good for me, to find myself. I dyed my hair back, and started dressing like I always had. This is who I am. This is the real Daisy. I bought a house in Oak Island a few months ago. It's my home. You're home has always felt like my home. I couldn't imagine living anywhere else."

I couldn't believe I just shared all of that with him, but Austin always had a way of making me feel comfortable in my own skin. It was easy to pour my heart out to him. He always made me feel like it was okay to share my thoughts and emotions with him like we had known each other for several lifetimes. Even then, after everything we had been through, it felt normal to tell him all that as if no time had passed between us at all.

No sad stories.

At least not anymore.

AUSTIN

I took in every word she said, trying to keep my emotions in check. When all I wanted to do was reach across the fucking table, and pull her into my arms. Hold her for as long as I could. Never letting her go.

She was single.

She was still mine.

"How about you? Hmmm? You seeing anyone?" she questioned, biting on her lip like she did when she was nervous.

I didn't hesitate. "I haven't been with anyone since you, baby." I told her the honest-to-God truth, needing her to know that there was no one else for me, but her. "I had every intention of reading 'our story' when Alex gave it to me. It was the same day I received my six-month sobriety chip. I tried to read it every day since then, but I wasn't ready to relive the past, when my future was finally full of possibilities. Up until three months ago, the book sat on my nightstand. When I finally decided to read it, I devoured the entire thing in one sitting. Staying up all night until I'd finished it. After that day, I read it again and again and again. You are so fucking talented."

Her eyes showed more emotion than I had seen in a long time. Her bright blue gaze intently focused on what I was saying. I leaned across the table, needing to feel close to her. Reaching for her hands to hold them in mine.

I recited from her book, "Have you ever met someone that you felt like you already knew with every fiber of your being? Knowing it was physically impossible, knowing it was the first time you had ever laid eyes on him, knowing that he was a complete and utter stranger. But, feeling it in your heart, in your mind, and in your soul that this person was a part of you. Someone you possibly met in a previous life, someone who may have meant something to you. I locked eyes with the guy across the room and a sense of deja vu hit me, I felt like I had seen him before, his presence was comforting and intriguing, although in my head I knew he was a complete stranger. I felt a pull towards him, like he was a piece of a puzzle that was missing from my life. I knew something was brewing.

Something big. Important. Life-changing. The way he looked at me, consumed me in ways I never thought possible. There was a predatory, yet captivating glare in his eyes. As if I was the answer to every question he ever had."

Her eyes widened in disbelief, tears pooling immediately.

"I felt every single one of those things you described in our love story, Daisy. Every last one of them. And yes, the second I laid eyes on you… you answered every question I ever had."

Tears fell from her eyes, and I squeezed her hand in comfort. Wanting to hold her anyway I could. I reached across the table, rubbing her tear-stained cheek with my thumb.

"I need to make amends with you. I can't pass my ninth step in my recovery until I do. I know I've said this to you a hundreds, thousands, possibly millions of times, but from the bottom of my fucking heart and soul, baby, I am so sorry. I needed to forgive myself from the guilt of everything I did to you. To my family, my friends, the car accident. Before I could love myself. Before I could feel whole again. I'm not asking for you to forget, I'm begging you to forgive."

She sniffled. "I forgave you a long time ago, Austin. I forgave you the moment I left your hospital room."

"I know it's going to take time for you to trust me again. Fuck… it's taken almost three years for me to trust myself again. But I need you in my life."

"Austin, I—"

"I'm not saying we go back to being what we were. I don't want to go back to the past. I want to move forward in the future with you. I want to be your best friend, Daisy. I miss your friendship more than anything in this world. Your love, your kindness, your smile, your laugh. Us. I miss hearing your voice, even your snoring," I chuckled.

"I don't snore. I have allergies," she giggled, sniffling again.

And it was still the sweetest sound I'd ever heard.

"Your allergies then. I miss those too. I just… I. Miss. You. If we could be friends again. Start from the beginning with a clean slate. If we could start in a new place, find our way back to whatever we're supposed to be to each other. I know in my heart, as well as in my mind, body, and soul that you're meant to be in my life one way or another. And you know that too. You wouldn't have written it, if you didn't."

She took a deep breath. I wasn't surprised in the least that she was hesitating. I couldn't blame her after everything I'd put her through. The emotional roller-coaster ride that was never-ending, all-consuming, held her hostage for years and years.

"Let's eat lunch, and then I'd like to show you something. Can we do that?"

She nodded, pulling her hands away.

We ate in comfortable silence both of us lost in our thoughts. Our plaguing emotions swirled all around us. I paid the bill and we walked out to my car. Once again driving in silence, I found myself reaching over the center console for her hand, kissing it before placing it in my lap. To my surprise, she let me. I couldn't fucking help myself, I needed to feel her.

As soon as I drove into my neighborhood, she knew where I was going. From the corner of my eyes, I caught her trying to hide a grin when she looked out the window. Parking my car in the garage we made our way into my house.

The home I purchased with a family in mind.

The same one I wanted with her.

Only her.

She slowly stepped inside through the garage door, immediately taking in all her surroundings from the kitchen to the dining room. Walking straight to the sliding glass door to gaze out at the dock she loved so much. Knowing she had already left a piece of her soul on the wooden planks. I watched her move to the living room, her fingers lightly skimming my furniture. Admiring the pictures on the walls and the shelves.

"This isn't what I wanted to show you," I stated, grabbing her hand.

I led her to the guesthouse I had built specially for her after I read her book. She peered around the spacious open room that I'd made into her office. It was a private writing space with huge bay windows that overlooked our dock and the water. She took in every last picture of all our happy memories throughout the years that were scattered all over the walls. She walked over to the reading chair in the corner and picked up her memory blanket that I'd given to her for her birthday a long time ago. She left it behind. I had it with me always. She brought it up to her cheek, snuggling into it as her eyes began to water. Placing it back on the chair, she continued over to the bookshelf that held all of her books that she'd also left behind. I pulled every last one of them out of storage.

"I made Lucas' company build this room for you after I read your book. I wanted you to have a happy place in my home," I informed, gazing at her as she continued to explore the room with her hand over her heart.

She stopped dead in her tracks when she saw what I really wanted her to see. I came up behind her, close enough to where she could feel my warmth, love, and devotion for her.

"See, baby, you've always been with me. Even when you weren't," I murmured into her ear as she stared at the Twilight Sparkle Briggs doll sitting on the shelf with a picture of us beside it.

Her hand went over her mouth as fresh tears erupted.

"I bought her on my way to rehab. I never needed you more than I did back then. I prayed that she could make me as happy as it made you the last time you were holding her. Hoping that maybe one day you could hold her again, knowing that this time she was yours. And you were going to be happy, forever. With me."

"I-I don't know what to say."

I turned her to face me, and there were tears streaming down her beautiful face. I resisted the urge to kiss them all away, so I wiped them away instead. She looked deep into my eyes, searching for something I hope she'd find.

"Okay," she whispered.

I pulled away her hair, caressing her cheek with my thumb.

"Okay, what, baby?"

"Okay, we can try to be friends again."

I smiled, pulling her into my arms. Feeling her against me for the first time in over three years was like coming home. She wrapped her arms around me, holding me in the exact same way. My girl was in my arms again. Where she belonged. I would prove myself worthy of her love and trust. I didn't care if it took the rest of my life.

She was mine.

There wasn't a chance in hell that I was ever going to let her go. I loved her too fucking much.

407

EPILOGUE

AUSTIN

Four and a half years later

"You ready?" I asked my baby girl.

She stopped building her sandcastle and looked up at me. She got her long, silky brown hair from her mama and the freckles sprinkled across her nose from me, but those bright blue eyes she shared with both of us. She fervently nodded, standing up, brushing off the sand from her chubby little legs and her purple two-piece bikini that Briggs insisted was the cutest thing she'd ever seen.

"Hold on, Amari," Briggs said to our almost three-year-old daughter.

She walked over to us from her beach chair and helped Amari wipe off the sand.

"Turn around, baby girl," she said, wanting to tie Amari's long hair up high on her head so it would be away from her face.

Briggs strapped on her life vest and I made sure it was securely in place, tight against her chest. Amari ran over and kissed her eight-month-old baby brother, Michael. We named them after Briggs' parents, and I was already trying to knock her up with a third. To give her the big family that she always dreamed of.

It took a little less than a year for her to tell me that she loved me again, even though I told her every fucking day. We started off as friends like we did when we first met, flirting relentlessly, cuddling, and laughing all the time. She slept in my arms every night like old times. The first time we kissed was on my birthday, exactly what I wished for when I blew out my candles. We had been together for three months by that time, but it felt like we'd never parted ways. It was as if nothing had changed between us.

The first time I tasted her again, bringing her to ecstasy with my tongue and fingers, was on her birthday. It was three months after mine. That was my gift to her. The best fucking orgasm she'd ever experienced. She wanted to make love right then and there, she actually begged me for it. It took everything inside me not to give her what she wanted. I told her she couldn't get my cock again until she told me she loved me.

Sound familiar?

She finally said it the day I received my four-year sobriety chip. I didn't waste any goddamn time. I asked her to marry me and knocked her up on our dock out back. We were married on those same wooden planks less than a month later. The same day she told me she was pregnant.

I was paranoid as fuck with her pregnancy. Since she had suffered a miscarriage before, she was a high-risk pregnancy. I barely let her lift a finger. I waited on her hand and foot, giving into her every crazy request. Turned out her pregnancy was normal, and she went full term without any complications. We both wanted to focus on Amari being the only child for as long as we could. Finally getting the baby girl that I'd dreamt about for years.

Amari was the spitting image of her mama. She already started asking to dye her hair bright pink, her favorite color. Briggs bought her some pink clip-in hairpieces instead. She was so damn cute when she wore them, carrying around her "Briggs doll" that she stole off of her mama's shelf in her office, claiming it was hers now. She took it everywhere, and it made Briggs smile every time she saw it. Our son, Michael, was the spitting image of me. Briggs claimed that he already had my "I-don't-give-a-fuck attitude."

"I'm ready, Daddy," Amari said in her tiny baby voice, standing in front of me with her arms up in the air.

I picked her up, placing her on my back. Her little arms wrapped around my neck while I held on to her under her butt. I crouched down kissing Michael on the forehead. Grabbing Briggs' chin to kiss her pouty pink lips.

"I love you," I rasped against her mouth.

She smiled. "Be careful."

"Always am."

I kissed her one last time. Grabbing my surfboard, we made our way into the water.

"You ready, baby girl?" I asked, lifting her higher on my back.

She nodded. "Yep! Let's do this," she replied, enthusiastically kicking her legs at my sides.

I laughed, strapping the leash on my ankle. Lying on my board, I paddled out with Amari safely placed on my back. Her arms were tightly wrapped around my neck, practically choking me. The first wave hit and I dropped in, holding onto Amari tight before I stood. I caught the wave with her on my back like I'd done countless times. Riding it all the way down the peak along the shoreline.

"Yeah, Daddy! Let's hit a big one!" she yelled in my ear.

Amari loved surfing. She was my little daredevil.

It was one of her favorite things to do with me. We had been surfing like this since she turned two. My baby girl was definitely going to be a surfer when she got a little bit older and could swim better. As soon as my son was old enough, I would do the same with him. All the boys had done this with their kids. It became our thing. Wanting to give our kids something that was so special and dear to our hearts.

We spent the next hour out there, laughing and having a good ol' time. I finally started going to therapy for my back while I was in rehab. Believe it or not, it worked wonders. I could do the things I loved again without the throbbing discomfort and pain. Sometimes I would lie about it just so Briggs would give me a massage. Naked. After the kids were in bed, sleeping.

"Mama! Mama! Mama! Did you see us? Did you see the big wave Daddy rode? Did you see, Mama? Did you see?" Amari shouted, running up the beach toward Briggs.

She caught her in the air, throwing our daughter up on her hip.

"I saw, baby girl."

"Mama, Daddy says that maybe I can learn to surf by myself when I'm this many." She held up five little fingers. "That's only…" Her eyes looked everywhere, trying to think of the answer. "That's only… a lot away," she simply stated, making us both laugh.

"You definitely got a minute or two, baby girl," I reminded, kissing the top of her head.

"How's Michael?" I asked, grabbing Amari from her arms.

I sat her on my lap to help her build her sandcastle like I'd promised earlier.

"He's lounging at the beach and has a full belly. He's the happiest baby in the world right now. Just like his daddy."

"Like father, like son, huh, buddy?" I cooed, leaning around Amari to blow raspberries on his chubby belly.

He flapped around everywhere, excited. Lying on Briggs' memory blanket that she now used for our babies.

I peered back at Briggs who was already looking at me adoringly. She was still breathtakingly beautiful, especially when she was wearing a bikini. Having two kids only made her curvier, she was sexier than hell now. I couldn't take my eyes off her heavy breasts that were spilling out of her top. Breastfeeding made her tits so fucking perky. All I could think about was motor boating the shit out of them later.

"Austin... stop," she giggled.

"What?" I glared at her with a predatory regard.

"I know that look! Your daughter is on your lap."

"Do you hear your mama's nonsense?" I whispered into Amari's neck, making her tuck her chin and laugh.

She hated her neck being touched as much as I did, but I still tortured her with it like my parents did to me.

"Mama, Daddy told me you belong to him so he can do anything he wants to you. But he said I belong to him too, and I need to remember that. So I can tell boys and he won't have to beat their ass'."

"Austin!" she reprimanded.

My eyes widened, trying to hold back a laugh.

"You're not supposed to repeat that," I murmured to Amari.

She looked up at me, smiling. "Oh yeah, I always forget that part."

"Psst... Amari, let's get Mama," I nodded toward Briggs.

"Yes, let's get her good, Daddy."

"On the count of three, okay?" I whispered again to her.

"Austin..." Briggs warned hearing our plot against her, knowing what I was implying.

Amari readily nodded, standing from my lap, counting, "One..."

"Amari," Briggs coaxed.

411

"Two…" I added.

"This isn't fair."

"Three!" we both shouted together.

Briggs instantly got up to take off running, but I grabbed her around the waist before she even took a step, flinging her up in the air.

"Austin," she giggled, loving this game even though she liked to pretend she didn't.

I placed her down on the ground, straddling her waist. Sitting over her legs, Amari and I attacked her, tickling her everywhere. Briggs thrashed around, screaming and laughing all at once.

"This isn't fair! It's always two against one! I need Michael to be on my team!"

"Michael will be on the A Team. Mine! Then there'll be three against one!"

I held Briggs' arms above her head, tickling her neck and face with my beard. Amari tickled under her arms.

"Oh my God! Stop!" She thrashed around more, moving her face side to side. "Well then it's a good thing I'm pregnant because this one will be on Team Kick A-S-S."

I jerked back, smiling. Not letting go of her wrists.

"Amari," I called out, locking eyes with a grinning Briggs.

"Let's give your mama a break. Can you check on your brother for us, please?"

"Yes," she replied, happy to help.

She loved Michael and being a big sister. She jumped up and ran over to her baby brother, not paying any mind to what Briggs just informed me.

I didn't falter. "You're pregnant?"

"Your baby is in my belly," she stated with the same phrase she used with all our babies. "Apparently, your boys really love me. The doctor was even shocked that it happened so fast."

I leaned forward. My cock throbbed to be inside her, and I hated that we were in public. I couldn't have my way with her.

"I fucking love you, baby."

I kissed her long and deep. Until Amari jumped on my back, tickling me under my neck. Causing us to break our connection. I threw Amari in the air, tickling her next. Kissing all over her face, rubbing her with my beard exactly like I did with her mama.

I had everything I ever wanted and more.

My wife.

My babies.

My family.

My life was finally complete, and I owed it all to my Daisy.

The girl with the tattoos and vibrant purple hair.

Briggs

I had never been so happy before in my entire life. My whole world was in front of me, and it was filled with nothing but happiness. The past didn't matter anymore. I truly believe with all my heart that it was what led us to this place and time.

My future.

Our future was with each other and our family. I wanted a whole soccer team. I wanted to be surrounded by our babies and my husband, that's all I needed. I loved being pregnant. I loved knowing that what was growing inside me, was a part of Austin and me. I loved hearing the heartbeat for the first time. Feeling the flutters and kicks. There was no feeling like it in the world. Austin would spend hours talking to our unborn babies so they would know who their daddy was. We had come full circle and nothing else mattered anymore.

He saved my life.

I saved his.

And then we saved our relationship.

"Austin, we got to go. I still have to go home and pack," I reminded him.

"What time does our flight leave tomorrow?"

"Noon."

My uncle was having a party for some unknown reason. When I asked him what it was about, he said I would find out soon enough.

Our relationship had changed so much it was hard to believe. He flew out the second I told him we were getting married and that I was pregnant. Since then he was there for every holiday, birthday party, any memorable event. Even for the birth of our kids. He was still the same man as always and still did the same shady shit.

A mystery.

413

But Amari had him wrapped around her little finger from the moment she was born. She didn't see the cold, soulless man behind the expensive suit. She would grab his hand, kiss his cheek, sit on his lap, tell him she loved him and to our surprise.

He let her.

And said it back.

Amari helped me pack when we got home, and Austin put the kids to bed so I could shower. I was lying on our bed waiting for him.

Naked.

He grinned, shutting and locking the door behind him. Crawling his way up my body. Kissing every last inch of my skin only stopping to linger on the tattooed dates of our babies' birthday's on my lower abdomen.

Giving me one hell of a wicked, mischievous glare. He kissed his way back down to where I wanted him the most.

"I want to fuck you with my mouth."

I bit my lip, peering down at him with hooded eyes.

"After I'm done making you come, over and over again, tasting you all around my tongue, I want to fuck you with my fingers and then have you lick them clean so when I claim your goddamn mouth. I can still taste you as I fuck you, hard and rough with my pierced cock. That you love so fucking much."

My breathing hitched, my chest rising and descending with each filthy word that left his lips.

"You think you can do that for me, baby?" he groaned, taking my clit into his mouth.

"Yes," I panted.

"Good."

He did everything he promised and then some. Until I begged him to stop, unable to come anymore.

He didn't.

I was exhausted on the flight to New York, but in the very best possible way. There wasn't anything better than to feel Austin for days after he made love to me like that. The thought alone made my belly flutter and my panties wet.

We made it to my uncle's penthouse around four in the afternoon. Traveling with two kids proved to be taxing, but I wouldn't have it any other way. He left a key with the concierge for us. We said we were going to get a hotel room while we were visiting, but he shot that idea down real quick. He argued that he would make sure that every hotel in New York would deny us a room. That we were to stay with him.

The sad thing was, he would actually do it.

"Mama, when will Unkey be here?" Amari asked as I opened the door.

She couldn't say uncle when she first started talking so the name stuck for him.

"He said later this evening."

"Can I wait up for him?"

"Maybe, let's see. Okay?"

She nodded, satisfied with my answer.

"He said he left a gift for me in his office when we talked on the phone, Mama. Can you go get it for me?" she asked as we stepped inside.

I looked back at Austin, and he reassuringly nodded.

"Yes, Daddy is going to go put down Michael for his nap. Will you help him?"

"Daddy, can I feed him?"

"Sure, baby girl."

"I'll be right back."

I kissed him, setting down my bag near the couch. I walked toward the back of the penthouse where his office was located. Even after all these years the penthouse still freaked me out. Maybe it was the soundproof doors and walls. The only thing that could be heard was your shoes echoing off the marble floors. Or maybe it was too many bad memories, lingering.

Although, having my family here with me made it less scary. I opened the door to his dark office and before I even stepped inside, a loud popping sound ricocheted off the walls followed by a hard thud.

My eyes widened and my heart dropped. I knew that fucking sound. It haunted my dreams for years.

A gun.

"Briggs!" Austin shouted, his pounding footsteps running towards me, echoing off the walls.

I didn't think twice about it, I fully opened the door and came face to face with my uncle lying in a pool of his own blood.

"NO!" I lunged into action, falling onto my knees. "NO! NO! NO! PLEASE NO!" I screamed, placing my hands over his wound. Blood gushed through my fingers as I applied pressure.

"Briggs!" Austin yelled, barreling into the room. Stopping dead in his tracks, peering from me to my uncle's body, to the person standing behind his desk.

The rest proceeded in slow motion.

I looked up never believing who was holding…

The. Fucking. Gun.

The end.

For Austin and Briggs.
It's only the beginning or is it *the end* for…
Alejandro Martinez
(Next is a Spin Off Standalone Series)
RELEASING AUGUST 30TH

Connect with *M*

Website:
www.authormrobinson.com

Like my Facebook page:
https://www.facebook.com/AuthorMRobinson?ref=hl

Join my VIP Group on Facebook:
https://www.facebook.com/groups/572806719533220/?fref=nf
I share EXCLUSIVES & hang out with my readers

Follow me on Instagram:
http://instagram.com/authormrobinson

Follow me on Twitter:
https://twitter.com/AuthorMRobinson

Amazon author page:
http://www.amazon.com/M.-Robinson/e/B00H4HJYDQ/ref=sr_ntt_srch_lnk_5?qid=1425429982&sr=1-5

Sign up for my newsletter:
http://eepurl.com/beltYj
Email: m.robinson.author@gmail.com

Printed in Great Britain
by Amazon